NORTHWEST
Readers

Other titles in the NORTHWEST READERS series
Series editor: Robert J. Frank

Wood Works: The Life and Writings of Charles Erskine Scott Wood
edited by Edwin Bingham and Tim Barnes

A Richer Harvest

AN ANTHOLOGY OF WORK
IN THE PACIFIC NORTHWEST

EDITED BY
Craig Wollner & W. Tracy Dillon

Oregon State University Press
Corvallis

TO PAT AND GRACE

The paper in this book meets the guidelines for permanence and durability of the Committee on Production Guidelines for Book Longevity of the Council on Library Resources and the minimum requirements of the American National Standard for Permanence of Paper for Printed Library Materials Z39.48-1984.

Library of Congress Cataloging-in-Publication Data
A richer harvest : the literature of work in the Pacific Northwest / edited by Craig Wollner, W. Tracy Dillon
p. cm. —(Northwest Readers)
Includes bibliographical references.
ISBN 0-87071-465-1 (alk. paper)
1. Northwest, Pacific Literary collections. 2. Labor—Northwest, Pacific Literary collections. 3. Working class—Northwest, Pacific Literary collections. 4. Working class writings, American—Northwest, Pacific. 5. American literature—Northwest, Pacific. I. Wollner, Craig, 1943- . II. Dillon, W. Tracy. III. Series.
PS570.R53 1999
810.8'09795—dc21 99-22451
CIP

 First edition 1999
Printed in the United States of America

Oregon State University Press
101 Waldo Hall
Corvallis OR 97331-6407
541-737-3166 •fax 541-737-3170
http://.osu.orst.edu/dept/press

Series Preface

In 1990 the Oregon State University Press issued its first two books in the Northwest Reprint Series, *Oregon Detour* by Nard Jones, and *Nehalem Tillamook Tales,* edited by Melville Jacobs. Since then, the series has reissued a range of books by Northwest writers, both fiction and nonfiction, making available again works of well-known and lesser-known writers.

As the series developed, we realized that we did not always want to reissue a complete work; instead we wanted to present selections from the works of a single author or selections from a number of writers organized around a unifying theme. Oregon State University Press, then, has decided to start a new series, the Northwest Readers Series.

The reasons for the Northwest Readers Series are the same as for the Northwest Reprint Series: "In works by Northwest writers, we get to know about the place where we live, about each other, about our history and culture, and about our flora and fauna."

RJF

TABLE OF CONTENTS

Introduction and Acknowledgments ix

1. CLEARING THE GROUND

To the Oregon Emigrants of 1846 2

FANNY ADAMS COOPER, West by Train 3

JAMES STEVENS, The Old Warhorse 13

ORLAND E. ESVAL, Member of the Crew 25

DENNIS "DINNY" MURPHY, I Found My Likings in the Mines 34

CLYDE RICE, from *Nordi's Gift* 42

SAM CHURCHILL, from *Big Sam* 55

WOODY GUTHRIE, Big Grand Coolee Dam 62

PAT KOEHLER, Reminiscence on the Women Shipbuilders of World War II 64

WILLIE DANIELS, from *Working on the Bomb* 70

KEN KESEY, from *Sometimes a Great Notion* 75

CLEMENS STARCK, Putting in Footings 85

KATE BRAID, *Girl* on the Crew 86

KIM BARNES, from *In the Wilderness: Coming of Age in an Unknown Country* 88

2. THE INDUSTRIAL FRONTIER

CHARLES OLUF OLSEN, Zero Hour in the Factory 104

HAZEL HALL, Instruction 105

FRANCIS SEUFERT, Chinese 106

H. L. DAVIS, Steel Gang 114

JOSEPH B. HALM, Recollection of the Fires of 1910 117

The Seattle General Strike of 1919 124

CHARLES VINDEX, Survival on the High Plains, 1929-1934 130

Oregon Labor Press, If America Should Go Red? 138

Ralph Winstead, Johnson the Gypo 139
Joe Hill, The Preacher and the Slave 146
Anise, Centralia Pictures 148
Howard Morgan, Recollection of Tom Burns of Burnside 156
Hamish Scott MacKay, from *My Experiences in the United States* 161
Gary Snyder, The Late Snow and Lumber Strike of the Summer of Fifty-Four 179
Robert Wrigley, The Sinking of Clay City 181
Tess Gallagher, Black Money 182
Henry Carlile, Graveyard Shift 184
Joseph Millar, Tax Man 186
Jesús María "El Flaco" Maldonado, Memorias de César Chávez 187

3. Working Ahead

Ernest Callenbach, from *Ecotopia* 190
Douglas Coupland, from *Generation X* 198
David Axelrod, Skill of the Heart 203
Craig Lesley, from *River Song* 205
Sherman Alexie, from *Indian Killer* 211
Kent Anderson, from *Night Dogs* 219
Jim Bodeen, Replenishing the Neighborhood 225
John Rember, from *Cheerleaders from Gomorrah* 227
Eileen Gunn, Stable Strategies for Middle Management 240
Ursula K. Le Guin, from *The New Atlantis* 252

Bibliographic Citations and Permissions 274

Van Camps Seafood Cannery, Astoria, 1952. Negative number OrHi 57010. Courtesy Oregon Historical Society.

INTRODUCTION

The literature of the Pacific Northwest reveals the rich and diverse themes that are the staple ingredients of life in the region. Typically, Northwest writers have reflected the especially close bond of humans to nature, the sense of abundance—of nature, of the human spirit—of the place, and the quest for a temporal paradise—a new Eden on the Pacific shore—that have always been hallmarks of the thinking about the region by its most articulate inhabitants.

An extraordinarily evocative element of this literature, but one that goes largely unappreciated, is the part of it dedicated to portrayals of the Pacific Northwest's work life. Among those who have labored on the region's farms, in its forests, on its waterways or in its offices, stores, and factories, mining the ground for precious minerals, fishing the rivers, lakes, and sea, cutting the plentiful timber, making the rich soil yield its bounty, or engaging in commerce, many have thought they were building a paradise inside time—as it were, a new Eden. When the *Oregon Spectator* extended its welcome "To the Oregon Emigrants of 1846," it did nothing to undermine that view. It promised an end to "weary pilgrimage and toil." The *Spectator's* anonymous poet painted a picture of "verdant prairie and prolific field, / Rich forest dells, where giant cedars stand, / Shading fresh treasures yet to be revealed."

The newcomers of 1846 may have been disappointed to find that the Northwest required of them no less effort to subsist than did their points of origin. They and their posterity were forced to grapple with the usual vagaries of human existence in a place just as beset by joys, sorrows, and tedium as every other part of the world. But this land is also one visited by the more than occasional hard rain. And yet, even when wet, it is one enveloped in beauty. So their written observations, those of their posterity, and those of others who have depicted workers' triumphs and frustrations in this place, are coupled with a frequently chaotic and sometimes bloody tradition of labor radicalism and organizing. Their accounts of rough and perilous employments, like fishing, mining, and lumbering, of workers, champions of workers, and shrewd observers of the working life, make unique and richly revelatory reading about the character of the region and its people. They add a compelling dimension to our knowledge of the Northwest's literature.

The editors of this anthology, which includes poems, excerpts from short stories and novels, manifestos, songs, memoirs, and oral histories, have tried, in the divergent works collected here, to represent the varied expressions of what it is like to toil triumphantly and sometimes fruitlessly in Oregon, Washington, Idaho, and Montana.

We have divided the selections into three parts with distinct motifs. Section I, "Clearing the Ground," concerns itself with expressions of optimism. Some selections betray an artlessness, a sense of grand enterprises, of self-identity through toil, of pride in work done well, and of nature seemingly at the service of man. In the second section, "The Industrial Frontier," the pieces display an awakening to a more worldly understanding of the intractability of nature and of humans' inability to master it. Frequently, work involves struggle: struggle between strong and weak, rich and poor, worker and boss; there are even moments when workers are pitted, or pit themselves, against each other. Work, to the voices raised here, is not a celebratory experience but a necessity to be endured. The readings in the third section, "Working Ahead," illustrate evolving attitudes toward work that range from the disillusioned to the whimsical. One finds a mix of realism, lively satire, even good-natured wit.

At any stage in the Pacific Northwest's life one can find hope and hopelessness coexisting, bone-weary pessimism and bursting optimism contending, edgy irony and the straightforward embrace of life comingling. In the culture of the Pacific Northwest, the literature of work represents not just an expression of a particular geography, but a region of the enigmatic, all-too-human heart.

ACKNOWLEDGMENTS

We are grateful for the help of many individuals in completing this anthology. Most notably, however, we wish to acknowledge the indispensable editorial assistance of Gwenn Stover, who contributed to the vision and contents of the volume while managing much of the daily business of tracking down permissions, contacting authors and publishers, and providing research. Grace Dillon at Portland State University offered valuable suggestions regarding content and coverage. Pat Wollner gave valuable research assistance in acquiring illustrations.

Donna Kiykioglu helped us gain financial support to acquire permissions through access to the Office of Academic Affairs Foundation Fund for Faculty Development at Portland State University. The Board of Friends of History at Portland State University also provided a grant to support permissions. We are indebted to our colleagues at the Oregon State University Press, Jo Alexander, Tom Booth, Jeff Grass, and Warren Slesinger, who patiently guided us through the publication process, and to Paul Merchant, who provided a keen editorial eye. Bob Frank deserves special thanks for encouraging us to pursue the project. We also are grateful to Michael Munk for contributing several pieces to this anthology. Our thanks for timely assistance in securing permissions also go to Alba Scholz, manager of the continuing education press at Portland State University; Rick Harmon, editor of the Oregon Historical Quarterly; Adair Law, OHS Press; Orvis Burmaster, co-editor of Ahsahta Press at Boise State University; and Tammy Ryan and Pam Otto of *Montana: The Magazine of Western History*. We also thank Lynne DeMont of the Portland State University library for helping us gain access to research material.

McCormick Lumber Co. C.K. Kinsey photo, Seattle. Negative number OrHi 51350. Courtesy Oregon Historical Society.

1

Clearing the Ground

The following poem appeared in the *Oregon Spectator,* a weekly newspaper published in Oregon City, the end of the trail for westward-trekking pioneers to the Pacific Northwest. It sums nicely the sentiment toward industry and the ideal of equality that many people associate with the immigrations of 1843, 1845, and 1846. Indeed, the promised land seemed to offer all people—artisans, professionals, the wealthy, and farmers and laborers who depend on plough, awl, axe, and spade—equal opportunity to the riches of wealth and ease.

To the Oregon Emigrants of 1846

Welcome! ye freeborn yeomen of the soil,
Right welcome are you to our new made home;
Here ends your weary pilgrimage and toil,
You've reached the goal, and need no longer roam.
O'er dreary wastes, and sterile sands,
O'er mountain crag, through torrents mad'ning roar
You've toiled undaunted in courageous bands,
To seek a home, on this far distant shore.
Here waits ye then, ye tillers of the land,
The verdant prairie and prolific field,
Rich forest dells, where giant cedars stand,
Shading fresh treasures yet to be revealed.
The cunning artisan of every trade,
The learned professions, and the man of wealth,
Will for his journey here, be soon repaid
With ample competence, and blooming health.
Unlike the bee, that daily roams the bower,
Culling the nectar from each blushing stem,
Forsakes the rose, to taste some brighter flower,
But finds that none are quite as sweet as them.
You leave the crowded towns and worn out fields,
Of *old* Columbia for our virgin soil.
Here industry, a richer harvest yields;
In *new* Columbia, health repays your toil.
Come seize the plough, the awl, the axe, the spade,
The pond'rous sledge, or what so e'er you please,
And soon your labour will be well repaid,
With showers of plenty in the lap of ease.

Then here united let us firmly be,
And when Columbia shall extend her laws,
We'll hoist the stars and stripes of Liberty,
From Old Atlantic, to Pacific's shores.

Fannie Adams Cooper
(1867-1942)

Fannie Adams Cooper was born July 23, 1867, in Kingston, Pennsylvania, but spent much of her life moving between the Midwest and the Pacific Northwest in search of the perfect homestead. The following recalls Fannie and her husband Everly James Cooper's 1889 trek to Tacoma, Washington, with Fannie's Uncle Evan Hughes and Aunt Emma. Fannie's reminiscence captures the day-to-day instability of lower class existence on the wage earner's frontier, and the mix of high hopes and hard-headed working class practicality that characterized many of the pioneering people who came to the region from easterly origins.

West by Train (from *My Life as a Homesteader*)

We arrived in Portland one rainy day and put up at a hotel till evening. Took a walk around the city in the meantime, and saw our first sturgeon and salmon. They looked like whales to me. Our train went to Goble and on to a ferry boat to cross the Columbia River. It was thrilling to me to see the big boat settle down in the water with the weight of the cars and I thought sure we would sink. The trip to Tacoma was such a change from what I had been used to. We had left snow and cold in Nebraska and found green grass and everything spring-like and lovely in Washington. We arrived in Tacoma late at night. The town was booming and streets so crowded and jammed we could hardly pass along, and the hotels, too. We put up at the Fifi Hotel. Uncle and Auntie got an outside room so had fresh air, but we had an inside room and nearly smothered. I don't believe it had been aired since the hotel was built, and we were glad to get out in the a.m. The halls were so full of cots and sleeping people we could hardly get by. After breakfast we went to Uncle's room and Auntie and I stayed there while Uncle and Ev went out to find a house for us.

They found a little four-room house just off Pacific Avenue (the main street) and one block from the streetcar line, and Ev found an old acquaintance who was a transfer man, and he said he would get our chest and trunks and take them up to the house, although it was Sunday. In those days transfer wagons did not run on Sundays. Uncle and Auntie stayed on at the hotel until they bought a lot or two and built a home. But Ev and I went to our house that night just about dark, got our trunks open, put some bedding on the floor to sit and lie on and wait till morning. I didn't want to be left alone, but Ev ran out to a bakery and bought some bread and a plum pie. We were eating in the dark when there came a rap on the door. Our next door neighbors had seen us come in and thought we had no lights, so came with a lamp for us and to tell us they would be pleased to do anything to help us until we got settled. They saw we were eating and hurried back and brought us a pot of hot tea and a plate of crackers and butter. They were fine people and we were friends for all the while we lived there. Their name was Meagher, and Mr. Meagher was a bookkeeper at Links Planing Mill.

It was so nice for us to be so close to young people who were acquainted with the city, and our houses were so close we could look in each other's windows and talk. Not more than ten feet apart, I think. We had such nice times together, Belle and I. Ev got work at building right away so I would have been alone most of the time if it had not been for them. We went for long walks and I loved the trees and spring water that bubbled up everywhere, and the moss and evergreen trees and etc. We were only two blocks from the Sound and could see the boats come in and the fishermen, and watch the tide, etc.

In May, 1889, my people rented their farms in Nebraska, sold their stock, etc., and came too. Papa traveled around looking for land for himself and for us. Most every place was timber or logged off land and corduroy roads or waterways to get to it. He finally decided to move onto a hay ranch at Stuck Junction, Washington (near Tacoma) and take more time to decide on a place. We had so much fog and dampness, the roof dripped every morning from the heavy dew. The grass was so rank and wet one almost drowned walking anywhere before noon, but was lovely the rest of the day. There were two houses. My folks moved into one and we moved into the other, and on August 18, 1889, Roy, my first child, was born there. We had one near neighbor; the Watkins. Mrs. Watkins was my age and we had good times together.

My father traveled around and decided to buy a place at Salem. His place was a ten-acre tract with a big house and two big barns, and an old orchard and nice meadow and garden and berry patches. The family moved there as soon as the haying was done on the ranch, but Ev and I stayed on at Stuck Junction until November, when we, too, went to Oregon, to Turner, where Ev got a place for us on a hop farm owned by J. R. Dickinson. The house was a big white one on top of a hill a half mile above the town. It was nicely divided... had two sitting rooms with fireplaces. The front sitting room had two bedrooms and the stairs went up from there to the hired men's room above. My part was an ell with big sitting room and fireplace, bedroom and dining room and kitchen, and a porch on each side of the living room. It was very pretty there and I was to cook and Ev was to have charge of the work outside. The Dickinsons occupied the front rooms when they were there, but that was only a short time. Mr. Dickinson and a son and daughter; they had a nice home in Salem and always went home after dinner Saturdays and did not return till Monday. As soon as the butchering was done and the late fruit canned they did not come back. They were very nice to us and I thought I'd like it there.

We were to have only one extra man to board for the winter and his name was Shepherd. We called him "Shep." He began to tell me about things after I had been alone one day and had heard someone walking about upstairs, and other strange noises and had become frightened. I took my baby and went to the hop field where Ev was, and he had to come to the house and search it before I'd stay in it again, and then we found the house was "haunted" and they could not keep anyone there any length of time. We did not believe in "haunts;" but there were tramps and the road so close, I was afraid. So we began to look for someone to stay with me. Got a little girl first, but she was lonesome and went home. Then I found the house was full of uncanny sounds and got so nervous Ev could not leave me alone and do his work, so we got a neighbor girl 18 years old to come and stay with me. We had to pay her two dollars a week, and Ev only got twenty a month, so we knew we couldn't keep that up for long.

We moved back to Salem to a double house on Court Street right in the business part of the town. A dentist had offices and lived on one side and we had an apartment on the other. No yard front or back, right on the street. Ev had his old job back at the Club Stables and he bought some lots in Knight's Addition, across the road from our friends, the Savages. The Building and Loan Company put us up a nice three-room, pantry and big closet, cottage there, and as soon as we could we moved there and we stayed until times got so hard there was no work and Ev lost his job. There was no work anywhere, every man hunting a job and none to be had. We had cleared our lots and had trees and grapes and flowers and lawn all lovely, and had added a nice porch and walks, etc., and when we could not meet our payments we lost it all and had to pull up and go home again.

Ev and Papa started out with the team to look for a homestead for us… thought if we could get in the country we could live some way. While they were gone I was taken down with typhoid fever, so when they got home there was nothing to do but wait for me to get well or die. Ev had all he could do to take care of the children. I was a long time sick and then got better. I had a relapse and they thought I was dying, but after a long while I got better.

The men had found a place near Holley [Linn County] in the Calapooia country, not a very desirable claim, but the old settlers showed them about and were nice to them and anxious for more settlers with children so they could have more school. They located them on this rough mountain place that was covered with big trees and logs and brush and only a small part that ever could be cultivated, but told Ev there would be good range for stock and he could get work on their farms. Anything looked better than what he had then.

An old bachelor whose place adjoined it, said Ev could use part of his ground for garden, etc. so he decided to file on it and start a home there. Ev did not look about the boundary lines carefully, just took the neighbor's word as to where they thought they should be.

We had a friend who would go with us and help us move, and Papa took his team and wagon and one day we started with all our worldly goods in two big wagons. We were three days going from Salem to Holley. It was a pretty road through Albany and Lebanon and up the Calapooia River; but an awful hard trip for a woman just able to sit up. And hard to care for two small children and ride on a bumpy loaded wagon and camp out nights. One night it rained and we were allowed to sleep in a farmer's barn and build a fire on the ground in a shed out of the rain. Then we finally pulled into the barnyard of our old bachelor neighbor; where we planned to camp until we could build a cabin on our homestead.

He came out to meet us from his cabin in a thicket of plum trees, a big fat hound that we later got acquainted with called "Sport," at his side. We learned to call the old fellow Uncle John Henderson, and wherever be moved, "Sport" was always beside him. He was a black, unkempt, dirty old man and looked as if he had never had a bath in his life. But he was kind and good to everyone. When he saw the babies and me he said, "You can't put your family in a tent here, there's hogs and cattle and horses running loose everywhere. My barn is full of straw, and there's never been any stock in it. Open the doors and move your things in there till you can build a cabin." So the men opened the barn door and took pitchforks and piled the hay all back into the main part of the barn, leaving a big lean-to empty for us. There was wide cracks between the boards, and the floor was very rough, but oh, I was glad I could get in where I could shut the doors and be out of the rain. The woods looked so dark and wild up towards our place. The cracks made all the light we had. There were no windows. They cut a hole in the roof and we put our roof tin in that we had brought for our cabin, and put our cookstove up and got our wagons unloaded and it was late. There was no partition in the barn. Our bed had a high head board and we put it against the straw piled high behind it and the mice often worried me nights. It was a wonder Uncle John ever let us put a stove and fire in there with all that straw so close. I guess we would have chilled to death if the barn had not been filled, though, to keep the wind from blowing through in all directions. News travels fast. The next day after Ev had got our boxes and furniture fixed so I could get at things, he and Uncle John went up to the homestead that was some distance away and on a hill overlooking Uncle John's place. It was nearly all bottom ground and quite level. They picked out a spot to build our cabin.

While they were gone someone rapped on the barn door with a heavy stick. I was a bit scared, but went to the door. (The doors were wide and hung on wooden hinges and had wooden hasps, and were cumbersome things to open.) There stood a man with a pack over his shoulder and a pail in his hand. He said, "I'm your neighbor, Minor McQueen, and we heard there were children here and Sary thought you'd like some milk, so I brought some, and some squashes, too, for you." I took the milk and squashes and thanked him. He asked me where to find "my man" and I told him, so he went on up to the homestead, and he and Ev made arrangements to work together; he to help get our house built and Ev to pay him later in clearing land, making posts and rails and later to build him a new house. I think it would have been better if they had gone ahead and built a cabin, but Mr. McQueen told Ev he should get out shingles and shave them and pull the poles for rafters and joists, etc., all of which took lots of time and shakes, etc. It would have been so much less work and answered the purpose. We had only twenty-six dollars in the world, but the next day Mr. McQueen and Ev went to a saw mill and bought twenty-five dollars worth of flooring and other lumber. Mr. McQueen brought it home with his team and they began to clear a place for our house, and get out poles and peel them and cut logs for shingle bolts.

It took all winter to get our house built—every shingle was shaved and every timber peeled and a good foundation built under the house. It was 15' x 25'. Living room 15' x 15' and bedroom 10' x 15', good floor and ceiling and window casing. We had brought the windows and nails and hinges, etc., from Salem. Our door was made of flooring and the walls were rough lumber, battened on the outside. But it was well made, tight and warm, and we were pretty proud of it when we moved in. We had brought some hens and the next thing was to get a place for them, so the men built a nice log cabin about sixteen feet square, perhaps it was longer. But it was built high and it was roofed with shakes and it only took a short time to build it. It was a pretty building, set below the house across the little creek, in the only level ground we had, and took the lush place for a barnyard. Our yard and garden was all on a slope. While we were at Uncle John's, he had Ev help him butcher three pigs, and gave us meat for Ev's help and gave me lard and the things he could not fix himself, like heads for scrapple and headcheese, livers, hearts, tongues, etc., for frying out his lard and fixing the meat for him.

McQueens gave us apples and vegetables and milk, until they sold us a cow that Ev was to pay for later in rails, etc.

We were much in debt to our neighbors by the time we were fixed so Ev could leave home to pay them back. We had no money at all. All winter if our folks had not sent us postage we could not have written any letters. My shoes wore out and Ev fastened the soles on with wire from a broom handle. But we lived through it and in the spring he cleared a garden spot and built a fence around it and got in a good lot of seeds. The neighbors gave us all kinds of seeds and sets, etc., that first year. Later we saved our own and shared with them. Ev worked from before dawn till long after dark every day, rolling logs and burning them. I never saw such big logs and so many piled over on each other any place, as on the spot he cleared for our garden, but he was more than one year getting it cleared and it was burned deep and black far in the ground. The ground was springy, dark soil and never a weed grew there. Just once in a while a fern. It had burned too deep, and when we finally did plant it, the vegetables grew to immense size and grand flavor. Besides his work at home, which McQueen insisted he do until he had things ready for making a living, Ev worked for him. After our first garden was planted he began to work away. He finally paid McQueen for all he had done for us... made rails and posts and cleared land and the last year we lived there we helped McQueen build a house. Took them all winter, but it was a good big frame house. He peeled "Chittim" (Cascara) bark, packed it out of the woods on his back, and I would scrape off the moss and spread it to dry, then Ev would put it in a big deep box and chop it with a sharp spade and sack it. Then McQueen would haul it to town and he would get groceries and shoes, etc., in exchange. It took a lot of bark at 2 cents a pound to buy things. My one and only dress was a brown denim. Ev was so reduced for shirts, as a last resort he had to wear a white one with stiff bosom (his wedding shirt) and before it fell to pieces he traded some eggs for a piece of pink calico to make another.

Holley was only a Post Office and store in a farmhouse, and the stock in trade was very small. A few pieces of calico or denim, thread, etc. Ev walked the four miles, carried the eggs, traded for the only cotton goods they had, and got home about noon. After dinner he worked without a shirt and I ripped up the only one he had and made a pattern of it and cut out the pink goods and made him a shirt. He put it on and went down to my folks to show it to them before dark. I'll confess it was not as well made as some I've made since, but it was pretty good at that, and I could see him a mile off in that pink shirt.

My folks had mortgaged their first ten-acre home in Salem before they left there and bought another tract of land, only partly paying for it. Later they lost both places, so in the spring after we went on our homestead they bought Uncle John Henderson's place and moved up near us and built a new house there. So we had them for close neighbors, which helped a lot for me, for Ev was away working so much, he only had time to burn and roll logs nights at home, which he did most every night... often till midnight, and then get up early and walk from one to three or four miles to work.

In a couple of years we finally got a team, first only a saddle horse, and then an old lynch-pin wagon, that the pin would drop out of and let the wheel come off about every mile or so. He worked for wheat to take to the mill for flour; and for pigs to make our meat and lard, and for more cows... everything was paid for with work as we had no cash. Chittim bark (Cascara) and eggs were all we had to trade at the store for groceries and dry goods. And only a few eggs, for we could not raise many chickens, the hawks took them so fast, and Chittim could only be peeled in the spring and summer. But Ev put out an orchard and put a picket fence around a big garden spot, cleared a field of two acres and fenced it with a high rail fence.

September 24, 1894, Eloise (Peg) was born at about 2 a.m. Roy and Ruth were asleep. We had a pair of little puppies that they were very fond of. When they woke in the morning the baby was crying and they heard their grandmother talking, and Ruth called out, "Grandma, is that Lassie's pup?" and Grandma said, "Come and see," so they got out of bed and ran out to the living room where she held the baby near the stove. They were very much interested in their new sister. That winter Ev got out timbers and lumber and made a new big barn... box stalls and stanchions for the cows, a big hay bay, etc., getting ready for a team and more cows. He had worked all over the country carpentering, or most all kinds of work, and we were getting along pretty nicely, though we had very little money.

Then the Malone Estate was settled up, new surveys made, and they found the boundary lines that the old settlers had made were all wrong. Uncle John Henderson had lived 18 years and proved up on a homestead and found he had been living on the Malone place all that time and never on his homestead, though his barns and cultivated ground were on his homestead. That made us way off, too. We found our new barn and garden were on Henderson's place, the field we had cleared on McQueen's place, and the new lines came across our door step. All our improvements and good land belonged to someone else. We wrote to the Government Land Office about it and they said if we would relinquish our claim back to the Government, we could take another homestead. There was land opened to homesteaders in Lincoln County. So we sold our stock, all but two cows, and the horses, and I canned everything I could and we saved everything possible from our gardens, and in November 1895 set out again, with three wagons loaded with supplies.

My father with his team took the children and me. Eloise was walking, but still a baby, and the two others, just the age to have to watch all the time. We had quite a load besides the camp outfit. Mr. Kuny and Ev hauled the household goods, tools, supplies, etc. We had a hard trip. We had heard there were homesteads in the Five River Country and headed that way through Philomath and Alsea country over mountains, forded rivers, and over the most dangerous places where there was no chance to pass a team if we met any, and did occasionally. Then the one who had the least load would have to unhitch and all hands lower the wagon over the grade and hold it there by some means until the others pulled their loads by, then help the other fellow get his wagon back on the road and ready to go on. It was awful, and I vowed if I ever got to my destination I'd never go over the road again, and I did not, only once, and that was to come back out and stay.

We were four or five days on the road and then at last came to the wagon road to a homesteader named Seits, and he came out to meet us. There was a log schoolhouse right by his house and no school at that time, so Mr. Seits told us we could move right in and stay until we found a claim and got a house built, and as soon as we could get unloaded he would take Ev up the creek [Cascade Creek near Fisher, Lincoln Co.] and show him a good place. The women and children came out and helped me get my things straightened around some, too, and my father wanted to see what kind of a place we would have before he returned home. So they all set out up the creek after Ev had cut me some wood from a nearby log... of which there were plenty lying about. After while I started out of the house to get some wood. There were goats all about in the brush but I paid no attention, but stooped over and gathered my armful of wood when I was rammed from behind and sent rolling, my wood going in all directions. The Seits children came yelling, "Billy, Billy quit that"; and they got hold of the goat, which was a pet, and a "butter." After that I shied clear of goats.

The Seits were good neighbors. There were two families. Frank Seits, who lived near the log school house had a big family, and Lincoln Seits, who lived up the creek nearer our place, had a smaller family. Both men dropped their own work and helped Ev build our house and make a sled road to it. The way was too rough for a wagon and the vine maple so dense it was like making a tunnel through it. They cleared a spot near Cascade Greek, in a cherry grove, and got out cherry logs and made shakes and boards from logs. Soon we had a cabin 16' x 22' of logs, up and roofed. Then the weather was so bad they put a lean-to on it of poles and shakes and boarded the lean-to up tight and good. Put in a good floor and we moved up the creek so the children could go to school in the school house. Ev made a window... we had taken panes of glass with us, and hewed out boards from logs and made all our lumber. That winter we finished our house. We had a living room downstairs and big room upstairs, and we were settled quite well by spring. The clearing there was easy and he had a good small team. Ev put in two big gardens, set out strawberry and other plants and some orchard.

The land was fine and soft and plenty of water to irrigate easy from the creek... all would have been fine if there had been roads and bridges to cross the rivers, but after the fall rains came the rivers were at flood stage and one could only cross by boat and go by trail from one river to another. There were three big rivers to cross to get to town. Corvallis, over sixty miles away, was our trading place, only we did no trading until spring.

We had lots of scares, lots of thrills and lots of hardships that winter. I was sick, suffered awfully with gall stone, but I didn't know what it was. Mr. Seits swam his horse behind a boat and made his way out to Alsea to a doctor for me, the doctor sent in morphine tablets and that was all.

Ev's brother, Frank Cooper [George Franklin Cooper, b. 17 April 1863 near Peru, Indiana] had written us that he would send us our fare if we wanted to come back to Nebraska where he could help us get another start.

So we went back to Ogallala, Nebraska where we rented a farm. Frank got us horses and mules and everything to work with to get in a crop. There, on the Fleharty place, June 9, 1897, Betty was born [later Mrs. Stephen M. Eby], two years and eight months younger than Eloise [later Mrs. Harold Frick].

We bought a dray line in Ogallala that fall and moved to town. Ev did well with it. We began to get good carpets and furniture, clothes etc. The next fall, September 5, 1898, at five p.m., Carl was born.

That winter all the children were sick most of the time. Roy had a bad cough and was anemic. Eloise had catarrhal fever that left her with an offensive ear; and totally deaf. Betty and the baby had the croup quite often. In February, the doctor told us that there were some cases of "Whooping cough" in town and he feared an epidemic in the school. The doctor said that if Roy got it he could not live and he said that Eloise would probably always be deaf if we stayed in that climate. There was so much wind there, but if we went to a milder climate she would probably recover. We were just getting our business paid for and having nice things in the house, good clothes, etc., and it was hard to think of another move with so many small children and little ahead to go on.

We had made good friends that we hated to leave, but we wanted to save the children. So we decided to come back to Oregon, but to a different part. I never wanted any more homesteading, and wanted to be near schools and churches etc. We had heard there were mills at Hood River and the valley was just settling up, and we could grow berries and fruit, so we decided to stop there. We corresponded with Mr. Byerlee who had been a friend of my sister's husband, Joe Tooley, in Nebraska. He wrote us there were good opportunities for work at Hood River, and small tracts of land suitable for garden and fruit could be bought reasonable.

James Stevens
(1892-1972)

James Stevens moved from Iowa to Idaho with his family and by age fifteen began working the logging camps and mills in Oregon and Washington. His four books on Paul Bunyan brought him literary fame, and popularized the myth of the larger-than-life Pacific Northwest lumberjack. Those themes dominate the following more poignant portrayal of the work ethic in the logging industry. The story appeared in his collection *Homer in the Sagebrush* (1928).

THE OLD WARHORSE

THE BIG MENOMINEE & TACOMA mill-sawing average—two hundred thousand feet, board measure, per ten hours—was roaring close to the end of a payday shift. It was a rainy February day and the lights had gone on at four o'clock. There was a white blaze of them over the markers at the head of the long green-chain, and over every sawing machine. Saw steel glittered from trimmer, edger, resaw, and slasher, as the sharp teeth of circulars and bands bit and ripped through boards, cants, and slabs. The screaming songs of the saws and the rumble of live rolls filled the big millhouse with a tumult of sound.

At the headrig the sixty-foot bandsaw was a silver flash of ripping steel. A brute of a stick seven feet through and eighty long was on the carriage. The two doggers and the setter had to climb the log's side to catch the signals from the head sawyer's cage.

In that cage, with the log deck on his left, the carriage and its gigantic burden squarely in front of him, and the wide silver ribbon of the big band flashing on his right, stood old Johnny McCann. He had stood his ten hours a day in this cage for twenty-five years. He had stood in others like it back in Saginaw for fifteen more.

Head sawyer. Boss of the millhouse floor. A great lumbering operation centering around the skill of his eye and hand. A mighty life. Ay, it was a tremendous job, this one of sawing up the big timber. You felt like a general or a king when you got a great beauty of a log like this one off the deck and lined up for the bandsaw. Your eyes sized up the hundreds of year rings in its end. An old-timer. A tall tree before Columbus hit this new world. Ripe for lumber now.

The sapwood is deep. Slab her heavy and hard. Square her down to the sweet fine-grained clear. Keep the figures of your orders in your head, Johnny, old horse! Get the taper of the log! Signal the carriage crew with your left hand—why the hell is the lad so slow, that setter, that boy of yours, young Johnny McCann? Ease over this lever in your right hand, now—she moves—the old headsaw sings—boom! down the live rolls goes the first slab! Back with the carriage, the big beauty of a log showing a face of clear sapwood. On again—down the rolls—back—ahead—now a jiggle of the left-hand lever to lift the mighty steel gooseneck hook of the turner—slab her on!

Forty years of it in a head sawyer's cage, still old Johnny McCann could thrill like a youth at the cutting of an ancient giant from the forest. The years rolled away from him then. So did his troubles. He even forgot the hot lead in his feet and the shooting pains in his legs. He forgot his worry about the superintendent bending over the sheets on the log-scaler's desk. He was a head sawyer in all the glory of fighting a great bulk of sawlog into lumber. He felt the levers in his hands, he saw the steel hook of the turner jerking the log down on its slabbed face, and the carriage plunging ahead; and he heard the screaming thunder of his bandsaw as it ripped through bark and grain; he felt, saw, and heard no more. He was a hero, a king—and then the quitting whistle boomed through the mill.

The roar of machinery and the screams of the saws died away in a drone. Old Johnny McCann leaned on his levers and gazed miserably at the great log on the carriage. He had lost it. The night shift head sawyer would have it now. The sawyers and helpers were streaming for the door, all black shapes in the glaring light. The broad-beamed young setter swung away from the carriage, calling over his shoulder:

"Won't be home for supper, dad. Eatin' downtown."

II

Old Johnny didn't hear. His gaze was on the superintendent, who was slowly approaching from the scaler's desk. Old Johnny felt his legs giving way under him. He gripped the levers hard. His mind seemed to be turning numb from the burning ache in his feet; they shot pain clear to his eyes. That's the way she goes, lads. Forty years of it, forty years of standing dead still and at a strain in a head sawyer's cage, then the old legs and feet give out, the old hands get a little shaky and slow, and the super comes up, flushes, hems and haws, and finally blurts out the sad, sad news. The time has come. Life's got you down at last. You're old, you're old. No use to buck it. But it's—well, hell, let 'er go....

Old Johnny McCann walked alone from the company office to his home above the tideflats. On other payday nights the blue check in his pocket had made a glow that spread all over him, but now it was cold. He hobbled along, the wind blowing rain over his bowed head. Back of him the great domes of waste burners and the small lighted squares of millhouse windows shone through smoke and darkness. Old Johnny McCann was feeling like an exile, a man driven from his native city. Forty years as the king of a millhouse floor, and now… the superintendent's words kept pounding in his ears….

"Sorry, Johnny. Sorrier'n hell. But you know yourself—we got to hold the cut up to two hundred thousand—you've dropped to one-ninety-five, then ninety—eighty-five—losing two hundred dollars a shift, the company is. … Hrrumph! … It's all right—all right! You've made us thousands extra in your twenty-five years. You've got a pension coming. You're going to be treated right. Take it easy rest of your days—that's better, huh? Hrrumph. … The lad? Sorrier'n hell about the lad, too, Johnny. Looked like he'd step into your shoes till a while back. Can't stand for head sawyers hitting the redeye now. Times have changed since the old Saginaw days…. Well, maybe you *have* got it coming. Well—I'll give you another month—one more payday, Johnny—just one more. A chance to go out sawing on your highest average—I'll give you that. … Forget it. Us oldtimers got to stick together, Johnny. …"

The words kept hammering through old Johnny's head. A chance. Not a chance to keep himself from the waste pile—the shooting pains in his legs, the hot lead in his feet told him that. But for young Johnny, the broad-beamed lad who thought he could lick anything in life with a grin, a joke, or at the worst with a swing of his big white fist—ah, the hell of it, thought Johnny McCann. Blowing his check all night over the bar of the Owl. Laughing and joking all he could think of; with that soft streak in him. Would it turn hard at the chance for a real fight? Would he be willing to stand and battle by the old man's side? Old Johnny had his doubts. He only knew that he himself would make one mighty effort to go out in a grand smash of sawing…. Well, a bit of supper, a spell of rest, then to look up the lad…. Old Johnny McCann hobbled on, his head bowed against the winter rain.

III

SHAG HOGAN, DAY EDGERMAN in the M. & T. mill, was picking a cigar from a box on the Owl bar. He was making his selection carelessly, without even examining the box, for he was gazing sideways at young Johnny McCann. The broad-beamed young setter had just ordered another round of drinks for the M. & T. gang. A contemptuous grin was on the edgerman's swarthy face. Old Johnny McCann saw that first, as he stepped through the swinging doors of the Owl. He knew what it meant; he knew what thoughts were in the edgerman's head. Something like:

"Keep it up, my fine buck. Drink the redeye down. But watch friend Shag take a cigar. Drink yourself out of your last chance at the headsaw, son; hop to 'er, lad, for that makes Shag Hogan boss of the big rig when your old man saws himself off his feet."

Sure, those were his thoughts, though he spoke aloud so friendly and fine:

"Certainly I'm a friend of yours, Johnny. I just ain't drinkin' tonight, that's all. Don't mind my takin' a cigar now, hey Johnny?"

"Cert'nly not, Shag. Good ol' Shag, bes' edgerman on the tideflats! Take dozen s'gars on me, good ol' Shag Hogan."

Old Johnny felt his hands unclench, turn nerveless and cold. What was the use? That was the nature of the lad—puling drunk one minute, the next slobbering over the man who was all set to knock him out. No use—so old Johnny turned to go. As he did so he noticed that J. Michael Murphy, proprietor of the Owl, was conversing grandly with a nabob. As he talked he pointed at a faded and streaked steel engraving that was framed above the bar mirror.

"That picksher yer inquirin' about—yeah, it's been in my fambly for a hundred years," J. Michael was saying. "A fine, rare picksher it is. Come from the old country. Can't ye smell battle in it, though? And look at the harse. Ye never saw a braver harse in a picksher. Yeah, a fambly heirloom."

Old Johnny's gaze followed the pointing finger, and he grinned. The steel engraving was familiar to him. J. Michael had bought it from a pedler and hung it in his saloon back in the old Saginaw days. J. Michael had risen in the world out here on the Sound; he was a political influence and conversed with nabobs. Family heirlooms! Old Johnny felt an impulse to tell the nabob the facts about the engraving, but it was smothered by a sudden swell of emotion in his heart. In an instant the engraving had come to life with meaning for him.

It pictured the repulse of a cavalry charge in one of Napoleon's battles. The thing was vivid with an illusion of movement in a mass of panic-stricken horses. The background showed the enemy cavalry looming in pursuit. The battlefield was strewn with wounded and dying

Bunkhouse, 1894, Washington. Negative number OrHi35971. Courtesy Oregon Historical Society.

horses and men. But it was a hamstrung old warhorse in the center of the scene which had caught old Johnny's eye.

He was an old warhorse by the saber scars on his flanks, which the artist had taken pains to distinguish from his new wounds. His hind legs were sprawled impotently under him. Yet the heart of the old warhorse still throbbed with the fire of battle. That was beautifully shown. His lean, scarred, bleeding body was braced up on his sound front legs. His mane waved like a torn banner from his proud, arched neck. His teeth were bared at the onrushing enemy.

"Ah!" whispered old Johnny to himself, with huge astonishment. "To have known that picksher for so long and to have never really *seen* it afore! Why—why, it's me!"

Old Johnny McCann half-closed his eyes. The shine of the mirror turned into a bright mist. He saw himself as Roaring Johnny, a bully young sawyer in the white pine country far away. He mingled with the gang of his youth again. Tramped along with it to the big, red mill, the frost steaming off the sidewalk boards. He saw the cool, clear blue of a morning sky, he stepped high as the keen, frosty air tickled his ribs, he lifted his chest and was Roaring Johnny when he "helloed" his friends. Far out and away a snowy peak rose against the blue. Then a dark-green ridge of virgin timber, then stump-speckled, cut-over hills rolled down, with a light-green blanket of second-growth on the older lands near town. Steam wafted up in the sunlight from the booms in the millpond, the quiet water shining between the logs. The big, red mill, the black smokestacks, the white drifts of sawdust smoke, the whiter clouds of steam that puffed out from the exhausts. And the smells. The keen breeze bore down fresh and balmy smells from the green woods. It blew into his face the rousing pungent smells of green lumber and green sawdust.... Ah, it was a life to live over again!....

The life of the timberlands. His no more. Only to remember. But was it now? Old Johnny opened his eyes and stared hard at the warhorse in the engraving. By thunder, there he was! There was his story! He, too, had a grand life behind him! And, by the holy old mackinaw, he was going down fighting in just that style! And right here and now he'd show the lad, Shag Hogan, and all the rest of the gang, who was still the head sawyer of the M. & T. mill! Yea, bullies! Sawdust and shavings are going to fly! Come on, old warhorse, look up at your old tilicum in the picture there, square your shoulders, shake the hobbles out of your legs, and horn in!...

IV

"Only takin' cigars to-night, huh? Better put some redeye under your belt, Shag Hogan, and get some life into your carcass! For you've got a month of hell ahead of you, old-timer!"

There was a hush of amazement among the M. & T. men at the bar. Only one or two of the old-timers among them had ever heard their head sawyer's Saginaw bully roar. And old Johnny appeared about six inches taller and ten years younger to-night, as he jammed in between young Johnny and Shag Hogan. Old Johnny saw the wide stares of the sawdust savages and he shot a grim glance up at the old warhorse. More and more he was knowing how the brave old devil was feeling. It was kind of glorious, actually. The last grand stab in a mighty game.

"What are you buggin' your eyes about, Shag? Ain't you heard? Hell, I thought everybody in the mill knew I was due for the waste pile in another month. But you don't know, huh, Shag—you don't know you was brought here to take the headsaw when I passed out? Damn' innercent, ain't yuh?"

"Why, Mr. McCann, what you talkin' of?"

"Don't 'Mr. McCann' me, old-timer! I ain't no super. You know what I'm talkin' of—my last month on the headsaw. And I'm here to tell you it's goin' to be one grand smash! I'm tellin' you and the whole M. & T.

outfit I'm out to bust all records for my finish! Two hundred thousand feet a shift won't be nothin' this next month! I'll send the cants down the rolls to the edger so fast you'll wish you'd never heard of a sawmill, Shag Hogan! You'll be skin and bone, time this month is out!"

The edgerman's pride was stabbed, and he roared.

"Th' hell I will! You never saw the day you could cover me up, you stove-up old Siwash! Nev—"

The last word was choked in the middle as he saw the flash of a big, white fist swinging at his mouth. Young Johnny had turned from puling to fighting. He bellowed and swung—but a gnarled old hand knocked the blow down and clamped his wrist.

"Just a minute, lad. I ain't ready to start on *you* yet." Old Johnny turned on the edgerman again. "I'm warnin' you fair, Shag. You'll have to cinch your leather apron up tight, spit on your hands and keep your carcass full of life if you handle the cants I'll roll down this month. Rest up good to-morrer, for Monday you ketch hell and hallelujah!"

Old Johnny smacked a double-eagle on the bar.

"Set 'em up, bartender! Three rounds for the house on Roarin' Johnny McCann! Promenade to the bar! Drink to a month of sawin' such as has never been seen this side of Saginaw! Drink 'er down with an old warhorse of the timberlands!"

Shag Hogan drank with the others. He felt kind of sick, like he needed something. He could swear that the old sawyer was drunk. But old Johnny was steady on his feet, though his straight body swayed like a pine in a big wind. Maybe it *would* be hell and hallelujah. It was almost that right now, wrestling the big cants and tugging on the heavy edger levers. The toughest edging job he'd ever seen. He wouldn't stay on it an hour if it wasn't for the chance at headsawing which the super had promised him soon. A few shifts of extra heavy cutting might do him up. He was no fool. There was more to this than just a grandstand play on the part of old Johnny McCann. The old stiff had more on his mind than that. The kid-that was it, by the holy old mackinaw! He wondered now. If the old head sawyer was playing a game for the kid—

"Outside with you, lad. I've something to say to you alone."

Young Johnny obediently pushed his big frame from the bar and unsteadily followed the old man out through the swinging doors. Shag Hogan scowled after them. He was suspicious. He had good reasons to be.

V

THERE WAS A SPACE of clear glass at the top of the glazed front window of the Owl Saloon. Standing on the avenue curb, one might look up and through the oblong of clear glass and see the steel engraving above the bar mirror.

The old sawyer kept his gaze fixed on the battle scene as he stood and talked to the big lad at his side. About them were the trolleys, the horses and buggies in the wide avenue, the black shadows of store buildings behind dim street lights, the bright spots along the sidewalks, marking the saloons, and the sawmill men stringing by, hilarious over a payday night. But neither man was conscious of the life of the avenue as old Johnny had his say. One looked at a picture that had come to life for him; the other grew sober under words spoken in a voice that carried him back to the years when he was a small boy flushed with the pride of his dad being the head sawyer in the biggest mill on the tideflats. Looking past the corner of the Owl Saloon, young Johnny McCann could see the red domes of the burners, the lights of millhouse windows. He began to feel something of what that meant to the old man. Maybe life was something more than blowing your paycheck, hogging down the redeye, sporting with the girls, raising hell, cocky and proud.

It had hurt when the old man talked to him about being an old warhorse on his last legs; then throwing it into him about having a soft streak, saying it looked like he'd need another setter to go out in the grand smash of sawing he'd planned. It was the hurt of a scolded boy, and something else from boyhood welled up in young Johnny now. That feeling of his dad being a hero-it had stirred again at this talk of ending up like an old warhorse. That was it, right enough. The old man had sawed his way from the white pine sticks of Bangor and Saginaw to the big firs of Puget Sound. Battled the big sticks from a sawyer's cage for forty years. Young Johnny wanted to throw his arm around the stooped shoulders. But you could only bristle and bluster when words were coming at you like the licks of an ax.

"Your cocky hell-raisin' has left you jug-headed on the setworks, and that's what's knocked down my cut more'n any failin' of mine! The super knows. He didn't bring Hogan here on my account! You ain't got a chance to step into my shoes now, son!"

"To hell with it!"

"Yeah. All right. Hold your dander down. I ain't out for no lecksher. I'm thinkin' of myself; my finish. How I make it is up to you. You *are* the best setter on the tideflats when you want to be; you're the only one, son, who can help me bust all sawin records this last month and go out like an old warhorse." Old Johnny's voice quavered a little there, then it sounded steady and hard. "If you're goin' to lay down, say so, and I'll find a setter who'll see me through, anyway. I want to know now."

"Who the hell you think you're talkin' to, some ten-year-old? Certainly I won't lay down!"

"That's all I wanted to know." Old Johnny felt his knees shaking with relief; but he wouldn't soften. "Then come on home."

VI

A HEAD SAWYER NEEDS LEGS like two tough timbers. He stands on one spot and in a strain all through his shift. When the last cant is dropped from a sawlog and the carriage is shot back and ground to a stop in front of the log deck, the sawyer steps on a plunger with his left foot and the dogs that hold the first of the log deck turn are released. The sawyer's left foot then shoves a foot throttle down, steam pounds into a cylinder below the mill floor, and huge steel arms leap up and shove the new sawlog against the carriage headblocks. The sawyer then has both feet to stand on until the log is ripped into cants. His right foot hardly moves in its place until the noon and night whistles blow. Forty years of it, and any head sawyer needs new legs for his job.

Old Johnny McCann was needing new legs on the eleventh day of his battle. The first ten had made sawmill history on the tideflats. Everything had been right. There had been a noble run of the logs from the woods, all sticks between four and six feet in diameter. The only orders on the boards were for small timbers. So old Johnny only had to grade the clears out of each sawlog after slabbing off a face, and then knock off four- to ten-inch cants for the edger.

It was beautiful sawing. And young Johnny had been with him all the way. Whenever old Johnny had felt that he couldn't last another minute, that he'd have to give in to the pains that throbbed to his bones, to the "weak trembles" of his knees and the burning numbness in his feet that made him feel like his shoe soles were hot lead—then old Johnny only had to look up and out of the cage, across the sawlog on the carriage, and see the broad-beamed young setter at his dial, showing new life in every move of him, and then the leg pains were fought down again.

It was marvelous what a change had shown in the lad that first Monday. Even the super had noticed it, remarking that it was too bad old Johnny hadn't got his hand in before Shag Hogan was put on the edger and promised the headsaw. Old Johnny had managed a twisted grin, though a ten-hour shift was done and his legs were about killing him. And he had said under his breath, "Don't be too sure who's to take my headsaw, Mr. Super. 'Tis only the first day of battle." A mighty day it had been. The cut had jumped to two hundred and twenty thousand feet, a record for the mill. And Shag Hogan was like a dishrag. He was more suspicious of old Johnny than ever. He had more reasons to be.

For the record was broken by two thousand feet the next day, and through the week it had climbed on, until two hundred and thirty thousand feet were marked up by the scaler for Saturday. It had been a good thing for old Johnny that shift was a Saturday. Young Johnny had to go for a livery rig to take him home. But it was all right; the lad stayed away from the saloons that night; and he stuck home all day Sunday. He still bristled and blustered at every word that was said to him, bragged about the big drunk he would have when this month was over, and the like of that. Old Johnny wished him in hell and declared he'd fire him off the carriage in a second, once another decent setter showed up in the mill. One would have thought the two were sworn enemies. But what a week of sawing it had been!

Monday was a blue day. The cut dropped to two-fifteen. Still high over the average, but not enough. Shag Hogan had been freshened by a Sunday's rest, also, and he left his edger with something of a swagger Monday night. Tuesday morning old Johnny's eyes were bleak and his face was drawn with desperate determination as he hobbled into his cage. That day he cut two-thirty-five, with the edger table choked every minute of the shift. Wednesday and Thursday the old sawyer held the cut up to the high mark, and last night Shag Hogan, his long body as limp as an empty sack, his face sweat-streaked, his hair a wet tangle over his eyes, argued furiously with the superintendent. The super shrugged his shoulders and turned away, meaning that if the wrathy edgerman didn't like it he could quit. Old Johnny had to be carted home again, but there was a thrilling hope in his heart that more than made up for his wrecked legs.

It was hot lead in his feet, running snakes of fire in his muscles and the palsy in his knees this afternoon of the eleventh day. There was a cold spot in his heart from the feeling that this day was his last one—the old warhorse was licked—enemy was looming closer and closer above him, like a black cloud. Still it was never-say-die with old Johnny. He was sawing away at a mightier lick than ever. At midafternoon the scaler's figures showed that one hundred and ninety thousand feet of logs had already gone through the big headrig. If he could shove them on as fast he'd hang up two-forty for the ten hours, maybe more. The edger table was choked with cants; the lineup men were stacking them; and Shag Hogan was hog-wild. Maybe it'll be his Black Friday, thought old Johnny. The thought was made like a prayer, for he could feel his own finish drawing near.

VII

HE MIGHT LAST THE DAY, but never the week, never tomorrow. Flesh and blood couldn't stand it. He could fight pain, fight it like an old warhorse, but when the old right leg began to sink under him as he tripped a log from the deck, he knew that the enemy was drawing close, ready to beat him down. Looking over at young Johnny, who was all wildfire for the grand smash of sawing his old man was making, showing it in the shine of his eyes, the flush of his face, his swagger and bluster forgotten now—that would make old Johnny fight pain, but it couldn't keep the strained old knees from buckling.... Was he going now? Not on your life! Be an old warhorse, Johnny McCann, to the last snort!... Rear up and show your teeth to the last damn' gasp!

He forced his mind back to the sawing. It slowed just so much whenever he let himself feel pain or think. His right hand quickened on the lever that stuck up from the floor by his right foot, and the carriage shot behind the flashing teeth of the bandsaw so much the faster. Quicker again, and the carriage hardly seemed to stop before it was plunging forward, then slowing at the instant the log's end touched the ripping teeth, then crowding through, and another cant boomed down the rolls. Back and forward, back and forward, signal the setter—he's just the setter now, and not the big lad—now that much quicker with the left-hand lever—the giant gooseneck hook of the turner leaps up, stabs down into the sawlog, twists it like a cat twisting a ball of yarn, lifts, drops from sight as the steel arms set the log against the headlocks.

Saw on! Saw on! Keep a-sawing to break another record to-day, Johnny McCann! Aye, old warhorse, you're Roaring Johnny again!

The whistle shrilled for the millwrights. Black smoke rolled up from the edger with a stink of burning leather. Shag Hogan had stuck a cant in his circulars and slipped his drive belt. Take just one glance at him, old Johnny! See him jumping and waving his fists like a maniac. Saw hard now, old-timer! Pile the cants ten feet high on the edger table! Beautiful logs on the deck! Roll 'em along!...

The super was bawling into his ears, so as to be heard above the singing roar of the big band. What say—ease up?

"Ease up, hell! You want your big cut, don't you, hey? I'm sawin' logs!"

Forget the burning aches and pains! Quick on the levers, now, like you had the youth of the lad there behind the setter's dial! Hearken to the old saw's song! Better than a bugle call, hey, Johnny McCann? See the cants drop and boom down the rolls not a dozen feet apart! Ain't that some heavy artillery, old Johnny? Pile 'em ten feet high on the edger table! Pile 'em up, you lineup men! Got to put 'em somewhere—the old warhorse of the timberlands is busting another record to-day—two-forty—two-forty—two-forty—you're going to make that figure, Johnny McCann!...

What's that down behind the edger table? Sneak just one look and see what's going on. Hell, it's Shag Hogan, shaking one fist at the pile of cants and his other in the super's face ! And the super's bawling back at him-good glory, Johnny McCann, it looks like—yea, lad, there he goes! Off comes his leather apron, he jumps on it, heads for his locker, grabs his hat and coat, and out he goes, still shaking his fists, through the millhouse door! The super's taking the edger....

Hey, old warhorse, you've licked 'em! Old-timer, the last battle is yours! It's yours....

Ah, Johnny lad, it's all right now... all right... and the old warhorse needs a bit of help... he's sinking down... can't you see, Johnny lad... it was all put on... where's your big young arm?...

The big, young arm was around old Johnny a second after he had fallen between his sawyer's levers. From out of the grip of it a weak, old voice whispered:

"Take the headsaw, lad. She's yours."

Orland E. Esval
(1904-)

Orland Esval was born in North Dakota and grew up in eastern Montana, where he built a career as an electrical engineer. The following memoir records his impressions of the ennobling power of labor, which he gained as a youthful member of a threshing crew that met each year near Scobey.

Member of the Crew

After reaching my teens, an annual obsession was to join the neighborhood threshing crew on its fall circuit. While I had wistfully aspired, ever since childhood, to be an engine operator, there was no chance for that. My only possible place on the crew was as a bundle hauler. It was very hard work, and any youth who could hold his own on that job through an entire threshing season was accepted as a man. No longer did he have to take second place boy status. Each year, it seemed, Papa would not let me join the crews, feeling that I just did not have the necessary stamina. It hurt, because I knew younger fellows who could do it. To be sure, they had short, stocky builds, and were physically well developed for their age. Papa, I knew, was a little disappointed in me, for I had not inherited his solid frame and was tall but very slender. Papa encouraged me to wrestle, and even bought me some boxing gloves. But nearly always I came out second best. I had helped only as an alternate for a few hours at a time on crews of previous seasons, until the summer of 1921, when I was sixteen years old. That year I finally wore Papa down. He had misgivings, but he agreed to equip me with a good team of horses and a wagon bundle rack and let me hire out as a regular on the threshing run.

Our neighbor, Loren Fladager, operated the local threshing rig. He was at our place one Sunday before the start of the run, and agreed, with some misgivings of his own, to take me on. The pay: $5.00 plus $2.00 for the team and bundle wagon—a grand total of $7.00 per working day. I was jubilant. For the first time in my life, a man's pay! I quickly calculated that if the season lasted thirty days I would have earned $210.00. It was an opulent, but really not an impossible, dream.

Loren, however, soon brought me back to earth: "We are starting at my place tomorrow morning. The wheels are rolling at six o'clock and you had better be there."

The alarm woke me up at 4:30 on Monday morning. After a quick breakfast, I harnessed Mable and Queen, hitched them to the wagon, and drove off in the brisk pre-dawn air. Papa had let me have two of his best work horses. I was also equipped with a bedroll, the essential three-tined pitchfork, and what proved to be my lifesaver—a canvas bag for drinking water. Mama and Papa wished me well on a venture they knew was going to be very rough on me. But I was on top of the world and could see no reason for their concern. As it turned out, it was a bumper crop year for Montana, and a vintage (although painful) year of growing up for me.

The sun, a huge golden orb, was just rising through the morning mists of this portentous day in late August. The horses trotted and the wagon rattled as we passed field after field of grain standing in shocks, waiting for threshing. This was a bountiful year, the growing crops having eluded a gamut of hazards throughout the season. The precious grain kernels would soon be stored in granaries, provided the threshers were allowed a few weeks of dry, clear weather.

Never had the farmers' outlook, or mine, been rosier. Proudly, I was taking Papa's place on the team. Moreover, for practical reasons, it was good that Papa had a replacement. The new County of Daniels had just been formed from portions of Valley and Sheridan Counties, and he had been elected to the first Board of Commissioners. Occupied in setting up the new county government, and establishing a new courthouse in Scobey, he had to do so much traveling that he bought his first automobile—a second-hand Model T Ford. Thus aside from the excitement of harvest, my ego was bolstered because I was *needed.*

True enough, as I approached the base of operations the "wheels were rolling," the endless belt on its perpetual journey from engine to separator and back. The separator was moaning, groaning and throwing out plumes of yellow straw. Loren Fladager, standing in the cab of his giant, rumbling, four-cylinder Avery traction engine, had a watchful eye on everything. The romantic steam threshing engines were already outdated; simpler to operate, more efficient, powerful gasoline tractors had taken their place.

Waving from the cab, Loren indicated to me the field from which I was to start loading. Following a row of shocks, I was soon pitching bundles into the rack as fast as I could. The reins were tied to the side of the rack so I could easily reach them in guiding the horses to follow the row. After a few days of training, they followed the row at proper distance with very little reining. Starting and stopping them by "giddup" and "whoa" was all that was necessary.

Soon I had the bundles piled high on my rack and the load was getting heavy for the horses to pull over the soft ground. But I wanted to be sure my load was a big one as I pulled up to the machine, because I knew all eyes would be on the "greenhorn" to see if he might try to get by with lighter loads than the other haulers. I knew their code and I was determined to abide by it.

Driving in on top of the swaying load, I had hopes of arriving soon enough to have a bit of rest before unloading. The line, however, was nearly empty. There was no time to sit on the ground or even to say hello to anybody. Immediately I had the precarious job of guiding the horses to the feeder box of the growling, shaking separator.

The first time of the season, this was a frightening experience, even for the gentlest of horses. It was necessary to approach as close as possible to the feeder without colliding with belts, pulleys, conveyers and shakers. Luckily I had Mable and Queen—fine, placid draft horses of the Belgian breed—but even for them, coming so close to the noisy monster and the blinding dust was asking too much. At the first pass, I was too far away. The next time I managed to get closer. After calming the mares the best I could and tying the reins back, hopefully to make them stand still until my load was emptied into the machine, I started pitching into the feeder.

I had been joined by a "spike pitcher" to speed up the unloading and to keep the separator working to capacity. Since my rack was still not close enough to the feeder conveyer and we had to pitch the extra distance, the helper gave me a disgusted Bronx cheer.

The grain bundles had to be tossed "heads first" into the feeder for efficient separation of kernels from straw and chaff. A canvas conveyer transported them head-on into revolving knives which cut the twine with which they were tied, then they disappeared into the machine. Presently the mass became a rubbing, tearing, shaking, screaming and blowing holocaust that eventually diverted the kernels into bags or wagon boxes. It was the farmers' "pay dirt."

Quickly my load was gone, and I was on my way for another. It was not yet 7:00 A.M., but the sun was climbing rapidly in a cloudless sky. The day was going to be hot, with little breeze, but there was no time to think about that. I rushed out to load as fast as I could. This time I pulled in before all those ahead were unloaded, so I gained some precious minutes of rest. And my mares allowed me to maneuver my rack closer to the feeder.

Things were going well. At each load I was earning two or three minutes of rest; Mable and Queen were behaving beautifully as we established ourselves in a slot behind Ole Lien and ahead of Nels Sundby. We were, however, on the belt side of the machine, where, because of the heavy drive belt from the engine, there was a greater distance for pitching the bundles. As it turned out, this was to be my working position for the whole threshing run.

I knew that Ole and Nels were very nice men and that gave me courage. Since Ole unloaded just ahead of me, it was my aim to arrive at the rig before he started to unload, affording a moment to chat with him. Most important, there would be rest during his unloading. But as the morning went on, it became harder and harder to get any rest between loads.

Already I was getting weary, plagued with incessant thirst. I gulped water time after time from my blessed canvas bag. Even so, after about seven rounds, I began to wonder if I could make it until noontime dinner. The bundles were feeling awfully heavy, and actually, because the crop was good, they were. The straw was short and every bundle compact, the heads heavy with ripe grain.

At midmorning there was coffee and donuts at the rig if you had time to get off your load and take some. But I was getting behind so I passed it up. At 10 o'clock the sun was blistering, my head aching. No longer could I toss the bundles up into the rack; they had to be lifted all the way. Sweat was in my eyes and dust was crusting on my face. I could hardly see.

Just as I was pulling in with my tenth load, the threshing stopped for dinner. Staggering, I unhitched the mares and took them to the long watering trough where they drank great quantities before they would leave it. With bridles off, I tied them to the feed box at the back of the rack and poured oats out for them. After washing my face in cool water, I was somewhat revived. The dinner was very good, a typical harvest time meal; but however tasty it was, I could scarcely touch it. I crawled under my rack, in the shade next to the horses, and rested.

In no time, it seemed, Loren started the engine, a signal to hitch up and start unloading into the machine. The afternoon was worse, the sun white hot in an ashen sky. The bundles were pitched, loaded, hauled and unloaded in endless repetition in a semi-conscious kind of daze. In my mind, the threshing machine became a hungry demon, demanding more and more bundles for its awful appetite. Unreasoning and unrelenting, it devoured everything in its gaping maw. To deny the monster its tribute was too horrible to contemplate.

So the day went on—aching muscles, pounding heart, ominous thoughts, continuous thirst. Coffee and cake—but it was ignored again. Finally, came the saturated state of fatigue. It could get no worse.

The sun was no longer so blistering, but the routine just as perpetual. Like a cog in a chain between Ole and Nels, I never got out of place or missed my turn. This was the code, especially for greenhorns.

Unbelievably, the moan and groan of the separator finally stopped, leaving a hollow, silent void. As everyone began unhitching, there was low talk and a little tired joking. The animals had to be attended to first—find them a sheltered place for the night, after watering them. Unharness and rub down the sweat-caked bodies, find hay and bedding, then give them their ration of oats.

At about 7 o'clock, with hands and face washed, I joined the rest of the crew for supper in the Fladager house. Mrs. Fladager gave me a concerned look and motioned me to come with her. Speaking as a former nurse, she said, "You look terrible. How do you feel?"

Without much conviction, I said I was all right. Giving me two white pills, she said, "Take these and go to bed right after supper."

What these pills were I never knew, but now it occurs to me that they might have been salt tablets. It is likely that I had a salt deficiency from perspiring and drinking so much water.

Again, I could hardly touch the good meal. Ignoring the banter around me, I left the table to find a place to unroll my bed. But first I had to lead the mares to the watering trough. That done, I laid down, but it was a restless sleep. I pitched heavy bundles all night, and tossed as if in high fever.

A loud clamor aroused me. The crew was getting up for the day's work, but even to move in my bedroll was painful. Pulling on socks, overalls, shirt and boots was agony. At 5:00 A.M. it was chilly, so I put on a warm jacket. Rolling up the bedroll was more misery. When I limped over to the horses, they were in surprisingly good shape and hungry for their oats. It took excruciating effort to lift the heavy harnesses over their backs, but after a face wash in cold water, I was rejuvenated enough to eat a fried egg and a pancake.

Sad to relate, however, the second working day was truly worse than the first. Loading the first rounds with stiffened muscles took painful effort. Then there was some limbering relief. But the day was even hotter. Somehow I survived, not thinking, not questioning. I continued as a cog, never slipping my place in the chain. This is not fantasy; it is fact, because Ole Lien was always about finished unloading as I drove up to the machine. Sometimes Nels Sundby was there ahead of me to enjoy a long breather while I unloaded.

At dinner the second day I still had no appetite. Lying in the shade until work started again, there were lurking thoughts of quitting, going home, being sensible; it would be so easy to end the agony. Mama would be relieved. But the idea had to be rejected. It would mean a permanent loss of status, and I simply could not disappoint Papa.

In my numbing weariness that second afternoon, I was, in fact, a menace to myself and others. In unloading at the machine I was unsure of my footing on the spongy load of bundles. A fall into the feeder was sure tragedy. Al Lawson was the spike pitcher on the belt side. Blinded by sweat and dust, I accidentally scratched him twice with my pitchfork. He was a great mountain of a man and my unfortunate jabs did not even cause him to break the rhythm of his pitching. But he edged over to me for a moment, and over the noise shouted, "Boy, you better not do that again!"

It was fortunate that Mama did not know about my travail. There was a story that circulated at harvest time about a hapless bundle hauler who, after accidentally jabbing a spike pitcher with his fork several times, was thrown to his destruction in the feeder. Such a thing could happen to Mama's one and only son.

At coffee time that afternoon, I climbed down and tried to swallow some of it. Others of the crew were standing around, Selmer Fladager one of them. He was one who enjoyed needling me, and he said as I was holding my cup, "Is that you or is it your shadow? You are so skinny I believe I can see right through you." The others laughed. The dried sweat on my face cracked as I smiled wanly and retreated up on my load, heart pounding.

Two days of heavy exertion in extremely hot weather, profuse sweating and little nourishment had indeed taken their toll. My shirt and overalls hung on me loosely. I had been thin, but now I looked like a cadaver.

While I avoided jabbing Al with my pitchfork again, there were other problems. In my fatigue, some of the bundles I pitched to the feeder landed on top of others or even lay crossways as they entered the machine. This caused the separator to snort and slow down. This was bad for the threshing process, causing loss of grain in the straw pile.

Witnessing all this, Loren ran from the engine, climbed up on my rack, came close to me and yelled, "You feed this machine right or get out of here! Understand?"

I did understand. Perhaps it was anger, causing the adrenaline to flow, sharpening my wits, that gave me strength to deliver the bundles in better position after that. And even this awful day came to an end, as the groaning rumble of the rig suddenly stopped. In my stupor, it gave me a start. But this time I was not quite so indifferent. There came a small restoration of my wits, and in my thoughts, even food took on a slight appeal. Caring for my two faithful mares took super effort, but at supper, I did more than just toy with my food. Almost oblivious to the table chatter, I hurried through the meal and quite literally hit the hay (straw).

Sleep this time was not quite so nightmarish, but waking up in the morning was just as miserable, my muscles sorer than ever. The harnesses were heavier, too, and the mares nuzzled me as if in sympathy.

But this day—it was Wednesday—was the turning point. The hot weather continued and the threshing was as steady as ever, but I was less an insensible robot. There was more appetite, and more consciousness of the whole operation. That morning there was one nagging worry: a substitute spike pitcher was on the job to replace Al Lawson, and he didn't have Al's skill. This bothered me, especially since I had heard the reason Al was absent. He had a weakness for liquor, and the night before had gone to the town of Tande and treated himself to a bottle of bootleg whiskey (this was during Prohibition). It took him half a day to sober up, but he was on the job in the afternoon as if nothing had happened.

The next day, although the work was steadily getting easier for me and I finally was really hungry before mealtime, the jabbing episode with Al and his brief absence from the job was still to haunt me. This mental misery was in some ways worse than the physical torture I had known. At supper that night, one of my tormentors turned to Al Lawson and said, "I hear you took off and went to Scobey to see a doctor yesterday morning."

Al looked up in surprise, since the statement was obviously not true. But he caught the drift, grinned, and growled into his plate, "Who me? Oh ya, ya."

Following up his chance, the wise one went on: "Yeah, and I hear you got stuck with a pitchfork and got blood poisoned." This brought down the house and, of course, it was at my expense. New-found hunger gone, I stared down at my plate and blushed to my ears.

Saturday night, after pitching the last bundle for the day, I headed straight for home without waiting for supper with the crew. Never had home been so appealing. Mable and Queen knew our destination at once and maintained a trot all the way. The rig was now at Willy Fladager's, a couple of miles further away.

I had a gala reception. Papa's oldest sister, my cultured Aunt Aagot, was there as well as my parents, my sisters and Uncle Torstein. A conquering hero could not have been better received. Papa even took care of my horses for me. I surprised Mama by requesting, first of all, a washtub full of water in the back shed. For the first time in my life I loathed being filthy dirty. It was a glorious feeling to be cleansed of six days of sweat and grime and to put on fresh clothes.

Mama peeked at me in the lantern light before I got dressed and gasped, "Orland, you have lost so much weight. I think this is bad for you. Please do not go back to it."

I brushed her off, but surprised her at the number of helpings I had of her delicious supper. She had all my favorites, including strawberry shortcake and heavy cream. After supper there was music and singing, a real party atmosphere, but I could not stay awake and went right to bed. I did not wake up until 4:00 the next afternoon, when it was nearly time to go back to the threshing location.

Mama pleaded with me to give it up, but although I had misgivings, I hitched my horses to the bundle wagon and drove off. At this point, I knew I could take the physical part of being on the crew. What I still could not handle was the mental part, the needling. This feeling could not be shared with anyone, not even my parents. The complete rest at home had, however, done wonders. Rolling out of bed so early in the morning was still painful, but endurance had been developed to cope with the hard labor and hot weather. Most important, while I knew I might still be needled, I would no longer be singled out for it.

In the third week of the run there was an early September snowstorm. Fair weather quickly followed it, but the operations were halted for several days, allowing a welcome vacation for me at home. With it came the opportunity to hear from Papa about his interesting work with the County Commissioners in setting up the new government of Daniels County.

After this hiatus, I was really glad when the harvested wheat, standing in shocks, was again dry enough so threshing could resume. What a great feeling it was to take my place on the crew again, this time as a regular. I was especially proud of this when, in due course, the operation got to our farm.

My chief problem now was a ravenous hunger that plagued me the last couple of hours before dinner and supper. The mares, too, were thriving in spite of the long hours of hard work. By now they were so accustomed to the routine that I scarcely had to speak to them as they pulled the wagon along the shock rows while I tossed the bundles into the rack. I loved the gentle brutes. I loved it all. Too soon it would end.

With a final groan the machine swallowed the last bundle and stopped for good. The crew dissolved in all directions, hurrying home to attend to many things that had been neglected during the run.

Until that instant I could not comprehend that the finish would be so complete and final. A sudden tight feeling in the throat betrayed the attachment I had formed for these men, machines and animals. There had been a challenge, a mountain to be climbed. With painful effort and teamwork, it had been conquered. But now at the pinnacle it had collapsed into a valley of emptiness for me. The crew had disbanded abruptly, indifferently, leaving a void of silent desolation. I felt let down, deflated.

Loren and Carl Lien stayed with the rig, coupling up everything, including the cook car, for towing back to the Fladager place. I lingered for my pay. All the rest of the crew were farmers who applied their wages on their threshing bill. Loren took out his worn timekeeper book and tallied up my working days. I had not missed an hour of threshing time and it totaled 25 and 3/4 days. I had earned $180.25. As he handed me the check, Loren paid me his best compliment: "You're gonna be a good worker."

Mable and Queen sensed the run had ended. They would have galloped all the way home if I had not held them in. For me, it was high time I entered school. I would be deprived, even, of the companionship of my beautiful horses. Did they know they would be enjoying a well earned vacation? It seemed so. Within an hour they were in the big pasture, reveling, whinnying, snorting, free of leather collars and straps. They rolled on the ground, squealing in ecstasy. In their freedom it would take days before the heavy harness marks would no longer mar their furry coats.

I did not know it then, but not only had I parted company with Mable and Queen, a fine crew and a great team spirit, but with the only lifestyle I had ever known. Never again would I harness and drive fine horses, or ride windswept prairies looking for stray cattle, or plow fields, or harvest tall standing grain. Never again would I see limitless winter whiteness, or sense the pungent barn smells where cows are milked while dogs and cats wait hungrily for their dish of foaming milk.

Most of all, I didn't realize, and it is well that I didn't, that those noble people, bonded together by an austere environment, would become for me only a misty memory.

Dennis "Dinny" Murphy

Montanan Dennis "Dinny" Murphy worked as a motor-man, a contract miner, and a "nipper"—someone who brought tools and supplies to miners underground. Mining, an arduous occupation under the best of circumstances, left an indelible impression on the history of Idaho and Montana, where, particularly in the late nineteenth century, violence in labor relations was a chronic presence in the copper and silver areas. In 1986, author and researcher Teresa Jordan recorded Murphy's recollections of labor in the Butte mines owned by the Anaconda Copper Mining Company.

I Found My Likings in The Mines

as told to Teresa Jordan

I always remember when I went to St. Mary's school, one day I was sitting in a desk looking out the window into the mine yard. I had an Irish nun for a teacher, Sister Laurentia, and she cracked me on the knuckles with her ruler and told me to sit up. Years later, I was on Park Street one day and I saw her. I told her that now I was in the mine yard looking up at St. Mary's. She grabbed my hand, she said, "Dennis, we all have to be something. Some of us had to be doctors and some of us had to be priests and you were put here—what you do is vitally important." She tried to make me feel good anyhow.

People use to always think that you had to be really dumb to be a miner, that you couldn't have an education, that it was nothing to go down and drill a round. But I saw some of these "old country men" who probably couldn't read very much, or maybe they didn't speak English too well, but on measuring day, they could figure in their way faster than the graduate of the School of Mines. Everybody down in the mine wasn't just an ignoramus.

I tell some of these kids, you ought to be pretty proud of your heritage. Your dad, he wasn't a slob, he worked in the mines. You should be as proud as your friend over there who says his dad is a doctor or his dad is a engineer. They wouldn't be doctors or engineers if it wasn't for miners, either. I looked for other things, but I found my likings in the mines.

They had pretty places down in the mine where copper water would drip and it would form crystal icicles. When you touched them, they'd disintegrate. They'd be the prettiest colors—amber, green, emerald, even flecks of deep red would flicker. There were places at the St. Lawrence that went back to the days of the Copper Kings. There had been fires in there that were just left to burn until they went out. You'd get a piece of wood, and the knot of the wood would be filled with pure copper. A fire had probably burned in there for years and years until it went out and had melted the copper right out of the rock. They were interesting mines, the St. Lawrence and the Anaconda and the Neversweat, they had a history. They weren't just holes in the ground.

Every mine probably smells different, but when you left surface and fresh air to go down, it had a real different smell. Nothing on surface ever reminds you of that smell. Whether it's the humidity in some of the hot places, the smell from copper water or from decaying timber in certain places, it just has a different aroma. It's hard to describe.

You could never understand how hot, how really hot and humid, it would be in some of these places. You work in your yard and the sweat might roll down your face. Well, down in the mine, it was nothing to take off your mine undershirt and ring it out. And when you take your mine hat off sometimes, the water would just fall right down from the band. Or you took your mine boots off and dumped the water out. People would probably think that you couldn't really sweat that much to pour water out of your boots, but you could. In some places it was so hot that the men would get cramps from the loss of salt in their systems. The Emma and the Travonia were cool mines. The Belmont was noted for being a hot box and then the Con, when it got down 5000 feet, had some pretty hot spots. Some of the places had names, like the Chinese Laundry at the Stewart mine, if you worked in there, you could work any place because that was one of the hottest spots.

Some days I would just hate to go to work because I knew where I was going to be working and I knew it was going to be hot and would probably be gassy. When I was servicing a drift, or even pulling out of a raise, the minute I started letting that rock into the mine car that gas would come out of the rock and my headache would start at the base of my neck and go up. I'd get a pounding, pounding headache. But then you get on surface and go up to Big Butte Tavern and have a beer and a hamburger sandwich and talk it over, and you were back the next day to hate the same thing all over again.

But there were good people you worked with underground. They used to really tease you (when you were green). You know, getting on the cage, you just shook with fright because you never knew what to expect and the older men would tease you and tell you stories about big wrecks they had going down. Just anything to frighten you more. But once you were down there, they were very, very concerned for your safety. All that harassing and teasing but they made sure that nothing was going to happen to you.

I'm five feet five, and I weighed then probably a hundred pounds. We used to have to dump these one-ton cars. The man I was put to work with was a big husky kid and he was very good to me and showed me how it's easy if you do it right. And if I'd be on the station and maybe be a little bit behind, these station tenders would stop and help me dump rock. Other men, like pipemen that took care of the water pipes and the air pipes, if I had a chute that was hung up or something, they'd come and give me a hand. They didn't ridicule you, say something like, "Look, Shorty, get out of the way," or "Here, weakling, let me do it." They used to just say, "Here, Murph, I'll give you a hand."

These older men are gone, that I think about. You know, they called them Bohunks, Harps, Cousin Jacks. Some people probably didn't like to be called a Bohunk or whatever, but underground, these men were loving guys. There were two guys, Gabe and Keiser, they were brothers. One was as round as a refrigerator. And that poor guy worked in the stope and you could hear him huffing and puffing, he used to have to take his mine lamp off to get through the landing. He'd struggle for 20 minutes to get his hind end down. And then he waddled. He was such a loving guy. If he knew you liked Povititza, he'd bring a piece in his bucket for you.

There was another guy there, Dago John, he took these quarter inch steel sheets they have in the mine and walled his house with them because of the bomb—the "bome," he'd say—the bomb was going to come, the end of the world. He used to take a can of beer wrapped in newspaper. One day, he put his bucket down, and I stole the can of beer and rolled a piece of wood up in the paper. He was going to kill me—not me, he didn't know I did it. I just did it to tease him. But he used to tell me about his inventions. Great big man that was more powerful than he himself actually knew. He could do things.

I used to work with a guy, he was a Montenegran, from Yugoslavia, and he used to grab me by the cheeks and say, "Murphy, good kid, son of a bitch. Too bad you Irish." I was always invited down to his home for their Serbian Christmas. Same way when I worked down at the Leonard and all those people down there would always want you to come home to eat, or they'd bring you whatever was good in their bucket.

The rope men were nearly all Norwegians and Swedes. Like Judge Arnold Olsen, his dad was a ropeman. And they were the ones that lowered all that stuff down the mine. You may have seen pictures where they moved a whole gallus frame without dismantling it. These are all guys that never got out of grade school, but with winches and different rope pulleys, they did marvelous things.

I worked with the Finnlanders at the St. Lawrence and they were the nicest, cleanest people. They would give you the shirt off their back, want to feed you. And boy, they would come to work soused. But I never saw any of them knocked down and dragged out like the Irish. Seemed like they always kept on working, where an Irishman would fall by the wayside.

When I think of people like Gabe and Keiser, and like this John—I get a lump in my throat. "Too bad you Irish, you son of a gun." That camaraderie—that's probably what made working in the mines so interesting. I could just never explain why I liked the mines.

MEN WERE DIFFERENT IN THE PIT. There were really nice, nice guys at the pit, but their work was so different. You know, down at the mine, at lunch time, there was a lot of tomfoolery, a lot of playing. They'd nail your bucket to a post or, if you were sleeping, they'd tie your boots together or build a fire under you.

Underground, you got together at lunchtime. You'd pick a spot that was well timbered and had good ventilation. All the motormen would eat at the motor barn because when you get your motor [ore train engine], you put your coat and your bucket there. A raise miner would probably just come down to the bottom of the raise, find a good cool spot, eat in there. In farther, maybe by the tool shed where it was always cool, the pipemen and the fan bag man and some of the miners would come out and eat there. Everybody had a laggin, that's a three inch board, probably six feet long, and you'd stretch your lag-gin out and you'd sit on it to eat your lunch. That's when the fantastic stories would come out. You'd hear all about their wives' fights, all about their broken hearts, how tough they were, what good miners they were. Just some good stories. And then everybody would sleep for half an hour. But down at the pit, they had a lunchroom. It was just a lot different.

WHEN I WORKED AT THE ST. LAWRENCE, we used to eat in a place that was the old horse barn. And there was five or six guys that worked there when they had the horses. And they'd tell you stories about the horses that would just make you wonder.

The Company treated the horses ten times better than they did the miners. They used to bring the horses up out of the mine and put them out here to pasture. A skinner could stay down in the mine until he died of silicosis.

I always remember some of my uncles, we were going to Gregson past the pasture where the horses were, they would say, "Yeah, look at them over there. They were only down five or six years. We've been down thirty and we're still down there. No one puts us to pasture."

But some skinners were as proud of their horses as they were of their kids at home. Well, I guess they just did some fantastic things. Renegade horses would break out of their stalls and sneak off into a corner some place because they didn't want to go to work. If they weren't tied in their stalls, they'd back out and walk around the level. And they'd tip the tops off of lunch buckets and eat what was in them. The horses would pull a six car train and the skinner might go back in the drift and find another car that he wanted to bring up, so he'd sneak the car up and put the chain on real slow, but every time that horse or mule started to pull, he'd almost count as the cars would click, click, click—he'd get to the seventh one, he'd stop. He'd pull six and that was all.

Some of those skinners, a horse would do something fantastic, and they couldn't wait to get home to tell their family about it. I guess the horses all had names, and when the skinner'd go down in the mines, he'd have a chew of Peerless, he'd give his horse a chew of Peerless also. That's the stories that they told me.

The poor oldtimer, he was the one who paved the way for all of us. Where I lived was what they called Corktown and it was mostly all Irish Catholics. And it was nothing to see the woman walk her husband to the door in the morning. She would always kiss him, always tell him "God bless you." Some women would flick holy water on their husbands. And when the men came home, they were entitled to their shot and their homemade beer. These are places I'm thinking about; this didn't happen to everybody, because some poor guys went home to nothing, you know.

My uncle was the most loving guy. I don't say this just because he was my uncle. He was stern and tough, but he was so loving. He was a station tender here in the mines.

He used to come home and he'd had a few drinks and one of his daughters would say, "Oh Papa,"—they always called him Papa—"you've been drinking." And my aunt would say, "The poor critter, he's tired and he had a few shots and that's all he needs." Now—now people are married six months and they want to try going another way.

My wife really didn't like the mines. I seldom worked overtime, but one night right at the outbreak of the war they came down and wanted us to work overtime. There was no way to call home. I worked four hours overtime and when I came up out of the mine, I heard somebody holler, "Anybody seen Murphy?" I couldn't imagine what they wanted, so I went over to the time keeper and he said, "Murph, your wife has been up here a hundred times." After I showered I went out, and my wife was standing out by the guard shack. It was snowing. She wouldn't go in. When we were walking down Excelsior Street from the Anselmo, she looked back at the mine and said "I hate those things."

Sometimes I think that the women had it tougher than the men. The men just did the work and that was it. But the women, they had to take care of the kids, do the wash and the cooking, see their husbands off for work. If their husband was late coming home from work, if they were drinking someplace—the wife didn't know. She couldn't call the mine to see if he was all right. She'd get killed if she did that. There were a lot of widows that you don't hear much about anymore. Some of the young kids that got killed left young women that never married again. I don't know how they did it. It was a sad thing.

I GUESS ANOTHER THING I LIKED about working in the mines, you'd come off work and everybody would be at a saloon, you know, a fifth of whiskey, a shot and a beer. Like Finntown, one bar right after the other. I was 24, come off nightshift, and you could get a shot and a beer for a dime. And then the bars always kicked back [bought you a drink for every two or three you bought]. So you'd have 50 cents, and you wouldn't even get out of Finntown. Hell, by the time you got down to Park Street, you were smashed. Then you'd go home and eat, take two hours sleep and go out and get smashed again (laughs). I worked when I wanted to work. And I never worked really steady until I got married the second time and had children. If I wanted to go to California and I had the money, I took off. You could always get hired again. You liked to drink so you'd just drink. I never ever thought I would turn out to be an alcoholic because I saw so much of it in the neighborhood where I lived. But I got to where I couldn't go to work without having a drink, couldn't come off of work without having a shot. Then I got so that I didn't work.

I got a lot of "quits" because I drank an awful lot. I'd work two days and I'd be gone for a week. I went to work so drunk, the shift boss would do me a favor and send me home. He wouldn't tell me to go down in the mine and sweat it out. I had my job held for three weeks one time.

AT ONE TIME, MY BELIEF IS, life didn't mean a lot compared to the profits of the company. Not only in the Butte mines, but any mines, any steel factories or anything else. Life was pretty cheap for the money that some of these companies were making. It was nothing to go into one of these miners' wards and see all the beds full. A lot of broken legs and broken backs. Before they had hard hats, it was nothing to see guys going up the hill with white cones on their head. If they got cut on the head, the doctor used to just shave around the wound and put the stitches in and then put this cone on the wound—I don't know how they made it, but it would foam and then turn hard. And then the miner'd go to work

Possible quarry for Newport jetty. Negative number OrHi 66609. Courtesy Oregon Historical Society.

the next day. Towards the end, after all these safety regulations came in, it wasn't that bad. There was guys that got hurt, but it really and truly wasn't that bad.

There was no competition for labor. At one time, you couldn't work for anyplace but the Anaconda Company. Nothing else could ever come in here. The Company had a labor monopoly they wouldn't let loose of. They would probably tell you that they welcomed other business, but they never. Because when a guy got in the mines, he stayed in the mines. He couldn't say, well, I'll quit and go to the sawmill or I'll quit and go to the glassworks, and he stayed. He stayed because he had his home here and he had his family started, he had kids in school. Not all the miners liked the mines. Some of them stayed here because they had everything here and couldn't leave. My uncle used to always say he'd rather have his kids any place but in the mines, but he didn't want them to leave Butte, so they had no choice.

I never ever thought I'd live to see the day that one wheel wouldn't be turning. When I was in my 50s, I never ever thought I'd retire. I thought, you know, I've been around a long time and I know some of the guys in the mine, some of the foremen, I can get a watchman's job. But then when they just pulled out and closed everything, I thought that was really a crying shame. I thought there'd always be one mine.

All these Irish people bought plots—did you ever go to the cemetery and see these plots that they bought? You could raise a couple of sheep on some of them. And now there's not going to be anybody buried in them.

We never knew how good Anaconda was until they left us.

Clyde Rice
(1903-1998)

Clyde Rice was born in Portland, Oregon, and wrote his first novel, *A Heaven in the Eye*, at the age of 81. In it he chronicled his life and times in the bay area of San Francisco in the 1920s. He followed this success with other autobiographical novels, *Night Freight* (1987) and *Nordi's Gift* (1990). The following excerpt from *Nordi's Gift* traces Rice's return to Oregon and the simple pleasures of life on a stump farm. Rice's self-declared purpose was "to tell people of the richness of ordinary living."

From *Nordi's Gift*

So I decided to join the human race, lower middle class, Protestant, sort of, and certainly not catholic in their views. I didn't gravitate, didn't lurch, into the Smiths' and Joneses' mundane sphere of activity. No, hunger and want drove me and my wife headlong into the somewhat reluctant arms of our parents and relatives and into the bailiwick of our neighbors around the stump ranch. A couple of over-thirty waifs with child had to be absorbed by people whose own provender was none too certain. To their credit they did what they could with thinning larders and half-time jobs.

Decided, did I say? Really the lay of things handled that problem for me. Now, in late April on a Sunday morning, we ended our trek from Tiburon, but turned from our stumpland destination because Nordi demanded a long, hot bath. She maintained she wanted to be clean and rested before her encounter with a stump.

So we arrived before my father's door, truck piled high with plows and mattress, axes and saws and various oddments and, coupled to it, the trailer we had dragged behind us holding our cow and goat and the dozen chickens and, latched to it, our still dependable bicycle.

"Hello, Pop," I said, when on his crutches he came to the door. He stared at me before he said, "Clyde," expressing the word quietly, thoughtfully, then looked out at all the disarray that was our equipage. "Everything but the kitchen sink," he said with no smile on his face.

"Yes, everything I figured we could use clearing land."

"Those animals thirsty?"

"No, Pop, we watered them a couple of hours ago."

"How about the chickens?"

"Forget it, Pop."

Then seeing my wife coming around the corner of the truck, he called out, "Why, Nordi! I'm glad to see you. Come in and meet 'the Little Lady.'"

"'Little Lady'?"

"Yes, Pearl and I divorced. Nordi, I want you to come in and meet the Little Lady."

Well, Nordi had her hot bath; we all did. We were asked to spend the night. After luncheon my father and I drove out to look for the best road to get the truck and trailer up the hill out of Oregon City, and chose one. He was serious, solemn, not at all as he had been the last time we had looked for land. That time we had driven out in the farmland on the edge of the Willamette Valley. As a young salesman, it had been part of his territory.

Here the exuberance of youth had been spent away from my frigid mother-towns like Whiskey Hill and Molalla, and Good Tidings, yes, towns like Peach Meadow, Hubbard, and Mulino. The land around these towns was rich and too expensive for me to buy. When we found that out, he still continued to drive around and began pointing out to me boarding houses and hotels where he had stopped and showing me windows he had jumped out of in the middle of night because of the sudden appearance of a husband. These reminiscences of sexual exploits seemed to do him a world of good. It was Mame here and Sarah there, and he told me an odd thing: that, when you had a quick one with the serving girl or the mistress of the boarding house and the lady was still encased in her corset, the sporting men called it a "turtle."

"Yes, I had a turtle with Josephine. Gosh! It must be four years ago." Then suddenly we drove on without words. He was never to speak to me in that cheerful manner again.

Now, painfully lame on crutches, he was thoughtful as we drove along. Being a Christian Scientist he wouldn't speak of his injury, but eventually I found out that he had been delivering an oration about how much better his brand of bottled flavors was than his competitor's, when feeling a mellifluous phrase emerging from his consciousness and oiling his tongue, he stepped back as if to speak to a large audience instead of mutton-faced Ed Gorse, the store's proprietor, and dropped ten feet through an open trapdoor and lit standing. His hip joints took the awful blow and, since then, Mrs. Eddy's beloved practitioners could do little about it.

As we rolled sedately along he presently began talking. His business, he said, was in difficulty, for although his mainstay and best seller, a very good imitation vanilla, commanded a sensible price, the market was lately being overrun by a product in a big thin bottle that looked like a lot but wasn't, selling at less than half the price of my father's product. He rummaged in the car's glove compartment and brought out two bottles of the cheapie.

"Don't just taste these. You gotta drink the darn stuff. There's nothing subtle here." I did. "How do you figure it, Clyde?"

"There's no flavor at all," I answered, "just mild color."

"It's Mississippi River water," he said. "The coloring is mud in the water. I had it analyzed. Times are hard. People think with their purses. That St. Louis outfit is going to break me if I'm not careful."

"Is there any way I can help?" I asked.

He turned his head as we drove along and looked me over, looked me up and down with distaste. We really didn't have much room for it, sitting as we were side by side, but it worked. I had been weighed on whatever scales and found wanting.

"Hell," he said, "you can't take care of yourself, and anyway you owe me money."

We drove along silently the rest of the way, and I had time to consider and do a little summing. Here I was back in Oregon after a dozen years in California. I could not deny that my father was right, but I hadn't lost my independence sitting on my ass. In the years of the great depression I had battled miserable odds and lost. Not just once, but five times I had taken a beating. Whether it was tuberculosis while fishing off the west coast of Mexico, or a coffer dam going out around one footing of the Golden Gate Bridge, or a temporary change in the laws concerning milk in San Francisco, I got it right in the teeth. To handle the problems of a stump ranch you needed to be a big brawny plugger, and here was I, an average guy of five-feet-eight and not overly muscular. By keeping myself always in condition I had so far made up for it, but against bad odds. Still, I could see no alternatives.

We reached his house where we had dinner and slept a troubled sleep from which I awakened hours before dawn. My mind kept going back to the little house we had built at Waterspout Point on San Francisco Bay. Losses during the depression had taken it away from us. Finally, with nothing more to lose, we left California. The long strange trip up here was not over yet.

"Are you awake?" Nordi whispered, turning slightly.

"Yes, full of questions and propounding inadequate answers." I paused. "But I can't kick. I've got you and Bunky. If I could only do better by you, merciful sleep would come."

She rolled over and drew my head down to her warm breasts. "We've made it, Clyde. We're back home! All those awful miles, hundreds of them, while you fought to keep our wreck on the road and rolling, are almost over. Sleep now, darling."

Well, she did, but I continued to go over the past remembering our early carefree years together. Time was fading some of Nordi's beauty. Ten years before she had been a rather famous artist's model. Our interest in art and painting, love of beauty brought us together when we met in art school and kept us close. Nordi's little ways of making me feel loved—her support, telling me she loved the twinkle in my deep-set gray eyes and my childish honesty. That was what kept me going, helped me roll with the punches life had been handing out.

After an early breakfast we were soon at Oregon City and the hill—Pop, in his car with my heavy rope to pull if need be, though we made it without his help. He turned back to vanilla, yeah, and twenty-five other flavors, while that little decrepit Ford engine strove clatteringly along in its last effort for mankind and, specifically, for me.

The country about was slightly rolling, but soon the road came down and out on the vast plain of the Willamette Valley, our road now following a finger of the valley as it reached in among the foothills of the mountains. We finally turned off the road and drove laboriously up into the hills—a turning road that we left at our own lane, which led into the eighty acres of stumps.

When we reached a small woodman's shack, we climbed out of our truck that was never to roll again, that had stayed in one piece for us until the journey was over. How can you love a battered piece of equipment? Well, we did. After all our belongings were out, we pushed our faithful truck into a little gulch behind the shack, where it came to rest standing. I suppose rust is still working quietly on its remains.

When everything was under cover with space for the cow and goat in the shed, we stared out over our land and it seemed each stump with its many great roots gripped the earth tighter, dared us. Then we looked long and hard at each other with Bunky staring up at us, and we laughed at ourselves and for ourselves, and because we had so little to do with and so much to do, we felt our frailty and we clung together as we girded our loins with laughter, for it was all we had.

Then Nordi started sweeping out the shack. I took my best axe and went out to consider a stump, but I looked at a hundred before I turned back to tackle one near the shack.

Smoke was pouring from the chimney as I came up. There was a pretty good kitchen range left in the shack and the smell of frying drifted to me. I rummaged among my tools for an old fashioned auger. The auger was a yard long and drilled a two-inch hole. The handle end was a crossbar of wood, which I twisted, forcing the auger into the stump while applying what pressure I could to keep it biting into the wood. One hole I drilled into the stump horizontally for over a foot. The next hole started over a foot above the first but angled down to it sharply did it right the first time. The holes met deep in the stump. I was tired but not completely frazzled by the grueling job, so I got a burning coal (in this case, from Nordi's stove) and shoved it in to where the holes met. Now I got out a tiny bellows I'd had for years and blew in the lower hole in the stump till it caught fire. Then sticking an iron pipe into the angled hole and another into the horizontal hole I had a little furnace burning, never wanting for fuel. After an hour I shoved the horizontal pipe farther in, directing the flame at the center of the stump. Several hours later I banked the stump with dirt and sod and let it consume itself down into its main roots. Sounds easy, but it demanded more from a man than I had or ever would have. "Just work slower. That's it," I said to myself, "and work more hours."

A week later we had seventeen stumps, with our help, consuming themselves. Two burned until they were only smoking craters, their deep roots still burning far underground. We turned from them to another endeavor, though still starting a new stump every day.

There were many great trees that had been left on the place, firs about four to seven feet through and extremely tall—old growth Douglas fir, they were called—too big for the former owner's sawmill. I decided to cut one down and make cordwood from it to sell in Portland. I chopped for two days making a big notch on the side toward where it would fall, then started sawing at the back side to sever the trunk. With the big crosscut saw, that was much longer than I am tall, Nordi and I were finally able to get the saw in about six inches, so that it was held in place while we pulled it back and forth.

That evening Nordi decided to go in and see her people, for she could ride in with Mr. Storter, who trucked the railroad ties from a nearby mill to the docks in Portland. So I was left with Bunky, Delia the cow, and Scheherazade, our Nubian goat of Egyptian descent nicknamed Zaddie, who, missing Nordi, followed me everywhere. Bunky kept himself busy for days damming an intermittent brook.

After many experiments I rigged two screen-door springs to a willowy sapling, which handled the other end of the saw after a fashion, and sawed through the trunk, though it took about forty rests to do it. When the tree looked to be ready to topple, I took our animals to the shack and tied them and checked on Bunky at his dam. Back at the tree, after a few dozen saw strokes, I withdrew the saw and hammered two wedges in the sawcut. Soon the treetop began to shake against the sky. I yelled, "Timber," in case anyone was near. The huge tree started to crash to the earth. There was a great whistling as the boughs that had soughed in the wind for a century screamed their way down to a mighty crash as the monarch hit the forest floor. Around the fallen tree was the debris of smaller trees it had broken and mashed into the sod. Some limbs that had been torn off in the fall and caught temporarily in smaller trees now fell here and there. Then all was quiet and in the silence I shuddered with awe, feeling puny indeed, but I climbed up on the trunk and marched down the length of it, marveling at its massiveness. I went to the shack and released the animals, who came with Bunky and me to see what the crash was about, the cow and the goat giving it a close inspection.

Next day, Tuesday, I started sawing the great log into four-foot lengths to be split up into cordwood. Starting at the butt I made one cut through. Wednesday I sawed through one and a half. I grew weary.

Thursday Nordi arrived in the morning with news that Pop wanted to see me. So, taking the same truck that she had arrived on, I argued my way into town. There my father confronted me with some facts.

"Look, Clyde," he said, "you're not built for it."

"You mean hard work? I've done it all my life. I've carried a lot of stones twice and three times as heavy as any cordwood."

"Perhaps, but you have to keep going with cordwood. With those stones you could rest between, but cordwood is a constant drudge if you expect to make enough to keep you through the winter."

"Yeah, but—"

My father waved me down. "Short arms, small hands, and an artiste. I tell you, Clyde, it won't work."

"Okay, Pop, you got any alternatives?"

"I don't know," he said, "I've been asking around. Seems nobody has a job opening in their places, and if they have, their or their wife's relatives are waiting in line to glom onto it."

"So I've got to keep cutting wood, Pop. Hell! I've got the trees. That's something at least."

"I see," he said grimly. "Come along."

We drove up in front of an agriculture equipment store. WADF said the sign on the worn building. We entered.

"Dragsaw, second hand? What have you got?" said my father to the clerk. Well, we picked one with three extra blades, files and saw set, and a splitting gun.

"A hundred bucks even," said the mechanic who had extolled its innards to us.

"A hundred and ten, if you deliver," said Pop.

"Where to?" The man was cautious.

"Near Wendel."

"Gosh, I can't deliver way out there."

"What's your competitor's address?" asked my father.

"Okay, tomorrow," the man said quickly, "but I'll need fifty dollars now, sixty on delivery. How do you get into your swamp?"

"Tell him, Clyde, if you think he can follow directions." Standing at the curb outside, my Dad, still grim, said "That's all I can do for you, son. Good luck!"

That dragsaw was a heavy wooden frame, a narrow triangle in shape, and like a wheelbarrow, it had a wheel in the narrow end. Where the handles of a wheelbarrow would be were the ends of the frame and attached to either of them were big moveable dogs—steel points. I could rest the handles on the log and drive in the dogs that would hold the rig in place on a log. Surrounded by the triangle of the frame was a simple little engine of ancient design that, through cams and levers, worked a saw heavier than the usual logger's saw. It moved the saw back and forth in the cut. It could cut through a four-foot log in less than ten minutes. The main problem with it was moving it to the next cut. It was too heavy for me and the handles were too wide apart and, when I backed up against the log with it, I was captured until I could drive the dogs into place.

Once, when I was doing this, both dogs swung down on my wrists, imprisoning me, and my back was arched against the big log I was cutting. No one was within a mile of me. I was on my own. I made one great effort with all my strength and forced one of the dogs up, or I'd be there yet. It skidded off on its wheel, and somehow no bones were broken. It was a tool for a big, rangy man. We medium-size and small guys took on a dragsaw at our peril.

I soon learned how to use a splitting gun—a round rod a foot long sharpened and deeply drilled at one end. At the inner end of the drilled hole was a tiny hole. You filled the big hole with blackpowder and pounded it into the center of the end of the log. This compressed the powder. You put a short blasting fuse into the little hole, lit it and retreated. When it exploded, it split the log into two or three pieces, usually throwing them up ten or twenty feet in the air. The wood could easily be split into cordwood after that.

Zaddie and Delia grazed a few feet from where I worked, and when I lit the fuse and ran back, they ran back too and with me stared at the log to be split by the explosion. After it happened the three of us rushed through the powder smoke to see how many pieces had been split out. When we had studied it all and seen just what had happened, they went back to grazing until the next explosion.

Bunky came every once in awhile, but his series of dams and pools was more interesting than mere explosions. Bunky was not on the team. In fact I was the team, but the goat and the cow were excellent sidewalk superintendents.

Soon Bunky met other young boys of the scattered farms around and went with them to a two-room school about a mile away, where there was a summer session. Before long he had many friends and was enjoying himself. We too met some of our neighbors and found most all of them interesting.

From the first tree I cut five and a half cords-a cord is four feet by four feet by seven feet. The second tree was a bit bigger and it had no brush to hinder it when it fell. It leaned in no discernible way. The only place I could fall it was near two tall stumps ten feet high, cut years ago when that was the fashion in dropping big trees. It was with a certain delicacy that I placed the notch to assure that the tree would fall where I wanted it, otherwise it would plunge into the canyon. I was so confident that the tree would fall according to my plan, that I set the peg out a hundred feet to drive into the ground when it came down on it.

I worked three days on the tree and had taken out the saw and was driving wedges in the sawcut to topple it when a sudden blast of wind came from another quarter and down it fell on the two stumps. Fifty feet of the top broke off and fell in the canyon. The massive log over a hundred feet long lay ten feet above the ground.

Next day I put the car jack under one side on the stump, and working at it, soon had the log in place for cutting up. So it went. In three months I had one hundred fifteen cords of fine wood seasoning, ready for market.

Two brothers had contracted to haul my wood to town. I had gotten enough customers to sell it all in Portland and everything seemed fine, but one of the brothers was jailed and the other one left the state with their truck. When I looked for other truckers, they were all engaged in getting cordwood to town, though one agreed to haul it if I waited a week.

Very early rain came that year. For two weeks it pounded down and my road to the highway became a quagmire. I cut the bark off stumps and filled the ruts with bark. By the time the road was passable and the cordwood brought into Portland, my customers, of necessity, ordered other wood, and I had to sell elsewhere at a lower price, because it was late in the season. My net was three hundred and fifty dollars with which to face the winter. Nordi despaired. If she hadn't put in a big garden behind the shack we certainly would have starved. She took fifty dollars and rented a furnished farmhouse nearby. I had cut up enough short blocks to make into stovewood, so at least we had a roof over our heads and fuel to keep us warm, four sacks of potatoes, a keg of sauerkraut, carrots and turnips without end. Now I decided to go into the mountains to get a deer for meat in our house.

"But, Clyde," Nordi objected, "you promised me you would never hunt out of season again."

"I know, but I figure I've got a right to feed my family. Look, Nordi, if we were from one of the old settler pioneer farms like down around Peach Meadow, I'd get my venison as a pioneer's right. Of course that's a thing of the past, but it's still honored in a left-hand way. What I mean is, the law looks the other way, and I do come from such beginnings, but where's the farm—the old ties to the land? I haven't any, so I'm fair game for game wardens."

In early afternoon I hid the tools and picked up my gun. I had told Nordi if I didn't get back to come looking for me around the Red House Trail in the morning, but I strayed in a northerly direction from the old pioneer trail. I wandered as quietly as I could into an area where a tornado must have struck fifty or a hundred years ago. The big tree trunks lay in ancient disorder. Over them in some recent storm alders had been uprooted and cast about like jackstraws.

In this odd maze I found my deer—a big buck—and a head shot dropped him. As I scrambled over a log to get to the downed buck I heard a car being started to the north and down below me. It immediately backed and filled, obviously turning around, and bumped away heading north, I gathered. *Game Wardens,* I thought. They must have been parked at the end of the road.

I had wandered too far into the Cooper Creek drainage and shot the deer above the town. The road from Wendel ended below me, stopped by cliffs, and the wardens knew that the way out of this part of the woods was the Red House Trail. They were driving around to intercept me, a matter of fifteen miles on rutted roads.

With my knife I cut off the deer's head and the scent glands on its hind legs, then opened it up and removed the viscera and heart and lungs. I lashed the left hind leg to the left foreleg, did the same to the right legs, slipped my arms in the apertures produced, and reared up with the heavy carcass on my back, grabbed my Winchester and started clambering up a log lying between me and the Red House Trail. But the neck of my victim and my family's food reached up much higher than my head. I would claw my way up to the top of a big, mossy log and start to jump down on the other side only to get that neck caught in branches or against the trunk of one of the uprooted alders, and back down I'd come with my burden breaking my fall. After this happened a few times, I knew I should have cut off the neck with the head; but now in a blind, unthinking rush to get out of the woods, I scrambled on another hundred yards or so, until completely winded, I lay down and the carcass lashed to me did too. I hadn't had time to drain it before my flight and now my back was soaked with blood and my shoes sloshed with it at every step.

As I lay with both arms numbed from the pressure of the leg bones on them, I laughed, admitting with disgust, "Clyde, you're in another mess. True to form, doing it the Rice way!" And then I thought of the waiting game wardens. (How I was certain that there were two of them, I don't know.) Anyway, thinking on game wardens I recalled that many minions of the law become plump, because theirs is not an active job. The word "Ah" was expelled from me—a very satisfied "Ah," for I saw a way out of my dilemma.

I waited for deeper dusk, so it would be hard to see through the woods, though I could still see twigs and branches that would crackle underfoot. One thing was obvious: I would not be able to carry this big buck home. I was hard put to carry him a hundred yards without resting. I must leave it to drain while I slipped past the wardens, got Nordi and a borrowed horse. Anyway, somehow we were going to get all that meat home.

I rolled awkwardly over and reared myself up, buck carcass and all, and staggering, stumbling I came to the trail, crossing it to a maple thicket where, after repeated attempts, I heaved the carcass up over two whittled vine maple crotches.

I believed I was about a half a mile from where the trail met the road. The woods were not as dark as I needed. It began to rain heavily, a soaking rain, still it couldn't wash the smile from my face, for this now seemed like a light-hearted game instead of one leading to jail. The rain brought the darkness I needed. Remembering carefully just how the trail ran, I began paralleling it by about a city block south. I figured that one plump game warden had stayed in the car at the end of the road, while the other one pussyfooted a goodly stroll up the trail to intercept me.

I had not gone far when through the trees I glimpsed the pussyfooter on my side of the trail making a hiding place from where, unseen, he could howl, "THROW UP YOUR HANDS."

He was much too close to where I was passing to make me happy. Scarcely moving, barely breathing I did finally pass him. Farther down on my parallel course, about between the wardens, my coat caught on a branch. Thank God! The branch was alive and could bend instead of breaking with a crack.

It was getting darker and I moved a bit faster to get out while I could see. After some time, when I was reasonably sure that I was past their car, I took to the road and continued down it. Well after complete dark, I heard a shot and an automobile horn answering it. I stepped into the brush when I heard them coming and watched them go by. After that I sauntered home, where I told Nordi we had meat, but I'd need help to get it. She said I was a sight, but blood is easily removed with cold water.

Half frozen, but clean once more, I sat down to a supper of bean soup with the small withered potatoes in a butter sauce.

We slept until the alarm went off at one o'clock. At Nordi's suggestion we forgot about a horse and got out our wheelbarrow. We skinned the carcass in the barn and took one beautiful roast to the house.

A couple of days later a plump man knocked at our door. I answered. I'd been expecting him. Now the dread was over. Nordi knew too.

"Hello," I said, "won't you come in and eat with us. She just put it on the table."

The mill's whistle blew for noon. He looked a little startled from his grimness of lip. "Do you ask people in to eat with you without knowing their names?" he asked.

I laughed, steady as a rock now. "Well, in the city I didn't, but in the country I do. It's a pleasure. Come on in."

He stepped in. I took his hat. "There's a basin and a towel on the back porch," I said.

He came back washed up, his hair neatly parted. The grim expression was oddly seated on his open jovial countenance. I saw he wasn't particularly fat, but compact, short-coupled with short arms. We sat down to the beautiful venison roast and the boiled weazened potatoes and hot biscuits. After all the plates were filled I sat down.

"What's your name?" I asked, buttering a biscuit. "Mine's Clyde Rice."

"My name's Johnson, the same as the people what built this house. You renting or did they sell?" he wondered, around a mouthful of venison.

"Renting," I replied, "we were buying eighty acres of stumps back of here." I caught Nordi's eye and smiled hope. At least I tried to smile hope.

Rather quizzically, he said, "Rice? You got relatives up Salem way? My father was born there."

"My grandfather was born at Scio in 1855. Is that close enough? His wife was born in a blockhouse near where Philomath is now. Guess an Indian raid brought the settlers in."

He was smiling into his plate as he said, "My grandfather settled in Salem. I was raised on a farm near Silverton." He lifted his smile, now a grin, and regarded me.

"That makes both of us webfoots, doesn't it?" I said.

"Well, I was away for awhile."

"Makes no difference," I grinned. "I was too—California—but I always dreamed of Oregon, Western Oregon. I took a hell of a beating down there and now here too. A guy just can't cut it anymore."

"Roosevelt's in there pitchin'," he said.

I agreed. "Wonder what would have happened if he hadn't taken hold when he did."

"Why, Stalin would be chopping us up just like we was Russian citizens," he answered as Nordi filled his cup. "Which reminds me," he said. "They solved that axe murder over in Molalla. Seems these guys fought over their different interpretations of a statement in the Koran. I thought that one stumbling block was enough, but now we've got another book to kill about or for. Oh, I forget. Here's your pocketbook," he announced and, after I took it, he went on. "Looked like you fell off a log and lost it. You know I'd stay out of those woods up there before you lose somethin' else."

"It's a healthy idea," I agreed, "and I'm going to observe it to the letter." We gossiped a bit then he got up. "I got to be getting along," he said. "Mrs. Rice, thank you for a most welcome meal. You sure know what to do with a roast of beef."

On the porch before he put on his hat, he said, "Now take that noon whistle. It reminded me how hungry I was and changed things. Well, so long, Rice." He put on his hat, stepped off the porch and was gone.

Sam Churchill
(1911-1998)

Sam Churchill's *Big Sam* (1965) tells the story of his father, Samuel J., and of his mother, Caroline Snow Churchill, a Pacific Northwest timber family that thrived during the boom of big business logging in the early decades of the twentieth century. Sam the younger was born in Astoria just twenty miles from the Western Cooperage logging camp where Big Sam worked. After a few years in college, Young Sam went to work as a logger, a miner, a bookkeeper, a variety store manager, a radio technician for the Navy in World War II, a radio announcer, and a journalist. He reported for the Yakima, Washington *Herald-Republic* from 1951-1974, and spent his remaining years in his hometown of Astoria. The following excerpt portrays camp life in Big Sam's woods.

FROM *Big Sam*

WHISTLE WHILE YOU WORK

IN THE WESTERN COOPERAGE camp life was regimented by whistles. When Mrs. Johnson wanted Fen or Jake she placed her thumb and index finger against her lower lip and tongue. Then she'd exhale a blast of air. The combination produced an earsplitting screech that would carry a mile or more.

Whistling was an accomplishment Mother never mastered. In fact it didn't seem to run in our family. Dad was no good at it and I could barely produce enough sound to carry a tune. Even though Mother couldn't whistle worth a darn she didn't have to take a back seat to any mother in the camp. When she'd stand on our front porch and yell out, "Saaaaaaaamm yoooooooool," it covered most of the nearby areas. I heard her once when I was at the Fischer and Leitzel camp and that was almost a mile away.

A stream of short blasts from the little Climax locomotive at Fischer and Leitzel would send all eight grades at the Western Cooperage school rushing to the south windows. The warning cry meant the little engine was out of control on the company's steep railroad grade and a wreck with flying logs and torn-up track was possibly minutes away.

Sometimes after such a mishap the Fischer and Leitzel camp would be quiet for days while the engine crew got the battered little veteran back in operating condition. The ingenuity and patience exhibited by the average logger in such situations never ceased to amaze Mother. She could never fathom how men, many of whom, like Dad, could barely read, could do such incredible things as build railroad trestles, repair smashed and broken equipment including locomotives and donkey engines, lay out camp sites and railroad lines.

To her way of thinking each of these accomplishments demanded a certain amount of education and great amounts of native ability and skill. In Boston a plumber was a plumber, a carpenter a carpenter, a construction engineer a highly trained individual. Each excelled in some one thing and knew very little about any other line of work.

At the Western Cooperage camp and in every logging camp from British Columbia to California each worker seemed to come equipped with a dozen skills. A hooktender could run donkey or take the throttle of a locomotive if he had to. Uncle Marsh could build a house, lay out a rough course for a railroad, or look at a block of timber and know immediately where to place a half-dozen or so donkey engines to log it most efficiently.

Dad, a man who suffered agonies and would sweat as though involved in hard labor whenever he had to write his name, could watch a straining main-line cable stretched tight as a bow string between a power-crazed donkey engine and twenty tons of stubborn log, and know almost to the pound when the line had reached the breaking point.

Mother was never hesitant in telling T. W. Robinson, the camp superintendent, that men with such diversity of talent and ability were entitled to more out of life than four dollars a day wages and the humiliation of being ordered around by a steam whistle.

"Oh, for heaven's sakes, Caroline," was Mr. Robinson's usual answer. If Dad happened to be handy, Mr. Robinson would turn to him in feigned exasperation. "Sam, why couldn't you have married some quiet, reasonable girl from Astoria?" But he was an admirer of Mother's.

"You do what your mother tells you," he often told me, "and you'll amount to something." That was almost like a command direct from Heaven, coming as it did from Mr. Robinson. There wasn't much I could say but "Yes, sir."

No matter what Mother contended in those early days, loggers have remained loggers and most of their working days continue to be dominated by whistles—electric these days, instead of steam.

Although all whistles may have sounded alike to a newcomer in camp they were as individualistic as night and day to us. The possibility of confusing the whistle call of a yarding donkey on Side One with that of a road donkey on Side Two was as remote as mistaking the voices of Mother and Mrs. Johnson. There wasn't an individual in camp, adult or youngster, who couldn't give you an instant status report on the day's logging operations from the constant chatter of steam donkey whistles.

Monitoring the whistle calls was a subconscious process. You were rarely aware that your mind was checking off each signal as it floated in from the logging areas. But it was. Throughout the working day the movement of every log from cutting area to railroad spur line where it was loaded onto rail cars was guided by shouted commands which were relayed to the distant donkey engine operator by triggering a steam whistle mounted on the engine's boiler. The triggering was done by a "whistle punk" jerking a wire stretched through the woods and leading from the work area to the donkey engine. Whistle punks were usually young fellows in their teens and "punking" or blowing whistle was the starting job in the woods. A whistle punk had to know some two dozen signal combinations and a dozen special calls in relaying shouted calls of the rigging crew to the donkey engineer. Each need—go ahead on the main line, slack the haulback, stop all lines, call the foreman—had its special call. Later, when giant multiengined machines mounted on rail cars and called skidders were in action, a whistle punk had to know dozens of complex signal combinations and his hand and reflexes controlled tons of lethal rigging both on the ground and overhead.

Sitting in the Western Cooperage school and trying to concentrate on arithmetic or geography while the shouts of a half-dozen donkey engine whistles yammered at you was often a problem. Mastery of the multiplication tables sometimes couldn't compete with a yarder having a tough time dragging in an oversized log that might weigh as much as thirty tons. Logs hung up on stumps or other obstacles on their way to the donkey engine would often send a whistle into a screaming tirade as the rigging crew worked to free the log and send it on its way.

Mother contended at such times that it was just as though the whistle were swearing. In the daily fury of logging it often seemed that the whistles of the various donkey engines were shouting to each other.

There was nothing pleasant or relaxing about the sound of a steam donkey whistle. It always sounded impatient, angry, and militant. It never requested; it ordered. High-pitched and nagging, it was no respecter of job rank or authority. It treated everyone exactly alike. When Mr. Irving was needed, a whistle would summon him with four long blasts repeated at intervals. If he didn't get there right away and the whistle kept calling, Mother and other wives in the camp might make comments such as: "I wonder where Mr. Irving is? Why doesn't he answer his call?"

Over the years a whistle signal had evolved for just about everything imaginable. Three short blasts in series of three meant the donkey engine was low on fuel and to hook on a waste log that could be dragged in and cut into long slabs for the firebox. Two long was a message to the man tending the gasoline water pump located at some nearby creek or spring dammed to form a pond; it meant start the pump and send us water. When the donkey engine's water tank was full, a long blast from the whistle meant to stop pumping water.

A long blast followed by a short one started the crews to work in the morning and announced quitting time at the end of the day. Three long bursts, repeated at intervals, was the loggers' way of requesting a locomotive to switch out loaded cars and bring in empty ones.

Out where choker setters were hooking the main-line rigging onto the ends of logs so that the donkey engine could drag them in, the whistle not only controlled log movement—it often regulated life and death. A wrong or misinterpreted whistle call might send writhing tons of rigging hurtling into a man. A big road donkey might drag logs for almost a mile. Once on the job the donkey engineer and the rigging crew might not see each other the rest of the day until the final whistle and quitting time; during this ten-hour interval the only line of communication was the thin stranded wire (similar to a backyard clothesline) that ran from the donkey engine whistle to the whistle punk.

Donkey engine whistles were the gossips. They couldn't keep a secret and they weren't meant to. Day after day they screeched, pouted, harassed, and assailed the ears and nerves of man and beast from the surf line of the Pacific to the snow line of the Cascade Range.

They had an entirely different personality in the middle of the night. Sometimes a tumbling sapling or a heavy limb would fall across the whistle wire at night. The weight of the intruder would absorb the slack and cause the wire to trip the donkey whistle. A whistle so tripped would send out a dead-of-the-night call eerie and ghostly enough to make your flesh crawl. Each logging side, or unit, had a night watchman. He made his rounds of the great resting engines, seeing that the wood fires were banked so there would be steam in the boilers when the crews reported for work in the morning. It was a lonely, scary job, tramping from donkey engine to donkey engine through the woods by lantern light all night long.

Whenever a donkey whistle was accidentally tripped in the middle of the night it would blow until the watchman could reach it and locate the trouble or disconnect the whistle wire. Sometimes it would be almost an hour before the whistle could be quieted and peace and quiet restored.

Even Dad, who seemed to fear nothing and could sleep through most any calamity including cougar calls, wind-storms, and I think even earthquakes, would wake up with nerves on edge when a night whistle sounded. "When's that watchman going to shut that thing off?" he'd snap irritably. Thinking of the watchman hurrying through the woods, surrounded by a tiny circle of kerosene lantern light in a forest of blackness, unnerved Mother more than the ghostly sound of the whistle.

"I wouldn't be out there alone for all the tea in Boston," she'd announce, snuggling up in a ball against Dad's back. The eerie call of a night whistle usually sent me scampering under the covers with Mother and Dad. Our cat, Muff, often made it a foursome.

"Git that cat out of this bed," Dad would roar. "Hush up and go to sleep," Mother would whisper, her voice muffled by the covers pulled up over her head.

Day or night the tone of a locomotive whistle was pleasing and implanted with warmth, friendliness, and indulgence. It was just as authoritative as a steam donkey whistle but it handled itself better.

"Whistles are no different than people," Mother used to point out. "Just remember, a whisper is often louder than a shout."

The throaty warning call of a logging locomotive as it neared the camp with a long train of loaded log cars would send us youngsters scampering for vantage points to watch its clattering passage through camp. The goings and comings of trains seemed to be of great interest to everyone. Housewives would stop their housework, cooking, or washing to step to the doorway and wave to the train crew. The office, cookhouse and shop crews always seemed to have a few spare minutes in which to watch. For the men this casual work stoppage two or three times a day was prompted by no more than idle curiosity and interest in locomotives and logging-railroad rolling stock. The log trains provided a clue as to how things were going at the logging end. Short trains of fifteen or twenty cars meant the donkey engines and their crews were in exceptionally rough country, or having breakdowns or other problems, that slowed production. On the other hand, long trains of twenty-five to thirty or thirty-five cars meant things were highballing, going full blast.

Passage of the log trains revealed the quality of timber coming out of the woods. Car after car of giant Douglas fir logs, fifty-two feet in length or even more, and of uniform size and yellowish in color, indicated highest quality, top price from mills and no interruption of pay checks.

Although it was God's forest Big Sam and the others were logging, each man on a logging camp crew took a personal pride in it. If the timber quality was poor the men often reacted as though in some way it was their fault. They tended to blame themselves as though they had failed somewhere along the way and were now being repaid with an inferior product.

Most of the whistle signals that bombarded the Western Cooperage camp were routine in nature and had to do with the day-in, day-out business of logging. But there were two that would immediately put our or any camp on edge. One was the repetition of long and short blasts which meant fire. The other, more feared than a dozen fires and affecting every household, was seven long followed by two short and repeated over and over. This signified, "Man injured. Send a stretcher."

A whistle call for a stretcher meant serious injury in a logging camp. Minor injuries such as broken arms, cracked ribs, broken jaws rarely interrupted the throb of the big yarding, road donkey, and loading engines. As long as a man was conscious and able to walk he usually made his own way to the railroad loading site. If a locomotive or speeder was on its way to camp he might hitch a ride. If not, he would walk the distance and think nothing of it.

When a man was hurt badly enough to require a stretcher he had to have at least a broken leg, smashed foot, skull injury, or crushed rib cage. In other words, he was so badly hurt he would have to be carried out.

Whenever the "dead whistle," as we youngsters called it, sounded the womenfolk of the camp would gather in little groups on the railroad track in front of their homes. They talked in low tones and kept close watch in the direction of the office. The goings and comings of camp officials such as T. W. Robinson or Jim Irving might suggest a clue.

There were other sounds worth paying attention to. The big machines in an area where a man had been seriously hurt would take their ease on their big wooden sleds while crews were bringing him out. It would take most of a crew to man a stretcher in the jumble of downed timber, logs, brush, and logging debris that cluttered a logging area.

If the machines resumed their work you knew the injured man had been removed to the safety of the railroad spur that served that particular logging unit and would soon be transported to camp by locomotive or speeder. If the great machines remained silent you knew the worst had happened—somebody's husband or father wouldn't be on the crew train when it rolled into camp at the end of the day. He wouldn't be on it ever again. It frightened you and made you sick inside. During those horrible, suspenseful periods of waiting, everyone looked at each other, hoping desperately and selfishly that God in His great wisdom and compassion had spared your loved one.

During these fearful moments I often found myself wondering in agony what life without Big Sam would be like. I suppose the same painful thought was in the mind of every boy and girl whose father worked in the ever present shadow of death or injury cast by the thunder-voiced machines. To me there just couldn't be a Western Cooperage camp with no Big Sam shouting and sweating and leaping from log to log and crashing through brush, or stamping down the railroad track from the crew train at the end of the day, as big as two ordinary men, swinging his empty lunch bucket and with love for me and Mother poking out of his eyes when he'd meet up with us.

On one such wait I tugged at Mother's hand and asked why we didn't go to our prayer garden, the way we did during the Camp 7 fire, and ask God to make it be somebody else, not Dad. She squeezed my hand until it hurt. We went behind the house to the garden but when we got there Mother didn't kneel and pray as she had during the fire. Instead she sat me on a block sawed from the end of a log. Dad sometimes used it for a chopping block for cutting wood and kindling.

Squatting down to where we could look each other square in the face, she explained that it wouldn't be right to ask God to spare you and hurt somebody else. These were times, she said, "When we put our full trust in God." I tried desperately to keep faith with God and do as Mother said. But I just couldn't. Every time the "dead whistle" would blow, I'd close my eyes and murmur a hasty, silent plea, "Please God, don't let it be Dad."

Most of the time when the locomotive or speeder arrived at camp the injured man would be in pain and misery, but alive. Usually after a brief stop the engine or speeder would hurry right on down to Olney where an ambulance would be waiting to take him by road to the hospital in Astoria.

But there were times when the figure on the flat car or speeder's deck would be motionless and covered from head to foot by a blanket. Then Mr. Robinson or Mr. Irving, or maybe both, would walk toward the group of waiting women. There is no reasonable way in which to tell a wife that her husband is dead. But Mr. Robinson and Mr. Irving did their best to ease the shock and pain.

The other camp women did what they could to comfort and help. Each knew that the others might be comforting her the next time the "dead whistle" blew.

Woody Guthrie
(1912-1967)

Woodrow Wilson Guthrie was a folk singer and composer whose songs and guitar style have exerted a great influence on twentieth-century America's best known musicians, including, for example, Bob Dylan. Guthrie gave common laborers in Depression-era America a voice of hope. The following song was recorded by ASCII Records for the U.S. Department of the Interior and the Bonneville Power Administration in Portland. Guthrie championed the building of the Grand Coulee Dam (Guthrie spelled it "Coolee" in his songs) and saw its power as progress for the working class. In fact, he used perhaps his best known song, "This Land Was Made for You and Me," as the anthem for a Public Utility Bond campaign to raise funds for the dam's construction and maintenance.

Big Grand Coolee Dam

Well the world has seven wonders that the travelers always tell
Some gardens and some flowers I guess you know them well
But now the greatest wonder is in Uncle Sam's fair land
It's that king Columbia River and that Big Grand Coolee Dam!

She heads up the Canadian Rockies where the rippling waters glide
Comes rumbling down her canyon to meet that salty tide
Of that wide Pacific Ocean where the sun sets in the west
In that Big Grand Coolee country the land I love the best.
She winds down her granite canyon and she bends across the lea
Like a silver running stallion down her seaway to the sea
Cast your eyes upon the greatest thing yet built by human hands
On that king Columbia River it's that Big Grand Coolee Dam.
In that misty crystal glitter of her wild and windward spray
We carved a mighty history of the sacrifices made
She ripped our boats to splinters but she gave us dreams to dream
Of the day the Coolee Dam would cross that wild and wasted stream.

We all took up this challenge in the year of thirty-three
For the farmer and the factory and all of you and me
We said, roll along Columbia, you can ramble to your sea
Now in Washington and Oregon you hear the factories hum
Making chrome and making manganese and light aluminum
And you see a flying fortress wing her way for freedom land
Spawned up on that king Columbia by that Big Grand Coolee
Dam.

Pat Koehler
(1925-)

Pat Koehler was one of the many women who went to work in the male-dominated industries when the needs of the armed forces depleted the work force in World War II. The following record recalls her labors in the shipyards in Portland.

Reminiscence on the Women Shipbuilders of World War II

We girls wore leather jackets, plaid flannel shirts, and jeans we bought in the boys department of Meier & Frank. It was 1943, we were eighteen years old, our first year of college was over. My girlfriend and her mother had moved in with my mother and me for the duration of the war. Housing was tight because of the influx of war-industry workers. Our fathers were overseas.

Three local shipyards were recruiting workers from the East Coast and the South. They advertised in Portland, too: HELP WANTED: WOMEN SHIPBUILDERS. Cartoons asked, "What are you doing to help win the war?" They showed women sipping tea, playing cards, and relaxing. "THIS?" And then a smiling woman worker with lunch box, her hair tied up in a scarf, a large ship in the background. "Or THIS?"

We were ready to do some war work, something more exciting than typing. One job description read:

> ELECTRICIAN HELPER
> Duties consist of installing cables and fittings on board the ship and the installation of electrical equipment and wiring according to plans and drawings. Should be good at working with small tools such as pliers, wire cutters, etc. Considerable work is done vertically and overhead, which requires the worker to be on step ladders. Must have capable hands. Exactness and a flair for detail are necessary. Much of this work is on small objects and deals with color combinations. Color blindness would be a handicap. Should have an alert mind in order to pass the required schooling prior to employment. Additional training within the yard is necessary to qualify for a journeyman electrician.

Women watching Liberty ship launch. *Oregon Journal*, June 6, 1943. Negative number OrHi 81549. Courtesy Oregon Historical Society.

Together my girlfriend and I applied to be electrician helpers at the Kaiser Vancouver Shipyards. Even though I have always had a streak of tomboy, I might not have had the nerve to try it alone.

The yards were impressive, like a small city. Hundreds of acres along the Columbia River were filled with rows of big white buildings, half-dozen shipways (we called them "ways"), and an outfitting dock that stretched three-quarters of a mile. It was a city that never slept. Twenty thousand workers labored around the clock to build ships—fast. At night the yards were lit up as bright as day.

To hire on we spent a day going from one building to the next: finger prints taken here, ID photos taken there, forms and more forms to fill out. Then back downtown to Vancouver to join the International Brotherhood of Electrical Workers, Local #48. We paid our initiation fee and first month's dues before we had earned a penny.

We started on the day shift at the electrical warehouse; our pay was 85 cents an hour. Electricians on the hookup crews came to the warehouse for materiel and parts. Since only one of each part was issued for each ship, if something was damaged in the outfitting process, either it had to be repaired in a shop or a new one made. We organized a salvage operation to recycle these parts, and to expedite the work we called for a cart driver. The cart was similar to a golf cart, and we made the rounds of machine shop, casting forge, rigging shop, feeling glamorous and important, even in our drab clothes. The yard could seem like a movie-studio lot, the huge lofts like soundstages all abustle. I learned to be resourceful and persistent, to get the job done at all costs.

It was a world of strangers who did not step aside for teenage girls. Coming from outside the Northwest, as most of them did, they spoke in accents we had never heard before. It became a game with us to listen and ask point of origin. Soon we could distinguish between a Brooklyn accent and one from New Jersey, Florida, or Oklahoma.

Besides the rich mixture of regional dialects (which TV has now almost obliterated), there was also the culture shock of rough language and obscenities. Some tried to make us blush. Most were considerate. Still, it was unsettling to have all conversation hush to silence when I entered an area. Our first leadman used "goddamn" as an adjective to modify almost every noun. It set my teeth on edge, until I learned to block it out.

When the whistle blew for quitting time, we crowded into the "Ladies" for a quick wash at the circular fountain, grabbed our lunch boxes, and headed for the gates. A wave of workers pressed toward the parking lot. Periodically the crowd moved slower than usual. A ripple passed through the ranks as person after person became aware of a looming lunch-box inspection. All around us lunch boxes snapped open and items were furtively slipped out and stuffed into pockets. Through the gate we went, holding open our lunch boxes for the inspectors. No one was searched.. Most of us did not steal, but it was common practice for some.

In the parking lot buses loaded workers for the housing projects and Vanport, then the second largest town in Oregon. Other buses went to downtown Portland. We hunted for our car pool. Four of us from North Portland rode with a man who lived in the Irvington district. He picked us up at our door in the morning and took us home at night. For this he received a fee from us and extra gas coupons. Traffic moved slowly until we crossed the Interstate Bridge, which, at that time; had only one lane, each direction. Army guard posts stationed at the ends of the bridge reminded those who passed that this was the only crossing between Longview and Cascade Locks. We were captive to our driver's car radio. Every evening we had to listen to the news in H. V. Kaltenborn's irritating, staccato delivery.

Along the outfitting dock were moored the LSTs (landing shiptanks), the newly launched on the east end and the completely outfitted on the west. The whole row moved downstream and backwards, prow into current, until they sailed away to Astoria for "shakedown." Each ship's complement of navy crew arrived regularly for the sailings. Their blue and white uniforms were a stark contrast to the worker's outfits.

At night we went to school to study electricity, both theory and practice. It was a crash course designed to equip us with the essentials. We earned Ohm's law—that "for any circuit the electric current is directly proportional to the voltage and is inversely proportional to the resistance." It had a fine ring to it. The practical lessons stayed with me, too. The most important was: unplug the power before making connections. Advancement up the ladder to electrician trainee brought us 90 cents an hour, then $1.10, and then $1.15. The day came, by dint of study, when we graduated to journeyman-electrician at $1.20 per hour. We celebrated by applying for jobs on the hookup crews, which worked aboard ships at the outfitting dock.

I was assigned to fire control. That meant guns! My leadman had never had a female working for him, and he was skeptical. Like a shadow, I followed his every move, anticipating what tool he needed next and handing it to him before he could ask. After a few days of this he relaxed and began teaching me the ropes—or, rather, the wires. The most important lesson was: do not cut the wires too short; leave a little extra curled up inside the box.

I liked working with my hands, and I liked the feel of the tools. I favored one tool especially: the wire stripper. When I used this tool to grab the wire, I would squeeze, pull, and all the insulating rubber would come off and leave the wire raw. Then I crimped a little connector tip onto the wire.

I wore steel-toed boots and a shiny hard hat made of rust-colored plastic, with a bright yellow stripe—the colors of my craft: marine electrician. We considered ourselves the elite craft. Only the riggers had more clout. They wore silver-metal hard hats and could order other workers around, for safety's sake, since they directed the huge cranes and fastened the slings of cables that carried everything aboard."

By 1944 aircraft escort carriers ("baby flat-tops") had replaced the LSTs on the outfitting dock. They were over 500 feet long, with a flight deck that was 400 by 480 feet. On both sides of the flight deck were four forty-millimeter guns and ten twenty-millimeter antiaircraft guns. On the fantail was one five-inch gun. That was all the weaponry. Their real fire-power were the thirty airplanes they would carry.

We had watched some of the carriers launched, with wartime ceremony, gold braid, and ribbons. There was no glamour for us, though, as we slipped on the cluttered decks, dodged, cables over our heads, and risked death crossing the tracks of the giant cranes. It was winter and the wind whipped down the Gorge. The push for completion grew even stronger. The goal—and it *was* reached—was a ship a week from the west end of the dock. We labored seven-days-a-week, ten and twelve hours a day. After eight hours we were paid time-and-a-half. The seventh day was double time.

It was no coincidence that the Kaiser Permanente Hospital (predecessor to Bess Kaiser Hospital) was built on the bluff above the Vancouver Shipyards. With thousands of workers and an emphasis on speed, even a vigorous safety program could not prevent accidents. We were encouraged to suggest safety ideas. I received a twenty-five-dollar war bond for my suggestion that the cranes not only clang when they began to move but also flash lights in the direction of their movement.

I saw one accident take place inside a crane. We were eating lunch seated on the steps of the office facing the dock, with a crane between us and the ship. A flash of light inside the cabin of the crane was followed by a scream. The crane operator came out holding up his hands. His arms were black up to the elbows. He screamed again and fainted. Rescuers had to lower him in a harness since they could not manage him on a ladder. We did not see the rescue. The 12:30 whistle blew and our half-hour lunch period was over.

My first solo assignment was hooking up the forty-millimeter gun directors on the starboard side. These weapons were in round pillboxes that hung out over the water. Occasionally I had looked down into the swift current of the Columbia River and noticed small boats dragging for a worker who had fallen in. In the spring the river rose and the gangways became steeper. Now I connected the electricity to the five-inch gun, the largest weapon on the ship. As I worked there on the fantail, fastening the red wire to the red wire and the yellow wire to the yellow wire, I fervently hoped that the five-inch gun would be well tested before battle. What was a nineteen-year-old girl doing up there in such a job, anyway?

Although the cranes were a genuine concern of mine, my injuries did not come by way of them. Once, when climbing down a ladder clogged with welding leads (large rubber hoses), I slammed a steel-toed boot against one of them and broke a toe. The doctor taped it to its neighbor, and I went on working. On another occasion I broke my elbow in a fall, lost a day getting it set, and learned to work left-handed. I worked graveyard shift until I became anemic and the Red Cross turned down my regular blood donation.

Since every night we fell into bed exhausted, our hands chapped and our hair smelling of paint, there was really no time to spend our money. So we invested most of our earnings in war bonds to be cashed in for college. After a year and a half we had enough for two years' tuition, board, room, and books. Best of all, we had acquired new confidence and maturity.

Kaiser Vancouver Shipyards built fifty escort carriers. They engaged in the tide-turning navy battles in the Pacific that helped to win the war in 1945.

Willie Daniels, Concrete Worker

In 1989, Stephen Sanger published *Hanford and the Bomb*, a book chronicling the Hanford Engineer Works, the site of production of the first atomic bomb during World War II. The bomb entered history over the skies of Hiroshima on 6 August 1945, with Hanford's plutonium contributing to the device that devastated Nagasaki three days later. Throughout the mid-1980s, Sanger conducted exhaustive interviews with workers who participated in the Hanford production. To preserve as completely as possible the original historical record provided by these interviews, Portland State University's Continuing Education Press published the supplemental book, *Working on the Bomb: An Oral History of WWII Hanford*, compiled by Sanger and edited by Craig Wollner. That resource offers an authentic record of those whose labors both made history and threatened to destroy it. The following representative excerpt is by Willie Daniels, a lively and talkative man in his 80s. Daniels was one of thousands of blacks who left low-paying jobs and a segregated society in the South for higher pay and better social conditions in the wartime industries of the North. The expected income boost was indeed a reality, but the treatment of black workers was little better than what they experienced under the Jim Crow regime of the South.

FROM *Working on the Bomb*

MY HOME WAS IN KILDARE, TEXAS. I grew up there, went to high school in Jefferson, to college in Prairie View, a segregated school. I took general education, and taught school for about four years in Texas. That was during the Depression, and man when you came out of school you had to scuffle and scuffle hard to get a job. Trouble was you only got paid for six or seven months teaching school in those days but you got to live 12 months a year. I worked anywhere I could.

I went to Texarkana and worked at the creosote plant and from there I worked up and down the railroad, loading ties. At Texarkana, I was working at a concrete plant, making $33.33 a week, that was good money then, working as a common laborer. I worked there a couple of years, and when I left there I heard about this job in McAlester, Oklahoma, in about '42, a naval air station. That job kinda went down, and we heard about this job in Washington state.

I had an uncle who come out here, and he wrote back and said they was paying a dollar a hour. I say, "What?" My brother say "A dollar an hour?" I say to my brother, "You going?" My brother was working on the railroad. He say, "I don't know. Them jobs don't last long." I say, "Man, I'm going, you do what you want. I got enough money for you to go." We got together, my brother, Vanis, myself and another boy. We came out to Hanford, in the late summer of '43. We went to work on Labor Day.

We came by bus, we paid our way. Du Pont was shipping some people, but we paid our way. Oh man, that bus broke down in the desert somewhere, and we sat a long while. We finally got to Umatilla, and we was looking at the country and we come around that road to Pasco alongside the river and that bus was leaning and it looked like that bus was going to jump over into that Columbia River. I know that man driving was looking at us back there, I imagine he was having fun looking at us so frightened.

I was so glad when we got to Pasco. We got off the bus at the station and looked around. I asked "Where that job is?" and nobody told us anything, so I went back to the bus station and said, "Lady, where's that big job going up around here." She say, "It's out at Hanford." I say, "Where's Hanford?" She says, "Sixty miles out. You go on the bus. One just left and the next one goes after midnight." I asked "Where do the colored people live around here?" She said, "Over across the track." We went across the track, and looked down the main street. We saw one or two houses. I said, "Let's go back."

I went back to the station and said, "Lady, when people come in, going out to Hanford, where do they usually stay until the bus runs?" She said, "Well, Du Pont's got a place up there by the railroad station." We went up to the place, and an old colored gentleman was in there. I said we wanted to stay the night until the bus goes. He said, "Did Du Pont send you?" I said, "No," and he said, "Well, I can't let you stay."

"Look," he said, "If you stay here and Du Pont didn't send you, that gets my job, if they find out. I'll let you stay, but be quiet about it." We lay down because we was tired. Along about two o'clock in the morning, this train came in from Chicago, loaded with fellows. The next morning, we got with those men and went to breakfast and didn't have to pay. We followed them around, and signed up to go out to Hanford on the bus. We went on out, no charges, and we got there and there was an old boy from home. I knew him from when I sold men's clothing. He says, "Hey, boy, did you bring your samples?" I say, "Yeah, I got 'em." "Well," he say, "Make me a suit."

They told us we would have to stay in tents that night. But I saw some barracks was finished but nobody was living in them. We got a blanket and slept in the new barracks in beds. The next morning there was so much wind and so much dust, everything was plowed up, you could write your name on our luggage.

We got signed up, and went to work for E. I. Du Pont. Our first day of work, we made $19.20, my brother and I together. They sent us to work on postholes, and we got some overtime. "Gee," my brother said, "$19.20 is more than I bring home in a month." I say to him, "I told you to come off that railroad."

The barracks were segregated. Lots of black people were out there, in construction, and lots more were just out there, not doing nothing. We would go to work and come back and some guy had been there ransacking our room. Once we came back to the barracks, and there were some guys in there scuffling. This guy had another one down, beating him, kicking him with steel-toe shoes, stomping him. He said, "I'll teach you to go in a room and take stuff, I'll bet you won't go in another one." In the barracks, there was drinking and fighting, and carrying on. Oh, man. There'd be gambling in the washrooms, and playing cards. Some of them were professional gamblers, out there to get all the money. I didn't mingle with that bunch, not at all.

No.5 mess hall was where most of the colored people ate. Some whites ate there and some coloreds ate up in No.2 mess hall. Generally, they ate separately. The food was good, and plenty of it. Long as you raise your hand up, they would bring you more.

I remember at Christmas, '43, some guys got to fighting in the messhall. Some guy with big ol' dark shades on, he was jumping on this little guy, and another guy was running from him, and this guy jumped up on a table and stepping from one table to another, trying to hit people, and everybody was running. He got close to where my uncle and I were, and I said I'm going to get that guy off that table, he don't have no business there. He got to the table next to us and threw a cup at the wall and almost hit my wife. I said I know I am going to get him off now, if he hits that little woman over there, I know what will happen to him. They'll take him to the cemetery and me to Walla Walla, cause I'm gonna eat him up. I had a jackknife, I still have it. It was sharp enough to shave a cat running. I used to trim carpet with it before I got into construction. You weren't supposed to carry a jack knife in your pocket, but I said this is a tool. In a few minutes, the security guards came and got him.

In those days, we worked about 12 hours a day, sometimes we worked more. Besides that, I was selling stuff, like toilet goods and I was working at that for Lucky Heart, cosmetics, perfume, hair dressing, powders. I was doing that on the side, some weeks I made as much at that as I did on the job. I was getting about $50 a week on the job, sometimes as much as $70 a week, with overtime. I was also selling men's clothing for Stonefield Corp. out of Chicago, and for W. Z. Gibson clothing company. I was selling men's shirts and ladies clothes, those Fashion Frocks. At night, when we come in for dinner, I'd get my little bag and go to the mess hall and recreation rooms and get some sales. Oh, yeah.

Where I was working was up at various places, pouring concrete flooring where they stored the trucks. We pushed wheel barrows through there and put matting down. Some of those guys didn't know how to push a wheel barrow. Boy, they was in trouble. That was hard work, yes, it was. I worked common labor when I wasn't in concrete. We worked at 2-East. My brother and I poured the first mud [concrete] there, and spread it out of the mixer truck. I also worked at the 100 Areas, all three of the reactors. My brother helped haul and unload the bricks that built that smokestack at 300 Area.

I knew what I was doing when it came to spreading mud. I spread the first load of mud at 100-F. They call concrete mud because it looks like mud. They hauled the mud in trucks, from a mixing plant at Hanford. When the buildings got high, they pumped mud through steel pipes. I worked high up, sometimes. They called that "pump-crete."

I thought working conditions was fair. We didn't have no cruel supervisors. I remember two of the guys in our crew, they'd get to telling tales, and everybody in our crew, including the supervisors, would stand there laughing. The supervisors would say, "Okay, boys, stop lying, and let's go to work." I remember Wyatt Durette, a white fella who was Du Pont's concrete supervisor. He used to get on a big box, one of those big ol' shipping boxes, and say, "All right, boys, I want you to go out and do a good job. Say, if you see a nail sticking up somewhere, take your time and bend it down because we don't want nobody hurt here. You got all your hands, fingers and toes, and we want you to keep 'em that way," I remember he would get on that big crate on a Monday morning. We got friends and brothers over yonder fighting and we want to do a good job here, he'd say. Sure, I remember Durette.

Only one time I remember any racial problem at Hanford. We was working on postholes and drains at the trailer camp. We had to pull a water line. I forgot his name now, but this white carpenter called one of our boys by name and the boy said "Yes."

And this carpenter said if you was back in Mississippi now, you would say "Yes, sir!" The boy said back to him, "But you ain't IN Mississippi now."

A lot of blacks worked in concrete. They didn't mind getting in that mud. We wore rubber boots, hard hats, slicker pants, gloves, to keep the concrete from messin' your clothes. We wore those steel-toed shoes. Durette always said "Be safe."

In the barracks, when I wasn't working, we'd play whist or dominoes. I didn't have a lot of spare time. I went to Kennewick once, Pasco once, I would go to Yakima because that was where my wife was when she first came. I was a church member, but out at Hanford they had one little house for a colored church, an old farmhouse. I understand some of the preachers got to fightin' and squabblin' over something. I never went to church while I was out there, unless I would go when I was in Yakima.

On Sundays, during the summer sometimes I watched baseball games. Whites and blacks played on the same teams. Some of the guys would go swimming. I never attempted to go swimming because they said that Columbia River don't give up the dead. No, sir.

None of us knew what we was doing. Durette tell us if anyone ask what you are doing, tell 'em you working. It was way along in the game when they told us we was building that bomb that was dropped on wherever it was, Nagasaki. I say "Is that right?" If we all would have known what we was doing, some of us would have been frightened and left. I would have stayed. I figured if it was safe for somebody else, it was safe for me.

I left Hanford the latter part of '44, when the job was kinda playing light. I went home to Texas, and I had more money than I ever had in my life. I was down there in Texas in '44, for Thanksgiving, and I took out my friends and told them to get what they want, this was my bill. I was spending money with both hands. At Christmas we went to see my wife's people in Alabama. After we stayed home for a while, I bought some hogs, some cows, put some wire around our pasture at Kildare. Said, well, I guess we'll be here a while. But I got to thinking and told my wife, why don't we go back where we can make some money. It's all going out, none coming in. She ask, "Where we goin'?" I say, "Well, there's a shipyard in Vancouver, Washington."

Ken Kesey
(1935-)

Ken Kesey's acclaimed first novel, *One Flew Over the Cuckoo's Nest* (1962), secured his position as a nationally recognized talent. A native of Oregon, Kesey graduated from the University of Oregon in 1957. His second novel, *Sometimes a Great Notion* (1964), examines the effects of a lumber strike on a small town on the Oregon coast, focusing on the Stampers, who defy their community and continue working. In the following excerpt, Henry, the patriarch, Hank, the favored son, and Leland, the returning son who had left the family business, share the bond that hard labor forges in working-class men.

FROM *Sometimes a Great Notion*

ON THE SLOPE HANK SMOKED in patient silence beside his father while he heard the dissonant squeak of Joe Ben's little radio draw closer through the dripping firs. (The old man still stood leaned up against the log, working his jaw in thought; his white hair was plastered to his bony skull now and hung streaming from the back of his head, sort of like wet cobwebs. "Steeper land like that over yonder," he kept mumbling. "Hm. Yeah. Over there like that. We can get half again the cutting. Uhuh. I bet we can...."

I was a little awed by the change that had come over the old coon; it seemed that the cast had broken to reveal a younger and at the same time more mature person. I watched old Henry appraise the land and announce which trees we was gonna cut, how, in what order, and so forth... and I got to feeling like I was seeing a once-familiar but almost-forgotten man. I mean... this wasn't the old yarn-spinning, bullshitting character that had been thundering damn near unnoticed through the house and the local bars for the last six months. Not the noisy joke of a year before either. No, I realized gradually, this is the boomer I used to follow on cruising walks twenty years before, the calm, stubborn, confident rock of a man who had taught me how to tie a bowline with one hand and how to place a dutchman block in an undercut so's the tree would fall so cunthair *perfect* that he could put a stake where he aimed for it to fall, then by god drive that stake into the ground with the trunk!

I kept still, looking at him. Like I was scared if I said something this phantom might disappear. And as Henry talked—haltingly, yet deliberate and certain all the same—I felt myself commence to relax. Like I'd had a couple quarts of beer. I let my lungs pull deep and easy and felt a kind of repose, almost like sleep, go running through me. It felt good. It was the first time, I realized, that I'd felt relaxed in—oh, Christ, except for last night with Viv rubbing my back—in what seemed years and years. Hot damn, I figured; the *old* old Henry is back; let him hold the handles a spell while I take a breather.

So I didn't say anything until Joby was almost there. I let him carry on for a while with his instructions before I reminded him that that slope me and Joby'd been working was exactly the one he'd pointed out for us to work that morning. "Remember?" I grinned at him. "You said just down from that outcropping?"

"That's all right, that's all right," he says, not the least concerned, and went on to say, "But I said that account of this place was *safest.* An' that was this morning. We ain't got time for that, not no more, not now. Down yonder she'll be a little trickier, hut we can fall half again the bastards we can fall up here. Anyhow I'll tell you when Joe gets up here. Now hush and let me think a minute."

So I hushed and let him think, wondering how long it had been since I'd been able to do *that*...

I left the school and playground and spent most of the rest of that lonely morn over dreary cups of drugstore coffee brought me by a dour Grissom who seemed to hold me solely responsible for his lack of business. During this time I revised and revamped my demon-teammate theory—improving on symbolism, sharpening the effect, stretching it to cover all possible woes.... I could stretch it far beyond grammar school. All through prep school, I avoided that playground, all through college I had stayed safely in the classroom, secure behind a bastion of books, and played no base at all on the field outside. Not first or second, not third. Certainly not home. Secure but homeless. Homeless even in the town of my home-town team, with no base to play. No arms in all the wet world to enfold me, no armchair by the cozy fire to hold me. And, now, on top of it all, I was deserted, deserted at the hospital, left to the merciless hoofs of galloping pneumonia, by my own pitiless father. Oh, Father, Father, where can you be... ?

"Gettin' drownt," I tell Hank. "Out in the weather thisaway, I should of brung more better gear." I lean my bum hip against the log again to take the weight offn the cast and I take me a little knit cap from my pocket and pull it on. It ain't gonna keep my head dry none, but it'll soak up enough rain to keep it from running into my eyes. Joe

Ben, he comes scrambling up the hill practically on all fours, looking like some kinda animal scared outa the ground. "What's up? What's up?" He looks from Hank to me, then settles himself on the log and looks down the direction we're looking. He's itching to pieces to know what's up but he knows he'll get told when I'm ready to tell him, so he don't ask again.

"Well sir." I pat my old cap into place and spit. "We got to finish our cuttin'," I tell them, "an' finish it today." Just like that. Hank and Joe Ben light up cigarettes and wait to see what it's all about. I say, "It's full moon, an' a poor time for it. I bet this mornin' was a good minus-one-five or minus-two tide. Real low. When we left the house this mornin' the river shoulda been low enough to show barnacles on the pilings, ain't that so? With a tide so low? Huh? But did we see any barnacles? Or did anybody look... ?" I look right at Hank. "Did you check the marker at the house this mornin' against the tide chart?" He shakes his head. I spit and look disgusted at him. Joe says, "What's it mean, anyway?" "What it means," I tell them, "is the game is all, is jick, jack, joker, and the game for Evenwrite and Draeger an' that bunch of goddam featherbeddin' *so-slists* is eg-zactly what it means! Unless we really get in high gear. What it means... is there must be damn heavy rain up country; there's *more water* comm' out'n the upper branches'n anybody figured. We're in for maybe one sonofabitch of a flood! Not tonight, probably, no, I doubt it tonight. Unless she really cuts loose a storm. And she could, but let's say not. Let's say it keeps on like it's goin'. By tomorrow or the next day nobody'll be able to hang onto a boom of logs, not us nor WP. So we got to deliver before it crests. Now. Let's say, oh, say, it's about ten-thirty now, so that means eleven, twelve, one, two... so let's say we get two of the bastards an hour, pushin' it, two of these...." I take me a look up one of the firs standing there. She's a good one. Like they used to be. "At seventeen board feet, times two, times—what did I figure? five hours' cuttin'?—times five hours, say six hours; we can have Andy to stay up all night at the mill with a boat and spotlight watchin' for the latecomers... yeah, we can do that. So. Anyhow. Figuring six real *highballin'* hours of cutting, nothin' goes wrong, we—let's see now... hum..."

The old man talked on, darting the brown tip of his tongue over his lips and occasionally pausing to spit, speaking more to himself than to the others. Hank finished his cigarette and lit another, nodding now and then as he listened (content to let the old guy call the shots and run the show. Damned content, to be honest with you.

Henry kept rambling on. After telling Joe and me all the details and outlining to us all the dangers and doubts, he finally got around to allowing, "But, yessir, we can hack it," like I knew he would. "With even a little margin, if we hump our tails. 'N' then tomorrow we got to rent a tug an' run the booms down to Wakonda Pacific, quicker the better. Not wait for Thanksgivin'. Get 'em off our hands before we lose 'em. Well… be tight, but we can whup it."

"You bet!" Joe said. "Oh yeah!" Business like this was right up Joby's alley.

"So… ?" the old man said, talking straight ahead. "What do you say?"

I knew it was me he was asking. "Be tough," I tell him, "with Orland and Layton and the others buffaloed by Evenwrite and the rest of the town. I mean, it'll be tough making a drive on that high a river, with that many booms and us so shorthanded…."

"I know it'll be tough, goddammit! That ain't what I asked…."

"Hey!" Joby snaps his fingers. "I know: we can get some of the Wakonda Pacific foremen!" He's excited and chomping at the bit. "See, they got to help us, don't you see? They don't want to lose their winter millwork. With Mama Olson's tug, and some of them WP bosses, we'll be pretty as you please, right in the good Lord's warm little fist."

"We'll take that jump," the old man says, pushing himself up from the log, "when it comes up. Right now I'm sayin' can we cut our quota today? All of it. Just us three?"

"Sure! Sure we can, oh yeah, there ain't nothing—"

"I was askin' you, Hank…."

I knew he was. I squinted through the blue film of cigarette smoke, out across the fern and salal and blackberry, through the brute black straight trunks of those trees down to the river, trying to ask myself, Can we or can't we? But I didn't know; I just couldn't tell. The three of us he said. Meaning two and one old man. Two tired jacks and one old *crippled* man. It's crazy, and I said to myself, and I knew I should say Nothing doing to the old man, say it's too risky, forget it, flick it….

But some way he didn't seem like an old crippled man to me then. It wasn't like I was standing there talking with the wild and woolly town character any more, but with some fierce young jack who had just walked up out of the years ready to spit on his palms and take over again. I looked at him, waiting there. What could I tell him? If he says we can whip it, all right, maybe he knows, let him take over. "I'm askin' you, boy…." Because all I know is that the only way you can keep this jack from out of the past from trying to whip it was with a club and a rope, so I say all right. "All right, Henry, let's try it." *You probably know more about this kind of logging than me and Joby put together. So all right, head out. You run it. I'm tired rassling it. I got other things on my mind. You take it. Me, just turn me on and aim me. That's how I'd like it, anyhow. I'm tired, but I'll work. If you take over. If you just turn me on and aim me it's fine and dandy with this boy....*)

After Grissom had the effrontery to ask me to pay for the magazine I spilled coffee on, I decided to go mope elsewhere. I crossed the street and entered the Sea Breeze Cafe and Grill, the very apotheosis of short-order America: two waitresses in wilted uniforms chatting at the cash register; lipstick stain on coffee mugs; bleak array of candy; insomniac flies waiting out the rain; a plastic penful of doughnuts; and, on the wall above the Coca-Cola calendar, the methodical creaking creep of a bent second hand across a Dr. Pepper clock... the perfect place for a man to sit and commune with nature.

I climbed onto one of the leatherette stools, ordered coffee and purchased freedom for one of the penned-up doughnuts. The shortest of the waitresses brought my order, took my money, made my change, and returned to the cash register to play her accordion of neck to her bored companion... never really acknowledging my presence to herself. I ate the doughnut and reiterated my woes with fresh coffee, trying not to think ahead, trying not to ask myself, What am I waiting for? The second hand creaked a meaningless dirge. An ancient refrigerator complained in the cluttered kitchen, and the second hand cranked out a dreary fare of short-order time—tepid seconds, stale minutes, the drab diet that He Who Hesitates must always be satisfied with. ...

As the rain quickened on the slopes the three men set about work. Hank jerked the starter rope on his saw and wondered why the saw should feel so feather-light (*just take it over and it's dandy with me....*) when his arms felt so heavy. Henry walked the length of the log, looking for a place to set a check, and wished he'd brought a plastic bag or some damn thing to wrap around his cast so's it wouldn't soak up water and weigh him down even worse than ordinary. On the other hand Joe Ben, leaping back downhill to the log he had been working on when interrupted by Hank's whistle, felt as though the mud caking his boots was actually becoming lighter. He felt even more nimble and buoyant than usual. Everything was going fine. He'd been worried over something earlier that morning—can't even remember now—but everything was turning out just the way he liked it: old Henry's dramatic arrival, the news of the tides, the planning in terse, muted voices, that brass-band feeling rising among them, beating out we got to make that first down, we got to, and you block for me, Joby, and I'll tear 'em apart! Yeah boy! That brassy beat of high-school idealism and determination that he liked best of all: beating out we got, got to, got to! over and over until the words became we will, we will, we *will!*—and when I put my hand on the log and vault over it I feel like if I don't hold back I'll just sail right off in the sky—the log's ready to go—it was ready when Hank whistled—all the dickens needs now's a good shove to get it over the rock it's hung against. Let's see here...

Joe circled the end of the log and looked at the jack. It was screwed out to its maximum length, with one end anchored against a rock and the other biting into the bark of the log. To unscrew it meant that the log would fall back a few inches while he anchored the jack against another rock. "Bug that," he said aloud, laughing, and told himself, "Don't give a *inch!*" He wedged his compact little body in on top of the jack, with his shoulders against the rock and his boots against the log. I give a yeah-h-h shove be thou you dickens cast into the uh uh *sea!* Yeah! She teeters over the rock, rolls against a stump picking up speed, spins—off the stump, and slides straight as an arrow *whew* down the hill to within a bare half-yard of the river! Good deal, I'd say. "Hey... " Joe stood up and shouted over his shoulder at Flank and old Henry, watching him. "See *that*? Oh man; no sense messin' around, the way I see it. Now, you fellas want me to kick that one downhill and save you the effort?"

Laughing, he skidded down the slope with the jack light under his arm and his boots flying. And the little transistor bumping and squeaking against his neck...

> *I know you love me*
> *An' happy we could be*
> *If some folks would leave us alone....*

All righty now—I *screw* the jack short again and wedge it under the log and *twist!* He watched the butt of it bite the juicy bark. The wooden screw of the implement lengthened out with his cranking. The log rolled a few feet, paused—this time she pitches crashing through shredding fern blackberry vines and into the river. Yes sir, all righty, there! He picked up his jack, slung it across his shoulder by the strap, and swarmed up the hill on all fours—who-so-*ever*!—snorting and whooping as he came, like a water spider fleeing to high ground. His face was scratched and red when he reached the second log, where Hank worked the saw. "Hankus, ain't you finished bucking this thing yet? Henry, it looks like me'n you have to carry our load an' then some to make up for this loafer!"

Then vaulted over the log, the mud on his boots turning to wings: and whosoever shall not doubt in his heart, he will, by golly, he *will...!*

In her shack Indian Jenny hummed over an astrologer's chart that was patterned mysteriously with glass rings *interlacing!* Lee sipped coffee at the Sea Breeze. At the house Viv finished up the last of the dishes and wondered what to start on next. With Jan and the kids staying at the new place, there's not so much rush. And it's nice to set my own pace. I enjoy Jan and the kids here, and I'll miss them when they move into the other place, but it's nice to be here and set my own pace. Boy oh boy, is it quiet just here alone...

Standing in the center of the big living room, watching the river, feeling distracted and flushed, anxious almost... like I'm expecting something to happen. One of the kids to holler, I guess. I know what'll calm me down; take a nice long hot soak in the tub. Aren't *you* the Miss Lazy Britches? But gee, is it still and quiet....

Hank wiped his nose on the wet cuff of his sweat shirt sticking from his poncho, then grabbed the saw again and dug into the trunk of the tree before him, feeling the relaxation of labor, of simple uncomplicated labor, run through his body like a warm liquid.... (Like a sleep, sort of. More relaxing than some sleeps a guy could name. I never minded work so much. I could of got along right well just doing a plain eight-to-five with the bull telling what to do and where to do it. If he had been a decent bull and fairly reasonable about that what and where. Yes I could of....) Everything was going pretty good. The logs fell good and the wind stayed down. Henry helped where he was able, picking the trees, figuring the troughs, arranging the screwjacks in place, using his experience instead of bones he knew were brittle as chalk—wheezing, spitting, thinking a man *can* whup it, even he don't have nothin' but knowhow left, even his legs like butter and his arms and hands like cracking glass and he don't have nothin' but his knowhow left—he can *still* help whup it! Downhill Joe Ben paced off twenty-five steps and cut through his log, feeling the screaming vibration of the chain saw tingle up his arms and accumulate in his back muscles like a charge of electrical power... building, yeah, rising oh yeah and a little more and I'll just grab this log up and *bust* it over my knee! Watch if I don't....

On the counter of the Sea Breeze Cafe and Grill was a selection box for our youth's music. To pass the wait (I told myself I was waiting for my father to show up at the Snag across the street) I took a survey of what Young America was singing these days. Let's see... we've got Terry Keller "Coming with Summer"—very neat—a "Stranger on the Shore" called—s'help me—Mister Acker Bilk. Earl Grant "Swinging Gently"; Sam Cook "Twistin' the Night Away"; Kingston Trio "Jane Jane Janing"... Brothers Four...Highwaymen (singing "Birdman of Alcatraz," a ballad, based on the movie, that is based on the book, that is based on the life of a lifer who has probably never even heard of the Highwaymen...) the Skyliners... Joey Dee and the Starlighters... Pete Hanly doing "Dardanella" (how did that slip in?), Clyde McSomebody asking "Let's Forget about the Past"... and currently number one, at least in the Sea Breeze Cafe and Grill, a waitress with three pounds of nose under thirty ounces of powder accompanying herself on a tub of dishes while she sings "Why Hang Around?"

I muttered in my coffee cup. "Because I'm waiting for my daddy to come get me." Which convinced no one....

The hillside rang with the tight whine of cutting; the sound of work in the woods was like insects in the walls. Numb clubs of feet registered the blow against the cold earth only by the pained jarring in the bones. Henry dragged a screwjack to a new log. Joe Ben sang along with his radio:

"Leaning, leaning,
Safe and secure from all alarms..."

The forest fought against the attack on its age-old domain with all the age-old weapons nature could muster: blackberries strung out barbed barricades; the wind shook widow-makers crashing down from high rotted snags; boulders reared silently from the ground to block slides that had looked smooth and clear a moment before; streams turned solid trails into creeping ruts of icy brown lava. And in the tops of the huge trees, the very rain seemed to work at fixing the trees standing, threading the million green needles in an attempt to stitch the trees upright against the sky.

But the trees continued to fall, gasping long sighs and ka-whumping against the spongy earth. To be trimmed and bucked into logs. To be coaxed and cajoled downhill into the river with unflagging regularity. In spite of all nature could do to stop it.

Leaning on the *ev-ver-last-ting arms.*

As the trees fell and the hours passed, the three men grew accustomed to one another's abilities and drawbacks. Few words actually passed between them; they communicated with the unspoken language of labor toward a shared end, becoming more and more an efficient, skilled team as they worked their way across the steep slopes; becoming almost one man, one worker who knew his body and his skill and knew how to use them without waste or overlap.

Henry chose the trees, picked the troughs where they would fall, placed the jacks where they would do the most good. And stepped back out of the way. Here she *slides!* See? A man can whup it goddammit with nothin' but his experience an' stick-to-'er, goddam if he can't.... Hank did the falling and trimming, wielding the cumbersome chain saw tirelessly in his long, cable-strong arms, as relentless as a machine; working not fast but steadily, mechanically, and certainly far past the point where other fallers would have rested, pausing only to refuel the saw or to place a new cigarette in the corner of his mouth when his lips felt the old one burning near—taking the pack from the pouch of his sweat shirt, shaking a cigarette into view, withdrawing it with his lips... touching the old butt for the first time with his muddy gloves when he removed it to light the new smoke. Such pauses were brief and widely separated in the terrible labor, yet he almost enjoyed returning to work, getting back in the groove, not thinking, just doing the work just like it was eight to five and none of that other crap to worry about, just letting somebody turn me on and aim me at what and where is just the way I like it. The way it used to be. Peaceful. And simple. (*And I ain't thinking about the kid, not in hours I ain't wondered where he is.*)... And Joe Ben handled most of the screwjack work, rushing back and forth from jack to jack, a little twist here, a little shove there, and whup! she's turnin', tippin', heading out downhill! Okay-get down there an' set the jacks again, crank and uncrank right back an' over again. Oh yeah, that's the one'll do it. Shooooom, all the *way,* an' here comes another one, Andy old buddy, big as the ark... feeling a mounting of joyous power collecting in his back muscles, an exhilaration of faith rising with the crash of each log into the river. Whosoever believes in his heart shall cast *mountains* into the sea an' Lord knows what other stuff... then heading back up to the next log—running, leaping, a wingless bird feathered in leather and aluminum and mud, with a transistor radio bouncing and shrill beneath his throat:

Leaning on Jee-zus, leaning on Jee-zus
Safe an' secure from all alarms...

Until the three of them meshed, dovetailed... into one of the rare and beautiful units of effort sometimes seen when a jazz group is making it completely, swinging together completely, or when a home-town basketball squad, already playing over its head, begins to rally to overtake a superior opponent in a game's last minute...and the home boys can't miss; because everything—the passing, the dribbling, the plays—every tiny piece is clicking perfectly. When this happens everyone watching *knows*... that, be it five guys playing basketball, or four blowing jazz, or three cutting timber, that *this bunch—right now, right this moment*—is the best of its kind in the world! But to become this kind of perfect group a team must use *all* its components, and use them in the slots best suited, and use them all with the pitiless dedication to victory that drives them up to their absolute peak, and past it.

Joe felt this meshing. And old Henry. And Hank, watching his team function, was aware only of the beauty of the team and of the free-wheeling thrill of being part of it. Not of the pitiless drive. Not of the three of them building toward a peak the way a machine running too fast too long accelerates without actually speeding up as it reaches a breaking point that it can't be aware of, and goes on past that breaking point, accelerating past it and toward it at the same time and at the same immutable rate. As the trees fell and the radio filled in between their falling:

Leaning on Jee-zus, leaning on Jee-zuz
Leaning on the everlasting arms.

Clemens Starck
(1937-)

Clemens Starck's poetry reflects the world of work he has experienced as a merchant seaman, a reporter on the Wall Street beat, a ranch hand, and a construction foreman. He currently lives in rural Oregon and works as a journeyman at Oregon State University in Corvallis.

PUTTING IN FOOTINGS

Jake is the superintendent on this job,
I draw foreman's wages.
Mack the carpenter, Tom the laborer,
and there are others
wet to the skin
and cold to the bone—
that's Oregon in December.

Be joyful, my spirit. Be of high purpose.
We are putting in footings—
slogging through mud, kneeling
in it, supplicants pleading for mercy,
brutal, cursing,
drizzle coming down harder.

This is the Project Site.
Tobacco-chewing men in big machines dig holes,
we build the forms.
Ironworkers tie off rebar.
This concrete we pour could outlast
the Pyramids.

*   *   *

After the weather
has cleared, and the concrete has cured
and the paychecks are spent—

millennia later,
after the Pyramids
have pulverized and Jake has disappeared
and reappeared many times,
as grouchy as ever,
angels will come to measure our work,
slowly shaking their heads.

Kate Braid
(1947-)

Kate Braid worked for fifteen years as a construction laborer, apprentice carpenter, and carpenter, working on high rises, bridges, and commercial buildings for the union. When there were not union jobs, she worked with another woman doing renovations and residential housing. She chronicled these experiences in *Covering Rough Ground* (1991), where the following poem first appeared. She has authored two other books, *To This Cedar Fountain* (1995) and *Inward to the Bones: Georgia O'Keefe's Journey with Emily Carr* (1998). She now teaches creative writing and writes poetry in Burnaby, British Columbia.

Girl on the Crew

The boys flap heavy leather aprons at me
like housewives scaring crows
from the clean back wash.
Some aprons. Some wash.
They think if the leather is tough enough
if the hammer handle piercing it is long enough
I will be overcome with primordial dread
or longing.

They chant construction curses at me:
Lay 'er down! Erect those studs!

and are alarmed when I learn the words.
They build finely tuned traps, give orders I cannot fill
then puzzle when a few of their own
give me passwords.

I learn the signs of entry,
dropping my hammer into its familiar mouth
as my apron whispers *O-o-o-h Welcome!*

I point my finger and corner posts spring into place
shivering themselves into fertile earth at my command.
The surveyors have never seen such accuracy.

I bite off nails with my teeth
shorten boards with a wave of my hand

pierce them through the dark brown love knots.
They gasp.

I squat and the flood of my urine digs
whole drainage systems in an instant.
The boys park their backhoes, call their friends
to come see for themselves or they'd never believe it.

The hairs of my head turn to steel and join boards
tongue-in-groove
like lovers along dark lanes.
Drywall is rustling under cover
eager to slip over the studs at my desire.

When I tire, my breasts grow two cherry trees
that depart my chest
and offer me shade, cool juices
while the others suck bitter beans.

At the end of the day the boys are exhausted
from watching.
They fall at my feet and beg for a body like mine.
I am too busy dancing to notice.

Kim Barnes
(1960-)

Kim Barnes is a poet and novelist who lives with her husband and children above the Clearwater River in Idaho. Her work has appeared in numerous journals including *The Georgia Review* and *Shenandoah*. In 1995 she received the PEN/Jerard Fund Award on the strength of her then forthcoming book, *In the Wilderness: Coming of Age in an Unknown Country* (1996). Based on her family's experience of the decline of the timber industry in mid-1960 Idaho where her father worked as a logger, the memoir gives a powerful portrait of the changes in life that accompany changes in labor.

FROM *In the Wilderness: Coming of Age in an Unknown Country*

IN LATE FALL KOKANEE THE COLOR of rosewood crowd the shallow tributaries of the North Fork of the Clearwater River. Landlocked salmon, they have made their way from deeper waters to spawn, and the beautiful mass of red they become is the result of their bodies' decay.

We lived for years along the banks of these creeks—Orofino, Weitas, Kelly—our destination determined by what timber sale my great-uncle had bid upon and, finally, by the lay of the land: we leveled our trailers atop the flatness of meadows, or maneuvered them between the stumps of a clearcut.

Perhaps because I was so young, what remains with me about those camps is not the trees and mountains, not the streams pulsing with red as the days shortened; what remains is a sense rather than a memory of place, a composite of smells, sounds and images: the closeness of my parents as they slept beside me when the temperature dropped below zero; my mother's hair tightly curling around my fingers; cigarettes, coffee, sweat, diesel, the turpentine scent of pine.

In winter, our shack darkened by early dusk, the single kerosene lantern illuminated my mother's face as she worked biscuit dough across the oilcloth table. The door would open and my father step in, shedding sawdust like snow. He'd lay down his black pail and steel thermos and grin at my mother as though he had something wonderful to tell, something to make us jump and clap, something so good she'd wrap her arms around his neck and he'd swing her in circles, knocking down chairs, tilting the nail-hung cupboard, causing the flour to fly.

He'd lean over the table, careful with his diesel-stained clothes, never moving his caulked boots from that one spot on the wooden floor, a place pocked and gouged, soft as tenderized meat. They would kiss, once, twice, and then he'd turn to where I played on our shared bed, nesting my doll in flannel shirts, covering her with tea towels, waiting for the grace of his smile.

Even now, my parents speak of those first years in the woods as somehow magical. As poor as we were, we ate well. In summer, we picked huckleberries big as cherries, jerked trout from the shadowed bends of creeks, wrapping them in leaves of skunk cabbage. For Nan and Aunt Daisy, the coldwater char were a delicacy, so different from the muddy catfish they lived on as children. Fried in cornmeal and lard, the small brookies turned golden. Each year until 1988, when my grandmother died, I took her my first catch of the season. She added nothing, only the fish neatly arranged across her plate—no fork or knife, only her fingers pulling from the bones sliver after sliver of pure white meat.

The men could step a few yards from camp and take their limit of deer and elk, enough to fill several town lockers with stew meat and roasts. I still associate the smell of blood, the mounds of entrails steaming in new snow, with fall. One season, it was a bear they hung from the loader's boom. Gutted and skinned, it swung in the cooling wind, pink and muscled as the body of a man. It was the one thing my mother could not eat, sweet and tallowy, like the mutton she despised as a child.

My mother found herself surrounded by mountains. The friends she had left in Oklahoma had by now finished their schooling. Most were having babies of their own, keeping house in Tulsa or moving into Oklahoma City to clerk at Woolworth's. The few letters she received she kept tied in a ribbon, tucked away in some secret place.

She rose before dawn each morning to fix my father's breakfast—venison steak and eggs, home-baked bread toasted on the cast-iron stove top, coffee boiled black in its aluminum pot. While he ate, she packed his lunch, filling the dented bucket with sandwiches and fried pies—golden half-moon pastries made with dried apricots. His work clothes hung from the beams, the thick flannel shirt and black pants washed the day before and ironed to a shine.

After his kiss at the door, she watched him climb into his truck, its blue exhaust disappearing into the dark sky like a heaven-bound spirit. When I awoke, she lay sleeping beside me. The kerosene lantern still burned, its reflection lost in the sunlit window.

We hauled laundry to the wash shed, where the gas-powered wringer washer sat like a giant toad, all belly and noise. Uncle Clyde had connected a large reservoir to the woodstove there, and by building a popping fire, we had enough hot water to wash our clothes and bathe. While I splashed in a small galvanized tub, my mother hummed in the makeshift shower stall fed by pipes running from the water tank.

When Nan first arrived in Idaho, Aunt Daisy had immediately set about matching her younger sister to one of the numerous eligible loggers. She settled on Elmer Edmonson, a widower, known locally as the Little Giant. His small stature belied his strength, and his reputation was that of a hardworking and fearless lumberjack. He and my grandmother moved out of the woods to Lewiston, into the house he had shared with his first wife, who had died of cancer. Nan set up housekeeping with the dishes and linens of another woman, grateful to have what was given her.

Soon after their marriage in 1956, while working a site near Craig Mountain, my step-grandfather was severely injured ducking beneath a log to secure a choker cable. The log rolled, crushing his skull. By the time they got him to the hospital in Lewiston, his head had swollen to the size of a watermelon, the flesh split from the pressure, yet he never lost consciousness. My parents shudder when they speak of it. No one less strong and determined could have survived, they say.

My grandmother nursed him constantly, and it was only as an adult that I was told how the kindly, shaking old man could turn suddenly manic, returning home from the grocery store with gallons and gallons of ice cream or giving away every dime in his pocket to strangers on the street. He had violent seizures and hallucinations, and the family would have no choice but to commit him to the state mental hospital at Orofino until his episodes subsided.

I don't remember his bizarre behavior or sudden, unexplained absences. Instead, I remember the evenings spent visiting Nan, waiting for Grandpa to come home from his rounds as a salesman hawking Rawleigh spices and liniment door-to-door. He would draw from his pocket a rolled purse of soft leather, jingling with coins that I dumped onto the floor, stacking the dimes and quarters into towering columns, breathing in the blood-sharp smell of copper.

In the camps, my mother was left with Aunt Daisy, who gave her little attention, believing that a woman's duty was to provide her husband with every bit and moment of herself, so that even in his absence her hands were busy making his meals, scrubbing the pitch from his clothes, snapping and smoothing fresh sheets for his bed. She counseled my mother to do the same, reminding her that the needs and love of a child must come second to the ties between husband and wife. She offered another piece of wisdom: the only power women have in this world is sex. A smart wife knew when to offer herself and when to hold back. There was little a husband wouldn't do if teased and denied enough.

By the time my father arrived home, my mother had cleaned the shack's every corner. Brown beans bubbled on the stove, and the room seemed honeyed with the smell of cornbread cooked in a cast-iron skillet. Her hair was neatly curled and combed, her fingernails painted. My own long hair she drew up in a bow so that my father might be pleased.

The trailer's size made it impossible to gather more than a few people in at once, but on weekends my uncles squeezed around the table for a game of cards. The bed was mine, an oasis of softness and warmth where I played with my dolls and listened to the men's stories. Their days were full of giant things—machinery and trees, the noise of saws and snapping cables. They wore their wounds, deep cuts and bloody gouges, with the nonchalance of immortals, doctoring themselves with turpentine and alcohol. I fell asleep, protected from the outside world by my father's strength, by his laughter, louder than the screech of tree against tree as the wind whipped the darkness.

INJURIES IN THE WOODS ARE COMMON and expected: deep punctures from snagged limbs, twisted ankles, bruises from falling off decked logs—traumas so small they rarely warrant mention. The real danger lies in the dance of machinery and wood. In the hands of a seasoned logger the saw seems tamed, teeth directed easily toward a precise and efficient cut. But green wood cannot be predicted, nor can the saw's instantaneous reaction to what lies hidden in the heart of fir, tamarack and pine. Kickback—the saw ricocheting off a knot or warp deep in the tree's interior—seldom leaves the logger unscathed. If he's lucky, he has no time to turn his head, and the razored chain cuts only his face. If instinctively he does jerk away, the teeth find a truer mark—the neck. Even with good roads and helicopters, help cannot reach a man fast enough to staunch the flow of blood from a severed jugular.

One local logger decapitated himself, slipping from a log, his chainsaw still running. Another died when a cable snapped and the loader's boom plummeted. Some are killed, simply and predictably, when the tree, set loose from its base, twists in an unexpected way. A tree will sometimes "barberchair"—splinter vertically from a perfect half-cut, catching the faller squarely in the chest with enough force to crush or impale him against the next nearest trunk. Bulldozers roll. An unstable slope gives way and sends the logs, loader and man tumbling down the mountain.

The year I turned four my father lay housebound, a cast from armpit to hip. He had ruptured a vertebra that winter while trying to turn a pole with a peavey. After his surgery, we moved to Lewiston, in with Nan and Grandpa Edmonson for the six months it would take for his back to heal.

Workman's Compensation paid only forty-one dollars a week, so while my father recuperated, my mother worked morning shift at Kube's Korner Kafe. I had never seen so much of my father. The smoke from his cigarettes filled the small house. He read every western he could get his hands on, played solitaire and watched without comment the dramas of other people's lives unfold on daytime television. What I recall most is the card table set up in the kitchen for his puzzles—thousands of intricately cut pieces sorted by edge and color, which he patiently worked into perfect pictures of mountains and wildflowers—near replicas of the landscape they had hauled him from.

He showed me how the pieces fit, taking my wrist in his fingers, swiveling my hand, redirecting a corner. He smelled different—still smoky, but less like earth than pot roast and my grandmother's sacheted linen. I forgot to miss that other father, the logger who came home in twilight, bringing my mother wild iris, bending easily to kiss me.

EVEN THOUGH HE WALKED with a noticeable hitch and lifting a saw made spasms ripple my father's rib cage, when the cast was off we headed back to the woods. This time we settled into a small green house in Pierce proper. Pierce was named for Captain Elias D. Pierce, a California prospector who discovered gold there in 1860; within a year of his discovery, the townsite had been cut and cleared, making room for the miners, gamblers and prostitutes who lived, at least for a short time, in the booming heyday of the town. Along with them came a large influx of Chinese workers, and for many of them the West and its riches also held horror: three miles southwest of Pierce is Hangman's Gulch, now a designated historical site. There, in 1885, five Chinese unjustly accused of brutally murdering a local businessman were dragged from their cells by vigilantes and hung on a makeshift gallows.

Placer mining came first, and soon the hills were pocked with lode claims and ore mining, sites with names such as the Democrat and the Mascot, the American, the Dewey, the Pioneer, the Ozark, the Crescent and the Wild Rose; the Oxford, the Klondike on French Creek, the Rosebud. Then came the dredges with their greater capacity to scoop the gold from its bed, working the waters of Canal Gulch, Rhodes Creek, the Orogrande.

My father remembers the early days in Pierce, when the road was mud in spring and dust in summer and boardwalks fronted the bars and the single hotel. Now we had the luxury of a sidewalk down both sides, which the merchants kept shoveled and salted in winter to encourage business. Rape's Grocery Store and Meat Locker, Durant's Dry Goods, a beauty shop, bar and the post office lined the street's north side. Across was the Clearwater Hotel and Cafe, where old-timers sat for hours behind the large front window, still uniformed in black denim and red suspenders, spitting into Folger's cans. Some wore hard hats. When they waved, light shone through where fingers once had been.

We settled into the boomtown gone drowsy, our rented house only slightly larger than the camp shacks. Perhaps this was done thinking that my mother would be happiest living in town, closer to stores and the company of other women, especially since my brother had been born and she now had two children to contend with. And maybe she was happier. Maybe it is only my own feelings I remember in that house—of being closed up, kept behind doors with locking latches.

We were less isolated—neighbors often stopped by for coffee, and ready-made bread and fresh beef were as close as Rape's store—but some part of the magic was gone. Unlike my mother and my aunts, "Pierce women" (as I heard them referred to in the coded kitchen conversation) did not live in the camps with their husbands, but took up permanent residence in town. Most were born and raised in the area and had married into other logging families. They learned to dress and order their households in deference to the mud and deep snow. They often wore their husband's clothing, as did my mother, but I remember them differently: their shirt cuffs hung unbuttoned; their pants sagged in the seat. They cut their hair into no-nonsense bobs permed tight to their heads, and their only makeup was an occasional slash of red applied haphazardly in the pickup's rearview. They sucked at their cigarettes like old men, eyes crinkling against the smoke.

My mother must have missed those first few years in camp, when she and her new husband slept snugged together on their single cot, never minding the thin mattress and close edges, forgetting there ever was another world. My father's injury made her realize how easily she could be left alone, and she awaited his return each evening with growing uneasiness. She listened to the stories other women told—how the wife had opened the door, already knowing with the first knock, already disbelieving the words she had always feared to hear: the dozer rolled; the chain snapped; that one tree, the *widowmaker,* gave in to the wind it had withstood for decades and came down like a javelin. Always, they told the grieving wife, death was quick, the one belief she could hold on to as she passed into her life like the newly blinded—feeling for thresholds, leaning heavily on the counter's edge.

When one day our town neighbor came running across the muddy yard, fear on her face that could mean only one thing, my mother fell against the window, clutching the curtain to her breast. In those few moments before the woman burst in, half her head still in curlers, the other half sprung loose in ribbons of hair, my mother donned the shroud of a widow.

But it was not my mother the woman mourned for but Jackie Kennedy, and as we all sat before the neighborhood's only television, my mother cried for the country, for the slain president, for the widow in her brain-spattered dress, for the long hours she herself had yet to endure, waiting for my father to come home.

There is a trileveled hierarchy in woodswork. True logging—falling, limbing, skidding and hauling timber to be made into lumber—is at the top; making shakes and shingles is at the bottom, and only those who for whatever reason cannot find work as lumberjacks split cedar. Between these two is pole-making: the cutting, skinning and hauling of cedar trees straight and uniform enough to be made into telephone and electrical poles. Uncle Clyde found that, with the help of his nephews, he could cut and skin record numbers of poles, taking advantage of an opportunity left open by the prejudice of others. Buyers were amazed by the loads hauled off the steeply pitched mountains—the long, thin trunks still whole, not cracked or snapped by carelessness—and paid my great-uncle well.

One summer, he bet my father and uncles a town dinner that they couldn't clear the pole sale on Mockingbird Hill in a single week. They began cutting at dawn, urging each other on, giving everything they had to beat the old man's bet, even though they knew the smallness of his wager. They worked steadily until the light drained from the trees and their backs ached with the weight of peaveys and saws, then drove back to camp to eat and sleep, happy as they had ever been in their lives.

They won the bet. Uncle Clyde took them to Lewiston and treated them to a platter of sweet red spaghetti at Italian Gardens. My father still laughs with pleasure at the memory of them all there together—

four young men, boys, really, the oldest just twenty-five—working their way through the dense underbrush, clearing and skidding with the skill of seasoned lumberjacks, at home in a land the folks back in Oklahoma could imagine only as full of bear and cougar, a wilderness so untamed a man could lose himself in broad daylight only yards from his doorstep. My father remembers how good that spaghetti tasted. He remembers a time when all that mattered to any of them was the sure strength of their arms and the direction a tree might fall.

BY THE TIME I WAS READY to start school, Uncle Clyde had established a more permanent camp just off the main road between Pierce and Headquarters. It was across from a pole yard, a large landing where thousands of peeled poles rose in decks stacked fifty feet high. We called our new home Pole Camp, and once again we circled and leveled the trailers, but this time they were more fixed. Uncle Clyde and Aunt Daisy built themselves a frame house and painted it green. The men erected a large, two-story garage in which they could work on machinery in the coldest weather. Some of the smaller shacks were pushed together; ours, two trailers connected to form a *T*, had an indoor toilet. We were close enough to town to have electricity. One day, Uncle Clyde ran a wire from trailer to trailer and into each of the long wooden boxes he had hung on our walls. The first time our new telephone rang, I held the black, bell-shaped receiver away from my ear, startled to hear my father's bodiless voice.

The shortest trailers, just large enough to accommodate a bunk, stove and wash pan, went to the itinerant sawyers who hired on for the season. Each in his turn was called "Swede," and when Aunt Daisy sent me to fetch them for dinner, the answer came from the doorway left open to air the smoke of their pipes and tightly rolled cigarettes: 'ah, um comm!" Their rounded consonants and opened vowels were a song to me, but I never worked up the courage to top the steps and pass into their secret lives: always dark, even the single square window curtained with a towel, the smell of woodsmoke and boot grease and that particular odor of old bachelors alone with their woolen underwear—sometimes, the whiskey on their breath, the heavy sharp scent of it as they came to the door, pulling up their suspenders, rubbing their teeth with rough knuckles.

My uncles each married women with children and soon brought their new families into our circle. Suddenly, my mother was rich in female companionship—women her own age to share her days with, other mothers struggling with the demands of young children. Suddenly I had cousins. My bed was no longer my own but a place where boys jumped with their dirty shoes and girls squabbled over my dolls. Aunts and uncles gathered close in our kitchen for long weekend games of pinochle and Monopoly, smoke from their cigarettes filling the air to a barroom haze.

IN WINTER, AFTER THE RAINS when temperatures dropped far below zero and the heavy freeze set in, the loggers could continue their cutting, shoveling snow from around the trees' base, moving equipment across the icy clearings with the help of studded tires and chains. But for the pole-makers, winter meant no work: when the slim and fragile poles began snapping like toothpicks in the crackling cold, we would pack what we could into the trunk of our car, resting our feet on boxes and paper bags, and be suddenly gone from the woods to Lewiston, where my father and uncles would work swing shift at the mill or pump gas at the Texaco until the weather moderated.

The road leading from Pierce to Lewiston is narrow and winding, descending from the Weippe Prairie (pronounced "Wee-ipe") to the Clearwater River in a series of steep and pitching curves. The last fifty miles is river road, the part of Highway 12 now referred to as the Clearwater Canyon Scenic Byway. The entire trip took less than three hours—across flat farmland nestled between stands of timber; past Fraser Park (named after David Fraser, the man supposedly murdered by the Chinese), complete with a rough baseball diamond, a single set of warped pine bleachers and a galvanized-pipe swing set; down the grade with its switchback turns so tight the trucks with their long loads of poles took both lanes at the curves; across the bridge at Greer and past Orofino with its doctors and tiny airport said to be cursed so that all owners died in fiery crashes while trying to maneuver their single-engine planes between the highway and parallel water; alongside the widening Clearwater to its confluence with the Snake at the mouth of Hells Canyon—out of the absolute blackness of nights in the forest into a city of twenty-four-hour markets and cars lined up at the intersections ten deep.

As the years of our travel passed, Greg, four years younger, would listen intently as I read to him from the Children's Library of Classics our parents had purchased with the set of encyclopedias we hauled with us from one place to the next. Arabian Nights, Robinson Crusoe, King Arthur, Robin Hood, Treasure Island, Swiss Family Robinson—the worlds I fantasized were lush with exotic flowers, full of giant pythons and man-eating natives, populated by gossamer fairies, men and women who conversed in words I had never heard spoken, words I mispronounce to this day because their sounds existed only in my mind's ear: *joust, vizier, yeoman.*

The books kept me anchored—not in the real world, but in worlds I carried with me, stacked neatly in a cardboard box I balanced on my knees as the heavy car leaned into the curves of the road. I marked the miles reciting lines from Tennyson's "The Idylls of the King":

> My good blade carves the casques of men,
> My tough lance thrusteth sure,
> My strength is as the strength of ten,
> Because my heart is pure.

The sentiment echoed that of the children's hymns we sang when my grandmother took us to Sunday school: *Onward Christian soldiers, marching as to war....* Reading the tales of Arthur, I mooned over the mystery of the Silent Maid, whose throat was as white and round as the cup of a lily and who waited silently for the arrival of Perceval. I thought that if I could not be a queen I might be the Maid, who "prayed and fasted till the sun/Shone and the wind blew through her."

My fantasies of feminine loyalty and sacrifice would be interrupted by my brother's yell that he could see the mill as we came into Lewiston. Its towering smokestacks belched out sulfuric steam, and the fog rising from the giant settling ponds shrouded the river and road in a foul mist. The lights seemed blinding, so bright they swallowed the stars and left nothing secret. Sometimes I'd move my box to the center of the seat and sink down to the floorboard, where I covered my head with my coat and made a night for myself: through the seams, pinpricks of light shone through and I imagined constellations of my own naming: *Avalon, Galahad, the Holy Grail.*

ONE WINTER THERE WAS NO TRAVEL. Instead of heading to Lewiston, we remained circled at the edge of the meadow, where elk grazed, herds of a hundred or more filling the evening air with high-pitched whistles and barks. The men had decided to wait out the cold. They pooled their dole, and for a short time we were rich in food: canned fruit filled the cupboards; bags of beans slouched in the corners of the rooms like woozy children. The single refrigerator we all shared burgeoned with carrots and cartons of Camels, so that the air wafting from the opened Frigidaire carried the mixed incense of sweet earth and tobacco.

My father and uncles filled their deer and elk tags, and then those bought in their wives' names. Night after night they came through the door, a haunch or back strap thrown over their shoulders, or the full body of a yearling, lean and tender. The women worked at the counter and table spread with butcher paper, trimming and boning. Whatever meat was left after the steaks and roasts were cut was fed into the hand-cranked grinder and mixed with pepper and sage for sausage.

Snow drifted against the windows, filtering the winter light to charcoal. The circle became a wheel with shoveled spokes leading from its center to each trailer door. As the days grew shorter the snow deepened until the pathways became corridors rising several feet above our heads.

My mother rose early enough to pack my lunch and send me off to catch the bus, but my father often slept past noon. On weekends, I watched them linger over their coffee before beginning their daily chores. While my father split and stacked another day's firewood, my mother prepared her share of the communal meal—mixing flour and shortening into pie dough, filling the shells with syrupy fruit, or sorting the beans as bacon browned in the bottom of the soup pot.

Those winter afternoons, the aunts and cousins arrived first, bringing with them the smells of woodsmoke and freshly baked bread. By the time the men had gathered in, slapping their hats against their knees, the snow on their backs already melting, the plates were laid out and the bread cut. The other children and I ate where we wanted—on the couch or cross-legged on the floor—and no one cared that we coaxed out thick wedges of pie with our fingers. Miraculously set free of baths and bedtime, we whispered secrets, shielded from our parents' view by a makeshift teepee of wool blankets. As long as we kept our quarrels to ourselves and minded the general rules of the household, we were blissfully ignored.

While the women cleared and washed the dishes, the men leaned back in their chairs, sucking on toothpicks. After the dishes were done and another pot of coffee put on to perk, the adults scooted their chairs closer around the table and began their game of poker or pinochle that would last long into the night. The snow and below-zero temperatures meant little more to them than inches and degrees: no matter how bad the blizzard, no matter how low the thermometer dropped, we were safe in the circle, with enough food and fuel to keep us for weeks, the gift of land to sustain us—wood to burn, package after package of frozen venison, spring water cold and plentiful running pure beneath a crystalline crust of ice.

Uncle Clyde had known what Idaho offered to people made poor by Oklahoma dust, and we were blessed to be there. What went on in the rest of the world—whatever wars raged in the jungles of foreign countries, whatever prices rose and fell—could not affect us. Our days were made of ourselves. There was little to pull us outside that circle.

I REALIZE NOW THAT MY MOTHER and aunts were some of the first women to reside in the camps. Before, without the machinery needed to punch through roads, the men left their families at home. Only men manned the cookstoves and loaders, made the coffee and skidded the poles. The closest women were town whores, who hung from upstairs windows and called sweet things to the loggers in their cleated boots, wages heavy in their pockets.

During the mid-fifties and early sixties, logging equipment became more advanced and efficient, capable of reaching into the deepest pockets of virgin timber. New roads crosshatched the mountainsides, and existing roads were improved to allow easier passage of the machinery. With the improvement in access, most of the camps were abandoned altogether, and those that remained served only as temporary shelter for the loggers, who arrived in town late Friday evening, spent weekends with family, and left hours before dawn Monday morning to begin the week's work. Pole Camp was a compromise, close enough for the men to make their daily commutes, but isolated enough to make us believe the wilderness still touched us.

Like my mother, my aunts were beautiful women. Dorothy, Ronnie's wife, had deep auburn hair, which she combed into an elegant chignon before breakfast. She was from Tennessee, and she carried herself with all the elegance of a horsewoman born to Southern aristocracy. I shivered at the pure beauty of her town clothes—matching high heels and purses, emerald greens, black patent leathers—and the way words dripped off her tongue, slow as winter syrup.

Aunt Bev was only slightly less displaced in the winter snow and spring mud than Aunt Dorothy. Born in Texas, she mixed her own Southern drawl with that of her new Oklahoma relatives, who teased her, as border-sharers often do, about her home state allegiances. She was barely five feet tall and even when pregnant never moved the scale above a hundred pounds. (Her husband, Roland, stood over six feet, as do all the Barnes brothers.) She reminded me of my Barbie dolls—a tiny waist and blond hair looped and pinned in a fashionable twist. She was the only woman I knew who wore false eyelashes, and she taught her sisters-in-law how to mend a torn nail with cigarette papers and clear polish. My strongest memory of her is shooing me and my cousins out the door and locking it behind us, ensuring that her newly mopped floors would remain spotless until her husband got home. I see her standing on the threshold in a summer top and tight knit pants, broom clutched in one hand, the other hand cocked on her hip, enchanting in her blue eyeshadow and pink lipstick.

Other than my father, Uncle Barry, the youngest brother, remained the longest. He brought to the woods a woman from Colorado named Mary, and with her came Lezlie, a little girl with startling white hair and green eyes. I was a year older than she was, and the relationship we established in our shared yard became less that of cousins than sisters, with all its inherent jealous rages and intimacies.

Mary had the high cheekbones of her Indian mother. She came without pretense, equally at home in the trees as on the sage and cinnamon plains of Colorado. Her beauty was enhanced only a little by makeup and polish: large brown eyes and dark lashes gave her an exotic appearance even when she fluttered at the door in her soot-streaked bathrobe, and no matter how long the winter, her face and arms seemed bronzed.

She, too, left a life less than fortunate. The women in her family had run their men off, sometimes with the help of a gun, and her first marriage had lasted less than a year. She entered into our family with the bravado of a woman used to making her own way, and her spontaneity and the childlike pleasure she took in games and holidays often lent a carnival-like atmosphere to our get-togethers.

Each morning, the wives rose first to make their husbands' breakfast, then stood at the door to see the men drive off into the pre-dawn light. They waved, hollering their day's plans to each other across the yard before turning back to wake the older children for school. After the dishes had been done, the laundry hung to dry or sprinkled and rolled to be ironed later, my mother would take the cap off the tea kettle and whistle from the door, then wait for the long, high-pitched reply to echo across the meadow.

What time they did not spend baking or sewing they filled with wishing: mail-order catalogs cluttered the table. I often came home from school to find one of the women perched primly in a child's high chair while another cut her hair, Sears models for inspiration, or one of the aunts straight-backed as a Buddha, clothespins numbing her earlobes, waiting for another to sterilize the darning needle over a kitchen match. I couldn't bear to watch the needle punched through to its backing of raw potato or cork, and hid in my room, covering my head with a blanket.

During the high-altitude heat of summer, we loaded the car with iced tea and root beer, sandwiches and fried pies, and drove to the creek. While my cousins and I waded the shallow current, hunting periwinkles and crawdads, our mothers lounged on old sheets, their bathing suit straps undone, draping their shoulders.

They seemed glamorous and distant then, leaned back on their elbows, one knee slightly raised, not at all like the same women we saw scooping up their husbands' piled work clothes, mixing batter for breakfast, still wearing long johns and flannel to fend off the night's lingering chill. On the banks and small pebbled beaches of the Musselshell they smoked and talked quietly, calling us in when we ventured too far, threatening early naps and spankings when we quarreled. I would look up from my pool of tadpoles and see them perfectly composed against the sheets' white backdrop, smooth legs positioned to flatter, as though the world might be watching, judging their flat stomachs and ruby nails.

Often I forget how young my mother and aunts were, barely into their twenties. Their men coming home must have meant everything, and to welcome them with golden shoulders and sun-tinted hair was an offering: *Even here, in the deep forests of Idaho, in the wilderness, I can give you what you desire, what you love the most.*

The men returned each evening to find them tanned, glowing, arranging children and pork chops with equal ease. They must have wondered what kept them there—women any man might long for. Certainly, my father and uncles were jealous of their wives' attention. I imagine that when the itinerant buckers and sawyers visited our camp, the women kept busy in the kitchen. All knew the few things that could fill a man's gut when the isolation and deep-woods silence set his teeth to chattering for something he could almost taste, like the sweet whisper of last night's whiskey: more whiskey came easy from the town taverns, but not the shoulder of a woman, bared for his mouth and no other.

EVENTUALLY, THE ISOLATION AND LACK of even minimal luxuries such as indoor toilets and hot running water took their toll. By 1966 my aunts and cousins were gone, settled into city homes with yards and draped windows. My father must have felt the circle tighten, at its center my mother—the one who stayed, who never asked for more, who had been raised to believe each kindness shown her a gift, every grace mercurial as moonlight.

2

The Industrial Frontier

Charles Oluf Olsen
(1872-1959)

Born in Lyngby, Denmark, Charles Oluf Olsen came to America at the age of sixteen and settled in Oregon in 1899. He worked as an ironworks laborer, cook, salesman, lumberjack, and blacksmith. Despite his ten years of blacksmithing experience, Olsen was unable to secure a blacksmith job in Portland, so he turned to writing instead. He published feature articles for the *Morning Oregonian,* technical articles for lumber journals, fiction, and poetry. His background as a laborer and his literary talent combined to give a voice of expression to the working classes of Oregon.

Zero Hour in the Factory

There's hissing and panting of steam
And a throbbing everywhere,
As I hang for a breath of air
Over a dusty window-sill
Out of a room that is never still
From whir of wheel and thump of press.

The whole thing seems so meaningless.
Below me on the railroad track
An engine tries to move a train,
But groans and coughs and pulls in vain,
The hot smoke spouting from its stack.

There seems no sense to life at all
Work and heat and smoke and sound.

I am one of the sparks that pour
From a belching stack, to glow and soar
For a moment, only to die and fall,
A cinder-speck on the sooty ground.

Hazel Hall
(1886-1924)

Portland poet Hazel Hall based her writing on her work as a seamstress. An invalid from the age of twelve, she stayed in her house and took in sewing jobs for area residents. Her poetry appeared in diverse publications including *The Nation*, *Dial*, *Harper's*, and *Yale Review.*

INSTRUCTION

My hands that guide a needle
In their turn are led
Relentless and deftly
As a needle leads a thread.

Other hands are teaching
My needle; when I sew
I feel the cool, thin fingers
Of hands I do not know.

They urge my needle onward,
They smooth my seams, until
The worry of my stitches
Smothers in their skill.

All the tired women,
Who sewed their lives away,
Speak in my deft fingers
As I sew to-day.

Francis Seufert
(1913-1974)

Francis Seufert was a principal in a family-owned cannery. His recollections of the Northwest canning industry, and of the Chinese emigrants who were the backbone of its labor force and made it thrive in the early years of this century, provide an intriguing glimpse into the work lives of members of an interesting and important regional subculture. The following excerpt from *Wheels of Fortune* (1980) is from a record told to Tom Vaughn, director of the Oregon Historical Society.

Chinese

The decision to use Chinese workers in the cannery was made in 1896. Seufert's built and operated their first salmon cannery up at The Dalles fishery. At the same time, in 1896, they took over the cannery which they had always operated down at Seuferts, Oregon. The two were about a mile apart. I believe that the cannery Seufert's built at the fishery was never used, but that the cannery at Seuferts was operated by the family from 1896 on. When they first started to operate this cannery in 1896 they used Chinese labor exclusively. The Chinese did all the butchering of salmon, the sliming, filling of cans, sealing of cans; they put them in the retorts and took them out, stacked them in the warehouse, put on the labels, put them in boxes, and loaded the boxes on freight cars. All the manual labor was done by the Chinese; the only exceptions were a white man who worked as steam engineer, a white foreman, white machinist and white bookkeeper.

All the Chinese came from Portland. They were brought out on passenger trains. In those days you went to Portland and bought tickets for the entire crew of about 50 men, notified the railroad what day they were to leave Portland. The railroad would put a passenger car on especially for the Chinese crew, and bring them up to The Dalles. The train would generally arrive in The Dalles about noon. The train then carried the car out to Seufert's where all the Chinese were then unloaded from the passenger car. The Chinamen brought all their own luggage, which was in the baggage car, and it was unloaded at the cannery when the Chinese got off. The luggage generally consisted of a three-gallon bucket for each man. In these buckets the China-men carried all of their clothes and personal belongings. The buckets were very important because when they reached the China house they were used as suitcases, then later as bathtubs, because a man could take a sponge bath from his bucket.

In those days you hired the Chinamen just like you hired the crew of a ship. They were hired to go to work in April, generally about the 25th, and then they were to work until the 15th of October. They were not paid at all during that time; on the last day they got their entire six months' pay in one lump sum, always in cash. As a rule they wanted 500 or 1000 dollar bills. As far as the pay of each individual was concerned, the Chinese boss and bookkeeper had all of the accounts, and if anyone deserved more pay because of particular extra work, the account was turned in and you paid it. When the crew was paid off, you went down to The Dalles, bought the tickets for the entire crew, notified the railroad and the passenger train was flagged at the cannery on whatever day you sent the crew back to Portland.

In the early days, up until World War I, the hours were from six in the morning until six at night. The men went to work at six, worked until noon, had an hour off, went back to work at one, and worked until six. That was an eleven-hour day. By the 1920s and on into the 1930s this dropped to ten hours, and then later to eight. They worked six days a week. It was up to you to keep them busy, since they got full pay whether or not they worked; if they worked overtime, they were paid for it.

Chinese cannery labor was not cheap labor. The Chinamen working in a salmon cannery received the same wages as men working outside the cannery—the fishwheel workers and the fish house workers. The Chinamen were used in a salmon cannery because a Chinaman has hands as nimble as a woman's, and he also had the power in his fingers and wrists of a man. Packing salmon all day into a tin can was hard work and needed nimble fingers and strong wrists.

Quite a few Chinese cannery workers would return and work for Seufert's year after year. It was always quite a thing for us at the cannery to wait out in front of the office for the train to arrive from Portland with the new China crew to see which Chinamen were returning to the cannery for another salmon canning season, and to see the new men arrive too. Of course these Chinamen worked for all the companies canning salmon on the Columbia River, one year for Seufert's, the next for Barbie, then the next year for CRPA. Then they would probably come back and work another year for Seufert's. Only the China bosses came back to the same company year after year. When you had a good China boss you kept him. Seufert's never thought of getting a new China boss as long as the regular China boss was ready and willing to come back.

In the late winter when you were thinking about opening the cannery for the coming season and you needed a China crew you just wrote your China boss a letter and told him to get you a China crew for the coming season. He would generally come up to The Dalles from Portland on the local passenger train and in the Company office he would tell you what the going wages were to be for the new season. You could argue about the crew's wages but whatever the China boss said he would have to pay the China crew was about what you were going to have to pay to get your crew. Then you decided how many men you needed, and what jobs were to be filled. After you and the China boss had decided on that, the China boss then returned to Portland on the train and down in Portland signed up the crew for you. When you were ready to open the cannery and start your canning operation, the China boss would bring the crew up for the new season.

I want to talk now just a little about the Chinese salmon butchers. A Chinese butcher could butcher a 30-pound Chinook salmon in 45 seconds, and the Company expected each man to butcher at least ten tons of salmon in a ten-hour day, or roughly one ton per hour. Three Chinese butchers could handle 30 tons of Columbia River salmon per day, which would produce at least 900 cases of 48 one-pound cans per day. On such a day the Company always had at least two men, usually white, who did nothing but pick up salmon from the fish room floor and put the fish on the butchering tables, always with the heads facing the Chinese butcher. The Chinese were hired to butcher, and they were too busy to stop and pick uncut salmon off the floor and heave them up on the tables. The Chinese butchers were the elite of the Chinese cannery crew.

The Chinese butchers always used a heavy knife of imported Sheffield steel. These were the finest butcher knives available. They had long heavy blades, curved at the end. They held a fine sharp edge, and the heavy blade would not nick when the butchers cut into the heavy backbone of a big Columbia River Chinook salmon. While the Chinese butcher was working he would sharpen his knife on a steel from time to time. Also these Chinese never washed the butcher knives in hot water. The knives were first wiped off on a wet burlap sack, then thoroughly washed in cold water, and then the knife was honed on an oil stone. Then the knife was put away by the Chinese butcher until the next day's work began.

These fine knives were hard to get after World War I, and by the 1930s it was nearly impossible to buy one. Price was no consideration as far as the Company was concerned; but the knives were just not available. The Company always bought the knives, but once the Chinese butcher was given his knife it became his personal property. He kept it in order, and when he left in the fall of the year and went back to Portland he took the knife with him.

There was always a grindstone down by the closing machines in the cannery. It sat on a wooden frame, and was pumped by one's feet while sitting on a little bicycle seat. There was a little tin can on the frame so you could put water on the stone while you were sharpening a knife. These stones were used for the big heavy butcher knives the Chinese used; they would take nicks out of the blades. They could also be used to sharpen a pike pole, but usually it was easier to sharpen those on an emery wheel.

We also butchered salmon in the cannery with a machine called an "Iron Chink." The machine got its name because it replaced Chinese butchers. The Iron Chink Seufert's used was purchased in 1918 and was still in use until the salmon cannery stopped operating. An Iron Chink would butcher about 15 salmon per minute, but it could only handle small salmon, so it was only used in the fall. Even then it was only used when the cannery was so busy you had all the salmon you could possibly handle in a day. It was used to butcher such small fish as jack salmon, small Chinooks and steel head. The Iron Chink stood about seven feet high. It only took two Chinamen to operate it; one white man would feed salmon to the Chinamen who operated the Iron Chink. These two Chinamen were always butchers. The first fed the salmon onto a butchering table where a knife on the side of the Iron Chink cut off the head. The first Chinaman passed the salmon on to the second, who fed the salmon into the Iron Chink tail first, belly up. The Iron Chink was basically just a large revolving wheel some six feet in diameter. The wheel seized the salmon and while the big wheel revolved slowly making one complete turn, the Iron Chink cut off the fins and tail, slit the belly open and removed the entrails. When the big wheel completed its revolution the salmon came out completely cleaned and butchered.

The Iron Chink, using two Chinamen to feed it and one white man to pike salmon to the Chinamen, would butcher as many salmon in a day as ten Chinese could butcher by hand. The Iron Chink was noisy, and it threw salmon guts all over the place. Sheets of tin covered the Iron Chink to keep the salmon guts around the machine. The shortcoming of the machine was that it tended to tear the salmon meat, and also that it was limited as to the size of fish it could handle. It was never used to butcher a fancy Columbia River Chinook salmon; these were always

Salmon canning, Astoria. Negative number OrHi 28194. Courtesy Oregon Historical Society.

butchered by hand so you were always sure of getting a nice fancy pack. Also, the Iron Chink was wasteful. When you butchered by hand you could save more of the salmon weight, so as long as the three Chinese butchers could butcher by hand all the salmon the can fillers needed, the Iron Chink wasn't used; but in the fall when you were running fall Chinooks and packing by automatic filling machines, then sometimes you had to use the Iron Chink to keep enough butchered salmon on hand for the automatic filling machines to stay busy.

There was never any goldbricking among the China crews who labeled cans and loaded cars. They all worked and each did his own share of the work. These Chinamen would just naturally go to work as a group on a job, with each man taking the job he was physically capable of doing. The old men all labeled cans and the middle-aged men stacked the salmon cases after the Chinese laborers had filled them with labeled cans. These middle-aged men also saw to it that each laborer had a full case of unlabeled salmon cans at his side, and took away the cases of labeled cans. They also manned the hand trucks and trucked the salmon cases ready for shipment in the freight cars. The young Chinamen and the husky ones did all the piling and stacking of the canned salmon cases into the freight cars. If there was a pile of canned salmon in the warehouse to be taken down onto the warehouse floor for labeling, it was the young men who lifted the cases down. Once in a while when you had to move some cases in the warehouse, but the distance was not far, instead of using a hand truck a number of young Chinamen would line up in single file and pass the cases down the line, one case at a time. It was surprising how many cases of canned goods a China crew could move this way.

In the 1920s when everything was still shipped in wooden boxes, the China crew made all the wooden salmon cannery cases. Also in those days all labeling was still done by hand, and the China crew did this. Of course hand labeling was slow and took a large number of men to label a car of salmon by hand, but then you had to pay the crew whether or not they worked, so they might just as well be in the cannery warehouse labeling cans than being down at the China house doing nothing. The China boss picked the crew; you had nothing to do with it. The men the China boss brought up from Portland were the ones you took, and no ifs about it. Before the days of our present social laws, the China crew always had a couple of old men, possibly as much as 80 years old, but the Chinamen's attitude was that a man should work, although he was not expected to do more than would be reasonable for his age. These old men got full regular wages and were hired as salmon fillers; but about all they could do was to sweep the floor. There were always one or two real old men. They kept the cannery floor clean and I must add that they might have been old and slow, but never could you find fault with the job they did.

These China crews were dependable, and hard workers, and once you signed a labor contract for your China crew, that worry was over for the season. The China boss always came with his crew the day you wanted them to arrive. He had all the men specified in the labor contract, and the men could and did do their jobs well, and the labor boss followed the contract to the letter. There was never any question of the honesty of the boss, or of the willingness of the crew to carry out all the provisions of the contract. And of course we also followed the labor contract right down the line. If there was ever a question about anything, you and the China boss discussed it, and when the China boss left he was satisfied. And I must emphasize that never under any conditions would the Company ever do anything they hadn't agreed to do in these Chinese labor contracts. In 58 years of salmon canning operations, Seufert's had only six China bosses. Five came from the same family, and during all those years I never heard of a disagreement between the China boss and the Company over a contract once it had been signed.

For some reason Chinese labor was always referred to as contract labor, with the hint that there was something bad about this. I never could understand why this was, at least in this day and age with labor contracts playing such an important part in our industrial labor relations. The China boss would meet in the Company office early in the spring and tell the Company what the China labor would cost for that coming season. You might argue about various Chinese labor costs, but when it was all over the China boss's ideas would prevail. These labor discussions were always friendly, although there could be arguing and some shouting. But the whole discussion never lasted more than an hour. By then you knew what the China crew would cost for the year and that was that.

Next the labor contract was drawn up, which was just a copy of the one used the previous year. You decided how many men you wanted on each job and marked it in the contract. You always needed three salmon butchers, and then you had to decide on the number of slimers you would need to handle the butchered salmon. Then there were the fillers who packed the salmon into the cans, the patch fish men, the cooler men, the test tub men and the retort men. The China boss also had to have a Chinese cook and a Chinese bookkeeper. (You always agreed to furnish all the wood needed in the China mess house.) This made up your crew for the coming year. Chinese labor of course included board and room. You had to purchase so many sacks of rice from the Chinese grocer in Portland, and then you bought some pigs from the local white farmers up the creek. There was also a bonus provision in the contract. Any Chinaman filling more than 3,000 cans of salmon in a standard working day got a bonus. The China boss kept these records, and you paid a bonus to whomever he said. You also agreed to purchase railroad tickets from Portland to Seufert's for each man. In the fall when you closed the cannery you agreed to purchase tickets for each man from Seufert's back to Portland.

By the end of World War II the old experienced Chinese cannery crews began to disappear. After World War II the young Chinamen had been Americanized. They didn't want to work in a salmon cannery out in some isolated spot for six months, with little or no chance to get into town to spend their money or to have a good time. By then jobs were plentiful in Portland, so they would just not leave the city to work in a cannery. By the late 1940s it was becoming harder and harder to get any China crews at all.

One time the salmon cannery was working nights. We had a Chinaman up in years taking salmon cans from the closing machines and racking the cans up in coolers. This Chinaman must have been nearly blind. His glasses had lenses so thick that when you looked at him his eyes were magnified. Once in a while when we were working at night the cannery machinery would stop. Then this old Chinaman would begin to do a Balinese dance, first one leg and then the other, with all the necessary postures required of a Balinese dancer. The other Chinamen would pay attention to him, but because the whole thing was happening in the dim light, and the dancer was not concerned with anyone about him, it made the hair on the back of your neck stand on end. Then the cannery machinery would start to operate again, and everyone would go back to work, including the dancer, just as if nothing out of the ordinary had happened. This Chinaman would put on his dance several times during the evening, but never during the day. I was fascinated by it. I could not help wondering if as a young man he had been trained as a dancer somewhere in the Far East, and then I would wonder how under the sun he had ended up as an old man working in a salmon cannery on the Columbia River.

H. L. Davis
(1894-1960)

H. L. (Harold Lenoir) Davis was born in Douglas County, Oregon, and grew up along the Umpqua River. His family later moved to Antelope and The Dalles, where he graduated high school in 1912. He later moved to Washington but continued writing about his native state. In 1919, he won the Levinson Prize for poetry, and his first novel, *Honey in the Horn* (1935), won the Pulitzer Prize. Davis is the only Oregonian ever to have received this award. Critic H. L. Mencken further distinguished this prize-winning debut as the best first novel ever published in America. Davis' work looked closely at the daily lives of common people. Davis' treatment of racism and work is set here in the context of railroad laborers. The poem appeared in *Proud Riders* (1919).

Steel Gang

The boss came over and called us out a little bit after dark.
He said, "I don't want you boys to think your work ain't up to the mark,
But Paddy Duffy goes bragging around, the steel his Mex can lay—
All how that spiggoty gang spikes down two miles and a half a day,
And how two miles and a half is more than any man's gang can tap.
So I want you men to help me out to make him shut his yap.
No matter what record a Mex gang makes, I claim white men can trim it.
What I want you to do is, prove I'm right—for one day, go your limit.
I want you men to go tomorrow and make that record climb.
You put it where these damn spigs can't reach, I'll pay you triple time."

We counseled it over and said we would. We hit the deck at three,
And the engineer whistled, "Let's go!" before it was light enough to see.

The tram rolled up to the head of steel. The ties came sliding off
And we had 'em laid and the steel half spiked before a man could cough.
The tram rolled over the spikers' work, and they never missed a lick.
Right under the wheels, they spiked right on, and drove 'em tight and quick.
When the surfacing-crew came up at a run, to raise and level track,
The tram was a dozen rails ahead, and never a man looked back.
We swung those hundred-and-ten pound rails like a grocery-clerk flips matches.
We grabbed those damned ties four at a time, and dealt them out in batches.

At half-past eight o'clock that night, the boss said, "Pull the cord!"
Said, "Call 'em off! Christ, four miles and a half! There's a record, by the Lord!
Call in the men and let's go in—they've earned a feed tonight.
You can boost for your goddam greasers, but I'll string with a gang that's white!"
The snipes let go their tools in the dirt, the hogs climbed down from the tram,
And they flopped in a heap in the outfit-train, too tired to give a damn.
Too tired to talk, too tired to wash, too tired to even eat.
The cooks had a feed shook up, supposed to be a special treat;
But victuals didn't have any taste. The men dragged off to bed.
Some had too much of an edge to sleep, and lay and gaped in stead,
Their eyes half-shut and their mouths ajar, too dead to fight the flies
That stuck and bored in the sweaty places, and crawled around their eyes.

For that day's work they paid three days; and then, they paid
full pay
For the following day, when none of the men would budge
out of the hay.
Then, for the day that followed that, they offered us double
jack
Because we had all lost heart in the work, and they wanted to
bring us back.
So we worked that day for their double time, and then pulled
up and quit.

The spig gang stayed and finished the job after us white men
lit.

Joseph B. Halm

Joe Halm, forest ranger in the Coeur d'Alene National Forest, published the following story of the fires of 1910, two decades after living the experience. This record provides a unique perspective on the dangers faced occasionally by members of the logging industry, and often by career foresters.

RECOLLECTION OF THE FIRES OF 1910

OUT OF THE UNDERBRUSH dashed a man—grimy, breathless, hat in hand. At his heels came another. Then a whole crew; all casting fearful glances behind them.

"She's coming! The whole country's afire! Grab your stuff, ranger, and let's get outa here!" gasped the leader.

This scene, on the afternoon of August 20,1910, Stands out vividly in my memory The place was a tiny, timbered flat along a small creek in the headwaters of the St. Joe River; in Idaho. The little flat, cleared of undergrowth to accommodate our small camp, seemed dwarfed beneath the great pines and spruce. The little stream swirled and gurgled beneath the dense growth and windfall, and feebly lent moisture to the thirsting trees along its banks.

For weeks forest rangers with crews of men had been fighting in a vain endeavor to hold in check the numerous fires which threatened the very heart of the great white-pine belt in the forests of Idaho and Montana. For days an ominous, stifling pall of smoke had hung over the valleys and mountains. Crews of men, silent and grim, worked along the encircling fire trenches. Bear, deer, elk and mountain lions stalked starry-eyed, glazed-eyed and restless through the camps, their fear of man overcome by a greater terror. Birds, bewildered, hopped about in the thickets, their song subdued, choked by the stifling smoke and oppressive heat. No rain had fallen since May. All vegetation stood crisp and brown, seared and withered by the long drought, as if by blight. The fragrance of summer flowers had given way to the tang of dead smoke. The withered ferns and grasses were covered by a hoar-frost of gray ashes. Men, red-eyed and sore of lung, panted for a breath of untainted air. The sun rose and set beyond the pall of smoke. All nature seemed tense, unnatural and ominous.

It had taken days to slash a way through the miles of tangled wilderness to our fire, sixty-five miles from a railroad. On August 18, this fire was confined within trenches; all seemed well; a day or two more and all would have been considered safe. Difficulties in transportation developed which necessitated reducing our crew from eighty-five to eighteen men.

I had just returned after guiding our remaining packers with their stock to one of our supply camps, when our demoralized crew dashed in. Incoherently, the men told how the fire had sprung up everywhere about them as they worked. The resinous smoke had become darker; the air even more oppressive and quiet. As if by magic, sparks were fanned to flames which licked the trees into one great conflagration. They had dropped their tools and fled for their lives. A great wall of fire was coming out of the northwest. Even at that moment small, charred twigs came sifting out of the ever-darkening sky The foreman, still carrying his ax, was the last to arrive. "Looks bad," he said. Together we tried to calm the men. The cook hurried the preparation of an early supper. A slight wind now stirred the treetops overhead; a faint, distant roar was wafted to my ears. The men heard it; a sound as of heavy wind, or a distant waterfall. Three men, believing safety lay in flight, refused to stay "We're not going to stay here and be roasted alive. We're going."

Things looked bad. Drastic steps were necessary. Supper was forgotten. I slipped into my tent and strapped on my gun. As I stepped out a red glow was already lighting the sky The men were pointing excitedly to the north.

"She's jumped a mile across the canyon," said the foreman, who had been talking quietly to the men. Stepping before them, I carelessly touched the holster of the gun and delivered an ultimatum with outward confidence, which I by no means felt.

"Not a man leaves this camp. We'll stay by this creek and live to tell about it. I'll see you through. Every man hold out some grub, a blanket, and a tool. Chuck the rest into that tent, drop the poles and bury it."

The men did not hesitate. The supplies, bedding, and equipment were dumped into the tent, the poles jerked out, and sand shoveled over it. Some ran with armloads of canned goods to the small bar in the creek, an open space scarcely thirty feet across. Frying pans, pails, and one blanket for each man were moved there. Meanwhile the wind had risen to hurricane velocity Fire was now all around us, banners of incandescent flames licked the sky Showers of large, flaming brands were falling everywhere. The quiet of a few minutes before had become a horrible din. The hissing, roaring flames, the terrific crashing and rending of falling timber was deafening, terrifying. Men rushed back and forth trying to help. One young giant, crazed with fear, broke and ran. I dashed after him. He came back, wild-eyed, crying, hysterical. The fire had closed in; the heat became intolerable.

All our trust and hope was in the little stream and the friendly gravel bar. Some crept beneath wet blankets, but falling snags drove them out. There was yet air over the water. Armed with buckets, we splashed back and forth in the shallow stream throwing water as high as our strength would permit, drenching the burning trees. A great tree crashed across our bar; one man went down, but came up unhurt. A few yards below a great log jam, an acre or more in extent, the deposit of a cloudburst in years gone by, became a roaring furnace, a threatening hell. If the wind changed, a single blast from this inferno would wipe us out. Our drenched clothing steamed and smoked; still the men fought. Another giant tree crashed, cutting deep into the little bar, blinding and showering us with sparks and spray But again the men nimbly side-stepped the hideous meteoric monster.

After what seemed hours, the screaming, hissing, and snapping of millions of doomed trees, and the shower of sparks and burning brands grew less. The fire gradually subsided. Words were spoken. The drenched, begrimed men became more hopeful. Some even sought tobacco in their water-soaked clothing. Another hour and we began to feel the chill of the night. The hideous, red glare of the inferno still lighted everything; trees still fell by the thousands. Wearily, the men began to drag the water-soaked blankets from the creek and dry them; some scraped places beneath the fallen trees where they might crawl with their weary, tortured bodies out of reach of the falling snags. The wind subsided. Through that long night beside a man-made fire, guards sat, a wet blanket around their chilled bodies.

Dawn broke almost clear of smoke, the first in weeks. Men began to crawl stiffly out from their burrows and look about. Such a scene! The green, standing forest of yesterday was gone; in its place a charred and smoking mass of melancholy wreckage. The virgin trees, as far as the eye could see, were broken or down, devoid of a single sprig of green. Miles of trees—sturdy, forest giants—were laid prone. Only the smaller trees stood, stripped and broken. The great log jam still burned. Save for the minor burns and injuries, all were safe. Inwardly, I gave thanks for being alive. A big fellow, a Swede, the one who had refused to stay, slapped me on the back and handed me my gun. I had not missed it.

"You lost her in the creek last night. You save me my life," he said, simply. His lip trembled as he walked away

The cook had already salvaged a breakfast from the trampled cache in the creek. Frying ham and steaming coffee drove away the last trace of discomfort.

"What are your plans?" asked the foreman, after several cups of coffee.

"First we'll dig out our tent, salvage the grub, and then look the fire over. We'll order more men and equipment and hit the fire again."

Little did I know as I spoke that our fire that morning was but a dot on the blackened map of Idaho and Montana. After breakfast we picked Our way through the fire to our camp of yesterday All was safe. We moved the remaining equipment to the little bar. Our first thought was for the safety of our two packers and the pack stock at our supply camp. The foreman and I set out through the fire over the route of the old trail, now so changed and unnatural. With ever-increasing apprehension we reached the first supply camp where I had left the packers. Only a charred, smoking mass of cans and equipment marked the spot.

What had become of the men? Not a sign of life could we find. They must have gone to the next supply camp. We hurried on, unmindful of the choking smoke and our burned shoes. We came upon our last supply camp; this, too, was a charred, smoldering mass. Still no signs of the men. A half mile beyond we suddenly came upon the remains of a pack saddle; then, another; the girths had been cut. Soon we found the blackened remains of a horse. Feverishly we searched farther. Next we found

High school boys heading out to plant trees on the Tillamook Burn, March 5, 1945. Negative number OrHi 63466. Courtesy Oregon Historical Society

a riding saddle. With sinking heart we hastened on. More horses and more saddles. The fire was growing hotter. We halted, unable to go farther. We must go back for help and return when the heat had subsided.

Smoke darkened the sky; the wind had again risen to a gale; trees were once more falling all about us. We took shelter in a small cave in a rock ledge where the fire had burned itself out. Here we sat, parched, almost blind with smoke and ashes. Once the foreman voiced my thoughts: "The wind will die down toward night, then we can go back to camp." This fury of the wind, however; increased steadily Fires roared again, and across the canyon trees fell by the hundreds.

After what seemed like hours, we crept out of our cramped quarters and retraced our steps. The storm had subsided slightly. If the remains of the trail had been littered that morning, it was completely filled now. We came to a bend in the creek where the trail passed over a sharp hogback. As we neared the top, we again came into the full fury of the wind. Unable to stand, pelted by gravel and brands and blinded by ashes, we crawled across the exposed rocky ledges. I had never before, nor have I since, faced such a gale. On the ridges and slopes every tree was now uprooted and down. We passed the grim remains of the horses and supply camps. In the darkness we worked our way back over and under the blackened, fallen trees. Fanned by the wind, the fire still burned fiercely in places. Torn and bleeding, we hurried on, hatless in the darkness, lighted only by the myriads of fires—me picking the way, the foreman watching for falling trees. While passing along a ledge a great tree tottered above us and rent its way to earth, rolling crazily down the slope. We ran for our lives, but the whirling trunk broke and lodged a few feet above. So absorbed were we with our plight that we nearly passed our camp on the little sand bar in the creek bottom.

By firelight we ate and related our fears as to the fate of the packers. As we talked, one of the men, pointing to the eastern sky, cried, "Look, she's coming again!" The sky in the east had taken on a hideous, reddish glow which became lighter and lighter. To the nerve-racked men it looked like another great fire bearing down upon us. Silently the men watched the phenomenon which lasted perhaps ten minutes. Then the realization came that the sky was clearing of smoke. In another brief space of time the sun shone. Not until then did I know that it was only 4 o'clock. A change in wind had shifted the smoke toward the northwest. We later found that the burn extended but a mile or two to the south of us.

Daylight next morning found us chopping and sawing a route back through the now cooled burn toward civilization, searching for our packers. That day I visited a prospector's cabin on a small side creek, a mile from the trail, to learn the fate of the man, a cripple. His earth-covered dugout by some miracle had withstood the fire. There were no signs of life about. Whether the man had gone out earlier in the week, or had suffered the same fate as our packers, I did not then know. Evening found our little party many miles from camp. We saw the remains of an elk and several deer; also, a grouse, hopping about with feet and feathers burned off—a pitiful sight. Men who quenched their thirst from small streams immediately became deathly sick. The cleat; pure water running through miles of ashes had become a strong, alkaline solution, polluted by dead fish, killed by the lye. Thereafter we drank only spring water.

Late that night, weary and silent, the men returned to camp and crept into their blankets. Daylight again found us on the trail equipped with packs and food and blankets. About noon we came upon an old white horse, one of our pack string, badly singed, but very much alive, foraging in the creek.

Late one day, the sixth since the great fire, a messenger; be-smudged and exhausted, reached us. From him we learned that Wallace and many other towns and villages had burned; that at least a hundred men had lost their lives and that scores were still missing. He had seen many of the dead brought in.

Our crew had been given up as lost. Several parties were still endeavoring to reach us from different points. Ranger Haines with his crew was then several miles back and would cut the trail to take us out. Our packers, he said, had reached safety The crippled prospector was still among the missing, and we were to search for him. For three days we combed the burned mountains and creeks for the missing man. On the third afternoon, weary and discouraged, we stumbled upon the ghastly remains, burned beyond recognition. His glasses and cane, which we found neat; told the mute story of the last, great struggle of the unfortunate man who, had he but known it, would have been safe in his little shack. In a blanket we bore the shapeless thing out to the relief crew

From Ranger Haines I heard the story of our packers. Shortly after I had left them they had become alarmed. Hastily saddling the fourteen head of horses, they had left the supply camp for Iron Mountain, sixty miles away Before a mile was covered they realized the fire was coming and that, encumbered with the slow-moving stock, escape would be impossible. They cut the girths and freed the horses, hoping they might follow. Taking a gentle little saddle mare between them, they fled for their lives, one ahead, the other holding the animal by the tail, switching her along. The fire was already roaring behind. On they ran, the panting animal pulling first one, then the other. Hundreds of spark-set fires sprang up beside the trail; these grew into crown fires, becoming the forerunner of the great conflagration. By superhuman effort they reached the summit on the Idaho-Montana state line. Here the fire in the sparse timber lost ground. On sped the men down the other side until the fire was left behind. Ten miles farther; completely exhausted, they reached a small cabin, where they unsaddled their jaded, faithful little horse, threw themselves into a bunk and fell asleep.

Two hours later the whinny of the horse awoke them. A glare lighted the cabin. They rushed out; the fire was again all around them! They rescued the little horse from the already burning barn and dashed down the gulch. It was a desperate race for life. Trees falling above shot down the steep slopes and cut off their trail. The now saddleless, frightened little beast, driven by the men, jumped over and crawled beneath these logs like a dog. Two miles of this brought them to some old placer workings and safety Exhausted, they fell. The fire swept on.

They had crossed a mountain range and covered a distance of nearly forty miles in a little over six hours, including their stay at the cabin—almost a superhuman feat.

The Seattle General Strike of 1919

The general strike of 6-11 February 1919 was one of the most spectacular events of American labor history. It arose from a demand for higher wages by shipyard workers following World War I. Their demand was backed by the government pay board, but ignored contemptuously by the employers. About sixty thousand workers walked away from their jobs under the leadership of James Duncan who, as head of the Central Labor Council, was closer philosophically to the radical IWW than the more conservative, but mainstream, American Federation of Labor, and was an admirer of the Soviet Union. Seattle was paralyzed for five calm, but for most citizens, disquieting days, owing in part to the posturing of Mayor Ole Hanson, who called the strike a bolshevist plot which he was heroically thwarting. After five days, the strike died without result as workers went back to their jobs, but they had shown resolve, discipline, and order. From the pages of the *Seattle Union Record,* the Seattle labor's official organ, comes a compelling profile of the first and only general strike in American labor history.

Seattle Union Record, 6 February 1919

Official Statement

Labor resents the suggestion that has been expressed by a number of public men to the effect that rowdyism will be the result of the cessation of work. We are confident that if the general public will keep their feet upon the ground the police division of labor will co-operate with the proper public officials in maintaining law and order.

The law and order committee that has been appointed by the executive committee of the general strike committee is now issuing a call upon all union men who have been discharged from the ranks of either the army or the navy of the United States government to place themselves at the disposal of the committee. These men will be requested to assist in preserving the peace and order for the duration of the strike.

All business agents and discharged soldiers and sailors belonging to the unions met at 7 o'clock last night to perfect their plans for the organization for policing.

Arrangements have been made for the supply of milk for babies and the sick, and also for the filling of prescriptions by drug clerks.

In conformity with the spirit of law and order committee's desire to prevent rowdyism by disinterested persons, it is the earnest desire, after conferring with the officials of the Telephone Operators' Union that they cooperate with the strikers' police division in maintaining order by placing their entire membership, not to include the telephone men, at the disposal of organized labor to postpone the entire shutdown of telephone dispatching wire, for the reason that the continuance of same is necessary for the dispatching of our committees. It must be understood that this is no exemption and the call to quit work must be effective at a moment's notice from the executive committee.

The welfare committee have charge of the health and sanitation of the city in regard to the garbage situation. The committee at this time asks the cooperation of the public to the extent of segregating the garbage; that is, do not put ashes, waste paper, or other trash in cans where you can place swill or other decaying matter, as our garbage man has instructions to collect nothing but garbage the decomposition of which tends to breed disease.

Notice is hereby given that the general strike is effective even with the property of organized labor, including the Mutual Laundry Company, Labor Temple Cigar Company, Metal Trades Hall Cigar Company, Seattle Union Record, and the janitor services applying to these establishments, also janitor service to Labor Temple.

With the early issue of Thursday of the Seattle Union Record, it will suspend publication by orders of the executive strike committee and will not be published until the general strike shall have been brought to a conclusion. This is published at this time to disabuse the minds of any who may think that labor intends to publish their own paper during the controversy.

W. F. De Laney, Chairman
W. C. Zimmer, Secretary

Seattle Union Record, 8 February 1919

TO THE MEN AND WOMEN OF LABOR!

THE HOUR HAS STRUCK!

You have ceased your daily labors as a protest against insufficient wages paid to your fellows.

You have quit your accustomed toil to lend your voice against the vicious prostitution of power on the part of the Emergency Shipping Board. Through its pernicious meddling a deadlock has resulted where an adjustment, no doubt, would have been arrived at.

YOU WANT TO WIN.

Your only chance to win is your willingness to—

OBEY ORDERS!

You have delegated to certain committees the duty of maintaining this strike.

This delegation of duties to these committees means that you have promised to OBEY ORDERS issued by those committees. Unless you do this, your fight is lost before it is begun.

The first and prime essential to the conduct of any strike is ORDERLY OBSERVANCE OF THE LAWS OF THE LAND.

If the least show of disorder is permitted to creep into the conduct of the men and women on strike, then this struggle WILL BE LOST.

The person who permits himself or herself to be pulled into any mode of conduct that will not square with what is commonly considered lawful and orderly procedure is a SCAB—of the worst possible kind.

YOU WANT TO WIN!

SHOW YOUR LOYALTY TO THE CAUSE OF LABOR BY—

STAYING AT HOME;

AVOID CONGREGATING IN CROWDS;

AVOID DISCUSSION THAT MAY LEAD TO DISORDERLY DISPUTES;

OBEY ORDERS!

REMEMBER—THAT THIS IS YOUR CITY AND THAT YOU HAVE STAKED YOUR REPUTATION AS A GOOD CITIZEN AND A GOOD UNIONIST ON THE OUTCOME OF THIS STRUGGLE.

Any show of disorder will result in chaos and will surely lead to defeat.

Thirty-eight thousand shipyard workers have been on strike for two weeks without a single case of violence being reported.

The members of the general labor movement should pattern after the shipyard workers—and they will.

Let us make this great strike an occasion for a display of discipline that finds its expression in implicit and ready obedience to orders of the committees and all lawful authority having this strike in hand.

STAY AT HOME!

BE QUIET!

OBEY ORDERS!

AND THE STRIKE IS WON!

Seattle Union Record, 11 February 1919

IN RETROSPECT

The first general strike in the history of the American labor movement has come to an end.

Perhaps it would not be amiss to stop just a moment and take a slant at what has happened—a post-mortem, as it were. It sometimes happens that much can be learned from a careful analysis of events that have transpired and, perhaps learn to avoid mistakes of both omission and commission.

Four things stand out above all others like a mountain in the center of a plain. These are:

First—The splendid solidarity evidenced by the 100 percent response to the strike call.

Second—The absolute orderliness of the workers on strike and their absolute refusal to be aggravated into any action that could in the least measure be interpreted as riotous conduct.

Third—The hysterical bombast and sometimes guttersnipe comment on events that emanated from the mayor's office down at the City-County building, and then retailed through the Seventh Avenue "friend of labor" that has at last been unmasked.

Fourth—The desperate efforts at "playing to the gallery" that was indulged in by the Star in an effort to curry favor with big business after the management had finally come to understand that its true character was known to the workers of the community.

Taking up these several points we cannot refrain from comment on them. As to the solidarity that was so much in evidence, it more than met the expectations of the of the most sanguine and exacting of the enthusiasts for the sympathetic strike. It was a magnificent and inspiring demonstration. It might, perhaps, have been even more impressive but for a slight anti-climax that arose through confusion at the last. This confusion was the inevitable result of the use of a weapon that was strange to most of those involved. In the light of the experience of the last week a like experience a like anti-climax would not be permitted to occur.

The orderliness of the men and women is just what was expected by those who really know the labor movement. Whatever of slander and wild stories of respective riot that sent broadcast throughout the land by those who hoped to temporarily disgrace the city by their occupancy of high place in the city government are in every case without foundation in fact.

The best answer to all this rot about the need of military protection and of extra police is the record of the arrests for the period that covered the general strike. The record shows that fewer men and women were arrested during the strike than had been the case for a like period in years—if ever. And not one of the arrests was traceable to the strike.

Then we come to a discussion of Mayor Ole Hanson and his idiotic, slanderous and silly mouthings. Perhaps the less said about such a noisome subject as the mayor's recent actions the better. Adequate description and analytical discussion is impossible for two very good reasons—first, the postal regulations prohibit, and second, the readers of the *Union Record* are perfectly respectable and clean-minded and clean-tongued men and women and it would ill become this publication to indulge in the language that would fittingly characterize the mayor's recent efforts to incite riots and act the ignoble part of strikebreaker. Many of the readers of the *Union Record* have insisted that steps be taken to recall the mayor. To these Earnest men and women we must say: FORGET IT! There is much constructive work that needs to be done in this city. The time and energies of the labor movement can best be used to do that work. Let Ole rattle around down at the City-County building like peas in a skillet, for if he doesn't rattle around there he will rattle around somewhere else, for rattle around he must. Besides, it is fitting that the citizens should be obliged to endure, with what patience they can command, that rattling for having indulged in the political spree that resulted in Ole's election to the office of mayor. We are firm believers in standing up to the rack and taking what is coming to us for our mistakes. Having taken our medicine, perhaps we won't eat green apples again—no matter if they do happen to bear the label "Ole." With all of the opportunity he has had for mischief he has not shown himself capable, as yet, of doing anything worse than running off at the mouth and indulge in bombast that is neither polite nor good rhetoric.

It might very well happen that a policy of "watchful waiting" will result in our doughty mayor drowning himself in his flood of words. So why worry about him? Nothing can be said or done that would so conclusively damn him in the eyes of the average fair minded man than his own ravings.

Then we come to that almost unmentionable subject—the *Seattle Star.* This rag has been attempting to preach "Americanism." As that wise old head, Sam Johnson, once said: "Patriotism is often the last refuge of the scoundrel." It would almost seem that Johnson had written this sentence for the express purpose of characterizing the sheet that has so successfully played the game of bunk on the workers of this community for so many years. At last it has been unmasked and stands forth in all its naked shame for the {harlot or varlet} it is, and always has been. Now it attempts to preach Americanism to the men and women who have built all the ships that were built in the time of the country's need; to have the men and women who went "over the top" 100 per cent strong for every Red Cross drive and war measure that was pulled off in this city. This, too, at the same time that the principal owner of the Star was using every bit of influence he had to get what his draft board would not give him. What does the *Star* mean by "Americanism?" The kind that stays at home while other young men go overseas to brave the dangers of the battlefield? Such piffle and rot as has been spewed from the Seventh avenue bunk-shop during the past week like the mayor's ravings, are best answered by a reading of the stuff. The good that comes of it all is that many of the workers who have fallen for the stuff in times past will never be caught again. Exit *Star*! As an influence in the ranks of labor it will be about as efficient as a last year's bird's nest is in moulding opinion.

Just one more thing seems to need passing comment. That is the general strike as a weapon. There has been a good deal of loose talk about the general strike in times past. There are some who have sought to bring about a general strike in any and all occasions. Many of these well-meaning but mistaken persons, now that they understand the immensity of the weapon they would use, will not lightly venture upon its promiscuous use. The immensity of the undertaking has sobered many enthusiasts. The general strike has proven to be an efficient weapon but it has also shown to many of the unionists that its useinvolves certain responsibilities that are not light and should not be assumed except under the necessity of the gravest industrial crisis. This general strike has cleared the air of much stuff that was floating about to the distraction of the movement. The trades union organizations of the city are better because of that clearing of the atmosphere and we will all be better off because of the close-up view we have had of he immensity of the weapon about which we have been talking and writing so much.

Perhaps we will get from our friends and "near friends" a lot of "advice" about how labor organizations should be conducted. This has been the case ever since Adam was a corporal, and the labor movement has, somehow or other, survived it all and is going steadily forward, growing increasingly efficient as the years go by.

Mistakes have been made. The man or woman who never makes a mistake never does anything. Earnest men and women prefer to play the role of a trout rather than that of a mud turtle. They want movement, they want to go forward. They may stumble, they may even fall, but ever will they go forward on the road that will finally lead to a world that is a better place for men and women to live and work in.

IT WAS ALL WORTH WHILE!

Charles Vindex

A native of Minnesota, Charles Vindex moved West where he held many miscellaneous jobs including teaching school. He retired to his home state and wrote his impressions of western life in a series of memoirs. The following account of rural Montana during the Great Depression recalls a bleak time when "Every man who sought a job, unless he could prove some special right to it, emerged willy-nilly as a threat to some other man's survival."

Survival on the High Plains, 1929-1934

At the end of October 1929 a plains blizzard drove southwest from Hudson Bay. To my family and me, then residents of northeastern Montana, it was far more swift in terms of disaster than the financial storm already sweeping America. I had just brought my wife and our week-old daughter home from the hospital in Plentywood when the warm blue afternoon haze dissolved into gentle rain—the first rain since early July. We welcomed its beginning as only plainsmen welcome rain. But about nightfall it turned to sleet, and the wind rose. Within moments the grim Montana winter burst about us. When that first fury abated, after seventy hours of wild opaque whiteness, the machines with which our road crew had gouged all summer at the brown prairie sod and gravel stood ice-encased and buried under snow. The work on which we had been living was not resumed until 1934.

My wife and I had been married seven days short of a year and had put much of that year's earnings into repairing and furnishing the house in which we lived. To supplement my very seasonal income we had bought a large incubator and 1,200 hatching eggs the previous spring. But white diarrhea had scattered half our downy flock in hideous bedragglement. Now, confused by cold, the brooder-accustomed survivors ignored their roosts, huddled together on the floor for warmth and smothered one another, ten to fifty at a time.

Early in April our landlord required his house. After a week of vain search we moved into a tall gabled four-room structure eleven miles northwest of town, which had stood gathering dust for years. All windows not boarded up were broken. With the hostile haunted air that grows in company with the smells of vacancy, mold, and vermin, it faced south near the northwest corner of a 160-acre wheat-field. A crude trail ran south toward the Plentywood road.

This region, short of manpower since its very beginning, had always imported help, had in consequence been devoted to the work ethic. Now with blinding suddenness came an ethical revolution: the simple and forthright obligation to work was ousted overnight by something describable only as the doctrine of the prior claim. Every man who sought a job, unless he could prove some speci-al right to it, emerged willy-nilly as a threat to some other man's survival.

1929-30

WEST OF THE HOUSE three stony acres sloped toward the road. I turned what I could of this ground with a battered walking plow, and planted most of our first garden about May 1. Earlier attempts were self-defeating; there seemed to be always another cold spell waiting to come back. The wind, which seldom died down for more than a few hours, whipped up incredibly penetrating dust. The best houses were not free of it; in ours it gathered daily on every level surface. It even came up through the floor.

A whole folklore of methods for shutting out dust grew up among our neighbors. For us the most effective immediate way was to enlarge and deepen the cellar, then bank the removed material around the house to close small wind-admitting gaps between its sills and the foundation. Meanwhile, cleaning remained a task without end.

Our surviving chickens were laying several dozen eggs daily. Local markets paid around 15 cents a dozen for them, in trade. There was no longer any market at all for the chickens themselves. As feed grew scarcer and values inexorably fell, while our new chicks grew to usable size, we ate so many chickens and eggs that both became tiresome.

The distance from suppliers made milk for the baby a problem from the start. There was a good dairy just outside Plentywood; but our wheat-farming neighbors kept few cattle. At length, one, only a mile distant over the fields, informed us that he had a young cow he disliked to milk because "her teats are so small you can't get hold of 'em." He offered us her morning milk if I would walk over and extract it myself. She gave two to four quarts that summer, depending on the changing quality of pasturage.

East of the house a 40-foot windmill tower surmounted a well 300 feet deep. The pump was out of order; without hoisting equipment I could not repair it. I carried drinking and cooking water from a neighbor's well; for other purposes I hauled water from a coulee dam which did not go dry until late summer. We caught every drop of the run-off from the roofs when, rarely, it rained. When winter came we continuously melted snow in a wash boiler on the kitchen stove and in a barrel beside the stove. We kept adding snow as the level sank; when we had a boilerful of water finally heated we poured it into the barrel to accelerate melting there. There were many steel barrels, once containers for oil or gasoline, blown into nearby coulees, where boys had used them for targets. I soldered metal patches on the smaller holes and bolted pieces of discarded tires over the large ones.

After midsummer most of our hens stopped laying; only the growing grasshopper infestation saved the flock. It was pathetic but comic to see twenty cockerels advance like a skirmishing party in the shimmer of heat—wings drooping, beaks panting— alert to pounce upon hoppers too drowsy with sunglare to escape.

Only a few people used poison against hoppers that first year, but during the following half-dozen years the method was adopted throughout the region. The active ingredient, arsenic, was mixed with a wet bran mash baited with amyl acetate. The hoppers went for the banana-scented chemical, voraciously took the arsenic with it, and died in such numbers that their corpses piled up in windrows, like drifted soil or snow. It developed later, however, that human skins could be badly injured by the mixture; I knew one man whose hands still suffered a disabling eczema three years after handling the mash.

1930-31

I STRIPPED THE EARS from the desolated corn and the heads from the sunflowers, and spread them to dry for chicken feed. At the same time I had to shut the chickens up in their shed to prevent them from eating the freshly poisoned hoppers; then I cultivated the rows deeply to turn the bodies safely under. Our roots (apart from the onions) yielded fairly well. We traded $11 worth of the best potatoes and carrots to a Plentywood grocer, and stored the rest. I helped a neighbor dig his potatoes and received in payment a sack of speltz, a valuable addition to our supply of chicken feed.

Cold weather multiplied our problems. Our cash income for 1930 had been about $65, a fact so truly ghastly that it did not at all amuse us to be told that we were safe from the internal revenue people. We could not buy winter clothing. The things that might have improved the house—stucco, plaster, paint—were as inaccessible to us as to the first settlers.

Wood is not plentiful in the Plentywood region. Except along stream courses, there aren't even bushes. Under the prairie lie veins of lignite coal from an inch to fifteen feet thick, but good ones are seldom available to the man who digs his own. The one I found, halfway up a coulee wall two miles east of us, was only one foot thick.

I tried to mine it by removing one foot of earth beneath the coal, but ended by removing two. Swinging a pick in a space three feet high and three feet wide, I still had to work in a difficult kneeling-crouching attitude. When my head touched the untrustworthy ceiling, cold grit showered down my neck. Taking out a ton of this fuel was a bitter twelve hours' toil. It meant knuckles flayed so often that they never really healed- hardly a day without its minor quota of blood lost. I did no blasting, but broke the coal down with a bar after removing the dirt beneath it as far back as I could reach with pick and shovel. Loading out was almost as bad as digging; I had to leave the wagon at the foot of the hill and trudge up and down, slipping, sliding, and being wrenched about. I was able to haul only when some neighbor could spare me a wagon and team.

In February, 1931, the temperature power-dived from summery readings to forty below zero in a single night; the wind mourned around our shell of a house. On the second day I made two trips to the mine on foot. Each time I brought home a large block of coal in a sack on my back, smaller chunks in a bucket. The path up from the coulee was coated with ice; the wind met me at the top with the spiteful authority of a whip. Every few hundred feet I had to swing my arms violently to restore circulation; almost before I could get the sack back on my shoulder my hands were chilled.

That night my wife wore overshoes and overcoat while washing dishes at the red-hot kitchen stove.

1931-32

MY WIFE'S TASKS INCLUDED such drudgeries as hair cutting, which she dreaded more than the severities of scrubbing floors. After midwinter she taught me such things as doing the laundry, but she continued her hardest job, the preparation of three meals a day from materials that grew more dismayingly scanty as the months wore on. The only variety possible lay in the choice of forms and combinations in which to serve the same carrots, potatoes, parsnips, beets. She made a mixture of finely chopped vegetables into a hauntingly delicious sandwich spread. Green tomatoes she transformed by some miracle into mince pie....

Our chickens, again on short rations, laid few eggs. By April only forty hens remained. We ate bread without butter, vegetables flavored only with salt, and an occasional jackrabbit. Rabbits were so plentiful that young people organized rabbit drives to get rid of them. Long lines of beaters trudged the dun prairies herding the animals into chicken-fence enclosures where they were clubbed to death by the hundreds. Fried rabbit was delicious, but many people rejected this "wild" food for fear of rabbit plague. We ourselves examined the meat very thoroughly and discarded more than we used.

The winter's light snow seemed not to thaw but to evaporate, moistening nothing. Throughout spring and most of summer it rained not a drop. But how the wind blew! The soil of neighboring fields swept over us in dense black clouds and pattered like sleet against the windows. Large but weightless thistles wheeled across the fields or bounded into the air like a new, insane bird life. They lodged high in the windmill and formed solid gray walls in fences. A screaming gale tore out miles of such fence and dragged posts, wire, and thistles far over the fields. It was like living in a permanent hurricane with grinding, sand-blasting dirt to face at each moment instead of salt spray....

At 3:00 A.M. on the first of May, I took my wife to the hospital in a neighbor's car. By the time I had hiked back to town after returning the car, our son was two hours old.

Any mother of two small children can arrive at my wife's problems thereafter by squaring the sum of her own. We had no new clothing for the boy; everything he wore was either taken from the older child's layette or adapted from things never meant for such service. Luckily he was a quiet fellow who, like his sister, set about life's beginning calmly....

A friend gave us five turkey eggs, of which four hatched. Our chicks and poults got through the early summer chiefly on milk and bread scraps. In June we used the last of our flour. For weeks we ate coarse cakes made of corn ground and reground in our own hand mill. Our young birds subsisted on insects.

Wells went dry all over the prairie that year. Knowing that ours was deep and had staying power, two neighbors helped me repair it in return for water for their stock. That saved us. I fitted up a conduit of bits of pipe, garden hose, old inner tubes, and wooden troughs, and pumped tons of the blessed fluid into the garden by the well. To the larger patch I carried it in buckets, a severely limited method of irrigation.

Suddenly in late summer it rained—rained briefly but so hard that the coulees ran like rivers. For minutes after the sky cleared the rush of water echoed among the hills. Almost overnight the scorched grass turned a rich green, and rectangles of countryside miles away had the brief heart-stopping beauty, the look of absolute freshness, that is never seen elsewhere to such advantage as on the Great Plains. Unhappily, it came six weeks too late.

One disaster remained to round out that wrenching summer. For two days we noticed army worms on roadside thistles; then as if these scouts had reported favorably, they attacked in force. They crawled so thickly over the fields, yards, buildings—always over; never, apparently, around—that it was impossible to avoid them, impossible not to touch the brown, greasy abomination. Wriggling food offered itself to our chickens in such abundance that they watched it with every sign of boredom. When the instinct to move on relieved us of the creatures, they left the same desolation that the hoppers had left the year before, except that where the hoppers had wiped out onions and other strong-flavored plants, the worms preferred the mild members of the cabbage family. They took every trace of our cauliflowers, for example, which I had babied along with hand watering all summer....

At this point, despite our terrible second summer, we fully intended eventually to raise everything we needed for food—salt excepted, of course. We hoped to make shoes and mittens of farm-tanned skins and to limit clothing purchases to textile fabrics. I did make sound bootees and slippers of the lining of an old sheepskin coat. My wife made attractive dresses from low-priced mill-ends; her old ones she made over for the children. My clothes became marvels of reconstruction. Small patches patched large patches, and larger patches covered all; these in turn were spotted with smaller patches until Joseph's coat of many colors wasn't a patch on my shirt. When all strata of a garment wore out, my wife tore them into strips and knitted them into thick warm rugs with a pair of needles I made of a springy wire barrel hoop.

In utilizing odds and ends I believe we went our pioneering forebears one better. Waste of many things was common on the frontier; for us any waste at all was felony. We made odd bits of metal, leather, wood, and what not into children's cribs, various garden and household tools, and innumerable repairs. Once I went too far: I experimented by half-soling a shoe with a piece of tin cut from an old oilcan. Every time I stepped with this shiny sole on snow or ice I became an irresistible force sitting down on an undentable surface.

The third winter was our nadir—the winter I cut ice for 75 cents a day. The house seemed colder; during storms we had to keep hot ashes and a lighted lantern in the cellar to protect our precious vegetables. Our chickens had starved too often, lost all resistance, and now died one by one. Somehow we saved the turkeys....

1932-33

By no standard was 1932 a good year. Cutworms menaced growing crops; some farmers had to plant their cornfields twice. Brassy-looking wireworms dug tunnels through the best potatoes until another shiny insect—the savage, venomous black larva of the click beetle—came along and killed them by the millions. But things grew despite worms, despite the continuing plague of hoppers. Knowing now what was too difficult or costly to produce, we traded off our 600-egg incubator and raised few chicks, but as many turkeys as possible. In the garden our mainstays were corn, potatoes, and carrots. Of other seeds we planted as much as space permitted. The vine crop was the surprise of the season. Pumpkins grew so large that our scales would not weigh them. We stored them upstairs, in the cellar, in the living room; we piled them outdoors. We ate pumpkin pies and pumpkin butter; baked pumpkins for the chickens, the turkeys; gave pumpkins to anyone who would take them. We traded vegetables in general for things we would ordinarily have had to buy; even the newspapers of Plentywood accepted vegetables for subscriptions that fall. We heard of others who traded produce to their doctor for medical attention. (Try that in 1978!)

Brief jobs became available several times that summer. The pay was a dollar for a ten-hour day until harvest, when it rose to a dollar fifty. One neighbor without money paid me in wheat valued at 25 cents a bushel and delivered it to the Plentywood flour mill, which ground it for us on shares. This solved the problem of bread for a full year. Another man paid me partly in cash, partly with a half-grown pig, partly by lending me a wagon and team for hauling.

We were by no means overprosperous during our penultimate winter on the land. Through the coldest months we had, for example, no eggs or milk. But we had plenty of bread, almost every vegetable of our latitude, a pig to slaughter, a few turkeys to sell. And at last we had hope: we and our neighbors had begun to take the measure of the Depression. We had proved that if the breadth of a man's shoulders and the nimbleness of a woman's hands are not salable for cash, they are not therefore valueless. Having something others needed, we did not really have to jingle coins to live.

In the spring of 1933 we found a better house on the edge of an irrigable coulee. This would have been an earth-shaking change for us except that the land belonged to others; our tenure there, as in our first house in 1930, would end at their need. Far more important in practical terms were the changes taking place in the whole community's approach to common problems. In 1933 something like two dozen of our neighbors pooled their resources of labor and equipment and opened a cooperative coal mine in a good vein. Some contributed horses, tractors, or trucks; others, like myself, only their own labor. My share was informally computed to be one week's work; then neighbors with trucks hauled the coal we needed and dumped it in our fuel shed. After the endless struggle of digging and carrying all winter for three years, it was like a personal emancipation proclamation.

Oregon Labor Press

The following political prophecy from the editors of the *Oregon Labor Press* appeared on November 17, 1933, at the height of the Great Depression. As the print organ of the state's American Federation of Labor (AFL) trade unions, the *Labor Press* took a conservative perspective, appealing to readers who worried about a radical solution to the nation's woes with the same concern as their employers.

IF AMERICA SHOULD GO RED?

IF AMERICA SHOULD GO RED?

What would you do? It is a fair question because you would have to take some part in the re-organization that would take place under COMMUNISM. It may sound ridiculous for intelligent persons to be discussing such a possibility, yet unless those who now hold the destiny of the country in their hands, take an intelligent and frank course of action to meet the serious and, economic crisis we are facing—America can go Red, just as other countries have—if enough of its citizens think RED.

If America went Red it would be the results of wrong THINKING on the part of Labor and Capital. Somewhere along the line you, Mr. Business Man, and you, Mr. Worker, have failed miserably. Now is the time to take serious thought of this matter and see to it that there will be no regrets when you look back a year from now upon the year 1933-1934 and its winter of discontent.

There isn't any question about your desire to Think Right and Build Right by your family and your neighbor's family. Few men that have enjoyed the advantages of individual initiative in these United States of ours, would exchange their state for one of Communal bondage, where the individual becomes a number and the family a memory—yet under the stress of repressed wrongs, injured feelings, and dire necessity many races have stepped from freedom into bondage that was smeared with the crimson stain of Revolution, have placed themselves at the mercy of dictators, men and systems, from which it was a long, long trail back to liberty again.

If America should go Red—What would be your role? Think it over. Heed the warning signs about you.

GET RIGHT WITH YOUR FELLOWMAN!

Ralph Winstead
(1894-1957)

Ralph Winstead was born in Spokane, Washington. His father was a prospector, and Ralph had to work throughout his youth to supplement the family's earnings. He worked in mining, lumber, and construction and became secretary of a coal miner's union in the Northwest sometime around 1918. He soon became active in the Industrial Workers of the World (IWW) Lumber Workers' Union #120. IWW members were known as Wobblies. Winstead's penchant for literary expression led him to join the editorial staffs of the *Industrial Worker*, *One Big Union Monthly*, and *The American Contractor*. But he is best remembered as the author of a short story series that appeared in various IWW publications from 1920-1923. Here he invented the character Tightline Johnson, a migrant Wobbly who worked as a smelterman, coal miner, and lumberjack. In the following story that appeared in the *Industrial Pioneer* (September 1921), Tightline addresses conditions in post-World War I lumber camps, where management had instituted a piecework system that offered workers extra pay for individual effort but was meant to undermine solidarity. The union called it "the gypo system."

JOHNSON THE GYPO

THIS HERE GYPO PROPOSITION reminds me of the old woman who had a peppy daughter. She used to moan and plead with the girl to change her state of mind and be a good girl. This old woman was faced with a condition of things, not a state of mind and the only way for to deal with condition is by the use of tactics, not by using a line appeals to be good.

Now there is one time honored tactic that has been used by old dames on their daughters since and before the human race had thumbs. This line of action was to turn the refractory young female over a bony knee and administer to the well being of her ideas by hand.

That ain't the only tactics to fit this particular problem by a whole lot but at least it has some advantages over appealing to 'em to be good. They got inside urges as to what they want and need and all the appeals in the world don't cut much ice in the face of a human urge. Tactics is what counts.

Now it's the same way with the Gypo proposition. These here bushel maniacs just naturally got the same sort of nature as John D. Rockefeller and a lot of other humans includin' all of us. They wants to get rich quick and are goin' to listen that interior urge to gather in the mazuma while the gatherin' is good in spite of any appeals to good saintly wobs and travel the narrow path.

But mostly we have been playin' the part of the noble mother and been pleadin' with these here almost human Gypo birds to be good, and spurn the pitfalls of their evil ways. What we got to do is use a few tactics on em. Maybe spanking would be justifiable but maybe it wouldn't get the goods as quick as a way that me and a bunch of other wobs tried up at Grinnon one time.

Of course, as I say, tactics is the thing to use and when tactics is decided on in a whole industry it takes a lot of organized action and working together that is a lot harder than just going around spoutin' about the humpbacked species that ruined the organization and is now keepin' us the bum. In order to put any real tactics across we got to have a real plan worked out and have got to put the thing over by co-ordinated action—and not by sanctimonious prayers to stay away from the sinful contract and keep pure and undefiled.

One time I blowed into Seattle with a short stake and was prepared to stick around town for a week or two. There was a good bunch in town and we lit out to take a little relaxation. Snowball Smith and me was roomin' together and was takin' the said relaxation mostly in company. About the first stunt we done was to go out to Alki point and gather an eyeful along the beach. Of course this was before the short skirts made the beaches unnecessary for purposes of sight seein' but even aside from this sight satisfaction we was both longin' for a salt water swim, and got it.

It was the next afternoon after this excursion amongst the darin' dressers that I was walkin' down the slave market when I noticed on old man Moore's board a sign that caught the eye: "Wanted eight men to take contract bucking and falling. Details inside."

There it was, straight Gypo stuff. Chance to make a co-operative fortune right in my hand. Me—well, I looked around real quick to see if there was a humpbacked Swede in sight and not seeing any I high balled right up to the room and got hold of Snowball.

Now Snowball is one of these here plugs that is ever restin' with his trigger on safety. They ain't no neutral gear in his make-up. Snowball is always ready to go and further more after the goin' a long ways from the start and gets rough, why, he ain't the bird to crawfish neither. Maybe he ain't exactly what you call an executive genius that can lay out and get others to carry through the big campaign but he don't need to ponder over the proposition for three weeks to see if it'll hold water. Snowball makes up his mind quick and stays with it.

So, when I suggests to him that we become the original humpies and go scabbin' on ourselves just for a little fun and tactical experience, why, Snow don't bat an eye but hustles his lid and we streaks for Moore's. Nobody had beat us to it so we got all the details.

Eight men was wanted to sign a contract to fall and buck a full section of timber up at Grinnon which as you know is a sort of steeple jack outfit up in the Olympics off of Hoods Canal. The ground was level we was told and the timber was good. The rate was 60 cents per thousand and we had bunk house all to ourselves.

The company furnished the tools but we had to the saw filing. We was to eat in the company boarding house and they would deduct the board bill at the pay off. We could draw only fifty percent of what our log scalein' called for till the job finished. Everything in regular Gypo style.

Snowball did most of the talkin'. He made rapid mates with greedy eyes at how much we could clean up in the summer. I almost got in earnest on the finance end of it myself. It sure sounded good the way he mentioned the thousands of dollars.

Moore agreed to hold the job till we got six other fellows to go in with us and so we set out to round up six good wobs that was willin' to mar their perfectly good reputations in order to put the Gypo game in bad at Grinnon. We had a hard time. Some of our best known wobs sneered at the idea and told us we was just lookin' for an excuse. But we kept travellin' in spite of little set backs and raised a crew.

The eight of us signed on and got our John Hancocks on a big contract that was goin' to make or break somebody. Then we separated and rustled our clothes and spent the night listenin' to advice not to go and tryin' to explain why we was goin' to the bunch, but they wouldn't pretend to believe us. Fainthearted wobs never went Gypoin' yet is my claim. The pressure was awful, but we stuck it out. A fellow's friends and fellow workers can always be depended on to state the right and wrong of things. Right and wrong I always claims is matters of gettin' results.

Next mornin' we grabbed the boat for the first lap of the trip and after changin' into busses and back onto boats a few times we made the landin' at Grinnon. We was met by the time keeper with a speeder and made the trip up over the steepest known loggin' track in the country and that is sayin' a heap.

We didn't see where the nice level ground mentioned in the sacred contract was comin' but we sure enjoyed the scenery which is sure pleasant in this section.

Mountains and valleys with clear tumblin' rivers and misty clouds hangin' half way up can sure wipe out the memory of a lot of squalid misery found in more civilized sections. Somehow they make a fellow feel that life is big and not exactly centered about himself.

And this feelin' is most necessary to get real action these days. Most of us like to stick our chests out about two inches further than is necessary for deep breathin' and seem to forget that there are others in the world that might be just as wise as—the big center of things—me. There are a lot of us that have to learn to think and act according to the biggest benefit to the greatest number instead of in the way that our own ideas points.

We made the camp alright and found a bunk house fixed up for us that was pretty fair. The boss give us the icy eye as if he was only in on this Gypo proposition by compulsion but the manager was all smiles and explained to us over and over that he had only left his office work in town to come up and see that we got a good start.

Of course we was grateful. We even told him so. The grub was good too but the flunkies set it down before us with a bang and the cook looked cross-eyed at the whole bunch of us. Sure a guy must have to suffer a lot from just wantin' to make a few lousy dollars via the Gypo route in some places. I even commenced to be scared somebody that knew me would write it up for the Worker and demand that I turn in my card. Such would have sure ruined me for life but then I been ruined more than once anyhow.

Well, we went out and looked over the ground. It was level, too. A fine bunch of trees in a level valley that just seemed to happened along by accident in the steep canyons. Then we organized ourselves. Snowball was elected to do the filing and the Bull buckin' and the rest of us scattered out in the trees.

I started in with the fallin' gang not knowing anything about this end of the loggin' game and we dropped the first tree fine except that the blamed thing hooked up and it took us most of the day to get it down where we could look at it.

Then we done better. The manager came around and found all of us sweatin' and puffin' so he went off to town satisfied that he had solved the problem of bustin' up these here pesky wobs by makin' 'em take an interest in the work. Yeah, we done better. In the afternoon me and my pardner dropped three fine big trees, every one of 'em with high grade timber in 'em—number one flooring stock, but the blame sticks dropped on stumps and was busted all to hell. It was sure tough but I cheerfully took the blame as I didn't know much about the fallin' game anyway.

When I looked over the rest of the crew's work I commenced to think that I had picked the biggest bunch of green horns that could be found in the whole organization. Not one of 'em seemed know as much about fallin' or buckin' as I used to.

The newly elected bull bucker came around me and he pulled his face into a sorrowful twist and explained that we wasn't makin' more than three or four dollars a day and was a dullin' of saws.

This of course was awful news as it meant that maybe we wouldn't make that young fortune we was a lookin' for here. I promised to speed up and we did manage by workin' a little overtime to drop another fir, but it was punky.

The funny part of the whole thing was that we didn't seem to improve as the days went by. Some of the gang got lazy and wouldn't drop as many as they should and then they would blame Snowhall for bein' a bum sawfiler but I couldn't see anything wrong with his filin'.

The boss dropped around and looked over the work we had done and I saw him goin' away with his hat off and him a scratchin' his head. He appeared to be plum puzzled by our progress. In the meantime I got friendly with the blacksmith's helper and he told me that the boss once carried a card in the early days and that there was a good bunch of wobs that had been sent down the road to make room for us damn scabs.

You bet I got *real friendly* with that helper. He made it a point to see that he wasn't handlin' any hot irons when I happened around. Well, we stuck to this job for a month. Things went from bad to worse. I commenced to lose faith in the co-operative movement when it comes to getting work done. We didn't seem to have the right spirit for work no matter which way we tried to bring it out. Still I learned a lot about fallin' trees but the fallin' pardner didn't seem to think so. He said that I couldn't hit even the ground more than one out of three times without him. Well, I thought if he was so wise I would try my hand at buckin'. So we made the switch.

I went on with a big Finn that agreed to show me how to buck. But I soon wished that I hadn't done it. Buckin' is even harder work to my notion than fallin', besides I was no good at it and didn't seem able to learn much. About every time that I got a real good log about half bucked out, why, somethin' was sure to happen to the wedges and the blame log would split. I must of spoiled a lot of 'em that way but I learned how to buck 'em off square at last but the bunch decided to let me buck on the split ones about this time so I didn't get any real practice at that.

In other ways, however, things went fine. For instance, the cook finally seemed to get over his grouch and was real friendly. He came out and looked over our job and even got jolly about it. Then we sort of decided to take it easy anyway. About this time, why, we got a good bunch of papers and magazines up and it got so it was harder and harder to tear ourselves away from the literary field. We enjoyed discussions on a lot of highbrow topics and sometimes when the job got irksome we took a hike up on some of the hills and looked around.

Maybe I am a little off on the subject but I sure admire the scenery in the Olympics. The more I saw of it the more I admired it. Finally it got so that it appealed to me more than even the buckin' did though I admit that that was sure fascinatin'. It certainly was wonderful to get away up on the mountain side and look down on the riggin' crew a sweatin' and strainin' like little ants down in the valley while the donkeys would shoot steam like these little peanut roasters on the pop corn stands in town.

Oh, it was a great life. I could see where there was all sorts of temptation to be a gypo. I commenced to think that I would like to do this regularly.

The good grub and the pleasant companionship sure didn't make none of us feel bad either. Snowball said that he wore a full inch off of some of the saws just to keep himself busy about the shack while we was out on the job but I think he was exaggeratin'. I never did think that he always told the whole truth about some things especially about how hard he worked but I will say that he changed the looks of some of them saws alright.

All good things come to an end at last, however, and one day the scaler come up to scale up our cut and see where we was at. He come out on the job unexpected but as it happened three of us was workin'.

He started to work scalin' the logs and seemed to grow real excited. He didn't stop, however, to make any remark to us but kept on all day. Well, he stayed with the job and so did we. When he got finished he come over to tell us about it. He was so mad he was almost happy.

"Well, you birds have sure got away with some-thin' this time," he tells us in our bunk house the night he finished. "You have been here thirty days and have eat up four hundred dollars' worth of grub. You have knocked down and mutilated a million feet of timber, whether from pure cussedness or because you are damned fools, I don't know and no one can prove. But I sure have a bright suspicion because none of you look like plum idiots to me.

"The foreman wrote into town advisin' the manager to abrogate the contract a couple of weeks ago but then the manager had an idea he was still opposed to the contract system. Now I know what he was opposed to, alright."

We all asked him what was wrong. We wanted to know if he was goin' to get us fired from our good job. In fact we made him feel that we sure enjoyed the stay up there but that didn't seem to help him any. He went away madder than ever. I heard later that he had three shares of stock in the company.

The manager came up and told us that our contract was not worth a damn and that the quicker we got out of camp the better he would be pleased. He said that if we wanted to collect the money for the trees that we had put down we could bring suit and see what we got.

We pulled out and blew into Seattle but so far none of us has taken up the matter of our legal rights to pay for our work. And on the other hand I saw the boards down at Moore's chalked up heavy for buckers and fallers workin' by the day at Grinnon right away after we hit town.

Tactics, I claims, will get the goods where dealin' out the sneers and peddlin' the holy solidarity stuff only makes a man feel ashamed and unnatural but don't stop him from wantin' to obey that inner urge. In fact some of the looks I got up in Grinnon made me think that maybe I was a superior bein' and not in the crude and unsophisticated circle of common workin' stiffs.

Providin' that I hadn't already known better I feel sure that that idea would have got stuck in me somehow or other. It's funny that way. Everybody is always ready to believe that he or she (especially she) is different from the rest of the people. You know the line of bunk I mean and how if you shoot it out just right, how it always gets results.

Well, Gypos don't want to get no chance to think that they are different from you and me. Just use a few organized tactics and the humps on some of the loggers' backs will look like a camel's that's has been through a famine worse than a term in the Spokane City jail in a free speech fight.

Suppose we just get together and put across a few tactical maneuvers on these birds and see that they don't obstruct the progress of the organization any more. That is my idea.

Joe Hill
(1882-1915)

IWW member Joe Hill wrote numerous songs communicating the Wobbly message of the state of labor in early twentieth-century America. Executed by firing squad on November 19, 1915 for the disputed murder of a Salt Lake City grocer, Joe Hill quickly became a martyr for the Wobbly cause. His most-loved song was "The Preacher and the Slave," also know as "Pie in the Sky" or "Long-Haired Preachers." It appeared in the third edition of the IWW songbook. Twelve years after Hill's death, Carl Sandburg included it in a 1927 collection, *The American Songbag*, establishing Joe Hill as part of American folk tradition.

The Preacher and the Slave

(Sung to the tune of "Sweet Bye and Bye")

Long-haired preachers come out every night,
Try to tell you what's wrong and what's right;
But when asked how 'bout something to eat
They will answer with voices so sweet:

Chorus:
You will eat, bye and bye,
In that glorious land above the sky;
Work and pray, live on hay,
You'll get pie in the sky when you die.

The starvation army they play,
They sing and they clap and they pray.
Till they get all your coin on the drum,
Then they tell you when you are on the bum:

Chorus:
You will eat, bye and bye,
In that glorious land above the sky;
Work and pray, live on hay,
You'll get pie in the sky when you die.

Holy Rollers and jumpers come out,
They holler, they jump and they shout.

Give your money to Jesus they say,
He will cure all diseases today.

If you fight hard for children and wife—
Try to get something good in *this* life—
You're a sinner and bad man, they tell,
When you die you will sure go to hell.

Workingmen of all countries unite,
Side by side we for freedom will fight:
When the world and its wealth we have gained
To the grafters we'll sing this refrain:

Last Chorus:
You will eat, bye and bye.
When you've learned how to cook and to fry;
Chop some wood, 'twill do you good,
And you'll eat in the sweet bye and bye.

Anise
(1885-1965)

Anna Louise Strong was a journalist and writer who used the pen name "Anise." She was feature editor of the *Seattle Union Record* from 1916 to 1921 and reported on the Montesano, Washington trial of the IWW unionists, or Wobblies, who were sentenced to prison following the Centralia Armistice Day massacre in November 1919. Fueled by anti-radical sentiment in the post-World War I climate, the massacre took place when citizens of Centralia, incited by a group of business leaders calling themselves the Centralia Protective Association and by members of the American Legion, stormed a newly opened IWW hall. Three legionnaires were killed in the initial skirmish. IWW member Wesley Everest, a war veteran, was tortured and hanged. In the days following the melee, over 1,000 suspected IWW members were detained by the legionnaires, who had taken over the town from local law enforcement. In the end, ten IWW members stood trial; seven received second degree murder sentences of 25-to-40 years in Walla Walla Penitentiary. Anise covered the trial and described some of the defendants in the following poems. As Anna Louise Strong, she lived her later years in and wrote about the People's Republic of China under Mao Tse Tung. She died there.

Centralia Pictures

1. Eugene Barnett

"I was born," he said,
"In the hills of Carolina,
And the schooling I got
In this great free land
Of compulsory schools
Was very simple;
My MOTHER taught me
Reading and writing
And I went to school
For a three-months' term,
And a five-months' term!
Then
I was EIGHT years old

And my father went
As a STRIKE-BREAKER
To the West Virginia mines.
I remember the TENTS
Of the UNION miners,
Driven from their homes
CAMPING
Over the river.
They put me to work at once
UNDERGROUND
And when the inspectors came
I had to HIDE
In the old workings,
For the legal age in the mines
Was FOURTEEN years,
But neither the BOSS
Nor my FATHER
Cared about LAW!
I was caught
In the Papoose explosion
At the age of eleven,
And I ran away from home
At thirteen.
I followed MINING
All over the country
Joining the UNION
In Shadyside, Ohio.
I was SIXTEEN then
And had worked EIGHT years,
And in all those years
My only chance for schooling
Was a short time
After a FEVER,
When I was TOO WEAK
To WORK!
But somehow I managed to get
A good-looking wife
Who encouraged me
To improve myself!
We had a little girl that died

And a boy that lived,
He's two years now
And a BRIGHT KID;
Can't keep still.
We took a homestead
Over in Idaho
Till the government called
For MINERS,
So I came to Centralia
At the country's call
And after the Armistice
There wasn't much work!
I saw the raid on the hall
And the starting
Of the MAN-HUNT,
And I rode home
For my GUN
To get some law and order
In Centralia!
When they arrested me
I didn't tell all I knew,
For I was afraid if I did
I mightn't live to see
A court-room trial!"

2. *Ray Becker*

It was through the bars
Of the county jail
That he told his story,
While the jailer waited
In a corner,
And the other boys
Were washing up
For supper:
"I'm twenty-five," he said,
"And I studied four years,
Intending to be
A SKY-PILOT!
But after I saw
The INSIDE WORKINGS

I quit!
Not overnight, of course,
Nor in a day,
It took some time.
For I come
From a preacher family!
My father has a pulpit
And one of my brothers
Has a pulpit.
But I found most people
Wouldn't practice
What you preach,
And I didn't see how
To get them to.
Besides,
To be real frank
I no longer believed
most of the stuff
And I didn't want
To preach it.
Since 1915
I've been in the woods
And I joined the Wobblies
In 1917.
After the raid on our hall
I was one of the occupants
Of the ice-box
And I had
An Iver Johnson .38!
That was how
I come to be here,—But I figure
The only practical Christians
today
Are the I.W.W.'s
And the Socialists,
And the folks
That are trying to get
A new world!
Anyway,
Christ was a tramp

Without a place
To 'lay his head,'
And WE are tramps,
And I guess
That fifth chapter
Of the epistle of James,
Telling the RICH FOLKS
To weep and howl
For what was COMING,
Must have been written
By a WOBBLY!"

3. Bert Bland

All life's uncertainties
Sat lightly on him,
He was of the WOODS
And YOUNG enough
To smile at danger,
Indeed, he smiled
On all the world
With joyous greeting
As if everyone he met
Gave him PLEASURE,
"I was three years old," he said,
"When they brought me to Washington
From the Illinois farm
Where I was born.
My father, too, was born
In Illinois
In Lincoln's time,
And my mother came
From the SOUTH,—
I guess I'm about as near
An American
As they make them,
And if I ever had ancestors
From any foreign land
They got lost somewhere
In the PRAIRIES!
I was sixteen

When I became a LOGGER
And for eight years
I've followed the WOODS,
It's a great life
If you don't weaken,
But the CAMPS
Are certainly ROTTEN!
Fourteen of us slept
In a 10 by 14 bunkhouse
Over in Raymond,
With our wet clothes
STEAMING
In the middle of the shack!
The bad conditions drove me
From camp to camp,
Twenty-two different ones
In a single year,—
And only one of them all
Had a BATH!
I've been a WOBBLY
For about three years
Hoping to change conditions.
When they raided our hall
I shot from the hill
To defend it
And then I fled to the woods!
A lynching party
Had me surrounded once
But I crawled through them
About 1 A.M.
On my hands and knees,
And lay out in the hills
For seven nights.
I was the lucky guy,—
For by the time they got me
In a train-shed,
Things had quieted some,
So I missed
The TERRORIZING
The others got

In the Centralia jail,
And the worst they handed me
Was watching **OILY ABEL,**
The Lumber Trust's pet lawyer
Helping the state hand
'JUSTICE'
To rebel Lumberjacks!"

4. Britt Smith

The weight of the world
Seemed resting
On his shoulders,
He was thirty-eight
And had followed the woods
For twenty years.
He knew to the full
The lumber camps of Washington,
And he had no more
ILLUSIONS
He sawed the timbers
To build the great flume
At Electron,
Where the mountain waters
Come pouring down
To give, light and power
In Tacoma,
And to carry
The **LUXURIOUS** Olympian
Over the Cascades,
Softly and smoothly,
With passengers warm
And **COMFORTABLE.**
But he and his fellows
Had slept in a **SWAMP**
On cedar **PLANKS,**
And had no place
To **WASH**
After their day's labor.
He said: "I have slept
WEEKS at a time

In WET CLOTHES,
Working
All day in the rain,
Without any place,
To DRY OUT.
I have washed my clothes
By tying them
To a stake in the river,
Letting the current
Beat them partly clean.
It was often the only place
We had for washing."
It was HE
The LYNCHERS sought
That night of terror
When the lights went out
And they broke into the jail
And dragged forth Everest
To torture
And mutilation
And hanging,
Crying:
"We've got Britt Smith!"
For he was Secretary
Of the I.W.W.s
And lived in a little room
At the back of the hall
Which he tried to defend
In the RAID,—
It was his only HOME
He had spent his strength
And used his youth
Cutting LUMBER
For the homes of others!

Howard Morgan
(1914-)

Howard Morgan, a political activist, was among a small group responsible for the revitalization of the Oregon Democratic Party following World War II, and served as head of the Oregon Public Utilities Commission. He delivered these remarks in the course of a symposium sponsored by the Oregon Cultural Heritage Commission, one of a series on "Oregon Originals" at the Oregon Historical Society on May 15,1997. They are reconstituted here from Howard Morgan's fragmentary notes.

RECOLLECTIONS OF TOM BURNS OF BURNSIDE

I MUST START WITH A BRIEF APOLOGY. This will not be a particularly scholarly or even an historical discourse in any real sense. I know very little of Mr. Burns' origins, the dates of his birth and death, formal education, his arrival on the Portland scene and so on. All I can offer are the recollections of adolescent contacts with him, beginning some seventy years ago at his watch repair shop and workmen's library on the skidroad section of West Burnside street when I was about fourteen, in the late 1920s.

During most of my grad-school and all of my high-school years I lived in the Albina neighborhood of Portland, just up the Russell street hill from the Union Pacific yards and shops where my father was employed as a railroad mechanic. When I was in the seventh or eighth grade, an instructor at one of the City's public swimming pools brought me to the attention of the Multnomah Athletic Club's world-class swimming coach, Jack Cody. The result was that I was given an athletic membership in the club—that is, a full membership with all privileges and absolutely free, so long as I could satisfy Mr. Cody's standards and requirements for his swimming teams. This lasted for the next ten years or so, at a time when the Multnomah Club was still, among other things, a serious athletic club rather than a social watering-spot with a five- to ten-year waiting period for costly membership.

Naturally membership in the Club was a welcome bit of class and luxury for me but it also required me to make at least three or four trips across town every week for extensive workouts. Street-car fare was something like seven cents each way, so I did a good deal of walking, except when it rained too hard, and I sometimes varied the route by taking one or another of the several bridges, ranging from the Broadway to the Hawthorne, for a bit of novelty.

In very short order I found the Burnside bridge to be the most interesting by far. It led to all the colorful features of the famous Skidroad: loggers in town from the camps, once-famous saloons like Erickson's and the Valhalla (by then much reduced by prohibition), medicine shows and kindred enterprises for separating suckers from their money, curbstone preachers, soap-box orators, hobo philosophers, Salvation Army bands, and always the curious and sometimes wonderful displays in the windows of Tom Burns' watch shop. I never failed to stop, or at least to walk very slowly, taking it all in.

Mr. Burns was obviously a man with a severe pedagogic itch. His windows were full of oddities and curiosities almost guaranteed to stop the passerby and give him a chuckle. But along with the chuckle the passerby would absorb, or be reminded of, some fact, insight or principle essential to a civilized understanding of the world he was living in. The constant theme was the history and current practice, good and bad, of labor relations. Clearly Tom Burns was an open and ardent admirer of the IWW and all the cantankerous free spirits who called themselves "Wobblies." He could very well have paraphrased Will Roger's remark about being a Democrat to say, "I am not a member of any *organized* labor movement, I am a Wobbly." Of course that was more than enough to send chills up and down spines in the Arlington Club, the Chamber of Commerce and the Portland Police Red Squad. Not to mention some of the equally conservative Labor Temple officials. If he ever gave a specific name to his political leanings I do not recall it. He did acknowledge that he was a radical—in the truest sense of the word—and he did understand what the word meant. If I were to guess at his political alignment it would be somewhere between ethical socialism and intellectual anarchy. But that's only a guess and a reluctant one at that. His admirers tended to take him as he was, without analysis.

I do not know the details of his formal education but he was obviously a well-read man of broadly humane and civilized outlook, sometimes roughly expressed. One of the permanent displays in his window was a plaque with a quotation ascribed to Plato but suitably translated for the loggers, longshoremen and other bindle-stiffs he was aiming at: "Empty Your Pocketbook into Your Brain."

A few years later, while I was doing just that as a student at Reed College, I came across the original quotation in one of the Dialogues, and my recollection is that it was almost as plain and direct as Tom's version. He occasionally quoted this opening couplet from a trenchant poem by Alexander Pope:

> Know then thyself; presume not God to scan
> The proper study for Mankind is Man.

Burns published a little newspaper at irregular intervals named *FAX*. I remember its masthead slogan as also borrowed from Pope:

> Fools be my subject,
> Let satire be my song.

He sometimes pasted sheets from this newspaper against the inside of his storefront windows so they could be read conveniently from the sidewalk. They generally were well worth reading. True to his masthead slogan, he lambasted stuffed shirts, punctured windbags and poked ribald fun at the local gentry in every issue. As Stewart Holbrook pointed out, there was an abundance of what lawyers term "actionable material," but no one is known to have taken action. The skidroaders and numerous others were vastly amused. The victims were vastly but silently outraged.

Mr. Burns' approach to journalism, as I deduced it, went something like this: "If William Shakespeare could construct highly suggestive scenarios populated by characters with highly suggestive names—Doll Tearsheet, for example—as a means of getting the English to attend good plays and read good literature, what was to prevent Tom Burns from doing the same thing for the much worthier objective of getting working stiffs to read about and understand the real world that they had to cope with every day, and which the stodgy daily press did its best to disguise and sugar-coat?" Such an approach could and did produce some fairly salty episodes.

One such episode remains a reasonably clear memory for me to this day. It concerned the visit to Portland by a personage bearing a most distinguished, ancient and exotic title: The Princess Cantacuzene. The title had been handed down from the glory days of Constantinople and the Byzantine Empire by way of Romanian royalty. As it happened there was something of a Romanian vogue in the U.S. at the time, and particularly in Portland. This stemmed from a visit by Queen Marie of Romania, who spent some time locally and at the strange palace of her infatuated admirer, Sam Hill, just up the Columbia.

The Princess, however, was every bit as American as Sam Hill himself. She was a granddaughter of Ulysses S. Grant, and in the fashion of the time among wealthy or notable American women, she had gone to Europe and returned with a husband. This gave her the choice of being addressed as either the Countess Speransky, in accordance with her husband's Imperial Russian title, or as the Princess Cantacuzene, in accordance with his other, more Byzantine encumbrance. Both jurisdictions being inoperative at the time, she had full freedom of choice. She chose to become a princess.

She was, of course, entertained royally on Portland Heights. Tom Burns could not have imagined better material for his newspaper and its few but avid readers.

He began by transposing a couple of vowels in her ancient title, thus intentionally misspelling it in a fashion to make Shakespeare's Doll Tearsheet seem positively demure by comparison. After a few paragraphs of this, as I recall it, he managed to link her with Portland's Mayor Baker.

Those old enough to remember him will recall that Mayor Baker was a man of considerable parts, some of which were not normally discussed in mixed company. Though an unusually homely man, he was large, forceful and had labored to establish a tradition that actresses and lady opera singers visiting Portland could, at worst, look forward to being soundly kissed by His Honor. The rest was left to their, and the public's, imagination.

We needn't go further into Mr. Burns' indelicate essay. Suffice it to say that this sort of thing furnished some pretty sprightly reading material for a 15 or 16 year old kid. Especially one accustomed to reading about local affairs in the sedate columns of the *Oregonian, Oregon Journal, News Telegram,* and soon.

By that time I had ventured inside Mr. Burns' establishment, had browsed through some but by no means all the books in his extensive library, and had even been allowed to borrow a few. My recollection is of being treated courteously, though he was naturally more attentive to the mature workingmen who frequented the place. They were his major interest and audience and I understood that my interest lay mainly in the books and pamphlets, which opened up parts of past and current history that nothing in my schooling had more than hinted at

In a short time I acquired more knowledge than I knew what to do with about the great Pullman strike for the 8 hour day, the associated bombing and riot in Haymarket Square and their aftermath; Homestead; Ludlow; private armies; the killings at Everett and Centralia; and much more. By the time I was seventeen or so I had learned enough that I was not in the least surprised when Henry Ford began turning virtually his entire enterprise over to the commander of his own private army, coming within easy reach of losing everything. Almost none of this information came from my classes at school or the daily press, but from what I found at Tom Burns' little watch repair shop on the skidroad. He was indeed a dangerous person, as is everyone who sets out to reveal what our betters prefer to remain hidden or at least obscured.

In short, enough of Tom Burns' itch had rubbed off on me to encourage me to look further and I did so at the Albina Branch Library, the largest branch library in town at the time and only three or four blocks from my home. There I encountered the great liberal periodicals of the time—*The Nation, The Progressive, The New Republic*—and the writing of progressive historians and novelists such as Lincoln Steffens, Upton Sinclair, C.E.S. Wood, the early works of John Dos Passos and many others. I have been an unrepentant liberal ever since.

So my association with Tom Burns was brief and sporadic, and I didn't learn as much about him as I later wished I had. But it did open doors and history for me and for that I have always been grateful to him.

In 1952, as Chairman of the Democratic Party of Oregon, I attended the Democratic National Convention at Chicago and listened as Add Stevenson, Governor of Illinois, gave the opening and welcoming address. In it he paid a brief, eloquent tribute to John Peter Altgeld, liberal governor of Illinois in the 1890s and the first Democrat to hold that office after the Civil War. Vachel Lindsay had called him "The Eagle Forgotten." In that convention audience, more than a half-century after the events Stevenson spoke of, I would guess that no more than a quarter of those present would have known that Altgeld had sacrificed the remainder of his political career when he pardoned the last three surviving prisoners, seven years after they were corruptly railroaded into prison, in connection with the long-ago incidents in Haymarket Square.

Stevenson knew, of course, and I honored him for it.

Except for my initiation into such matters in Tom Burns' skidroad watch shop I might still, like millions of others, not have fully understood what Stevenson was talking about. But I did understand. And I like to think Mr. Burns would have been pleased to know that he had helped to pass that understanding on to me. Those who suffer a pedagogic itch can usually look forward to no other compensation.

My one regret is that it didn't occur to me to tender my small contribution until it was too late to be received.

Hamish Scott MacKay
(1905-1984)

In a dramatic and poignant scene at Portland International Airport on the evening of November 18, 1960, the United States government tore Hamish Scott MacKay from the arms of his young sons and deported him for having belonged to a "proscribed organization" in Oregon. He was flown to Vancouver, British Columbia, where he lived until his death in 1984. Mr. MacKay was born in Alberta, Canada in 1905 and came with his parents and younger brother to the United States at the age of eighteen. His father had come from Scotland in 1893, settling in North Dakota, where he met his American-born wife, who was related to a signer of the Declaration of Independence. After their marriage, they moved to Alberta and returned to the United States in 1923.

Following his deportation, Hamish MacKay wrote a memoir entitled *My Experiences in the United States*. Michael Munk edited the following excerpts from that memoir. The story begins in Chicago —where, at 25, McKay found himself jobless after the stock market crash of 1929—and covers the decade of the 1930s in Oregon

FROM *My Experiences in the United States*

To Portland

EVERYONE I KNEW IN CHICAGO lost his job in 1929. With the Depression staring me in the face, far pastures looked greener and the West was the only place to be. My brother Roderick had a friend, Clarence Lasalle, whose wife was from Portland, and Clarence was sure there was work for all of us there. So we all started out at the end of October, driving two Yellow Cabs from Chicago to Los Angeles for their owner.

In L.A. I bought a 1924 Model T Ford for $25, loaded it up with camping gear, blankets, Clarence and his wife, their 10 year old son and their Collie and, together with Roderick, we all started out on the last leg of our trip to Portland. Since I was a mechanic, a burned out connecting rod and a new set of transmission bands were no problem and the trip was a pleasure. But we arrived in Portland with no more than $40 between us and all of us found ourselves sponging off Clarence's mother-in-law, Mrs. Kemmel, since there were no jobs anywhere.

I walked the streets of Portland, trying to get work as a auto mechanic but ready to take anything. Everywhere I went during the spring and summer of 1930 there was a line of laid off workers who right-ly had first dibs on any rehiring by their former employers. My only job, taking up bearings on old Chevys for the Veterans Administration, lasted just one day and you can bet I spent all my pay for food for all of us. When that was gone—toward the end of September 1930—I got the uneasy feeling I wasn't wanted around Mrs. Kemmel's house any more.

Farm Work Around Tigard

THAT HELPED ME REMEMBER a farmer from Tillamook who had told me my feet would be welcome under his table anytime, so I borrowed 50 cents from Mrs. Kemmel for carfare, left her house and started out. My first stop was a chicken farmer who told me he had already hired somebody, so now being down to 30 cents, I had to hitchhike if I was to get to Tillamook. But broke and unemployed as I was, I couldn't get anyone to stop, because I was still too green to know the tricks of hitchhiking. So I walked each of the ten miles to Tigard, where finally one old farmer gave me a ride for all of 200 yards. On the way I walked by about 50 men lined up in what I found out later was a soup line, something I also hadn't heard about before.

I never made it to Tillamook. About a mile past Tigard, I asked a farmer what people were doing on Bull Mountain up behind his yard and learned that was Mr. Dono's "tater" digging. He then introduced me to his neighbor, Mr. Scott, a fine, good natured farmer, whose hired man had quit that morning. So I put in a full day's work milking his cows and digging potatoes. While he was having his supper he asked me if I had had anything to eat. I was hungry as a bear since I hadn't eaten since I left Portland at six that morning, but I said "Sure, I found an apple going to waste on the ground, so I picked it up, looked around to see that no one would see me stealing and ate it." I was sure glad he was good natured and gave me my dinner.

Mr. Scott called Mr. Dono, who asked me to come over to his place and offered to hire me for $10 a month and room and board. Since my other choice was $2.50 a day digging potatoes, which wouldn't last more than a few more days around Tigard, we agreed on $10 during the winter and $20 a month for the summer. When I told my brother Roderick about my job he came out and took a similar one with Mr. Bill Holtz a few miles away. It lasted for the next five years.

I worked for Dono only for about a year, until the fall of 1931. Soon after my wages went back down to the winter rate of $10, Dono had me help the neighbors with the later digging but collected the $2.50 a day for himself, claiming he was paying me steady wages and even let me use his digging fork. That upset me so much I quit and went back to Portland.

State Emergency Relief Work

BACK IN PORTLAND, I STAYED WITH Oscar and Lotie Hoch, acquaintances who were friends of Mrs. Kemmel, in their house at 4314 N. Mississippi street. They were well-known musicians in Portland who conducted the orchestra at Cotillion Hall [today's Crystal Ballroom] on W. Burnside street. In return for a roof over my head, I painted their home which later became a music conservatory and historic building. And just about then, my mother got a ride to Portland from Riverdale, Maryland, to live with me.

So how was I going to feed her, or myself, on nothing? Mrs. Hoch suggested that I see Mrs. Kemmel who now had a job signing up people for State Emergency Relief Administration (SERA) work. Because I had to support my mother, I qualified for two weeks of work a month—anyway better than nothing.

Now I was wading in the Columbia River Slough up to my hips, cutting brush so we could put sacks of sawdust soaked with oil along its banks to kill mosquito larva. We burned the brush in the pouring rain and at first I couldn't believe my eyes that it burned as wet and green as it was. Many people were getting this much needed relief work and I began to listen to some of them talking about the Depression.

Next, I went to work tearing down old buildings and docks at $2 a day, but I didn't even get paid that for several years. So while I couldn't even buy my food, my mother got another house cleaning job and I rented her an old Grange caretakers' house in Tigard for almost nothing. When she went to live there I got the job of painting the roof shingles on the Hoch's house. It was a steep roof and not knowing how to build a proper scaffold, I had some hair raising experiences up there.

One day I was dangling dangerously by a rope on that roof when Sylvia Tuaminen came by and saw me. That night we met at the Finnish Federation meeting, danced and got acquainted.

Back to the Land

THE NEXT SPRING (1931) I went out to Charlie Lieberman's farm for $30 a month and room and board and my mother worked as a housekeeper for a woman in Tigard for room and board and $10 a month spending money. When haying season came around, I went to work for Harry Kuhni out at Yamhill. I was very strong and in good physical shape so I got to buck hay bales 11 high. They averaged about 165 pounds a bale but some weighed as much as 210 pounds so to stairstep those bales took some doing.

Harry was a light- or medium-weight wrestler and wanted me to play around with him but, not having any training in that line, I didn't take a chance on breaking my neck. I could box, though, and tried out against one of the men there. He was a hard hitter, so I didn't encourage any more of that: I still have a scar from that encounter.

My mother lost her job in Tigard so I was able to get Harry to hire her to cook for our baling crew. They would scare her out of her wits with harmless garter snakes. She also bragged to the men about how I broke wild horses back in Alberta, but didn't tell them I trained them slowly and with kindness—not the rough and wild way the old time westerners did. So she put me on the spot to show my stuff to the baling crew and that didn't work out very well. Harry's horses were rough and ready and, I must say, fearless. After my mother's buildup, I was embarrassed.

During the winter of 1932-33, in partnership with Mr. and Mrs. Stowie and their daughter, I rented a place on Parret Mountain east of Newberg and later a stump farm two miles southeast of the town. Our idea was to beat the Depression by going "back to the land." The Stowies led me to believe they owned the cows, pigs, goats, chickens, turkeys and rabbits outright but when the creditors came to take away the cows in the spring of 1932, I learned they had gone deeply into debt to buy the livestock. In fact the cows and pigs were owned by my old boss Harry Khunie and my partners hadn't even rented the land—they just squatted on it. So we lost everything.

Wheat Harvest in Wasco

In the summer of 1933, my brother and I decided to go to eastern Oregon to take in the harvest. We took my old Model T, and the strong winds there did a good job of blowing us around. In Wasco we got jobs sack-jigging on a horse drawn combine; I'd jig the sacks and my brother would sew them. At $3.50 a day and room and board the pay wasn't very good but better than nothing. Roderick got to drive a string of about 16 horses pulling a wheat thresher. When you could sell wheat in that harvest at all, you got 25 cents a bushel. After most of the Oregon wheat was harvested, we moved up to Washington. But in the Hoovervilles we found there were 10 men for every job, and it seemed one of them always got to the jobs before we did.

We were about to run out of gas money when I got some sack needles from a guy for 65 cents and practiced sewing sacks of hay so I could get the feel of it. So the next farmer who came to town asked if anyone was a fast sewer since the last six men had failed to keep up with his fast 48-inch separator. "You bet I can do it," I told him, not letting on I had never sewn sacks at the side of a separator. So the next morning I went to work and before the day was over another fellow and I sewed some 800 sacks between us. We had to do our own jigging, and after sewing the sack had to shoulder it up three tiers on a flatbed truck. Not having worked so hard in a long time, I was so tired I went to sleep on the straw stack by the separator. It was a moonlit night and I soon woke up itching all over. Taking off my shirt I saw what I thought were lice on the collar but it turned out to be chaff that had worked into my pores. I finally found some black gear grease, smeared it over my neck and ankles and slept sound as a log the rest of the night. I kept that job at $3.50 a day until the harvest was over and I had enough money to drive back home through Spokane (where I stopped and listened to a socialist open forum debate among Wobblies, Socialists and Communists) to Portland, where, with my mother and Sylvia, we went out picking raspberries. Some we canned for the coming winter, and some we got paid pin money to pick. I also worked on a few odd jobs like digging taters.

The Unemployed Councils & the Oregon Workers Alliance

BUT SOON ENOUGH SYLVIA AND I got the idea of getting married, and so we did. We decided to settle down in Portland because we had made many good friends by then by going to meetings at the Finnish (Finn) Hall (and in fact we went to almost all the public meetings in town) because the Depression was now, in the fall of 1933, on in full force and we got interested in what caused it and what could be done to get us out of it. So many men were unemployed that they filled freight trains, riding the rods to find work, and setting up makeshift camps called "Hoovervilles" out of old boards, sheets of tin and anything else they could find for shelter. These were usually near a railroad where they could build fires and cook a stew and catch a train out of town. The soup lines were getting longer and more businesses and factories were closing. There were suicides and bank failures and many people lost their life savings. People who had worked hard all their lives were facing real hunger and actual starvation.

So this fall, farm work with room and board was not enough to meet the new obligation I had made. Since I was married, I was able to apply for relief and for a few months Sylvia and I got rent and grocery orders. But when I was out trying to do someone else out of a job by being the best "wage slave" for a boss, I wondered how the man I beat out was making it. These questions attracted me to meetings where I heard demands that if "private enterprise" couldn't create jobs then the government had to be responsible to put America back to work. Up to now I was kind of an individualist but now the conditions caused me to do a lot of thinking and I decided individuals couldn't get this message across to the politicians by themselves. So as Sylvia and I were both interested in the same program, we decided it was better to be fighting together and our duty, as we saw it, was to get people jobs so they could live normal lives. From that decision, Sylvia and I went on to put our lot in with others and we joined the Unemployed Councils of Oregon, part of a national movement to create jobs with public money.

The Unemployed Councils also took up the problems of families that were out of work or on relief. We had committees that would first ask the city not to turn off the water for those who couldn't pay the bills, but if they did, we would turn it back on ourselves. Finally, we won when the City stopped turning the water off. We also investigated cases where families were turned down for relief and took them to city commissioners or county officials. If they wouldn't help, we organized demonstrations at their offices to publicize the poor families. That often got a better response from the politicians.

That winter, in January of 1934, the Unemployed Councils and the Civic Emergency Federation, which represented people on relief jobs, joined together in the Oregon Workers Alliance. By then, a broader organization was needed because of all the New Deal programs starting up. In addition to the Works Progress Administration (WPA), we had the Youth Workers Administration (sic), the Federal Writers, Theater and Arts Projects, and all of these needed support and a push to keep them on the straight and narrow. That's what the Oregon Workers Alliance tried to do, and we gained recognition from the staff of relief stations because we visited the homes of the families whose cause we took up and our facts could be verified and relied upon. Of course, we faced the opposition of employers who wanted cheap labor and opposed relief because it made the unemployed less desperate to take starvation wages. And some politicians who tried to make a name for themselves by promising to cut relief spending on what they called "lazy bums" who didn't want to work.

The Oregon Workers Alliance proposed a minimum wage of 50 cents an hour and union scale at any employer whose workers belonged to a union. We even helped organize the relief workers themselves into an AFL union. We boycotted restaurants which discriminated against colored people and, in general, our slogan was to do something for the working class every single day—while not rejecting middle-class allies.

Back in Tigard

IN 1934, SYLVIA AND I rented a place in Tigard, where on top of the relief, I did some seasonal work for the farmer Mr. Lieberman. I was on the local relief welfare grievance committee. Then the local relief office told me that, since I was "able bodied" and had a car I had to take a job splitting wood because they didn't have the funds to continue paying our rent or groceries anymore. So I borrowed splitting wedges, a sledge and a tent (since the weather was good) and we went up into the woods. I started to work and my wife cooked the bacon as I brought it home because she wasn't a wood cutter. It's mighty hard work for someone who weighed only 130 pounds, as she did.

Pay was $1 a cord for trimming, splitting and piling, but it was old growth timber and most of it was grained like a rope—the hardest to split of any wood I had come across. I worked as hard as I could but couldn't even cut a cord a day. On top of that, I found the harder I worked, the more I had to eat and we couldn't buy enough to feed us from the Tigard store. I even borrowed a power splitting gun and still couldn't make a cord a day.

The Longshore Strike of 1934 & the DeJong Case

IN THE SUMMER OF 1934, when the longshoremen in Portland had their big strike many of us unemployed came to their picket lines and told them we supported their demands and would not scab on them. I was on relief when their appeal came for food for the Longshoremens' soup kitchen. Could we help? Yes, we could. We went to the farmers and quickly got a full truck full of garden vegetables, which was appreciated by the strikers since Portland Mayor Joe "Bloody Shirt" Carson was trying to break the strike. The city's big businessmen hired scabs and, with Carson's police providing protection, tried to run the picket lines at Terminal Four in St. Johns. On "Bloody Wednesday," July 11, they shot and wounded four longshoremen and their leader, Matt Meehan, confronted Carson in City Hall with their bloodstained shirts.

A protest meeting was called for July 28 at a hall on SW Alder. The Police "Red Squad" came early and planted baseball bats and clubs so they could later claim falsely that the protest leaders advocated violence. One of the speakers protesting police violence on Bloody Wednesday was

Dirk DeJong, a single war veteran born in Holland who was a leader of the Bonus March on Washington in 1933 and a working class Communist. As he spoke the Red Squad raided the peaceful meeting and arrested Dirk and 10 others under the Oregon Criminal Syndicalist Act, enacted in the "Red Scare" of 1919. DeJong was sentenced in November to seven years in the Salem pen by Portland Judge Jacob Kenzler. His lawyers—Harry Grossman, Ben Anderson and especially Irvin Goodman—got the US Supreme Court to reverse Dirk's conviction. They did a good job done with very little money. The now famous DeJong Decision proved to some that although the legal costs were usually out of reach of most workers, with the backing of a strong organization, some of them could get their free speech rights protected even by a capitalist court.

And where was I on July 28? I had been invited to come to the hall in support of the longshoremen but I had just finished a long hard day's work and was too tired to travel the ten miles to Portland and so I stayed home. I suppose if I had gone I would have been arrested along with the 11 others and maybe deported a lot sooner than I was.

A Strike in the Hop Fields

Since I couldn't earn enough to live on from wood cutting around Tigard, I got desperate, and really sore about being cut off the relief rolls. Faced with going hungry, I went back to the relief office with my demands and, to my surprise, they gave me an order for groceries and suggested I look for work in the hop fields near Salem. So I loaded up the old Model T, filled both running boards with pots, pans, chairs and car tools, tied our bed springs and mattress on top and headed south to pick hops. On the way, I wondered what I would have done if the relief office had turned me down for food. How many others were in my position without a car? Some men I talked to told me they would have got hold of a gun if it came to starving. I think there were many poor and unemployed people who did take to crime just for the right to live. There were many bank robberies and even some violence against the relief workers who were doing their job of keeping as many off the rolls as possible.

But as someone already known in the fight for relief, I would have tried to rally the unemployed to demonstrate since the relief offices hated the publicity. I believed in facing obstacles in an organized way and not by force and violence.

It was in the fall of 1934 that my wife and I started looking for work in the hop yards several miles north of Salem. They had to be picked

Wool being unloaded at Terminal #4, July 12, 1931. Negative number OrHi 49074. Courtesy Oregon Historical Society.

before the rains came, and the weather was nice as my trusty Model T purred along the dirt road with its heavy load. Since I had been a car mechanic I always kept it in good shape because I knew the Ford was a big advantage when you didn't have steady work and had to travel from job to job. On the other hand, without a car I wouldn't have had to take the woodcutting job and be cut off relief.

I saw lots of workers picking hops and stopped the car. Mr. Goully and his son hired me. Sylvia and I were shown a cabin with a stove to cook on and a water tap outside. But the water was alkaline and it caused us problems later when Sylvia got sick from the bad water and I didn't feel good myself when the doctor charged us $4 for a checkup and some medicine.

We picked all the next day, filling large gunny sacks with about 100 pounds of hops for a crew that weighed, loaded them into trucks and drove them to market. We then went to a small store nearby and charged all the food we could, but it became clear that even with both of us picking all day we couldn't do much better than break even after buying enough to eat. Then we heard that hop yard workers at nearby Independence had gone out on strike for $1.50 per 100 pounds.

A few days later, we went out to work at about 6:45 in the morning. A barber whose name I've forgotten came up to me and said, "There's a strike on at Goully's. Aren't you going to stay off work today?" I told him that's the first I heard of it and since the other pickers were all starting work, the strike seemed to be pretty poorly organized. The barber was the organizer, so I suggested he call a meeting at noon in the fields to talk about a strike because I was afraid it would fizzle out otherwise. He agreed and we passed the word around the hop yard.

But when noon came around only a few pickers came to the middle of the field, together with the boss, Mr. Goully, himself. Thad Grub, a man who knew me from the Unemployed Councils demonstrations, asked me, "What do we do now?" and I could see that because the workers were afraid of sticking their necks out in front of the boss my plan was not going to work. I felt responsible for holding the strike back that morning and reminded myself that I promised to do something for working people every day. And here was my chance to do something.

So I told Thad to go around one side of the field and I would go around the other, and shout at the top of our voices for all pickers to come to a meeting at the camp and decide whether to strike for higher wages. We would vote the strike up or down.

Our calls brought every one of the 200 pickers to the camp except for a man and his wife who were friends of the Goullys, but with a little coaxing even they showed up later. I called the meeting to order and was elected chairman. After I gave a little talk about prosperity needing to start from the bottom with working people because it would never trickle down from the top, the pickers voted to strike. They drew up a demand for $1.50 per hundred pounds after I told them that Goully was getting $16 a ton for his hops this year—much higher than last year—but we were getting only $1 per hundred, the same as last year. The service crew demanded a 25 cents an hour raise.

Then someone reported that one family of Jehovah's Witnesses was still working in the fields and the strike committee was instructed to go out and ask them to stop and join the rest of us. While I was trying to persuade them not to get their hops weighed up, the State Police arrived from Salem to break our strike. Mr. Goully was pointing out members of the strike committee but all of them, including the barber, were surrounded by hundreds of pickers who protected them from arrest. But I was just getting back to the camp alone and the police handcuffed me like a common criminal and tossed me roughly into the back of their police car. My wife was having a fit and the police tried but failed to arrest anyone else. The strikers told the cops I was just doing my job as their elected representative and so they better arrest all of them.

Someone must have called off the police because while I was handcuffed in the back of their car they told me that since I was new at organizing a strike, they had some good advice for me: don't ask for too much. The cops tried to get me to settle for a 5 cent raise. After I told them we were asking for 50 cents, they told me they heard Goully would offer 30 cents, and let me out of the car to tell the strikers. I put the offer to them and they accepted and we all went back to work. Our strike lasted only two hours.

Fixing Streets in Portland

WHEN HOP PICKING WAS OVER, Sylvia and I went back to Portland and rented a house at 2828 N. Kerby Avenue in the Albina neighborhood for $10 a month. I got on relief again and was put to work tearing up streets and putting them back in shape again. We had a machine to dig up the streets and trucks to spread gravel but we had to use a shovel and wheelbarrow to level the gravel. So we shoveled all day long—leveling one hole after another which wouldn't have been necessary if we had had a grader. Though a machine would have finished the work in half the time and done a better job, we couldn't complain because we needed work and didn't care how it was done. The whole idea was to create jobs and make us work off our rent and grocery orders from the relief office.

It was now the fall of 1934 and the rains had begun. I remember the foreman telling us to work harder because there were busybodies in the neighborhood complaining that relief workers were lazy and leaning on their shovels. But the truth is that some of our work was a credit to the workers and is still admired today, like Timberline Lodge and the Johnson Creek riprap. We worked for two weeks, and then were off three weeks when other men took our places. Relief was just enough to keep us from going hungry if we pinched pennies, and we wouldn't have gotten that unless the public had put pressure on the politicians. The papers kept saying, "Recovery is just around the corner," but it wasn't.

But there was also another side to the relief work: it could not compete with "free enterprise." That's why when we cleared old growth timber to build roads, we had to burn it rather than sell it on the market or use it ourselves. So, like farmers paid to plow under every third row of cotton or slaughter pigs to keep up prices, we burned hundreds of cut up cords of the best wood in a terrible waste of labor and raw materials just to protect the profits of private industry. But since we got paid enough to live, all we could do was wonder about how much our society wasted during the Great Depression.

We also wondered why workers had to accept wages so low they couldn't pay their grocery bills, while businesses didn't have to invest money unless they thought they would earn big profits. The Oregon Workers Alliance, had already called for the 50 cent minimum or union scale, and refused to scab when the AFL unions were on strike. We boycotted and publicized restaurants which refused to serve colored workers and in general followed that policy of doing what we could for the working class every day.

The national Workers Alliance called a big strike for the 50 cent minimum wage in every state where there was an organization and we won it in only one day. Despite opposition by some right wing and anti-union groups in Oregon who tried to start fights on the picket lines, all relief work projects would pay 50 cents from now on.

Picketing Fascist Ships in Portland

The OWA was not just a bread and butter outfit. By 1935 we were also concerned about the rise of fascism in Germany and Italy and the danger of war, so we affiliated with the League Against War and Fascism. At that time, many American corporations were doing big business with facets countries, who were throwing Communists, socialists and democrats into concentration camps. So we tried to organize boycotts against the Fascists.

We got word that one of Mussolini's ships, the *Cellini*, was headed to Portland to pick up supplies for his war against Ethiopia, after Seattle longshoremen refused to load her. I got a call from a friend in Astoria one afternoon, telling me the ship had just cleared the Columbia River bar and asking me to organize a picket line to prevent it from loading. I borrowed a big car, recruited a driver and seven other men and we went out to meet it at the Dominion Dock at 4pm, but it didn't show up. We then were told it was to dock at Terminal 4 in St. Johns that evening at 8. We got there and put up our signs declaring the League was protesting the loading of supplies to support the war against Ethiopia.

Soon a hired guard came over with two vicious-looking police dogs on leashes, told us we were on private property and ordered us to move our line about three-quarters of a mile to the outer gates of the Terminal. Then a carload of company goons drove up to beat us up but luck was on our side that day because they were followed by 10 more pickets and we had them outnumbered. We were ready to defend ourselves and our cause very well, and they took off as if something had hit them.

We picketed for two and a half days and our line turned back many gangs of longshoremen who understood the issue and supported us. For that, a lot of credit went to the progressive leadership of the Portland local of the International Longshoremen's and Warehousemen's Union which was established in a strike the year before. We also had arguments with some of the Italian ship's officers who knew English and who claimed Mussolini was bringing "civilization" to the backward Ethiopians!

Finally, the ship owners persuaded a few longshoremen to cross our picket line, so we were only able to delay loading the ship. We told ourselves that we'll win some and lose some, but we felt satisfaction that we had tried to act for peace over the opposition of our own government and those who called us "just a bunch of Reds." We were right and we knew it.

Later the same year, the same "Bloody Shirt" Carson invited the officers of one of Hitler's battleships to wine and dine with city officials. Many anti-fascists picketed that ship too and this time Carson's cops arrested quite a few of them. My wife came down and warned me to be careful and I heeded her and they didn't get me that time. We also protested the shipping of scrap metal from Portland to Japan, where it was used in the war against China.

Fighting for Relief

AFTER WE GOT THE 50 CENT minimum wage, we had to fight even harder for relief money orders for rent and groceries when we weren't on work relief. The relief workers, usually young women, were always trying to find some reason to cut you off the rolls. If you didn't argue back and have someone to take your side, you usually lost your orders and all but occasional day jobs. The unemployed couldn't count on anything so when people needed help, I was often asked by the Albina branch of the OWA to serve on its family case committees. Our job was to investigate cases of people being cut off the rolls and then demand their reinstatement if it was justified.

One evening a man, about 40 years old and saying he was very religious, came to an Albina branch meeting and asked for help to settle his dispute with the relief office. So as usual we elected a committee to investigate—this time Art Foster, Lillian and myself. He told us he had just moved from Salem, where he was threatened with being committed to the insane asylum in Pendleton because of his argument with the relief office there. In his home we noticed he had a very large Bible on the table and half a box of corn flakes was the only food in the house. We knew that one of our most active members had been committed on a single doctor's word that she was "paranoid," and we had to raise $75 at a public meeting to hire a lawyer to get her out. In those times, it was easy to understand that desperate people might get mad at those who were condemning them to homelessness and hunger, so were inclined to believe the man from Salem without much checking. He told us that the Portland relief office turned down his family because he hadn't been a resident here for six months.

We did verify that he had been turned down and then went to Mr. Shull, the City Commissioner most sympathetic to people turned down by relief, and he trusted us to investigate the actual facts of the case. Commissioner Shull sent us to the Sunshine Division of the Police Bureau who gave the man emergency food. The next day he received a $10 money order for groceries and was reinstated on the relief rolls.

I investigated another family that was refused relief. When I visited them at home I was shocked to see with my own eyes they were cooking a dog in a big stew kettle. I immediately called the newspapers and the police and the OWA told the relief office they would make a photograph of the scene public. Since they didn't want the people of Portland to know that some of their fellow citizens had to kill their pet to feed themselves, the relief office quickly changed their minds about that family. We had many desperate cases, but only one like this!

My Family Grows

Ever since the fall of 1934 Sylvia and I were getting more concerned about the expected increase in our family. Like millions of others on relief (as welfare was called), we hoped for the best and expected the worst. Whether we would have one child, twins and even more come to life, we had to go on. Sylvia got regular checkups through the relief office and we prepared to go the Multnomah County Hospital for the birth. Our son James arrived there on the morning of April 14, 1935 and we were really happy that everything went nicely with a medical doctor in attendance. I visited Sylvia and James every day at the hospital and after 10 days my wife and baby came home to Kerby Street. Jimmy became our main attraction, especially after he began to notice the world around him. I have many memories of watching him grow and hoping the world would be better for him.

My First Arrest

RIGHT AROUND THAT TIME the lumber and sawmill workers in the Northwest decided to strike for, as I remember, a 50-cents-a-day increase on their three dollars for an 8 hour day and union recognition. The lumber barons, of course, figured many of the unemployed could be persuaded to scab and they got help from the relief administration. Hundreds of men on the relief rolls in Portland who had done any previous work in the woods were told to answer the ads for scabs or be cut off, and the OWA received more and more complaints about that.

But this time the relief offices began to refuse to recognize the OWA grievance committees. So we organized sit-ins at every relief office in Portland by groups of at least four protesters and refused to leave until they held hearings on our cases. They called the cops instead and we were arrested on disorderly conduct charges when we continued our sit ins and were taken down to SW Second and Oak, where our lawyers got us out with suspended $5 fines. As soon as we got out, we went right back out to the relief offices and sat in again. This went on for another day before they decided they didn't want us telling the papers they were herding scabs and agreed to grant relief orders to workers who refused to help break the timber strike. The OWA won because we were able to get large numbers of people to protest. When deep cuts for relief spending were announced, ten thousand people marched in the streets of Portland to protest.

Arrested Again

A FEW MONTHS LATER I was passing by the Albina relief office and saw Mrs. Minny Shank, a single mother of 7-and 8-year olds, picketing on behalf of families cut off the rolls. I asked her if the police had been bothering her and she said no, everything had been peaceful all morning. She asked me if I could take her place while she went home to feed her two children, who were coming from school at noon. Some friends had warned me to be extra careful about being arrested because I wasn't a US citizen—something I hadn't thought about much before—although I filed for naturalization (my first papers) soon after coming to Portland in early 1930. But I figured that since nothing had happened to Mrs.

Shank for four hours, I could take the chance and, besides, I didn't want her to think I was shirking my duty and principles.

So I put on her picket sign, which was called a "sandwich" because you put it over your shoulders so people could read it front and back, and started walking because the law said you could picket only if you kept moving. I wasn't there 10 minutes before a police car pulled up and arrested me for illegal picketing, took me back downtown where our lawyer, Irwin Goodman, once again got me off with a suspended fine. I'm sure the Albina office, where both Mrs. Shank and I got our money orders, called the cops because the office supervisor knew I was foreign born and an arrest would teach me a lesson.

Family Problems

It was tough on anyone on relief, but it was especially hard for the younger families with small children. Parents started to blame each other for being out of work rather than the "free enterprise" system itself. Some people began to believe the propaganda that they were lazy and not as good as those lucky enough to have jobs—even if they worked hard for very little. Families quarreled and my own family was no exception.

I may have been spending too much of my time fighting for other poor people who needed help, but once I decided to apply myself to one of life's battles, I did it wholeheartedly. It seems my wife Sylvia didn't see things that way and she complained I was neglecting our home life. She didn't even give me any warning when she asked me to drive her to visit her father in Greyland, Washington. After a few days I had to go back to Portland, but she said that she and Jimmy would stay a few more days. A few days later she wrote to say she wasn't coming back and I was really upset; I felt most terrible.

I wrote her many letters imploring her to come back, wondering how she could make out without me, whether she planned to team up with someone else or what she planned to do. But before too long, I was greatly relieved when Sylvia and Jimmy came back home.

Discrimination

I also got involved in the cases of some colored people that were more serious than Portland restaurants refusing to serve them. Vernon Jordan, a Negro from Klamath Falls, was framed on a murder charge and sentenced to be hanged in the prison in Salem. The International Labor Defense, which I supported, helped Irwin Goodman get his sentence commuted to life in prison, and we held many meetings to raise money for his defense. Later on, we also had local meetings for the Scottsboro Boys and Angelo Herndon, who were framed in the South.

My First Brush with Immigration

ON MARCH 9,1936, I was working on a WPA project at Johnson Creek in southeast Portland. This was one of the really worthwhile projects designed to put many unemployed to work because we lined the banks of the creek with stones to keep the spring floods away from the surrounding residential neighborhoods. We called it "rip rapping Johnson Creek." Of course, it couldn't compete with private industry and we couldn't use any heavy machinery except for pickup trucks that some of the unemployed owned—and which broke down every minute.

I was pushing a wheel barrow that morning when a stranger with an armed guard walked up to my crew boss, Tom Spears, and I saw Tom point to me. The stranger came over, called me aside, and asked in an unfriendly voice: "Are you Hamish MacKay?" It turned out he was Roy Noreen ("Mister Noreen to you," he told me), the head of the Immigration Service in Portland and he wanted to know when and where I had entered the US from Canada and whether I was a "Communist."

I told him I wasn't but also that I had to get back to work now, and he said that if I didn't come to his office and answer his questions he would come back after me.

At the time, we had moved to another rented house at 5425 SE Henderson Street. For $10 a month, we had hot and cold water, a wood stove, a flush toilet and bathtub. Our son was almost a year old and we were barely scrimping by without a penny to waste. When I got home that night Sylvia was terribly upset because Noreen had also been there with his bullying manner and she had told him where I was working. Worse than that, he spotted some copies of the Daily Worker newspaper in the house, which he told Sylvia was a Communist paper and could get me deported from the US. Instead of standing up and telling Noreen it wasn't his business whether we wanted to read a working class paper, she was so frightened she said the papers weren't ours and had been left on our porch that morning. I tried to assure her we were law-abiding people and our only crime was fighting for the rights in the US Constitution and we had many friends to help us. But that night I spent a long time in the Central Library at SW 10th and Yamhill reading up on immigration laws, although I wouldn't have believed anyone who told me then the outcome of that day's events would be my deportation 24 years later on November 18,1960.

Eventually Noreen interrogated me in his office in May and September of 1936, and I put in my second papers in July. But Mr. Langoe, a friend who was active in the Oregon Commonwealth Federation, told me my case had been "salted down" and getting my citizenship would require a really good lawyer. In any case, my next contact with Immigration wasn't until late in 1940 when everyone had to register for the Draft.

My First Steady Job in Oregon

My brother Roderick had gotten married in 1935 and managed to get a regular job at the B.P. John furniture factory on SW Macadam Avenue. In the fall of 1936 he told me there might be an opening there so I showed up at the plant gate every morning for two weeks until Old Man John figured out I needed a job real bad. I was husky and strong, and with my brother pulling for me I guess John figured he could give me a try.

I started on October 3rd and I was kind of glad to be doing some steady work after more than six years in Oregon. With all the wood dust, it wasn't very healthy and I got only 35 cents an hour for a 48-hour week, five-and-a-half days a week with some overtime but not much. I had more expenses for work clothes and driving to work, so it wasn't much better than relief. Still, it was a real job and I kept it for over six years until January, 1942, when I went to work for the war effort in the Swan Island shipyard. I joined Local 1482 of the Furniture Workers, an AFL Carpenters union, which included the Lumber and Sawmill Workers. The local had its office in room 211 of the Portland Labor Temple at SW 4th and Jefferson and by 1938, I was elected its Recording Secretary.

When the CIO started up, the AFL started to demand that the furniture factory had to have six separate craft unions, which sounded crazy to us who worked in an industrial plant. But a major and bitter fight developed between the two labor federations and it seemed to us all that money and energy would be better spent fighting the bosses. So my brother and I, as delegates to the Central Labor Council, voted against the expulsion of the CIO proposed by the AFL leadership—and for our vote we and 36 other delegates were expelled from the Council.

Right after that the leaders of the Furniture Workers Unions talked me into resigning as the local's secretary because of my trouble with the citizenship papers. Others also warned me to lie low because Immigration usually targets union leaders first for deportation. So I withdrew and the members elected a replacement, but I still got a pretty good vote.

Gary Snyder
(1930-)

Gary Snyder was born in San Francisco but soon moved with his parents to a farm north of Seattle, where he spent most of his youth. He graduated from Reed College in 1951; from 1951 to 1956, he attended Indiana University and the University of Berkeley; from 1956 to 1968, he studied in Japan, where he pursued Mahayana-Vajrayana Buddhism. The author of fifteen books of poetry, Snyder is best known along with contemporaries Jack Kerouac and Allen Ginsberg as members of the Beat movement in literature. "The Late Snow & Lumber Strike of the Summer of Fifty-Four" was copyrighted by the author in 1965. One of his lesser-known poems, it nevertheless reflects many of the themes in his ongoing examination of the working life.

THE LATE SNOW AND LUMBER STRIKE OF THE SUMMER OF FIFTY-FOUR

Whole towns shut down
          hitching the Coast road, only gypos
Running their beat trucks, no logs on
Gave me rides. Loggers all gone fishing
Chainsaws in a pool of cold oil
On back porches of ten thousand
Split-shake houses, quiet in summer rain.
Hitched north all of Washington
Crossing and re-crossing the passes
Blown like dust, no place to work.

Climbing the steep ridge below Shuksan
          clumps of pine
          float out the fog
No place to think or work
          drifting.

On Mt. Baker, alone
In a gully blazing snow:
Cities down the long valleys west
Thinking of work, but here,
Burning in sun-glare

Below a wet cliff, above a frozen lake,
The whole Northwest on strike
Black burners cold,
The green-chain still,
I must turn and go back:
            caught on a snowpeak
            between heaven and earth
And stand in lines in Seattle.
Looking for work.

Robert Wrigley
(1951-)

Robert Wrigley teaches at Lewis-Clark State College in Lewiston, Idaho, and lives in Clarkston, Washington, with his wife and son. His work has appeared in the *Anthology of Magazine Verse and Yearbook of American Poetry*. He received two poetry fellowships from the National Endowment for the Arts and won the 1985 Poetry Society of America's Celia B. Wagner Award. His collection of poetry entitled *The Sinking of Clay City* (1979) explores life in a mining community.

THE SINKING OF CLAY CITY

When the last mine closed
and its timbers turned pliable as treesap,
the town began to tilt, to slide
back into its past like a wave.

Old men, caught by the musk
of seeping gas, arrived at the mainshafts
hours before dawn. Their soft hands
turned the air like handles on new picks.

Here and there a house split,
a cracked wishbone,
and another disappeared like crawlspace
behind a landslide.

So the townspeople descended the sloping entrances,
found them filled with a green
noxious water. Each drank a little
and forgot about the sun.

Some dug at rusted beercans
or poked at a drowned rat, more patient
than dedicated archaeologists,
and waited for their other lives to join them.

Tess Gallagher
(1943-)

Born in Port Angeles, Washington, well-known poet Tess Gallagher is the author of several books. "Black Money" is from *Instructions to the Double*. In it, the author focuses on growing up in a tense working-class milltown family.

Black Money

His lungs heaving all day in a sulphur mist,
then dusk, the lunch pail torn from him
before he reaches the house, his children
a cloud of swallows about him.
At the stove in the tumbled rooms, the wife,
her back the wall he fights most, and she
with no weapon but silence
and to keep him from the bed.

In their sleep the mill hums and turns
at the edge of water. Blue smoke
swells the night and they drift
from the graves they have made for each other,
float out from the open-mouthed sleep
of their children, past banks and businesses,
the used car lots, liquor store, the swings in the park.

The mill burns on, now a burst of cinders,
now whistles screaming down the bay, saws jagged
in half light. Then like a whip
the sun across the bed, windows high with mountains
and the sleepers fallen to pillows
as gulls fall, tilting
against their shadows on the log booms.
Again the trucks shudder the wood-framed houses
passing to the mill. My father
snorts, splashes in the bathroom,
throws open our doors to cowboy music
on the radio. Hearts are cheating,
somebody is alone, there's blood in Tulsa.
Out the back yard the night-shift men rattle

the gravel in the alley going home.
My father fits goggles to his head.

From his pocket he takes anything metal,
the pearl-handled jack knife, a ring of keys,
and for us, black money shoveled
from the sulphur pyramids heaped in the distance
like yellow gold. Coffee bottle tucked in his armpit
he swaggers past the chicken coop,
a pack of cards at his breast.
In a fan of light beyond him
the *Kino Maru* pulls out for Seattle,
some black star climbing
the deep globe of his eye.

Henry Carlile
(1934-)

Henry Carlile is an accomplished poet whose work includes three books of poetry and numerous articles and reviews that have appeared in nationally and regionally prominent magazines and journals. His poems have appeared in numerous periodicals and have been included in seventeen anthologies. He is the recipient of the Oregon Arts Commission Poetry Fellowship (1994), the Pushcart Prize (1992), and the *Crazyhorse* Poetry Award (1988). He now works as a professor of English and teaches creative writing and literature at Portland State University. "Graveyard Shift" (1994) is based on his experience working in a paper mill.

Graveyard Shift

I never met you but heard the story often
of the boots and wallet and the note
beside the chipper chute, no explanation,
no clue why you died with your boots off
as if you had merely gone to bed with blades
like a forty-foot hemlock chipped in seconds.
I imagine you were lonely or betrayed
or afflicted with some terminal illness—
who knows what?—or with the need to disappear
so completely no trace might improve
the claim of your absence.
Unable to cheat death you could at least
cheat those of us who make a living from it.
I do you a disservice then in writing this:

asking why you chose that way,
a brief red stain in a blur of chips,
riding the high-speed conveyer, poured
level to level, rising above us until
you dropped into the chip bin and from there
into the tall iron digester,
cooked with steam and caustic soda
and bleached white as an angel, unrecoverable
from the paper machine and the paper cutters,
reamed and packaged and sold—a rag-bond

reduction of your former self, for business,
for profit, for this present monstrous need
to scribble something out of nothing
and resurrect you, emptied from the page.

Joseph Millar
(1945 -)

Joseph Millar left a job as a telephone installation foreman to teach and concentrate on writing poetry. His poems, which focus mainly on the workplace and family, have appeared in such literary journals as *Ploughshares*, *DoubleTake*, and *Shenandoah*. He lives with his family in Eugene, Oregon.

TAX MAN

Thunder Bob used to drive for Consolidated Freight
before the small bones began to press against the nerves
in his lower back and his right foot went numb.
Now he slouches by a computer in suspenders and a red shirt,
grizzled forearms propped on a steel desk, doing my taxes

His wife watches the Simpson trial in the den
and he wants to get me done, squinting down
at last year's forms and muttering to himself.
He leans his thick neck back, looks up at the Cadillac sign
and the photo of his youngest grandchild, a Chesterfield
burning between his fingers.
You need more write-offs, he says,
peering sideways through the smoke. Since
you can't afford a house, why not have another kid, eh?
Rain blowing in off the bay rattles the windows
and the branches of the pin oaks moan in the dim light.
He knows my wife moved out last year. The kids
I've got are waiting, eating leftover Chinese by the TV.

You watch, he tells me. Soon there'll be no more
Social security. I can hear the lawyers' voices
quarrel through the airwaves in the next room
and I think sometimes in winter a hunched
mudcaked creature prowls the landscape.
Maybe it enters our homes through the cellar,
leaning over us in its ragged fur, the smell
quicklime and swamp water rising,
misting our faces as we sleep.

I drive home through the storm, wrestling the wind
in the center lane, and think of him standing on his dark porch,
telling me to be careful. Try to kick down more cash
into Retirement, he'd said, bracing himself
on his good foot. Nobody knows for sure
what the hell's going to happen.

Jesús María "El Flaco" Maldonado
(1944-)

Born in Mission, Texas, Jesús María "El Flaco" Maldonado has lived in Eastern Washington since 1970. One of the pioneer Chicano *movimiento* poets, he has published two books, *Sal pimienta y amor* and *In the Still of my Heart* (1993), which chronicles three decades of Raza survival. The following poem is written in memory of César Chávez's speech.

Memorias de César Chávez

Memorias calientitas
        cold Seattle, winter 1970
Voces unidas
        black eagle proudly flying
    waving high
        so high like our dreams
Bronze bodies pounding the pavement
        voces gritando, gritando
            JUSTICIA
César animando
        hombre de barro
            como esta tierra que nos nutre
        hombre de corazón tan grande
            como la CAUSA de tu gente
Hombre querido / sufrido
        regalando su corazón al pueblo
Aquí en Seattle
        con tu gente caminando
    gritando / animando

Brown memories
 keep ringing loudly / proudly
 today in Pullman, 1993
The voices keep singing in Union unison
 JUSTICIA pa' nuestra gente
Tu dedicación
 tu memoria
 keep flying high like an eagle
Y tu espíritu de bronce
 permanece calientito
 en cada noble corazón.

(12 de noviembre de 1993,
cub auditorium, Pullman, wa)

3

Working Ahead

Ernest Callenbach
(1929-)

Ernest Callenbach lives in Berkeley, California, and edits *Film Quarterly*. An advocate of ecologically friendly life styles, he frequently travels to lecture and promote his writings, including *Living Poor with Style*. Published in 1975 and set in 1999, his novel *Ecotopia* imagines a Pacific Northwest that has seceded from the United States and has constructed a stable-state government founded on ecologically friendly policies. The story is told from the point of view of outsider Will Weston, the first journalist allowed to investigate the goings-on in this brave new world. The excerpt included here suggests how workers generally might fare in an environmentally centered society, especially in a key Northwest industry.

From *Ecotopia*

The Ecotopian Economy: Fruit of Crisis

San Francisco, May 12. It is widely believed among Americans that the Ecotopians have become a shiftless and lazy people. This was the natural conclusion drawn after Independence, when the Ecotopians adopted a 20-hour work week. Yet even so no one in America, I think, has yet fully grasped the immense break this represented with our way of life, and even now it is astonishing that the Ecotopian legislature, in the first flush of power, was able to carry through such a revolutionary measure.

What was at stake, informed Ecotopians insist, was nothing less than the revision of the Protestant work ethic upon which America has been built. The consequences were plainly severe. In economic terms, Ecotopia was forced to isolate its economy from the competition of harder-working peoples. Serious dislocations plagued their industries for years. There was a drop in Gross National Product by more than a third. But the profoundest implications of the decreased work week were philosophical and ecological: mankind, the Ecotopians assumed, was not meant for production, as the 19th and early 20th centuries had believed. Instead, humans were meant to take their modest place in a seamless, stable-state web of living organisms, disturbing that web as little as possible. This would mean sacrifice of present consumption, but it would ensure future survival—which became an almost religious objective, perhaps akin to earlier doctrines of "salvation." People were to be happy not to the extent they dominated their fellow creatures on the earth, but to the extent they lived in balance with them.

This philosophical change may have seemed innocent on the surface. Its grave implications were soon spelled out, however. Ecotopian economists, who included some of the most highly regarded in the American nation, were well aware that the standard of living could only be sustained and increased by relentless pressure on work hours and worker productivity. Workers might call this "speed-up," yet without a slow but steady rise in labor output, capital could not be attracted or even held; financial collapse would quickly ensue.

The deadly novelty introduced into this accepted train of thought by a few Ecotopian militants was to spread the point of view that economic disaster was not identical with survival disaster for persons—and that, in particular, a financial panic could be turned to advantage if the new nation could be organized to devote its real resources of energy; knowledge, skills, and materials to the basic necessities of survival. If that were done, even a catastrophic decline in the GNP (which was, in their opinion, largely composed of wasteful activity anyway) might prove politically useful.

In short, financial chaos was to be not endured but deliberately engineered. With the ensuing flight of capital, most factories, farms and other productive facilities would fall into Ecotopian hands like ripe plums.

And in reality it took only a few crucial measures to set this dismal series of events in motion: the nationalization of agriculture; the announcement of an impending moratorium on oil-industry activities; the forced consolidation of basic retail network constituted by Sears, Penneys, Safeway, and a few other chains; and the passage of stringent conservation laws that threatened the profits of the lumber interests.

These moves, of course, set off an enormous clamor in Washington. Lobbyists for the various interests affected tried to commit the federal government to intervene militarily. This was, however, several months after Independence. The Ecotopians had established and intensively trained a nationwide militia, and air-lifted arms for it from France and Czechoslovakia. It was also believed that at the time of secession they had mined major Eastern cities with atomic weapons, which they had constructed in secret or seized from weapons research laboratories. Washington, therefore, although it initiated a ferocious campaign of economic and political pressure against the Ecotopians, and mined their harbors, finally decided against an invasion.

This news set in motion a wave of closures and forced sales of businesses—reminiscent, I was told, of what happened to the Japanese-

Americans who were interned in World War II. Members of distinguished old San Francisco families were forced to bargain on most unfavorable terms with representatives of the new regime. Properties going back to Spanish land-grant claims were hastily disposed of. Huge corporations, used to dictating policy in city halls and statehouses, found themselves begging for compensation and squirming to explain that their proper ties were actually worth far more than their declared tax value.

Tens of thousands of employees were put out of work as a consequence, and the new government made two responses to this. One was to absorb the unemployed in construction of the train network and of the sewage and other recycling facilities necessary to establish stable-state life Systems. Some were also put to work dismantling allegedly hazardous or unpleasant relics of the old order, like gas stations. The other move was to adopt 20 hours as the basic work week—which, in effect, doubled the number of jobs but virtually halved individual income. (There were, for several years, rigid price controls on all basic foods and other absolute necessities.)

Naturally, the transition period that ensued was hectic—though many people also remember it as exciting. It is alleged by many who lived through those times that no one suffered seriously from lack of food, shelter, clothing, or medical treatment—though some discomfort was widespread, and there were gross dislocations in the automobile and related industries, in the schools, and in some other social functions. Certainly many citizens were deprived of hard-earned comforts they had been used to: their cars, their prepared and luxury foods, their habitual new clothes and appliances, their many efficient service industries. These disruptions were especially severe on middle-aged people—though one now elderly man told me that he had been a boy in Warsaw during World War II, had lived on rats and moldy potatoes, and found the Ecotopian experience relatively painless. To the young, the disruptions seem to have had a kind of wartime excitement, and indeed sacrifices may have been made more palatable by the fear of attack from the United States. It is said by some, however, that the orientation of the new government toward basic biological survival was a unifying and reassuring force. Panic food hoarding, it is said, was rare. (The generosity with food which is such a feature of Ecotopian life today may have arisen at that time.)

Of course the region that comprises Ecotopia had natural advantages that made the transition easier. Its states had more doctors per capita, a higher educational level, a higher percentage of skilled workers, a greater number of engineers and other technicians, than most other parts of the Union. Its major cities, except for Seattle, were broadly based manufacturing and trading complexes that produced virtually all the necessities of life. Its universities were excellent and its resources for scientific research included a number of the topnotch facilities in the United States. Its temperate climate encouraged an outdoor style of life, and made fuel shortages caused by ecological policies an annoyance rather than the matter of life or death they would have been in the severe eastern Winters. The people were unusually well versed in nature and conservation lore, and experienced in camping and survival skills.

We cannot, however, ignore the political context in which the transition took place. As Ecotopian militants see the situation, by 1980 there had been almost a quarter century of military action in Indochina. American involvement in Southeast Asia was in its fifteenth year. Cease-fires had come and gone. Evading Congressional fiscal controls, the U.S. administration had continued with attempts to find a "final solution" to Asian uprisings. The burden of military outlays to support an enormous arms establishment caused economic disruption even after the citizenry lost the power to control them. The persistent inflation and recession of the seventies had caused widespread misery and undermined American confidence in economic progress; wildcat strikes and seizures of plants by workers had required the almost constant mobilization of the National Guard. After the abortive antipollution efforts of the early seventies, the toll of death and destruction had resumed its climb. Energy crises had bred economic disruption and price gouging. And chronic Washington scandals had greatly reduced faith in central government

"All this," one Ecotopian told me, "convinced us that if we wished to survive we had to take matters into our own hands." I pointed out that this had always been the claim of conspiratorial revolutionaries, who presume to act in the name of the majority, but take care not to allow the majority to have any real power. "Well," he replied, "things were clearly not getting any better-so people really were ready for change. They were literally sick of bad air, chemicalized foods, lunatic advertising. They turned to politics because it was finally the only route to self-preservation."

"So," I replied, "in order to follow an extremist ecological program, millions of people were willing to jeopardize their whole welfare, economic and social?"

"Their welfare wasn't doing so well, at that point," he said. "Something had to be done. And nobody else was doing it. Also,"—he shrugged, and grinned—"we were very lucky." This gallows humor, which reminds me of the Israelis or Vietnamese, is common in Ecotopia. Perhaps it helps explain how the whole thing happened.

In Ecotopia's Big Woods

Healdsburg, May 17. Wood is a major factor in the topsy-turvy Ecotopian economy, as the source not only of lumber and paper but also of some of the remarkable plastics that Ecotopian scientists have developed. Ecotopians in the city and country take a deep and lasting interest in wood. They love to smell it, feel it, carve it, polish it. Inquiries about why they persist in using such an outdated material (which of course has been entirely obsoleted by aluminum and plastics in the United States) receive heated replies. To ensure a stable long-term supply of wood, the Ecotopians early reforested enormous areas that had been cut over by logging companies before Independence. They also planted trees on many hundreds of thousands of acres that had once been cleared for orchards or fields, but had gone wild or lay unused because of the exodus of people from the country into the cities.

I have now been able to visit one of the forest camps that carry out lumbering and tree-planting, and have observed how far the Ecotopians carry their love of trees. They do no clear-cutting at 41, and their forests contain not only mixed ages but also mixed species of trees. They argue that the costs of mature-tree cutting are actually less per board foot than clear-cutting but that even if they weren't, it would still be desirable because of less insect damage, less erosion and more rapid growth of timber. But such arguments are probably only a sophisticated rationale for attitudes that can almost be called tree worship—and I would not be surprised, as I probe further into Ecotopian life, to discover practices that would strengthen this hypothesis. (I have seen fierce-looking totem poles outside dwellings, for instance.)

Certainly the Ecotopian lumber industry has one practice that must seem barbarian to its customers: the unlucky person or group wishing to build a timber structure must first arrange to go out to a forest camp and do forest service—a period of labor during which, according to the theory, they are supposed to contribute enough to the growth of new trees to replace the wood they are about to consume. This system must be enormously wasteful in terms of economic inefficiency and disruption, but that seems to disturb the Ecotopians—at least those who live in and run the lumber camps—not a bit.

The actual harvesting of timber is conducted with surprising efficiency, considering the general laxness of Ecotopian work habits. There is much goofing off in the forest camps, but when a crew is at work they work faster and more cooperatively than any workmen I have ever seen They cut trees and trim them with a strange, almost religious respect: showing the emotional intensity and care we might use in preparing a ballet.

I was told that in rougher country ox-teams and even horses are used in lumbering, just as they were in Gold Rush times. And in many areas a tethered balloon and cables hoist the cut trees and carry them to nearby logging roads. But in the camp I visited (which may be a showplace) the basic machine is a large electric tractor with four huge rubber tires. These are said to tear up the forest floor even less than oxen, which have to drag timber out on some kind of sled. Though heavy, these tractors are surprisingly maneuverable since both front and rear wheels steer. They have a protected operator's cabin amidship; on one end there is a prehensile extension bearing a chain saw large enough to cut through all but the hugest trees, and mounted so it can cut them off only a few inches above ground level. (This is of course pleasant aesthetically, but it is also claimed that it saves some millions of board feet of lumber each year, and helps in management of the forest floor.) This saw can also cut trees into loadable lengths.

On the other end of the tractor is a huge claw device that can pick up a log, twirl it around lengthwise over the tractor, and carry it to the logging road where big diesel trucks wait to be loaded. Ecotopian foresters claim that this machinery enables them to log safely even in dry weather, since there are no exhausts likely to set fire to undergrowth. It does seem to be true that their methods disturb the forest very little—it continues to look natural and attractive. Several types of trees usually grow in stands together, which is supposed to encourage wildlife and cut the chances of disastrous insect and fungi invasions. Curiously, a few dead trees are left standing—as homes for insect-gobbling woodpeckers—and there are occasional forest meadows to provide habitats for deer and other animals. The older trees seed young ones naturally, so the foresters generally now only do artificial planting in areas they are trying to reforest The dense forest canopy keeps the forest floor cool and moist, and pleasant to walk in. Although it rained for a few hours during my stay, I noticed that the stream passing near the camp did not become muddy—evidently it is true, as they claim, that Ecotopian lumbering leaves the topsoil intact, cuts down erosion, and preserves fish. (I didn't actually see any fish—but then I am the kind of person who seldom sees fish anywhere.)

The lumber camps themselves do not have saw mills, though they possess portable devices with which they can saw rough boards in small quantities for their own needs. The main squaring and sawing of timber, and the production of slabs for pulp, takes place at mills located in more open country, which buy logs from the forest camps. The resulting boards are then sold, almost entirely in the county-sized area just around the mill. Lumber sales are solely domestic; Ecotopia ceased lumber export immediately after Independence. It is claimed that, since the U.S. formerly exported half as much lumber as was used in housing, much of it from the West, some surplus actually existed from the beginning of the new nation. Ecotopian foresters argue that their policies have, since then, more than doubled their per capita resources of timber. There are, however, no present plans for a resumption of export.

Interestingly enough, the Ecotopians themselves have a debate in progress about the huge diesel trucks they use to haul logs. Several forest workers apologized to me that they are still dependent on these noisy, smelly, hulking diesels. Yet there are people all over them at the end of the work day, shining them up—one of the few outlets still allowed in this carless society for man's love of powerful machinery. One truck I saw has lost its bumper, and the replacement is a large, sturdy piece of wood. As they wear out, the trucks will be eliminated in favor of electric vehicles. Meanwhile, people argue hotly over the bumpers—extremist ideologues saying that the bumpers (which are actually stainless steel, not chrome plate) should all be replaced with wood, and the traditionalists maintaining that the trucks should be treated as museum relics and kept in original condition. The factions seem about equally matched, which means that the traditionalists have won so far—since a change on such a "drastic" matter is only carried out if there is a virtual consensus.

Our economists would surely find the Ecotopian lumber industry a labyrinth of contradictions. An observer like myself can come only to general conclusions. Certainly Ecotopians regard trees as being alive in almost a human sense—once I saw a quite ordinary-looking young man, not visibly drugged, lean against a large oak and mutter "Brother Tree." And equally certainly, lumber in Ecotopia is cheap and plentiful, whatever the unorthodox means used to produce it. Wood therefore takes the place that aluminum, bituminous facings, and many other modern materials occupy with us.

An important by-product of the Ecotopian forestry policies is that extensive areas, too steep or rugged to be lumbered without causing erosion, have been assigned wilderness status. There, all logging and fire roads have been eradicated. Such areas are now used only for camping and as wildlife preserves, and a higher risk of forest fire is apparently accepted. It is interesting, by the way, that such Ecotopian forests are uncannily quiet compared to ours, since they have no trail-bikes, all-terrain vehicles, airplanes overhead, nor snowmobiles in the winter. Nor can you get around in them rapidly, since foot trails are the only way to get anywhere.

Has Ecotopian livestock or agricultural production suffered because of the conversion of so much land to forest? Apparently not; vegetables, grains and meat are reasonably cheap, and beef cattle are common features of the landscape, though they are never concentrated in forced-feeding fattening lots. Thus an almost dead occupation, that of cowboy, has come back. And cattle ranches in the Sierra foothills have reverted to the old summer practice of driving their stock up to the high valleys where they pasture on wet mountain meadow grass. Grasslands research is said to be leading to the sowing of more native strains, which are better adapted to the climate and resist the incursion of thistles. Pasture irrigation is practiced only in a few areas, and only for milking herds. But the true love of Ecotopians is their forests, which they tend with so much care and manage in the prescribed stable-state manner. There they can claim much success in their campaign to return nature to a natural condition.

Douglas Coupland
(1961-)

Douglas Coupland is from British Columbia, Canada, but placed the origins of the "hero" of his influential first novel, *Generation X: Tales for an Accelerated Culture* (1991), in Portland, Oregon. The story traces the quest for happiness undertaken by twenty-something Andy, Dag, and Claire, who want release from their pointless jobs and have come from around the country to Palm Springs, California, which provides a way station en route to better lives. This coming-of-age analysis of working-class babies born in the late 1950s and in the 1960s coined the phrase "Generation X." Coupland's later works include *Shampoo Planet*, *Life After God*, and *Microserfs*.

FROM *Generation X*

IT WAS A FRIDAY MORNING and I, being a dutiful foreign photo researcher, was on the phone to London. I was on deadline to get some photos from Depeche Mode's people who were at some house party there—an awful Eurosquawk was on the other end. My ear was glued to the receiver and my hand was over the other ear trying to block out the buzz of the office, a frantic casino of Ziggy Stardust coworkers with everyone hyper from ten-dollar Tokyo coffees from the shop across the street.

I remember what was going through my mind, and it wasn't my job—it was the way that cities have their own signature odor to them. Tokyo's street smell put this into my mind—*udon* noodle broth and faint sewage; chocolate and car fumes. And I thought of Milan's smell—of cinnamon and diesel belch and roses—and Vancouver with its Chinese roast pork and salt water and cedar. I was feeling homesick for Portland, trying to remember its smell of trees and rust and moss when the ruckus of the office began to dim perceptibly.

A tiny old man in a black Balmain suit came into the room. His skin was all folded like a shrunken apple-head person's, but it was dark, peat-colored, and shiny like an old baseball mitt or the Bog Man of Denmark. And he was wearing a baseball cap and chatting with my working superiors.

Miss Ueno, the drop-dead cool fashion coordinator in the desk next to mine (Olive Oyl hair; Venetian gondolier's shirt; harem pants and Viva Las Vegas booties) became flustered the way a small child does when presented with a bear-sized boozed-up drunk uncle at the front door on a snowy winter night. I asked Miss Ueno who this guy was and she said it was Mr. Takamichi, the *kacho,* the Grand Poobah of the company, an Americaphile renowned for bragging about his golf scores in Parisian brothels and for jogging through Tasmanian gaming houses with an L.A. blonde on each arm.

Miss Ueno looked really stressed. I asked her why. She said she wasn't stressed but angry. She was angry because no matter how hard she worked she was more or less stuck at her little desk forever—a cramped cluster of desks being the Japanese equivalent of the veal fattening pen. "But not only because I'm a woman," she said, "But also because I'm a Japanese. *Mostly* because I'm a Japanese. I have ambition. In any other country I could rise, but here I just sit. I murder my ambition." She said that Mr. Takamichi's appearance somehow simply underscored her situation. The hopelessness.

At that point, Mr. Takamichi headed over to my desk. I just knew this was going to happen. It was really embarrassing. In Japan you get phobic about being singled out from the crowd. It's about the worst thing that someone can do to you.

"You must be Andrew," he said, and he shook my hands like a Ford dealer. "Come on upstairs. We'll have drinks. We'll talk," he said, and I could feel Miss Ueno burning like a road flare of resentment next to me. And so I introduced her, but Mr. Takamichi's response was benign. A grunt. Poor Japanese people. Poor Miss Ueno. She was right—they're just so trapped wherever they are—frozen on this awful boring ladder.

And as we were walking toward the elevator, I could feel everyone in the office shooting jealousy rays at me. It was such a bad scene and I could just imagine everyone thinking "who does he think he is?" I felt dishonest. Like I was coasting on my foreignness. I felt I was being excommunicated from the *shin jin rui*—that's what the Japanese newspapers call people like those kids in their twenties at the office—new *human beings.* It's hard to explain. We have the same group over here and it's just as large, but it doesn't have a name—an X generation—purposefully hiding itself. There's more space over here to hide in—to get lost in—to use as camouflage. You're not allowed to disappear in Japan.

But I digress.

We went upstairs in the elevator to a floor that required a special key for access, and Mr. Takamichi was being sort of theatrically ballsy the whole way up, like a cartoon version of an American, you know, talking about football and stuff. But once we got to the top he suddenly turned Japanese—so quiet. He turned right off—like I'd flipped a switch. I got really worried that I was going to have to endure three hours of talk about the weather.

We walked down a thickly carpeted hallway, dead silent, past small Impressionist paintings and tufts of flowers arranged in vases in the Victorian style. This was the western part of his floor. And when this part ended, we came to the Japanese part. It was like entering hyperspace, at which point Mr. Takamichi pointed to a navy cotton robe for me to change into, which I did.

Inside the main Japanese room that we entered there was a *toko no ma* shrine with chrysanthemums, a scroll, and a gold fan. And in the center of the room was a low black table surrounded by terra-cotta colored cushions. On the table were two onyx carp and settings for tea. The one artifact in the room that jarred was a small safe placed in a corner-not even a good safe, mind you, but an inexpensive model of the sort that you might have expected to find in the back office of a Lincoln, Nebraska shoe store just after World War II—really cheap looking, and in gross contrast to the rest of the room.

Mr. Takamichi asked me to sit down at the table whereupon we sat down for salty green Japanese tea.

Of course, I was wondering what his hidden agenda was in getting me up into his room. He talked pleasantly enough... how did I like my job?... what did I think of Japan?... stories about his kids. Nice boring stuff. And he told a few stories about time he had spent in New York in the 1950s as a stringer for the *Asahi* newspapers... about meeting Diana Vreeland and Truman Capote and Judy Holiday. And after a half hour or so, we shifted to warmed sake, delivered, with the clapping of Mr. Takamichi's hands, by a midge of a servant in a drab brown kimono the color of shopping bag paper.

And after the servant left, there was a pause. It was then that he asked me what I thought the most valuable *thing* was that I owned.

Well, well. The most valuable *thing* that I owned. Try and explain the concept of sophomoric minimalism to an octogenarian Japanese publishing magnate. It's not easy. What thing could you possibly own of any value? I mean *really.* A beat up VW Bug? A stereo? I'd sooner have died than admit that the most valuable *thing* I owned was a fairly extensive collection of German industrial music dance mix EP records stored, for even further embarrassment, under a box of crumbling Christmas tree ornaments in a Portland, Oregon basement. So I said, quite truthfully (and, it dawned on me, quite refreshingly), that I owned no *thing* of any value.

He then changed the discussion to the necessity of wealth being transportable, being converted into paintings, gems, and precious metals and so forth (he'd been through wars and the depression and spoke with authority), but I'd pushed some right button, said the right thing—passed a test—and his tone of voice was pleased. Then, maybe ten minutes later, he clapped his hands again, and the tiny servant in the noiseless brown kimono reappeared and was barked an instruction. This caused the servant to go to the corner and to roll the cheap little safe across the tatami mat floor next to where Mr. Takamichi sat cross-legged on the cushions.

Then, looking hesitant but relaxed, he dialed his combination on the knob. There was a click, he pulled a bar, and the door opened, revealing *what,* I couldn't see.

He reached in and pulled out what I could tell to be from the distance, a photograph—a black-and-white 1950s photo, like the shots they take at the scene of the crime. He looked at the mystery picture and sighed. Then, flipping it over and giving it to me with a little out-puff of breath meaning "this is *my* most valuable thing," he handed me the photo and I was, I'll admit, shocked at what it was.

It was a photo of Marilyn Monroe getting into a Checker cab, lifting up her dress, no underwear, and smooching at the photographer, presumably Mr. Takamichi in his stringer days. It was an unabashedly sexual frontal photo (get your minds out of the gutter—black as the ace of spades if you must know) and very taunting. Looking at it, I said to Mr. Takamichi, who was waiting expressionlessly for a reaction, "well, well," or some such drivel, but internally I was actually quite mortified that this photo, essentially only a cheesy paparazzi shot, unpublishable at that, was his most valued possession.

And then I had an uncontrollable reaction. Blood rushed to my ears, and my heart went bang; I broke out into a sweat and the words of Rilke, the poet, entered my brain—his notion that we are all of us born with a letter inside us, and that only if we are true to ourselves, may we be allowed to read it before we die. The burning blood in my ears told me that Mr. Takamichi had somehow mistaken the Monroe photo in the safe for the letter inside of himself, and that I, myself, was in peril of making some sort of similar mistake.

I smiled pleasantly enough, I hope, but I was reaching for my pants and making excuses, blind, grabbing excuses, while I raced to the elevator, buttoning up my shirt and bowing along the way to the confused audience of Mr. Takamichi hobbling behind me making old man noises. Maybe he thought I'd be excited by his photo or complimentary or aroused even, but I don't think he expected rudeness. The poor guy.

But what's done is done. There is no shame in impulse. Breathing stertorously, as though I had just vandalized a house, I fled the building, without even collecting my things—just like you, Dag—and that night I packed my bags. On the plane a day later, I thought of more Rilke:

> *Only the individual who is solitary is like a thing subject to profound laws, and if he goes out into the morning that is just beginning, or looks out into the evening that is full of things happening, and if he feels what is going on there, then his whole situation drops from him as from a dead man, although he stands in the very midst of life.*

Two days later I was back in Oregon, back in the New World, breathing less crowded airs, but I knew even then that there was still too much history there for me. That I needed *less* in life. Less past.

So I came down here, to breathe dust and walk with the dogs—to look at a rock or a cactus and know that I am the first person to see that cactus and that rock. And to try and read the letter inside me.

David Axelrod
(1958-)

David Axelrod was born in Alliance, Ohio, where he worked in his family's used-auto parts business for fifteen years. After obtaining an MFA from the University of Montana, he settled in La Grande, Oregon, and now teaches creative writing at Eastern Oregon State University. His works include a chapbook, *The Kingdom at Hand* (1993), and a poetry collection, *The Jerusalem of Grass* (1992), where the following poem first appeared.

SKILL OF THE HEART

The morning I lost my job,
I glanced up absently
thousands of feet above me
into the Bitterroot Range,
where winter retreated
and snowmelt erupted from canyons.
Stranded in the anxious lines
of automobiles, idling
side-by-side at traffic lights,
I knew I might never change,
like my father, who stammered
until words twisted his face.
A freak to men who jeered,
he was always filled by
a rage that corrupted every
hope he ever held long enough
to value or recklessly love.
I was laid off from my job
the morning my son spilled
free from his mother's body
and drew the inevitable
knife-edged air in his lungs.
Through his first hour, he slept
in an exhausted repose
unlike any other he or
I would ever know again.

All the length of the valley
to where the Bitterroots
vanished on the earth's curve,
wide fault-lines of light streaked
through low clouds and rushed over
foothills blotched green with sage,
a landscape as intent
and overflowing with the skill
of its own inexhaustible heart
as vistas painted by Sung
masters, who washed raw silk
with India ink and fled
this world a thousand years ago.

Craig Lesley
(1945-)

Craig Lesley lives with his wife and daughters in Portland. His works include the acclaimed novels *Winterkill* (1984), winner of the Pacific Northwest Booksellers Association Award, and *The Sky Fisherman* (1995), winner of the Pacific Northwest Book Award. The following excerpt is from his first novel, *River Song* (1989), which tells the story of Danny and Jack Kachiah, contemporary Nez Perce who must deal with changes in the Columbia River that threaten traditional Native American ways of life.

FROM *River Song*

Fishing

A COUPLE OF SPORTFISHERMEN passed the point and then they saw a fast boat on the far side of the river. It was the Oregon Fish and Game Department's Jet-Sled, the fastest boat on the Columbia. The wardens were coming down from Memaloose Island toward Mosier and every so often they stopped.

"Checking the nets, I guess," Willis said. "Making sure everybody's got his net tagged right." The boat left the site and roared downriver toward the next net. "They probably started at The Dalles and are checking the pool down to Bonneville. That sled's sure fast. It'll outrun any other boat."

"You could give them a run with your new Evinrude," Danny said.

Willis laughed. "For about twenty yards. I put that little Evinrude on because those big old Mercs were keeping me broke. The big motors always go clunk, and they cost more to fix. Damn gas-hogs, too. I used a tank and a half just to run the nets. The harder I worked, the behinder I got."

"Your old boat seems solid."

"Those tri-hulls they made on the reservation were darn good," Willis said. "I don't know why that plant went broke. Poor management, I guess. It's a good thing a few of them are still around, though. Stablest boat on the river. The Yakimas got the original design from the Lummis. Puget Sound gets mighty rough."

A couple of windsurfers came into view, their bright sailboards skimming the water like paper boats.

"They're not paying any attention to those nets," Willis said. "They'll hit the cork line and foul it up—jiggle the net just when a fish is about to go in. Sometimes I'd like to sit up here with a rifle and make it hot for them."

"I can loan you my .30-.06," Danny said. "You could sink them with that."

"I think a varmint rifle is about right for those pests."

As Danny and Willis watched, the windsurfers tacked so they were approaching the small island on the Oregon side, just downstream from Mosier.

"That was my grandfather's island once," Willis said. "He was chased off in the early thirties. Shotgun deed. Now the people who live there actually think they inherited it fair and square from their relatives. Same with those people who planted their orchards on Indian land. Short memories."

He tossed a loose rock into the water. "I've talked with those island people a few times. They stand on the dock and try buying fish off me. Let 'em catch their own. But I wish I had that island now—it's nice and secluded. The wardens couldn't keep such close tabs on my place. Since they put Orville in jail, it seems like they're watching me all the time."

"How do you think that's going to turn out?"

"The feds had no jurisdiction, really. If we get him into tribal court, he's got a chance." Willis smiled a little. "I heard the cops spent a quarter-million dollars catching Orville. They even practiced raiding an old fish hatchery up near Mount Saint Helens. Different ones took turns pretending to be Orville. When they finally got it right, they busted into his place with twelve cop cars and a seaplane. They arrested Orville, and they terrorized his family. The government sure knows where to spend money.

Danny shook his head. "Twelve cop cars and a seaplane. You'd think he was selling bomb secrets to the Russians."

Willis held three fingers. "Three years just for selling a few salmon. They only gave that Rajneeshee woman five years for trying to poison the whole town of The Dalles. Anyway, it's Orville's religion to fish. The Creator sends the fish and Orville keeps catching them. He will keep sending more as long as Orville stays faithful and practices the old ways."

"Do you really think the Creator sends fish because Orville and some of the other old-timers catch them according to the old ways?"

Willis squinted at Danny, as if surprised he had even asked the question. "When the first fish comes up the river every spring, you have to treat it right—say some words over it and lay it on the rocks with its head pointing upstream so others can follow. It's always been that way on this river. In the old days, the men got their spears and nets and waited on the platforms. Some listened to the old singing river channel because its voice changed pitch when the fish came upriver. My father said they'd first see the fish way off downriver. Gulls wheeled overhead, and in the water, the salmon gleamed like ribbons of light."

"PUT BIG SMOKEY JUST ABOVE Preacher's Point," Willis said. "It's a killer net because the Japs make the webbing out of supercrystal, like Trilene. It just about disappears when it hits the water, and the fish swim in like churchgoers on Sunday."

Danny nodded. Taking its name from the gray tint of the sixstrand nylon webbing, Big Smokey was four hundred feet long with nine-inch mesh, sixty units deep. Willis gave all his nets nicknames: Big Smokey, Little Smokey, Backstop, Blondie and Little Blondie, Frog (named for its green tint), and the Sub. While the others were floaters, with their cork lines visible above the water, the Sub was a diving net, designed to lie close to the riverbottom. Its "floats" were made from hard black rubber so the water pressure a hundred feet beneath the surface wouldn't collapse them. When the water temperature rose or the surface chop calmed over several days, the salmon tended to congregate near the bottom, and the diving net caught more fish than all the floating nets combined. In addition, it was difficult to detect, so the fish and game officers never knew exactly how many nets Willis had out or their exact locations. Willis told Danny that he planned to buy some more divers with the season's profits.

Danny and Jack were standing in the boat, folding the nets onto the bottom. Willis and Velrae worked beside the boat, unfolding the nets from the blue plastic tarps the fishermen favored and handing the lead line to Jack, the float line to Danny. Now and again, Willis stopped to untangle the mesh or pick out seaweed strands that might scare off the wary salmon. Since this was a calm day, they could load all seven nets at once, separating them in the boat's bottom with the bright plastic tarps. When the water turned rough, they would carry four nets the first load, three the second.

Once the boat was loaded, Danny and Jack took the nets to the designated fishing sites and attached the cork lines to the wire cables sunk in shore rocks or to the white Styrofoam blocks that served as buoys. After attaching one end of a float line, Danny slowly backed the boat toward another buoy while Jack played out the net, taking care not to cross the float line with the lead line. In the water, the heavy lead line sank, stretching the mesh net to its full depth. With calm weather, it took between twenty minutes and half an hour to set each net. When whitecaps knuckled the surface, it might take twice that long.

"Great work," Danny said after they put out three nets. "Just taking a little boat ride while the salmon swim into our nets. That's easy money."

"Easy for you, maybe," Jack said. "My arm feels like it's made of rubber. I must have put out a quarter mile of lead line."

"Before long, your hands will hang below your knees," Danny said.

They laid out Big Smokey at the bluff where Willis had talked about the Wet Shoes, and Danny's neck tingled a little, thinking about Willis's stories. He watched the basalt rock column disappear into the gray-green water and he wondered how deep the Old People's pictures were. Even in the daytime the place gave him an eerie feeling.

"What are you gawking at?" Jack said. "You look like you're about to fall out of the boat."

Danny made a note to pick up the fish here in twilight. He didn't like the idea of being around the site in the dark. If he mentioned the old stories to Jack, the boy would just laugh and call him superstitious.

Jack was halfway through playing out the Frog by the Dynamite Shack when he turned to Danny. "I think you're going to have to take over. My arms are cramping."

Danny put the motor in neutral. "Let's not trip over the net while we swap places." He and Jack moved carefully past one another in the boat, and Danny slipped on the soft rubber fisherman's gloves they used to handle the nets. "Go slow, now."

When Jack put the motor in reverse, he gunned it, and Danny tipped against the front of the boat, catching his arm in the webbing. "For Christ's sakes. You trying to drown me on a milk run?"

"Sorry." Jack looked sheepish. "I didn't realize it had this much power."

"That's a two-thousand-dollar motor," Danny said. "But when this boat's loaded with fish and we're nose into the wind, it'll seem powered by a rubber band."

After putting out Frog, they set Blondie and Little Blondie near the Spring Creek Fish Hatchery. Even though the tule fish caught nearby would bring low prices, Willis said some upriver brights followed the spawning tules, so it was still a good place.

On the way back to camp, Danny had time to study the sides of the Columbia Gorge. Some of the scrub oaks had started to turn doe-brown and a few vine maples were already tipped with crimson. He liked the fall's cool days and crisp nights because he seemed to get another burst of energy. September always signaled the Round-Up, and after that he enjoyed hunting along the reservation ridges, where the fallen leaves' earthy smell lingered on the cool air and startled coveys of mountain quail exploded from the thickets. He'd get out Red Shirt's old pump shotgun, he decided, and fry up some quail in the cast-iron skillet.

The catch seemed to always depend on the light. They would run the nets just before daybreak each morning and again after dark, usually finishing past midnight. During the day, the swimming fish might detect the nets and avoid them, but after dark they could no longer discern the webbing. Danny quickly learned that a gray day meant better fishing and a bright moon signaled a poor catch.

For most of the runs, Danny drove the boat while Jack pulled in the lead line and float line together, drawing them across the center of the boat and disentangling the salmon. Usually, the mesh strands had snagged their gills, so they suffocated without damaging the net, but some of the smaller fish struggled through the mesh, weaving sections in and out until they became hopelessly tangled and broke nylon squares as Jack struggled to free them.

Cursing and complaining, Jack and Danny would flop the lead line over the cork line, trying to free the trapped fish. Their efforts popped nylon strands, ruining sections of the net, but the salmon were running heavy, leaving no time for repair, so they tried to minimize the damage and get the torn nets back in the water.

When a salmon was barely hooked, perhaps caught by its teeth or a fin, they gaffed it before it slipped free, the dead fish sliding from the net toward the riverbottom. A lost fish meant as much as a fifty-dollar waste, and Danny took satisfaction in knowing they didn't miss many. They gaffed the tangled sturgeon, too, sometimes out of quick anger, because these sharp-buttoned fish shredded the nets. Less than half the ones they caught were legal—four to six feet—and Danny thought dealing with sturgeon was a waste of time when the salmon were running. Moreover, it unnerved him to see how long the sturgeons lived out of water, their primitive slitted mouths opening and closing hours after they had been weighed at the fish buyers' scale and packed in ice.

Danny had heard stories about gutted sturgeons somehow managing to swim off into deep water, leaving their entrails on the banks for the gulls and swarming flies.

If the river was calm, Danny helped Jack pull in the nets, but when the wind stirred whitecaps, he stayed at the wheel, keeping the boat steady while Jack struggled to keep his balance and preserve the catch. On a bad night, they might lose a gaff or spotlight, so they carried spears.

With the wind whipping stinging water into his face, Jack often avoided picking the net clean of seaweed and river gunk, but a dirty net meant a sparse catch the following day, so Danny had to shout sharp reminders into the blow.

Jack would cast furious glances over his shoulder and mutter words the wind snatched away. Looking sullen, the boy kicked his gumboots at the big Chinooks underfoot and flung strands of seaweed over the gunwales.

DANNY COULDN'T COMPLAIN about the money they made from commercial fishing, but it was hard work. Sometimes, as they approached the nets, the floats were bobbing with the struggles of a recently netted salmon. Most of the time, the corks were still; the salmon had already drowned and become dead weights, dragging at the float line. Danny preferred sportfishing with a spinning pole and lures, giving the fish a chance to fight and spit the hook. Now he avoided looking at the salmon opening and closing their gills, suffocating on the boat's bottom.

Sherman Alexie
(1966-)

Sherman Alexie lives in Seattle, Washington. The author of novels including *The Business of Fancydancing, The Lone Ranger and Tonto Fist Fight in Heaven*, and *Reservation Blues*, as well as poetry collections including *Old Shirts & New Skins, First Indian on the Moon*, and *The Summer of Black Widows*, Alexie has emerged as a major new voice of Native American writing in the Pacific Northwest. The following excerpt from his 1996 novel *Indian Killer* tells the story of John Smith, an orphan adopted by whites and unsure of his Native American heritage. John works to help build the last skyscraper in Seattle as he puzzles out his purpose in life.

FROM *Indian Killer*

JOHN NEVER DID BECOME a good basketball player, but he graduated from high school on time, in 1987. Since he was an Indian with respectable grades, John would have been admitted into almost any public university had he bothered to fill out even one application. His parents pushed him to at least try a community or technical college, but John refused. During his freshman year in high school, John had read an article about a group of Mohawk Indian steel workers who helped build the World Trade Center buildings in New York City. Ever since then, John had dreamed about working on a skyscraper. He figured it was the Indian thing to do. Since Daniel Smith was an architect, he sometimes flattered himself by thinking that John's interest in construction was somehow related. Despite John's refusal to go to college, his parents still supported him in his decision, and were sitting in the third row as he walked across the stage at St. Francis to accept his diploma. Polite applause, a few loud cheers from his friends, his mother and father now standing. John flipped his tassel from one side to the other, blinked in the glare of the flashbulbs, and tried to smile. He had practiced his smile, knew it was going to be needed for this moment. He smiled. The cameras flashed. John was finished with high school and would never attend college. He walked offstage and stepped onto the fortieth floor of an unfinished office building in downtown Seattle.

JOHN SMITH WAS NOW TWENTY-SEVEN years old. He was six feet, six inches tall and heavily muscled, a young construction worker perfect for all of the heavy lifting. His black hair was long and tucked under his hard hat. When he had first started working, his co-workers used to give him grief about his hair, but half of the crew had long hair these days. Seattle was becoming a city dominated by young white men with tiny ponytails. John always had the urge to carry a pair of scissors and snip off those ponytails at every opportunity. He hated those ponytails, but he did not let them distract him at work. He was a good worker, quiet and efficient. He was eating lunch alone on the fortieth floor when he heard the voices again.

John swallowed the last of his cold coffee and gently set the thermos down. He cupped his hand to his ear. He knew he was alone on this floor, but the voices were clear and precise. During the quiet times, he could hear the soft *why-why-why* as Father Duncan's leather sandals brushed against the sand on his long walk through the desert. Once, just once, John had heard the bubble of the baptismal fountain as Father Duncan dipped him into the water. Sometimes there were sudden sirens and explosions, or the rumble of a large crowd in an empty room. John could remember when it first happened, this noise in his head. He was young, maybe ten years old, when he heard strange music. It happened as he ran from school, across the parking lot, toward the car where Olivia waited for him. He knew this music was especially for him: violins, bass guitar, piano, harmonica, drums. Now, as he sat on the fortieth floor and listened to those voices, John felt a sharp pain in his lower back. His belly burned.

"Jesus," said John as he stood up, waving his arms in the air.

"Hey, chief, what you doing? Trying to land a plane?"

The foreman was standing in the elevator a few feet away. John liked to eat his lunch near the elevator so he could move quickly and easily between floors. He always liked mobility. "Well," said the foreman. "What's up?" John lowered his arms.

"On my break," John said. He could still hear voices speak-to him. They were so loud, but the foreman was oblivious. The foreman knew John always ate lunch alone, a strange one, that John. Never went for beers after work. Showed up five minutes early every day and left five minutes late. He could work on one little task all day, until it was done, and never complain. No one bothered him because he didn't bother anyone. No one knew a damn thing about John, except that he worked hard, the ultimate compliment. Not that the hard work mattered anymore, since there would be no more high-rise work in Seattle after they finished this job. They were building the last skyscraper in Seattle. Computers had made the big buildings obsolete. No need to shove that many workers into such a small space. After this last building was complete, the foreman would take a job for the state. He did not know what John had planned.

"Well," the foreman said. "Lunch is over. Get in. We need you down on thirty-three."

John was embarrassed. He felt the heat build in his stomach, then through his back, and fill his head. It started that way. The heat came first, followed quickly by the music. A slow hum. A quiet drum. Then a symphony crashing through his spinal column. The foreman brought the heat and music. John looked at him, a short white man with a protruding belly and big arms. An ugly man with a bulbous nose and weak chin, though his eyes were a striking blue.

John knew if he were a real Indian, he could have called the wind. He could have called a crosscutting wind that would've sliced through the fortieth floor, pulled the foreman out of the elevator, and sent him over the edge of the building. But he's strong, that foreman, and he would catch himself. He'd be hanging from the edge by his fingertips.

In his head, John could see the foreman hanging from the fortieth floor.

"Help me!" the foreman would shout.

John saw himself plant his feet just inches from the edge, reach down, take the foreman's wrists in his hands, and hold him away from the building. John and the foreman would sway back and forth like a pendulum. Back and forth, back and forth.

"Jesus!" the foreman would shout. "Pull me up!"

John would look down to see the foreman's blue eyes wide with fear. That's what I need to see, that's what will feed me, thought John. Fear in blue eyes. He would hold onto the foreman as long as possible and stare down into those terrified blue eyes. Then he'd let him fall.

"Let's go, chief," the foreman said, loud and friendly. "We ain't got all day. We need you on thirty-three."

John stepped into the elevator. The foreman pulled the gate shut and pressed the button for the thirty-third floor. Neither talked on the way down. John could feel the tension in his stomach as the elevator made its short journey. He fought against the music.

"Chuck needs your help," the foreman said when they arrived. John looked where the foreman pointed. The thirty-third floor was a controlled mess. Chuck, a white man with a huge moustache, was pounding a nail into place. He raised a hammer and brought down on the head of the nail. He raised the hammer, brought it down again.

Metal against metal. John saw sparks. Sparks. Sparks. He rubbed his eyes. The sparks were large enough and of long enough ration to turn to flame. The foreman didn't see it. The rest of the crew didn't see it. Chuck raised the hammer again and paused at the top of his swing. As the hammer began its next descent, John could see it happening in segments, as in a series of still photographs. In that last frozen moment, in that brief instant before the hammer struck its explosion of flame, John knew exactly what to do with his life.

John needed to kill a white man.

John sat alone on the fortieth floor. He could see a white man working at a small desk in an office across the street. A small man from any distance. John knew he could kill a white man, but he was not sure which white man was responsible for everything that had gone wrong. He thought hard that day, could barely work, and often stared off into space, trying to decide. Which white man had done the most harm to the world? Was it the richest white man? Was it the poorest white man? John believed that both the richest and poorest white men in the country lived in Seattle.

The richest man owned a toy company. No. He owned the largest toy company in the world. It had thousands of employees. John saw the rich man on television. In commercials. On talk shows. On goofy game shows. His wedding was broadcast nationally. He had married a movie star, one of those beautiful actresses whose name John always forgot. Julie, Jennifer, Janine. The rich man's name was short and masculine, a three-lettered name that was somehow smaller and still more important than John. Bob or Ted or Dan or something like that. A monosyllabic, triangular monument of a name. A name where every letter loudly shouted its meaning. John could not understand how a man named Bob or Ted became rich and famous by selling toys. How can a toy maker meet and marry a beautiful actress? John knew that Bob or Dan must have sold his soul, that slaves worked in his factories. Thousands of children. No. Indians. Thousands of Indians chained together in basements, sweating over stupid board games that were thinly disguised imitations of Scrabble and Monopoly, cheap stuffed monkeys, and primitive computer games where all the illegal space aliens were blasted into pieces. But John could not convince himself that the richest man in the world deserved to die. It was too easy. If he killed the richest white man in the world, then the second-richest white man would take his place. Nobody would even notice the difference. All the money would be switched from one account to another. All the slaves would stop making toys, move to another factory, and begin making car alarms, director's chairs, or toasters. John could kill a thousand rich white men and not change a thing.

The poorest white man in the world stole aluminum cans from John's garbage. Well, that was not exactly true. Every Monday, John set the cans outside his apartment building for the recycling truck to collect, but the poorest white man always arrived first. John watched him from his bedroom window. The poorest white man dressed in ragged clothes. His skin diseased, face deeply pockmarked, hair pulled back in a greasy ponytail. The poor man would pick up the aluminum cans one by one and drop them into his shopping cart. Empty Campbell's tomato soup cans, Pepsi cans, cans that once held stew or creamed corn, hash or pineapple chunks. One by one, carefully, as if the aluminum cans were fragile, priceless. John hoped the poorest white man sold the cans for cents on the pound, and then bought some food. The poorest man might have a family, a white wife, white kids, all starving in some city park. But John knew the poorest man sold the cans for booze money. He just drank and drank. Fortified wine, rubbing alcohol, Sterno. John hated poor white men, but he knew killing them was a waste. They were already dead. They were zombies. John could stick a bomb in one of his aluminum cans. A mercury switch. When the zombie picked up the can, the switch would move, and boom! But it would be a small gesture, little more than waving good-bye to someone you had just met.

Rich man, poor man, beggarman, thief. Lawyer, doctor, architect, construction foreman. John knew this was the most important decision in his life. Which white man had done the most harm to Indians? He knew that priests had cut out the tongues of Indians who continued to speak their tribal languages. He had seen it happen. He had gathered the tongues in his backpack and buried them in the foundation of a bank building. He had held wakes and tried to sing like Indians sing for the dead. But Father Duncan was proof of something bigger, wasn't he? Father Duncan, an Indian, had walked into the desert like a holy man and disappeared. Whenever he closed his eyes, John could see the desert. The cacti, lizards, washes, and sand dunes, the lack of water. John knew what water meant to life. A man could have a camel loaded down with food, enough for weeks, but that same man would die without water. A man without water could last for two days, three days, four days at most. Father Duncan did not take any water into the desert with him. He left behind his paints and an empty canvas. He left behind his hat and shoes. But there was no water in the desert, not for miles and miles.

How could Father Duncan have survived such a journey? How was he saved? How had he arrived in John's dreams, both awake and asleep? John could see the stand of palm trees at the horizon, either an illusion or a place of safety. Could see Duncan in his black robe staggering across the hot sand. If John concentrated hard, he could see Father Duncan's red-rimmed eyes, cracked lips, burned skin. So much thirst.

After quitting time, John rode the elevator down through the unfinished building. He rode with the foreman and a couple other co-workers named Jim and Jerry. Nobody knew the foreman's name. He was simply known as the foreman. John knew these white men were mostly harmless and would live forever. They would leave work and have a few beers at the same tavern where they had been drinking together for years. They were regulars. Jim, Jerry, and the foreman would walk into the bar and all the patrons would loudly greet their arrival.

John stepped off the elevator, ignored offers to go for beers, and walked through the downtown Seattle streets. There were so many white men to choose from. Everybody was a white man in downtown Seattle. The heat and noise in his head were loud and painful. He wanted to run. He even started to run. But he stopped. He could not run. Everybody would notice. Everybody would know that he was thinking about killing white men. The police would come. John breathed deeply and started to walk slowly. He was walking in work boots and flannel shirt through Seattle, where men in work boots and flannel shirts were often seen walking. No one even noticed John. That is to say that a few people looked up from their books and a couple drivers looked away from the street long enough to notice John, then turned back to their novels and windshields. "There's an Indian walking," they said to themselves or companions, though Indians were often seen walking in downtown Seattle. John the Indian was walking and his audience was briefly interested, because Indians were briefly interesting. White people no longer feared Indians. Somehow, near the end of the twentieth century, Indians had become invisible, docile. John wanted to change that. He wanted to see fear in every pair of blue eyes. As John walked, his long, black hair was swept back by the same wind that watered his eyes. He walked north along the water, across the University Bridge, then east along the Burke-Gilman Trail until he was standing in a field of grass. He had made it to the wilderness. He was free. He could hunt and trap like a real Indian and grow his hair until it dragged along the ground. No. It was a manicured lawn on the University of Washington campus, and John could hear drums. He had been on the campus a few times before but had never heard drums there. He walked toward the source of the drums. At first, he thought it was Father Duncan. He was not sure why Father Duncan would be playing drums. Then he saw a crowd of Indians gathered outside a large auditorium, Hec Edmundson Pavilion. There were two drums, a few singers and dancers, and dozens of Indians watching the action. So many Indians in one place. There were white people watching, too, but John turned away from their faces. He stepped into the crowd, wanting to disappear into it. A small Indian woman was standing in front of John. She smiled.

"Hey," she said. "Hey," he said.

"I'm Marie. Are you a new student here?"

"No."

"Oh," she said, disappointed. She was the activities coordinator for the Native American Students Alliance at the University and thought she'd found a recruit. A potential friendship or possible romance.

"What's your name?"

"John."

"What tribe are you?"

He could not, would not, tell her he had been adopted as a newborn by a white couple who could not have children of their own. Along with the clipping about Father Duncan's disappearance, John always carried the photograph of the day his parents had picked him up from the adoption agency. In the photograph, his father's left arm is draped carefully over his mother's shoulders, while she holds John tightly to her dry right breast. Both wear expensive, tasteful clothes. John had no idea who had taken the picture.

His adopted parents had never told him what kind of Indian he was. They did not know. They never told him anything at all about his natural parents, other than his birth mother's age, which was fourteen. John only knew that he was Indian in the most generic sense. Black hair, brown skin and eyes, high cheekbones, the prominent nose. Tall and muscular, he looked like some cinematic warrior, and constantly intimidated people with his presence. When asked by white people, he said he was Sioux, because that was what they wanted him to be. When asked by Indian people, he said he was Navajo, because that was what he wanted to be.

"I'm Navajo," he said to Marie.

"Oh," she said, "I'm Spokane."

"Father Duncan," said John, thinking instantly of the Spokane Indian Jesuit.

"What?"

"Father Duncan was Spokane."

"Father Duncan?" asked Marie, trying to attach significance to the name, then remembering the brief fragment of a story her parents had told her. "Oh, you mean that one who disappeared, right?"

John nodded his head. Marie was the first person he'd met, besides the Jesuits at St. Francis, who knew about Father Duncan. John trembled.

"Did you know him?" asked Marie.

"He baptized me," said John. "He used to visit me. Then he disappeared."

"I'm sorry," said Marie, who was definitely not Christian. With disgust, she remembered when the Spokane Indian Assembly of God Church held a book burning on the reservation and reduced *Catcher in the Rye,* along with dozens of other books, to ash.

"I know a Hopi," said Marie, trying to change the subject. "Guy named Buddy who works at the U. He's a history teacher. Do you know him?"

"No."

"Oh, I thought you might. He hangs around with the Navajo bunch. Jeez, but they tease him something awful, too."

John barely made eye contact with Marie. Instead, he watched all of the Indians dancing in circles on the grass. It was an illegal powwow, not approved by the University. John could figure out that much when he noticed how the dancers were trampling on the well-kept lawn. Indians were always protesting something. Marie had organized the powwow as a protest against the University's refusal to allow a powwow. Only a few of the Indians had originally known that, but most everybody knew now, and danced all that much harder.

Kent Anderson
(1945-)

Kent Anderson lives in Idaho and is author of *Sympathy for the Devil* (1987) and *Night Dogs* (1996), from which the following is excerpted. A former police officer and Special Forces sergeant in Vietnam, Anderson creates the character of Officer Hanson, a Vietnam veteran who finds himself fighting a personal war for his career and his life within the North Precinct of Portland, Oregon. *Night Dogs* offers a disturbing view of the work routine of the police force.

FROM *Night Dogs*

HANSON HAD BEEN SO HUNG OVER when he got to work he knew he'd made a mistake not to call in sick. Sitting through roll call he tried not to look as bad as he felt while he copied down suspect information and license plate numbers. Sweating, and trying to smile, he checked out his shotgun and avoided Sgt. Bendix on the way out to his patrol car.

But the street was worse. The late afternoon sun seemed to scream at him through the bug-smeared windshield, boiling off the asphalt like kerosene. The hot patrol car smelled of cigarette smoke, vomit, and blood. He stopped at a gas station bathroom and forced himself to throw up in the filthy toilet. He splashed some water on his face and looked at himself in the cracked and peeling mirror over the sink, his faint reflection trapped deep in the dirty glass.

"Hey! How's it goin', officer?" the teenage attendant said as Hanson came out of the bathroom.

"Pretty good," Hanson said, "pretty good," heading towards the sanctuary of the patrol car.

The kid walked alongside. "How do you like the new Chevys?" he said.

"Okay," Hanson said. "I wish they'd clean 'em up once in a while."

"They're pretty hot little cars though, aren't they?" the kid said. He was chewing gum and smoking a cigarette, the smoke blowing into Hanson's face like sewer gas.

"Yeah," Hanson said, getting into the car, "better than the Fords."

"I'm planning to take the test for the police department the day I turn twenty-one," the kid said. "I've wanted to be a cop ever since I was a kid."

"Oh yeah?" Hanson said, starting the car. "I've got a call waiting for me. Better get going. Good luck on that test. See you later," he said, and drove off, the kid still bent down to talk to him through the window.

Hanson bumped over the curb, fumbling for his sunglasses, and a car he hadn't noticed had to swerve to the far lane to avoid the patrol car.

Great, Hanson thought, *a real inspiration to the future crimefighter back there.*

He should have been nicer to the kid, he thought. He'd never pass the written test and the interview, but why not let him have his cheap dream until the assholes and his own stupidity took it away from him? *I'm* an asshole, he thought, but there was something wrong with a person who'd wanted to be a cop ever since he was a kid. What kind of fucked-up ideas did he have? He probably had a police scanner in his car, one of those guys who show up at traffic accidents in a station wagon with an amber light bar on top, wanting to "help."

Up ahead, an Al's Haul-it rental truck full of collapsible wheelchairs was weaving in and out of the right lane. Hanson pulled around to pass and the truck lurched into his lane, forcing him into oncoming traffic, the wheelchairs rocking and clattering above him like some language of dread. He managed to pass, then took the next left, into the sun, hoping the truck wouldn't follow him. He didn't want to spend the next two hours processing a drunk driver with a load of wheelchairs.

He drove past littered yards and sagging porches where old black men spent the days watching traffic and drinking from bottles in paper bags. Then, way up the street, a runner took shape in the glare, coming out of the sun, down the street towards him, shimmering like a wraith. It was Aaron Allen, a concrete block in each hand, his bare chest sweating as he pumped the heavy blocks, dodging traffic and parked cars.

He sprinted through the intersection straight at the patrol car, looking at Hanson with perfect hate. He kept coming until Hanson hit the brakes, but Aaron pivoted away and past. Hanson looked for him in the mirror, but he was gone, vanished like the Spirit of Will-In-The-Ghetto.

Maybe hate could save him, Hanson thought. Maybe hate was the only way anyone could escape. Probably it would only get him killed, but that was a way to escape too.

* * *

ON THE WAY BACK to the precinct at the end of the shift, he got a call to cover the state police on an accident on the freeway. It was a fatal, they said. He was glad to see the flares and state police cars and ambulances as he came down the on-ramp. He would hate to get stuck with the paperwork on a fatal, especially this late at night.

Traffic was backed up, people trying to get a look. He drove along the shoulder of the freeway, lights silently flashing, into the hissing funnel of flares. The overhead lights, he thought, sounded sad. They moaned as they slowly turned, grinding on the roof above him, *Row-Raw, Row-Raw.*

He pulled up behind a state police car and got out, putting on his hat. There'd probably be a sergeant or lieutenant by on this one, and they'd chew him out if he wasn't wearing his hat.

One of the state cops, wearing his wide-brim Smokey the Bear hat was leaning against the car, watching a wrecker hook up to a demolished pickup truck. The patterns of hissing red flares sent up an acrid, eye-stinging smoke that hung over the freeway, catching the yellow beams of headlights as it drifted into the dark. His uniform, Hanson thought, would still stink of it in the morning.

"Looks like you guys have got it under control," Hanson said to the state cop. Out in the smoke another cop in a Smokey the Bear hat was pacing down the freeway, pushing his wheeled measuring device like some kid's toy. A technician was taking flash pictures of the scene. Each time the light strobe on his camera flared, it highlighted the boiling patterns of smoke and seemed to stop time for an instant.

"Yeah," the cop said, "I'll be doing paperwork on this all night. Thanks for swinging by though," he said. The state cops and the city cops didn't really like each other very much, but most of the time they tried to be courteous. You never knew when you might need help fast.

"Migrant workers," the cop said, gesturing towards three lumps covered with gray blankets, one of them smaller than the other two. "Mexicans. Pickup full of them. Probably on their way north to pick apples."

Paramedics were lifting a woman on a stretcher into the back of an ambulance van. *"Alicia,"* she moaned, *"Alicia. Pobrecita."*

"Shit," the cop said, "probably none of 'em speak English either. I'll be all day *tomorrow* trying to get statements. And they're probably illegals. We'll have to fuck around with the INS too." He laughed. "Poor me. Life's a bitch and then you die. Guess I better quit whining and get to work."

"Nothing I can do?" Hanson said, as a formality.

"Naw. Thanks, though. Take care," he said, walking off through the smoke and headlights towards the ambulance, a clipboard in his hand. He seemed like a good guy, Hanson thought, for a state cop.

An eighteen wheeler hissed and groaned as it downshifted, inching along, a white convertible behind it blushing pink from the truck's brake lights. Four girls in the convertible were trying to see around the truck, to get a look at the wreck. They were all blond. College girls, Hanson thought, on their way home from a party. They were excited, talking and straining for a look. The passenger in the front seat was standing up, holding on to the top of the windshield. Hanson turned to walk to his patrol car, then stopped and looked back at the girls in the convertible. All four of them were beautiful.

Hanson got in the patrol car and, overhead lights streaking the ground cover and trash along the shoulder of the freeway-red and blue, red and blue-rolled past the wreck and back out onto the highway. He thought about going north to pick apples. He imagined the weather would be warm, but cooler in the apple orchards, fragrant, sounds muffled by the leaves and branches like they are in a silent snow. Voices calling out in soft Spanish from the trees as if the trees were talking to each other.

He realized that his overheads were still on, traffic pulling over to give him room. He speeded up and took the next exit ramp so he'd look like he knew what he was doing.

He took one of the main streets through the ghetto. He was already on overtime, and the streets were empty. The barred and boarded-up windows of shops were dark, half of them out of business. Miz T's Love Wigs, Living Art Tattoo Parlor, Flint's Ribs, Billy Cee's Detail Shop, broken down-gas stations with Out of Order signs on the pumps, handwritten on pieces of cardboard. Hanson imagined the celebration, the hope of the people who opened the businesses and how it must have faded just like the paint on the storefronts. Maybe it was better not to have had any hope at all than to feel it die. The wind was blowing from the freeway, bringing with it the sour stink of the huge Holsum Bakery on the edge of the district.

It was at about the point where the shops thinned out and the street became residential that Hanson saw the dogs. For a moment he thought it was shadows on the street, light coming through the scrawny trees. But it was dogs, a pack of twenty-five or thirty of them, walking up the middle of the street as if they owned it. Like a flock of sheep out in the eastern part of the state, clogging a country road as they are herded to winter pastures.

Hanson slowed and pulled behind them, big dogs and little ones, mongrels and purebreds, cute and ugly. Some wore collars while others were obviously wild, feral, abandoned, their fur tangled and matted like a wino's hair. Like a gang of thugs, leaders and lieutenants and hangers-on, some running ahead like point men, the leaders walking steadily as if they were on their way to a confrontation. Hanson honked his horn and flicked his headlights bright and dim. One or two of them looked back at the car, but they all stayed in the middle of the street, walking, as if they knew Hanson wouldn't run them down, that they held the power out there.

Whenever they passed a fenced-in dog, a half-dozen of them charged the fence, spraddle-legged. They snarled and slathered, bounced on stiff front legs, their snouts piglike, distended, lips flared over teeth and purple gums, striking like snakes at the fence. Then, as if on some signal, they turned away and trotted back to rejoin the pack.

Hanson accelerated slightly, into the pack of dogs. It was like taking a lifeboat through a school of sharks, like one of those encyclopedia illustrations where all the species of shark are swimming in the same small patch of ocean-great white, crescent-tailed thresher, mako, mongrel dog shark, tiger, mustached nurse shark, a hammerhead with stemmed eyes. The dogs slowly parted for the patrol car as if it was a minor annoyance, one of many in their brutal night-shift existence. A cocky Welsh terrier looked up as Hanson rolled past, then snapped at a mangy cocker spaniel who yelped and ran under the patrol car. Hanson jerked to a stop and honked the horn. He tapped the siren, then stuck his head out the window.

"Come on, god *dammit.* I'll run your asses *over,*" he yelled, fear in his voice. "I'll squash you, motherfuckers, then I'll call for a confirmed dog kill . . ."

A half-breed Doberman leaped up, snarling, his claws raking the door of the car, and Hanson jerked his head back. The Doberman was missing an ear, the side of his head scarred and furless. He dropped back to the street where he cocked his damaged head and regarded Hanson with something that looked like a smile.

Hanson rolled through the dogs until he was ahead of them, watching his rearview mirror until they were gone.

The parking lot at North was quiet, graveyard shift already out on the street. He unloaded his shotgun and wondered if he'd really seen the dogs.

Even if he hurried, the police club bar would be closed before he got there, Debbie Deets and the other girls from Records or Radio gone home with someone else. After the last time, he'd promised himself he wouldn't call Sara again, but he didn't want to sleep alone tonight.

When he dialed Sara's number, a man answered and Hanson asked him if she was there. Sara sounded surprised, but happy to hear from him. She told him to "wait half an hour" before he came over.

* * *

HE BEGAN USING the cocaine to sober up for the drive home after the police club closed. The nights he didn't go to Sara's house, he sat up until dawn, studying the tables in *Steam,* or reading books about the war, cross-indexing conflicting accounts of enemy offensives and firebase sieges, hoping to find some agreed-upon "truth." Truman watched from across the room, listening, smelling the air.

He tried to stay away from Sara, but up in her little room, lizards watching them from the walls, he was able to forget the chirping in his ears, the knot in his stomach. The stairs creaked when he tried to slip out afterwards, past Tiny Tim's friends sleeping on the couch or floor, the stale air heavy with marijuana smoke. Too many people knew he was a cop.

When he woke up after three or four hours of fitful sleep, groggy and hung over, he'd snort more cocaine and go to work, resisting, for a while, the temptation to take a little with him for later in the day.

He watched himself more and more carefully as the days passed, but on the street, that was dangerous. Second-guessing himself, questioning his decisions, could cause him to hesitate when he couldn't afford to.

Jim Bodeen
(1945-)

Jim Bodeen is the publisher and printer of Blue Begonia Press, which creates original chapbooks to showcase his and other artists' poetry. His own chapbooks include *Our Mother Blooming*, *Hammer & Praise*, and *Lockup*. He teaches English at Davis High School in Yakima. The following poem portrays work in agriculture that involves migrant laborers who visit the Pacific Northwest for the harvests.

REPLENISHING THE NEIGHBORHOOD

In late May
the young Mexican
comes to the door
in the evening
selling asparagus.
Orchard this morning

He gives the price
and I give him the money
wondering
if these tender spears
came wild
from the side of the road
filled with pesticide
and spray, or from
the cutters in the fields,
and I think of the picture
they ran in the paper:

women strapped, harnessed,
dangling from irrigation pipes
hovering inches from the grass,
an innovation
to save their backs.

Packed in the Del Monte Box,
stalks to the outside,
delicate tips like feathered hands
clasped, true produce
of our labor.

Taking the lug from his trunk
grateful for no common language,
we shake hands, look at the stalks
and smile at the precision
of the mitered cut.

He drives off to his own life
under the safe light
of the evening street
and I carry the asparagus,
this slashing meditation,
to the back porch.

John Rember
(1950 -)

John Rember spent his childhood in Sawtooth Valley, Idaho, living alongside the Salmon River. A graduate of Harvard University, he received an MFA in fiction from the University of Montana. He has worked as a bartender, a ski patrolman, and a wilderness ranger. His first book of stories, *Coyote in the Mountains*, was published in 1989. He is currently writer in residence at Albertson College in Caldwell, Idaho. The following excerpt from his second novel, *Cheerleaders from Gomorrah: Tales from the Lycra Archipelago* (1994), depicts working class life in a genre that has been characterized as the "post-ironic recreational western."

FROM *Cheerleaders from Gomorrah*

Post Cowboy Dreams

A HARD RAIN CAME OVER MOUNT MAMMON and onto Gomorrah, soaking the hot bleached grass of backyards and turning the gutters in the middle of town into small rivers carrying beer cans, Styrofoam cups, and crumpled Bible Days programs. Bicyclists began pedaling for coffee shops. Down in the city park, a city league softball game, rugby practice and a pick-up game of basketball were all rained out.

And in the middle of Main Street, Sonny Cogan, who should have been glad it was raining, was instead cursing, trying to get his horse turned around and off the water-slick asphalt. His hat was starting to feel soggy. Rain was oozing through his Levi jacket and into his new cowboy shirt. A car went by too close, spraying an even band of mud across the horse and Sonny's pantleg.

The horse jumped and turned and made a little experimental hop toward the curb. Then it started bucking for real, but Sonny was already out of the saddle and into the air. He landed on his feet just as the horse slipped and fell to its knees. As it struggled to get up, he jumped back in the saddle and pulled hard on the reins, screaming, "Buck, you nervous son of a bitch. Buck!" He pulled the reins up until the horse started jerking backward, fighting the pain of the bit, blowing hard.

Sonny backed the horse across the street, stopping traffic. The drivers of motorhomes began honking their horns. The horse flinched and jumped. Sonny kept its head high and raked its flanks with his spurs. It reared again, and touched the far curb with its rear hooves. Sonny released the reins, and when the horse touched down, he whirled it around and onto the sidewalk, right into the middle of a Japanese tour group that was standing under the awning of The Slaver's Rest Saloon.

They scattered. Sonny could hear the clicking of Nikons and shouts of "Cow Boy! Cow Boy!" and "Shane come back. Shane come back!"

Sonny eased the reins and the horse, wild-eyed, stood on the slick concrete, legs wide and trembling. He dismounted to applause. Sonny doffed his hat and bowed to them in the way he'd been taught by the representative of the Japanese Consul at the Chamber of Commerce meeting. Then, showing off, he led the horse over to a parking meter and tied the reins to it and put a quarter in the slot. He undid the cinch and pulled the saddle and blankets off and leaned them against the wall underneath the awning, out of the rain.

"Watch he doesn't kick somebody's head off," he said to the Japanese.

"Cow Boy!" they said.

Sonny pulled open the heavy door of The Rest. It was dark and silent and empty inside. He stood for a moment, letting his eyes adjust to the reduced light, then remembered and took off his sunglasses. Jimmy the Bartender looked up, saw him, and without words poured a beer for him. Sonny sat down.

"Raining out there," said Jimmy. "Hard."

Sonny didn't say anything. He looked at Jimmy for a long moment, then took off his hat, shook a fine spray of water off it, and placed it on the bar to one side of him.

Jimmy shrugged. "You work in a bar with no windows," he said, "and you have to get your weather reports from the humidity of your customers.

Sonny still didn't say anything. He sipped from his beer and stared off into the dark corners of the bar. He was the only customer. Most people didn't show up in The Rest until after dark.

"How's business?" asked Jimmy.

"Dirty," said Sonny. "Dust six inches deep on the trails."

"Rain help?" asked Jimmy.

"Mud tomorrow," said Sonny. "Dust the day after." He shrugged. "It ain't so bad. I get to ride in front."

He stared deep into his beer, watching strings of bubbles. "Today my clients were twelve little kids. I rode them around the loop behind the stables until they all had a nice even coat of dust. Couldn't tell them apart. When their parents got there, they'd point out one that looked a little familiar, and I'd get on my horse and cut him out of the herd."

Sonny thought of his horses in the pasture north of town. He had turned them loose an hour before and had looked on as they had bucked and snorted their way through the sagebrush toward the river. Watching them, he had thought it might rain, but he'd ridden into town anyway, on a skittish new horse. Now his new cowboy shirt was wet. He put his beer on the bar and took off his jacket. Water had soaked into the piping of the shirt and had carried little blue stains into the silk, making it look tie-dyed.

"It could rain for the next forty days and nights," said Sonny, "and I wouldn't care."

"Season over?" asked Jimmy.

"Soon," said Sonny. "A couple of weeks and I'll take the horses to fall pasture."

"Where's that?"

"South. In-laws own some ranches down there."

"In-laws?" asked Jimmy. "Thought you were divorced."

Sonny nodded. "Ex-in-laws. They still like me, though. I still pay them money. They still winter my horses."

"Maybe they just like your horses."

"Maybe. But her brother tells me not to worry about any hard feelings on his part. He says it's nothing personal. It's just that I don't have what she wants."

"Nothing personal," said Jimmy.

"It's true," said Sonny. "I don't have what she wants. I don't think the man's been made who has what she wants. She's been gone a year now, and unless I've missed somebody, she's run with four different carpenters. And a real estate developer. Her ski instructor. And some kid who lets her snort his cocaine and ride his motorcycle."

Jimmy nodded. "She brings them in now and then. Not all at once, though. You say you did finally get divorced?"

"It was final last week," said Sonny. He grinned at Jimmy. "That tell you anything about the weather?"

Jimmy grinned back. "That it hasn't rained in years," he said. "That tumbleweeds are blowing down Main Street, and all the windows in all the houses are dark and frosted with fly shit."

Two women came through the door with bicycles, dripping water. Sonny thought of his string, by now huddled under the big trees on the river bank. The new horse outside was probably not enjoying the weather on Main Street, but he would be all right. Dude horses had to learn to put up with a lot.

"Lovely creatures, aren't they?" said Jimmy.

"Horses?"

Jimmy pointed. "Women."

"I like them," said Sonny, not turning to look.

Jimmy laughed. "You sure pick some winners."

"I even like the winners," said Sonny.

The women sat down on the two stools next to Sonny. The one closer to him said her name was Kim. The other one was Janice.

"Call me Sonny," said Sonny.

"Is that your horse outside?" asked Kim.

Sonny nodded. "One of them," he said.

"You mind bikes in here?" Janice asked Jimmy.

"We serve anybody," said Jimmy. "Long as their money's good."

"BIKES," said Kim.

"Their money's no good," said Sonny, putting a bill on the bar. "Take it out of this."

"Thanks, cowboy," said Kim.

"It's a pleasure, ma'am," said Sonny, and he picked up his hat and placed it over his heart.

Kim and Janice wanted vodkas with a twist. They were flight attendants, they said, and had both been to Russia, and that was where they had learned to like vodka.

"It was either that or drink the water," said Kim.

"Those people over there," said Janice, "are unlucky. Very unlucky."

"They'll do anything for a pair of blue jeans," said Kim.

"What's your horse's name?" asked Janice.

"Don't have a name," said Sonny. "What will those people over there do for a pair of blue jeans?"

"Anything," said Kim. "Take you around Moscow. Give you their AK-47. Marry you."

"They only want to marry you," said Janice, "to get out of Russia. What do you mean your horse doesn't have a name?"

"He just don't have a name," said Sonny. "Ain't named him."

"A horse has got to have a name," said Kim.

"Did you get yourself an AK-47?" asked Sonny.

"You can't take them on the plane," said Kim. "Even when you work on the plane. I got taken around Moscow instead."

"So what are you going to name your horse?" asked Janice.

"Ain't."

"Aint? What kind of a name is that?"

"Ain't gonna name him."

"A horse has got to have a name," said Kim again.

"You name him, then," said Sonny. "He's just a dude horse."

"George?" asked Kim.

"Already got a horse named George," said Sonny.

"How many horses do you have?" asked Kim.

"Call him Dude," said Janice.

"Fourteen," said Sonny. "Call him what?"

"Dude," said Janice.

"Dude the Horse," said Jimmy the Bartender. "It does have a ring to it."

"That's good," said Sonny. "Dude he is."

"How'd you get fourteen horses?" asked Kim.

"I'm an outfitter," said Sonny. "I sell horse rides. You show up tomorrow morning, I'll let you ride for free."

"I want to ride Dude," said Janice.

"You can't," said Kim. "We've got a charter flight to work tomorrow. You know that."

"Let's ride tonight, then," said Janice.

"It's raining," said Kim.

"I bet it's stopped," said Janice. She jumped off her bar stool and walked to the door. When she pushed it open, sunlight came streaming in, blinding them all.

"C'mon," said Janice. "Let's go tell Dude his name."

Kim jumped off her stool. "She's crazy about horses," she said. "And she's never even been on one.

"Can we ride him?" asked Janice.

"No," said Sonny. "And stay away from his heels."

"I used to have a horse," said Kim. Then she looked at Sonny. "You married, cowboy?"

"Was once," said Sonny. "It was the only way I could get out of Russia."

"I had a horse for two years," said Kim. "Then my parents got a divorce and they sold him. It broke my sixteen-year-old heart. That was ten years ago, and I still remember it every day." She turned and walked to Janice, and they disappeared into the light.

When the door had closed behind them, Sonny said, "Every girl has a horse story."

"Even Catherine the Great," said Jimmy.

"No," said Sonny. "They really do. It's like a boy and his dog. A girl and her horse."

"I think she likes cowboys," said Jimmy.

"She just likes horses," said Sonny.

Jimmy put another beer on the bar, took Sonny's money, and rang up the drinks. "I think you better go check on your horse," he said.

"Dude can take care of himself," said Sonny. But a little later he stepped off his stool and walked to the door, shaded his eyes, and opened it. The first thing he noticed was that his saddle was gone. So was his horse. But he looked down the block in time to see it go around the corner in a hard trot, with Kim and Janice bouncing on its back, one up, one down. Sonny shrugged and went back in the bar.

"They've gone for a ride," said Sonny.

"I thought you said they couldn't."

"I did. But it don't matter. Perfectly good women go bad, you get them around horses."

"Horses, too?" asked Jimmy.

"I'll tell you a story," said Sonny.

"While you're waiting for your horse to come back," said Jimmy, and poured him another beer.

"It's a sad story," said Sonny. "My wife had a dream of horses."

"Ex-wife," said Jimmy "Please. I see guys in here calling their ex-wives their wives, and the next thing I know they're in jail."

"Ex-wife," said Sonny carefully. "But she still dreamed of horses. A whole herd of them. Arabians. And they'd roam over a big ranch full of mountains and meadows, and it would be her ranch, and she'd ride on the whitest Arabian, and she'd ride the world until she found Her Cowboy."

"Are Arabians white?" asked Jimmy.

"These were. Every one of them. Clearcoat metallic white. And maybe they had wings, too. In fact I think they did. Every one of them had wings. They cost a little more that way, but it's worth it on hot days."

"Like Pegasus," said Jimmy. "The horse with wings."

"That's probably where she got the idea," said Sonny. "Off an old gas station sign."

"A whole herd of Pegasuses," said Jimmy.

"Pegasi," said Sonny. "A flock. That's what she wanted." He looked straight at Jimmy, and for a second his mouth became just a scar. "But she was a practical woman. She knew winged horses are rare and hard to catch and aerodynamically suspect anyway. So she decided she would search for Her Cowboy on a regular horse."

"Sounds practical," said Jimmy.

"Because cowboys hang out at rodeos, she learned to barrel race. She became a rodeo queen."

"She was a rodeo queen?"

"The Sodom Stampede. 1972. She never got over it."

"You married a rodeo queen," said Jimmy. "There are worse claims to fame."

"I used to come home," said Sonny, "and catch her in front of the mirror with her queen's outfit on. You know what? She still looks good in hot pink polyester. Snakeskin boots and a black felt hat and a neat little riding whip...." He stared into his own reflection behind the bar. Then he looked at Jimmy, grabbed his hat and put it over his heart again. "I still love that woman," he said.

"Your story," said Jimmy.

"The story," said Sonny, "is that we met at a rodeo. I'd gotten stomped on by a bull and she took pity on me." He put his hat back on. "We met. We married. She thought I was Her Cowboy.

"We leased a little ranch south of town. It was our homestead. I was going to break and train horses. We built corrals together. Bought a brood mare. Bought a stallion. Arabians. Didn't have any wings. But I think she thought we were going to breed them until they did have."

"You make money?" asked Jimmy.

"No," said Sonny. "We lost our asses.

"I thought they were Arabians."

Sonny took a long look at his beer. "This story is more than sad. It's tragic. You should remember that."

"You lost your Arabians."

"And our asses. We had to sell our brood stock. I took the money and bought a dude string and started taking tourists out on trail rides. She took it hard. First the horses didn't grow wings, and then Her Cowboy stopped being a cowboy."

"She didn't really think they were going to grow wings," said Jimmy.

"It's a metaphor," said Sonny.

"Pretty stupid metaphor if you ask me," said Jimmy.

"It's not stupid," said Sonny. "I knew what she was talking about."

"You thought they had wings, too?"

"Once when I was in high school," said Sonny, "I climbed over a fence and jumped on a horse. No saddle, no bridle, no nothing. It was dark. No moon.

"Is this part of the story?"

"Shut up. The horse stood there for a moment. I could feel him breathing under me, the night was so still. I don't think the horse knew he didn't have a saddle or a bridle on. Then I kicked him in the flanks, and he gave a big snort and we took off."

"It was dark?"

"Couldn't see a thing. And it seemed like he ran forever. It was a spring night. Warm and black and feeling like it was about to be full of rain. The best feeling I've ever had. I remember thinking I could die right then and it would be all right."

"You wanted to die on a horse," said Jimmy. "That's a tragic story. A truly tragic story.

"Didn't you ever feel anything you wanted to last forever?" asked Sonny.

"Once," said Jimmy. "It didn't."

"Jimmy," said Sonny, "That night, that horse had wings."

Jimmy picked a beer glass from the rack above his head and stared at it. He grabbed a bar towel and began polishing the water spots off it. Then he put it under the beer tap and carefully filled it. Then he drank from it and put it down in front of him. "That's not tragic," he said. "It's not even sad."

"Wrong. It is tragic. Because after the horse ran and ran that night, and after I felt those great wings on either side of me, and the whole world far below me, and the power of that big wild beating heart between my legs, then we ran into a barbed-wire fence. I was thrown free, and landed on my back in an irrigation canal. I got wet. But the horse broke both front legs."

"Not his wings."

"The wings are a metaphor. Legs are harder to fix."

"So it is a tragic story," said Jimmy. "What's it got to do with your ex-wife?"

"My ex-wife," said Sonny, "doesn't believe in fences. Or tragedy either. If she'd told the story, she'd still be flying up around the moon and you-just because you sat and listened to her-you'd be there with her and you'd be in love with her and the horse would be in love with you both instead of having to be shot because both front legs were broke-because it would have never have hit the fence, and never would have had to be put out of its misery, the way she'd tell it."

"I have not fallen in love in years," said Jimmy.

"How about misery?"

"Misery," said Jimmy, "is an occupational hazard."

"Then you'll understand what it had to feel like when I come home one day and find her putting her stuff in a carpenter's pickup. The carpenter's sitting at the wheel and he won't look at me.

" 'You're not a cowboy,' she tells me when she sees me. 'Cowboys herd cows. You're just a people-boy.' "

" 'I'm trying to make a living,' I tell her.

" 'Running pony rides?' she says. 'Riding little kids off into the sunset while their parents play golf?' Then she says, 'It's just not the great glowing West with you in it.' "

"Nothing personal," said Jimmy.

"It gets worse," said Sonny. " 'Don't leave,' I tell her. 'I love you.'

"She starts crying. 'Damn you,' she says. Then she says, 'I knew you were going to be a shit about this.' And still the carpenter won't look at me."

There was a silence. Finally Jimmy asked, "End of story?"

"Sure," said Sonny.

The door opened. A softer light pooled in front of the doorway. Kim walked in and stood still, her blonde hair glowing until the door swung shut and the dimness of The Rest closed upon her.

"Look," said Jimmy. "A woman. With wings."

"We've lost Janice," Kim said.

"She fall off the horse?" asked Sonny.

"She fell in love with the horse," Kim said. "She's out there now, talking to him. I don't think you'll get him back."

Sonny shrugged. "I can write up a long-term lease, if she wants. Unlimited mileage, and a buy-back option at the end of three years."

"When you talk to her," said Kim, "don't put it that way."

Janice pushed open the door and walked toward them, with a smile on her face that was like no smile Sonny had ever seen on a flight attendant. She sat down on the stool next to Sonny's and touched him on the arm.

"I like your horse," said Janice. "I want you to take me for a ride."

"I can do that," said Sonny.

"There's a beautiful sunset going on outside," said Janice. "I want to ride off into it."

"Sunset rides are my specialty," said Sonny. "You're in luck."

"You're not in luck," said Kim. "It's going to get dark before you get even halfway to the sunset. And we have a flight tomorrow."

"My horses can see in the dark," said Sonny. "Anyway, there's a moon," said Jimmy the Bartender. "That's right," said Sonny. "There is a moon. Which means you can have a moonlight ride. A moonlight ride with a real cowboy. Silhouettes of pine trees and the river rippling silver in the moonlight. A few strums on the ol' git-tar, big ol' mountains with snow on their tops, hoot owls and—"

"Can I ride Dude?" asked Janice.

"You can ride Dude," said Sonny. "Dude is mighty good on moonlight rides."

"Dude is barely broke," said Kim. "He is a nervous son-of-a-bitch. He bucked us off."

"But he didn't mean to," said Janice. "He told me he didn't."

"I can't stand it," said Kim. "You did this to me in Russia, too. You'd never ridden on a tank before, you said. If we miss our flight-"

"It's going to be a warm night with a big moon," said Janice. "Think about it. Riding along with a beautiful animal under you-"

"I'll take you," said Jimmy the Bartender. "Forget the horse."

"It's got to be with a real cowboy," said Janice. Jimmy grabbed Sonny's hat off the bar and put it on his head. "How's this?" he asked.

"Gimme that," said Sonny, reaching.

"It isn't the same. You're a bartender." said Janice. "You've probably never even been on a horse. I have. Sonny has."

"Goddammit," said Sonny, "gimme my hat."

Jimmy ducked away from Sonny, then took the hat off and put it over his heart. "I luhuvved that woman," he said.

"What woman?" asked Janice.

"Sonny's been telling me about his wife," said Jimmy.

"Ex-wife," said Sonny. "And give me my hat."

Jimmy handed the hat back to Sonny, who brushed dust off it and put it on his head.

"Don't mess with the hat," said Sonny. Then he turned to Janice and pointed off into a dark corner of The Rest. "Out there, west of town, there's a trail that runs up into the mountains, up to a little lake surrounded by big old pine trees. It's a secret place. Found it one day when I was looking for a lost pony. We'll ride up there and build a fire and watch the big moon come up.

"I'll bring the marshmallows," said Kim.

Janice ran her fingertips up and down Sonny's arm. "I like your shirt," she said.

"We'll look at the stars. Gaze into the fire. Lean back against a tree and look up yonder, and wonder if there are people like us on other planets, out there in the Milky Way—"

"That's what you do on moonlight rides?" asked Jimmy. "I never knew that."

"It's in my brochure," said Sonny. "The package includes a genuine Western midnight snack."

"I think I'd like that," said Janice. "I think I'd like that a lot." Sonny turned to Janice, looked into her face as if he were looking at her for the first time, and ran the tip of his little finger down her neck to her shoulder. She arched her neck in the direction of his hand, closed her eyes, and shivered at him.

"I guess we'll find out," said Sonny.

"Janice," said Kim, "not again."

Janice ignored her. "C'mon, cowboy," she said. She grabbed Sonny by the elbow and pulled him off his barstool. His spurs jingled against the silence. Janice walked him a little way toward the door, stopped, and looked up at him. "You're really tall in those boots," she said. Then she turned toward Kim. "Don't wait up," she said.

She pulled Sonny toward the door. When they reached it, Sonny pulled it open. A silver and rose glow framed Sonny and Janice for a moment. Then the door swung shut behind them, and the only light that Kim and Jimmy could see was after-image.

"Oh, to be a cowboy," said Jimmy.

"It's not the cowboy," said Kim. "It's the horse."

"For a minute there," said Jimmy, "I thought it was the boots."

"Is there really a lake up there?" asked Kim.

"It's not a very big lake," said Jimmy. "More like a pond. And it's going dry."

"I thought so," said Kim.

"And there's only one tree," said Jimmy. "And it's dead. The drought got it."

"And it's not a secret place," said Kim. "Is it?"

"It's got a road to it, if that's what you mean. And you have to build your campfire in one of those little concrete fireplaces the Forest Service put there."

"And Sonny's not a real cowboy," said Kim. "Is he?"

"Originally he's from Pennsylvania," said Jimmy. "Grew up in the suburbs." He poured her another vodka. "On the house," he said.

Kim toasted him. "To a real bartender," she said.

Jimmy smiled. "Sonny believes in himself," he said. "He believes in his own reality. He believes he came West by choice. Bought a horse. Bought a hat. Married a cowgirl. It's part of a story that he thinks he's making up as he goes along."

"Divorced a cowgirl," said Kim.

"Actually, she divorced him," said Jimmy. "But that doesn't matter."

"He's still got the hat," said Kim.

"That's right. And when he sees that pond it still looks like a lake to him. It'll look like a lake to Janice, too."

"I don't think Janice is looking for a lake tonight," said Kim.

"You're right," said Jimmy. "She's looking to belong to a story that has a cowboy and a horse in it. The lake's just a prop.

"So's the cowboy," said Kim.

Jimmy looked at her with respect. It was not a look he often gave customers. "You're right," he said. "It's all props, isn't it? Sonny's got the hat and the boots and the belt buckle the size of a pie plate, and somewhere out by his stables he's got a four-horse trailer and a pickup. Take them away, and what do you have?"

"The horses," said Kim.

"The horses," said Jimmy. "I forgot the horses. But they're props, too. Sonny grew up watching westerns on TV; and the little kids that he takes on rides probably watch the same westerns on their family cable channel, and Janice has probably watched them, too. But out there, when they all ride the trails outside of town and the dust drifts up like hazy dreams from their horses' hooves, and they hear the soft squeak of leather and smell the hot smell of sagebrush and dry pine, and they see dust-matted flanks and a sunset that look like it's a studio set-how could you say that they're not in a kind of movie? That what they're being and doing isn't something made up by some guy writing for television? That what they think is their own story is simply something out of an old cultural textbook, and it was written by somebody else?"

Jimmy stopped and looked at Kim. She was looking across at the dark wall and didn't seem to be paying attention to his words. But he had a lot of time to think during afternoons in The Rest, and sometimes it seemed that if the ideas he came up with during that time weren't important, then there was nothing in his life that was important at all. He shrugged. That was just on sad days. Sometimes there were other days-and other movies, ones involving bartenders and flight attendants. He wondered how he could get her to hang around until closing time.

"But don't you wonder," he said, "if there isn't some original Text, something that began the whole story-some moment, four hundred years ago, when some long-dead gold-seeking Spaniard got tired of chasing runaway horses, and saw, there in the empty Western Desert, three or four of them on a far ridge, and said to hell with it and went back to camp? That there was, in that first tired and angry release of horses that had escaped their corral, the beginning of all our Western lives? Wasn't that the Original Text from which all our stories came?"

Kim turned slowly toward him, as if being pulled away from a movie screen full of horses that were swift and sleek and beautiful and hers.

"You ever been on a horse?" she asked him.

When Jimmy confessed that he hadn't, she asked, "Then who's this guy Tex anyway?"

Eileen Gunn
(1945-)

As a Seattle resident, Eileen Gunn has been employed as a writer and manager in advertising agencies and at several large companies not unlike the one described in "Stable Strategies for Middle Management," which first appeared in *Isaac Asimov's Science Fiction Magazine* (1988). She wrote the story in 1987, and, yes, she sometimes refers to it as her "Microsoft story." Like most writers, she has also worked on assembly lines, performed manual labor, done temp clerical work, and spent a lot of time reading the want ads. She appreciates the not-so-subtle difference between working for herself and working for someone else. Her stories have twice been nominated for the Hugo Award of the World Science Fiction Association.

Stable Strategies for Middle Management

Our cousin the insect has an external skeleton made of shiny brown chitin, a material that is particularly responsive to the demands of evolution. lust as bioengineering has sculpted our bodies into new forms, so evolution has shaped the early insect's chewing mouth-parts into her descendants 'chisels, siphons, and stilettos, and has molded from the chitin special tools—pockets to carry pollen, combs to clean her compound eyes, notches on which she can fiddle a song.

—*From the popular science program* Insect People!

I AWOKE THIS MORNING to discover that bioengineering had made demands upon me during the night. My tongue had turned into a stiletto, and my left hand now contained a small chitinous comb, as if for cleaning a compound eye. Since I didn't have compound eyes, I thought that perhaps this presaged some change to come.

I dragged myself out of bed, wondering how I was going to drink my coffee through a stiletto. Was I now expected to kill my breakfast, and dispense with coffee entirely? I hoped I was not evolving into a creature whose survival depended on early-morning alertness. My circadian rhythms would no doubt keep pace with any physical changes, but my unevolved soul was repulsed at the thought of my waking cheerfully at dawn, ravenous for some wriggly little creature that had arisen even earlier.

I looked down at Greg, still asleep, the edge of our red and white quilt pulled up under his chin. His mouth had changed during the night too, and seemed to contain some sort of a long probe. Were we growing apart?

I reached down with my unchanged hand and touched his hair. It was still shiny brown, soft and thick, luxurious. But along his cheek, under his beard, I could feel patches of sclerotin, as the flexible chitin in his skin was slowly hardening to an impermeable armor.

He opened his eyes, staring blearily forward without moving his head. I could see him move his mouth cautiously, examining its internal changes. He turned his head and looked up at me, rubbing his hair slightly into my hand.

"Time to get up?" he asked. I nodded. "Oh, God," he said. He said this every morning. It was like a prayer.

"I'll make coffee," I said. "Do you want some?"

He shook his head slowly. "Just a glass of apricot nectar," he said. He unrolled his long, rough tongue and looked at it, slightly cross-eyed. "This is real interesting, but it wasn't in the catalog. I'll be sipping lunch from flowers pretty soon. That ought to draw a second glance at Duke's."

"I thought account execs were expected to sip their lunches," I said.

"Not from the flower arrangements... " he said, still exploring the odd shape of his mouth. Then he looked up at me and reached up from under the covers. "Come here."

It had been a while, I thought, and I had to get to work. But he did smell terribly attractive. Perhaps he was developing aphrodisiac scent glands. I climbed back under the covers and stretched my body against his. We were both developing chitinous knobs and odd lumps that made this less than comfortable. "How am I supposed to kiss you with a stiletto in my mouth?" I asked.

"There are other things to do. New equipment presents new possibilities." He pushed the covers back and ran his unchanged hands down my body from shoulder to thigh. "Let me know if my tongue is too rough."

It was not.

FUZZY-MINDED, I GOT OUT of bed for the second time and drifted into the kitchen.

Measuring the coffee into the grinder, I realized that I was no longer interested in drinking it, although it was diverting for a moment to spear the beans with my stiletto. What was the damn thing for, anyhow? I wasn't sure I wanted to find out.

Putting the grinder aside, I poured a can of apricot nectar into a tulip glass. Shallow glasses were going to be a problem for Greg in the future, I thought. Not to mention solid food.

My particular problem, however, if I could figure out what I was supposed to eat for breakfast, was getting to the office in time for my ten A.M. meeting. Maybe I'd just skip breakfast. I dressed quickly and dashed out the door before Greg was even out of bed.

Thirty minutes later, I was more or less awake and sitting in the small conference room with the new marketing manager, listening to him lay out his plan for the Model 2000 launch.

In signing up for his bioengineering program, Harry had chosen specialized primate adaptation, B-E Option No.4. He had evolved into a textbook example: small and long-limbed, with forward-facing eyes for judging distances and long, grasping fingers to keep him from falling out of his tree.

He was dressed for success in a pin-striped three-piece suit that fit his simian proportions perfectly. I wondered what premium he paid for custom-made. Or did he patronize a ready-to-wear shop that catered especially to primates?

I listened as he leaped agilely from one ridiculous marketing premise to the next. Trying to borrow credibility from mathematics and engineering, he used wildly metaphoric bizspeak, "factoring in the need for pipeline throughout," "fine-tuning the media mix," without even cracking a smile.

Harry had been with the company only a few months, straight from business school. He saw himself as a much-needed infusion of talent. I didn't like him, but I envied his ability to root through his subconscious and toss out one half-formed idea after another. I know he felt it reflected badly on me that I didn't join in and spew forth a random selection of promotional suggestions.

I didn't think much of his marketing plan. The advertising section was a textbook application of theory with no practical basis. I had two options: I could force him to accept a solution that would work, or I could yes him to death, making sure everybody understood it was his idea. I knew which path I'd take.

"Yeah, we can do that for you," I told him. "No problem." We'd see which of us would survive and which was hurtling to an evolutionary dead end.

Although Harry had won his point, he continued to belabor it. My attention wandered—I'd heard it all before. His voice was the hum of an air conditioner, a familiar, easily ignored background noise. I drowsed and new emotions stirred in me, yearnings to float through moist air currents, to land on bright surfaces, to engorge myself with warm, wet food.

Adrift in insect dreams, I became sharply aware of the bare skin of Harry's arm, between his gold-plated watchband and his rolled-up sleeve, as he manipulated papers on the conference room table. He smelled greasily delicious, like a pepperoni pizza or a charcoal-broiled hamburger. I realized he probably wouldn't taste as good as he smelled, but I was hungry. My stiletto-like tongue was there for a purpose, and it wasn't to skewer cubes of tofu. I leaned over his arm and braced myself against the back of his hand, probing with my styles to find a capillary.

Harry noticed what I was doing and swatted me sharply on the side of the head. I pulled away before he could hit me again.

"We were discussing the Model 2000 launch. Or have you forgotten?" he said, rubbing his arm.

"Sorry. I skipped breakfast this morning." I was embarrassed.

"Well, get your hormones adjusted, for chrissake." He was annoyed, and I couldn't really blame him. "Let's get back to the media allocation issue, if you can keep your mind on it. I've got another meeting at eleven in Building Two."

Inappropriate feeding behavior was not unusual in the company, and corporate etiquette sometimes allowed minor lapses to pass without pursuit. Of course, I could no longer hope that he would support me on moving some money out of the direct-mail budget....

DURING THE REMAINDER OF THE MEETING, my glance kept drifting through the open door of the conference room, toward a large decorative plant in the hall, one of those oases of generic greenery that dot the corporate landscape. It didn't look succulent exactly-it obviously wasn't what I would have preferred to eat if I hadn't been so hungry-but I wondered if I swung both ways?

I grabbed a handful of the broad leaves as I left the room and carried them back to my office. With my tongue, I probed a vein in the thickest part of a leaf. It wasn't so bad. Tasted green. I sucked them dry and tossed the husks in the wastebasket.

I was still omnivorous, at least—female mosquitoes don't eat plants. So the process wasn't complete....

I got a cup of coffee, for company, from the kitchenette and sat in my office with the door closed and wondered what was happening. The incident with Harry disturbed me. Was I turning into a mosquito? If so, what the hell kind of good was that supposed to do me? The company didn't have any use for a whining loner.

There was a knock at the door, and my boss stuck his head in. I nodded and gestured him into my office. He sat down in the visitor's chair on the other side of my desk. From the look on his face, I could tell Harry had talked to him already.

Tom Samson was an older guy, pre-bioengineering. He was well versed in stimulus-response techniques, but had somehow never made it to the top job. I liked him, but then that was what he intended. Without sacrificing authority, he had pitched his appearance, his gestures, the tone of his voice, to the warm end of the spectrum. Even though I knew what he was doing, it worked.

He looked at me with what appeared to be sympathy, but was actually a practiced sign stimulus, intended to defuse any fight-or-flight response. "Is there something bothering you, Margaret?"

"Bothering me? I'm hungry, that's all. I get short-tempered when I'm hungry."

Watch it, I thought. He hasn't referred to the incident; leave it for him to bring up. I made my mind go bland and forced myself to meet his eyes. A shifty gaze is a guilty gaze.

Tom just looked at me, biding his time, waiting for me to put myself on the spot. My coffee smelt burnt, but I stuck my tongue in it and pretended to drink. "I'm just not human until I've had my coffee in the morning." Sounded phony. Shut up, I thought.

This was the opening that Tom was waiting for. "That's what I wanted to speak to you about, Margaret." He sat there, hunched over in a relaxed way, like a mountain gorilla, unthreatened by natural enemies. "I just talked to Harry Winthrop, and he said you were trying to suck his blood during a meeting on marketing strategy." He paused for a moment to check my reaction, but the neutral expression was fixed on my face and I said nothing. His face changed to project disappointment. "You know, when we noticed you were developing three distinct body segments, we had great hopes for you. But your actions just don't reflect the social and organizational development we expected."

He paused, and it was my turn to say something in my defense. "Most insects are solitary, you know. Perhaps the company erred in hoping for a termite or an ant. I'm not responsible for that."

"Now, Margaret," he said, his voice simulating genial reprimand. "This isn't the jungle, you know. When you signed those consent forms, you agreed to let the B-E staff mold you into a more useful corporate organism. But this isn't nature, this is man reshaping nature. It doesn't follow the old rules. You can truly be anything you want to be. But you have to cooperate."

"I'm doing the best I can," I said, cooperatively. "I'm putting in eighty hours a week."

"Margaret, the quality of your work is not an issue. It's your interactions with others that you have to work on. You have to learn to work as part of the group. I just cannot permit such backbiting to continue. I'll have Arthur get you an appointment this afternoon with the B-E counselor." Arthur was his secretary. He knew everything that happened in the department and mostly kept his mouth shut.

"I'd be a social insect if I could manage it," I muttered as Tom left my office. "But I've never known what to say to people in bars."

For lunch I met Greg and our friend David Detlor at a health-food restaurant that advertises fifty different kinds of fruit nectar. We'd never eaten there before, but Greg knew he'd love the place. It was already a favorite of David's, and he still has all his teeth, so I figured it would be okay with me.

David was there when I arrived, but not Greg. David works for the company too, in a different department. He, however, has proved remarkably resistant to corporate blandishment. Not only has he never undertaken B-E, he hasn't even bought a three-piece suit. Today he was wearing chewed-up blue jeans and a flashy Hawaiian shirt, of a type that was cool about ten years ago.

"Your boss lets you dress like that?" I asked.

"We have this agreement. I don't tell her she has to give me a job, and she doesn't tell me what to wear."

David's perspective on life is very different from mine. And I don't think it's just that he's in R&D and I'm in Advertising-it's more basic than that. Where he sees the world as a bunch of really neat but optional puzzles put there for his enjoyment, I see it as... well, as a series of SATs.

"So what's new with you guys?" he asked, while we stood around waiting for a table.

"Greg's turning into a goddamn butterfly. He went out last week and bought a dozen Italian silk sweaters. It's not a corporate look."

"He's not a corporate *guy,* Margaret."

"Then why is he having all this B-E done if he's not even going to use it?"

"He's dressing up a little. He just wants to look nice. Like Michael Jackson, you know?"

I couldn't tell whether David was kidding me or not. Then he started telling me about his music, this barbershop quartet that he sings in. They were going to dress in black leather for the next competition and sing Shel Silverstein's "Come to Me, My Masochistic Baby."

"It'll knock them on their tails," he said gleefully. "We've already got a great arrangement."

"Do you think it will win, David?" It seemed too weird to please the judges in that sort of a show.

"Who cares?" said David. He didn't look worried.

Just then Greg showed up. He was wearing a cobalt blue silk sweater with a copper green design on it. Italian. He was also wearing a pair of dangly earrings shaped like bright blue airplanes. We were shown to a table near a display of carved vegetables.

"This is great," said David. "Everybody wants to sit near the vegetables. It's where you sit to be *seen* in this place." He nodded to Greg. "I think it's your sweater."

"It's the butterfly in my personality," said Greg. "Headwaiters never used to do stuff like this for me. I always got the table next to the espresso machine."

If Greg was going to go on about the perks that come with being a butterfly, I was going to change the subject.

"David, how come you still haven't signed up for B-E?" I asked. "The company pays half the cost, and they don't ask questions."

David screwed up his mouth, raised his hands to his face, and made small, twitching, insect gestures, as if grooming his nose and eyes. "I'm doing okay the way I am.

Greg chuckled at this, but I was serious. "You'll get ahead faster with a little adjustment. Plus you're showing a good attitude, you know, if you do it."

"I'm getting ahead faster than I want to right now—it looks like I won't be able to take the three months off that I wanted this summer."

"Three months?" I was astonished. "Aren't you afraid you won't have a job to come back to?"

"I could live with that," said David calmly, opening his menu.

The waiter took our orders. We sat for a moment in a companionable silence, the self-congratulation that follows ordering high-fiber foodstuffs. Then I told them the story of my encounter with Harry Winthrop.

"There's something wrong with me," I said. "Why suck his blood? What good is that supposed to do me?"

"Well," said David, "*you* chose this schedule of treatments. Where did you want it to go?"

"According to the catalog," I said, "the No.2 Insect Option is supposed to make me into a successful competitor for a middle-management niche, with triggerable responses that can be useful in gaining entry to upper hierarchical levels. Unquote." Of course, that was just ad talk—I didn't really expect it to do all that. "That's what I want. I want to be in charge. I want to be the boss."

"Maybe you should go back to BioEngineering and try again," said Greg. "Sometimes the hormones don't do what you expect. Look at my tongue, for instance." He unfurled it gently and rolled it back into his mouth. "Though I'm sort of getting to like it." He sucked at his drink, making disgusting slurping sounds. He didn't need a straw.

"Don't bother with it, Margaret," said David firmly, taking a cup of rosehip tea from the waiter. "Bioengineering is a waste of time and money and millions of years of evolution. If human beings were intended to be managers, we'd have evolved pin-striped body covering."

"That's cleverly put," I said, "but it's dead wrong."

The waiter brought our lunches, and we stopped talking as he put them in front of us. It seemed like the anticipatory silence of three very hungry people, but was in fact the polite silence of three people who have been brought up not to argue in front of disinterested bystanders. As soon as he left, we resumed the discussion.

"I mean it," David said. "The dubious survival benefits of management aside, bioengineering is a waste of effort. Harry Winthrop, for instance, doesn't need B-E at all. Here he is, fresh out of business school, audibly buzzing with lust for a high-level management position. Basically he's just marking time until a presidency opens up somewhere. And what gives him the edge over you is his youth and inexperience, not some specialized primate adaptation."

"Well," I said with some asperity, "he's not constrained by a knowledge of what's failed in the past, that's for sure. But saying that doesn't solve my problem, David. Harry's signed up. I've signed up. The changes are under way and I don't have any choice."

I squeezed a huge glob of honey into my tea from a plastic bottle shaped like a teddy bear. I took a sip of the tea; it was minty and very sweet. "And now I'm turning into the wrong kind of insect. It's ruined my ability to deal with Product Marketing."

"Oh, give it a rest!" said Greg suddenly. "This is *so* boring. I don't want to hear any more about corporate hugger-mugger. Let's talk about something that's fun."

I had had enough of Greg's lepidopterate lack of concentration. "Something that's *fun?* I've invested all my time and most of my genetic material in this job. This is all the goddamn fun there is."

The honeyed tea made me feel hot. My stomach itched—I wondered if I was having an allergic reaction. I scratched, and not discreetly. My hand came out from under my shirt full of little waxy scales. What the hell was going on under there? I tasted one of the scales; it was wax all right. Worker bee changes? I couldn't help myself—I stuffed the wax into my mouth.

David was busying himself with his alfalfa sprouts, but Greg looked disgusted. "That's gross, Margaret," he said. He made a face, sticking his tongue part way out. Talk about gross. "Can't you wait until after lunch?"

I was doing what came naturally, and did not dignify his statement with a response. There was a side dish of bee pollen on the table. I took a spoonful and mixed it with the wax, chewing noisily. I'd had a rough morning, and bickering with Greg wasn't making the day more pleasant.

Besides, neither he nor David has any real respect for my position in the company. Greg doesn't take my job seriously at all. And David simply does what he wants to do, regardless of whether it makes any money, for himself or anyone else. He was giving me a back-to-nature lecture, and it was far too late for that.

This whole lunch was a waste of time. I was tired of listening to them, and felt an intense urge to get back to work. A couple of quick stings distracted them both: I had the advantage of surprise. I ate some more honey and quickly waxed them over. They were soon hibernating side by side in two large octagonal cells.

I looked around the restaurant. People were rather nervously pretending not to have noticed. I called the waiter over and handed him my credit card. He signaled to several bus boys, who brought a covered cart and took Greg and David away. "They'll eat themselves out of that by Thursday afternoon," I told him. "Store them on their sides in a warm, dry place, away from direct heat." I left a large tip.

I walked back to the office, feeling a bit ashamed of myself. A couple days of hibernation weren't going to make Greg or David more sympathetic to my problems. And they'd be real mad when they got out.

I didn't use to do things like that. I used to be more patient, didn't I? More appreciative of the diverse spectrum of human possibility. More interested in sex and television.

This job was not doing much for me as a warm, personable human being. At the very least, it was turning me into an unpleasant lunch companion. Whatever had made me think I wanted to get into management anyway?

The money, maybe.

But that wasn't all. It was the challenge, the chance to do something new, to control the total effort instead of just doing part of a project....

The money too, though. There were other ways to get money. Maybe I should just kick the supports out from under the damn job and start over again.

I saw myself sauntering into Tom's office, twirling his visitor's chair around and falling into it.

The words "I quit" would force their way out, almost against my will. His face would show surprise—feigned, of course. By then I'd have to go through with it. Maybe I'd put my feet up on his desk. And then—But was it possible to just quit, to go back to being the person I used to be? No, I wouldn't be able to do it. I'd never be a management virgin again.

I walked up to the employee entrance at the rear of the building. A suction device next to the door sniffed at me, recognized my scent, and clicked the door open. Inside, a group of new employees, trainees, were clustered near the door, while a personnel officer introduced them to the lock and let it familiarize itself with their pheromones.

On the way down the hall, I passed Tom's office. The door was open. He was at his desk, bowed over some papers, and looked up as I went by.

"Ah, Margaret," he said. "Just the person I want to talk to. Come in for a minute, would you." He moved a large file folder onto the papers in front of him on his desk, and folded his hands on top of them. "So glad you were passing by." He nodded toward a large, comfortable chair. "Sit down."

"We're going to be doing a bit of restructuring in the department," he began, "and I'll need your input, so I want to fill you in now on what will be happening."

I was immediately suspicious. Whenever Tom said "I'll need your input," he meant everything was decided already.

"We'll be reorganizing the whole division, of course," he continued, drawing little boxes on a blank piece of paper. He'd mentioned this at the department meeting last week.

"Now, your group subdivides functionally into two separate areas, wouldn't you say?"

"Well—"

"Yes," he said thoughtfully, nodding his head as though in agreement. "That would be the way to do it." He added a few lines and a few more boxes. From what I could see, it meant that Harry would do all the interesting stuff and I'd sweep up afterwards.

"Looks to me as if you've cut the balls out of my area and put them over into Harry Winthrop's," I said.

"Ah, but your area is still very important, my dear. That's why I don't have you actually reporting to Harry." He gave me a smile like a lie.

He had put me in a tidy little bind. After all, he was my boss. If he was going to take most of my area away from me, as it seemed he was, there wasn't much I could do to stop him. And I would be better off if we both pretended that I hadn't experienced any loss of status. That way I kept my title and my salary.

"Oh, I see." I said. "Right."

It dawned on me that this whole thing had been decided already, and that Harry Winthrop probably knew all about it. He'd probably even wangled a raise out of it. Tom had called me in here to make it look casual, to make it look as though I had something to say about it. I'd been set up.

This made me mad. There was no question of quitting now. I'd stick around and fight. My eyes blurred, unfocused, refocused again. Compound eyes! The promise of the small comb in my hand was fulfilled! I felt a deep chemical understanding of the ecological system I was now a part of. I knew where I fit in. And I knew what I was going to do. It was inevitable now, hardwired in at the DNA level.

The strength of this conviction triggered another change in the chitin, and for the first time I could actually feel the rearrangement of my mouth and nose, a numb tickling like inhaling seltzer water. The stiletto receded and mandibles jutted forth, rather like Katharine Hepburn. Form and function achieved an orgasmic synchronicity. As my jaw pushed forward, mantis-like, it also opened, and I pounced on Tom and bit his head off.

He leaped from his desk and danced headless about the office.

I felt in complete control of myself as I watched him and continued the conversation. "About the Model 2000 launch," I said. "If we factor in the demand for pipeline throughput and adjust the media mix just a bit, I think we can present a very tasty little package to Product Marketing by the end of the week."

Tom continued to strut spasmodically, making vulgar copulative motions. Was I responsible for evoking these mantid reactions? I was unaware of a sexual component in our relationship.

I got up from the visitor's chair and sat behind his desk, thinking about what had just happened. It goes without saying that I was surprised at my own actions. I mean, irritable is one thing, but biting people's heads off is quite another. But I have to admit that my second thought was, well, this certainly is a useful strategy, and should make a considerable difference in my ability to advance myself. Hell of a lot more productive than sucking people's blood.

Maybe there was something after all to Tom's talk about having the proper attitude.

And, of course, thinking of Tom, my third reaction was regret. He really had been a likeable guy, for the most part. But what's done is done, you know, and there's no use chewing on it after the fact.

I BUZZED HIS ASSISTANT on the intercom. "Arthur," I said, "Mr. Samson and I have come to an evolutionary parting of the ways. Please have him re-engineered. And charge it to Personnel."

Now I feel an odd itching on my forearms and thighs. Notches on which I might fiddle a song?

Ursula K. Le Guin
(1929-)

An acclaimed author of science fiction, fantasy, and children's books, Ursula Le Guin is perhaps best known for her *Earthsea* series (1968-1990). Two of her novels won both the Nebula and Hugo awards: *The Left Hand of Darkness* (1969) and *The Dispossessed* (1975). LeGuin lives in Portland, Oregon. In the following excerpt from her 1975 novella, *The New Atlantis*, Le Guin imagines a dystopian future for work, politics, and life generally—one in which state control figures prominently.

From *The New Atlantis*

Coming back from my Wilderness Week I sat by an odd sort of man in the bus. For a long time we didn't talk; I was mending stockings and he was reading. Then the bus broke down a few miles outside Gresham. Boiler trouble, the way it generally is when the driver insists on trying to go over thirty. It was a Supersonic Superscenic Deluxe Longdistance coal-burner, with Home Comfort, that means a toilet, and the seats were pretty comfortable, at least those that hadn't yet worked loose from their bolts, so everybody waited inside the bus; besides, it was raining. We began talking, the way people do when there's a breakdown and a wait. He held up his pamphlet and tapped it—he was a dry-looking man with a schoolteacherish way of using his hands—and said, "This is interesting. I've been reading that a new continent is rising from the depths of the sea."

The blue stockings were hopeless. You have to have something besides holes to darn onto. "Which sea?"

"They're not sure yet. Most specialists think the Atlantic. But there's evidence it may be happening in the Pacific, too."

"Won't the oceans get a little crowded?" I said, not taking it seriously. I was a bit snappish, because of the breakdown and because those blue stockings had been good warm ones.

He tapped the pamphlet again and shook his head, quite serious. "No," he said. "The old continents are sinking, to make room for the new. You can see that that is happening."

You certainly can. Manhattan Island is now under eleven feet of water at low tide, and there are oyster beds in Ghirardelli Square.

"I thought that was because the oceans are rising from polar melt."

He shook his head again. "That is a factor. Due to the greenhouse effect of pollution, indeed Antarctica may become inhabitable. But climatic factors will not explain the emergence of the newer, possibly, very old continents in the Atlantic and Pacific." He went on explaining about continental drift, but I liked the idea of inhabiting Antarctica and daydreamed about it for a while. I thought of it as very empty, very quiet, all white and blue, with a faint golden glow northward from the unrising sun behind the long peak of Mount Erebus. There were a few people there; they were very quiet, too, and wore white tie and tails. Some of them carried oboes and violas. Southward the white land went up in a long silence toward the Pole.

Just the opposite, in fact, of the Mount Hood Wilderness Area. It had been a tiresome vacation. The other women in the dormitory were all right, but it was macaroni for breakfast, and there were so many organized sports. I had looked forward to the hike up to the National Forest Preserve, the largest forest left in the United States, but the trees didn't look at all the way they do in the postcards and brochures and Federal Beautification Bureau advertisements. They were spindly, and they all had little signs on saying which union they had been planted by. There were actually a lot more green picnic tables and cement Men's and Women's than there were trees. There was an electrified fence all around the forest to keep out unauthorized persons. The forest ranger talked about mountain jays, "bold little robbers," he said, "who will come and snatch the sandwich from your very hand," but I didn't see any. Perhaps because that was the weekly Watch Those Surplus Calories! Day for all the women, and so we didn't have any sandwiches. If I'd seen a mountain jay I might have snatched the sandwich from his very hand, who knows. Anyhow it was an exhausting week, and I wished I'd stayed home and practiced, even though I'd have lost a week's pay because staying home and practicing the viola doesn't count as planned implementation of recreational leisure as defined by the Federal Union of Unions.

When I came back from my Antarctican expedition, the man was reading again, and I got a look at his pamphlet; and that was the odd part of it. The pamphlet was called "Increasing Efficiency in Public Accountant Training Schools," and I could see from the one paragraph I got a glance at that there was nothing about new continents emerging from the ocean depths in it—nothing at all.

Then we had to get out and walk on into Gresham, because they had decided that the best thing for us all to do was get onto the Greater

Portland Area Rapid Public Transit Lines, since there had been so many breakdowns that the charter bus company didn't have any more buses to send out to pick us up. The walk was wet, and rather dull, except when we passed the Cold Mountain Commune. They have a wall around it to keep out unauthorized persons, and a big neon sign out front saying COLD MOUNTAIN COMMUNE and there were some people in authentic jeans and ponchos by the highway selling macrame belts and sandcast candles and soybean bread to the tourists. In Gresham, I took the 4:40 GPARPTL Superjet Flyer train to Burnside and East 230th, and then walked to 217th and got the bus to the Goldschmidt Overpass, and transferred to the shuttlebus, but it had boiler trouble, so I didn't reach the downtown transfer point until ten after eight, and the buses go on a once-an-hour schedule at 8:00, so I got a meatless hamburger at the Longhorn Inch-Thick Steak House Dinerette and caught the nine o'clock bus and got home about ten. When I let myself into the apartment I flipped the switch to turn on the lights, but there still weren't any. There had been a power outage in West Portland for three weeks. So I went feeling about for the candles in the dark, and it was a minute or so before I noticed that somebody was lying on my bed.

I panicked, and tried again to turn the lights on.

It was a man, lying there in a long thin heap. I thought a burglar had got in somehow while I was away and died. I opened the door so I could get out quick or at least my yells could be heard, and then I managed not to shake long enough to strike a match, and lighted the candle, and came a little closer to the bed.

The light disturbed him. He made a sort of snorting in his throat and turned his head. I saw it was a stranger, but I knew his eyebrows, then the breadth of his closed eyelids, then I saw my husband.

He woke up while I was standing there over him with the candle in my hand. He laughed and said still half-asleep, "Ah, Psyche! From the regions which are holy land."

Neither of us made much fuss. It was unexpected, but it did seem so natural for him to be there, after all, much more natural than for him not to be there, and he was too tired to be very emotional. We lay there together in the dark, and he explained that they had released him from the Rehabilitation Camp early because he had injured his back in an accident in the gravel quarry, and they were afraid it might get worse. If he died there it wouldn't be good publicity abroad, since there have been some nasty rumors about deaths from illness in the Rehabilitation Camps and the Federal Medical Association Hospitals; and there are scientists abroad who have heard of Simon, since somebody published his proof of Goldbach's Hypothesis in Peking. So they let him out early, with eight dollars in his pocket, which is what he had in his pocket when they arrested him, which made it, of course, fair. He had walked and hitched home from Coeur D'Alene, Idaho, with a couple of days in jail in Walla Walla for being caught hitchhiking. He almost fell asleep telling me this, and when he had told me, he did fall asleep. He needed a change of clothes and a bath but I didn't want to wake him. Besides, I was tired, too. We lay side by side and his head was on my arm. I don't suppose that I have ever been so happy. No; was it happiness? Something wider and darker, more like knowledge, more like the night: joy.

It was dark for so long, so very long. We were all blind. And there was the cold, a vast, unmoving, heavy cold. We could not move at all. We did not move. We did not speak. Our mouths were closed, pressed shut by the cold and by the weight. Our eyes were pressed shut. Our limbs were held still. Our minds were held still. For how long? There was no length of time; how long is death? And is one dead only after living, or before life as well? Certainly we thought, if we thought anything, that we were dead; but if we had ever been alive, we had forgotten it.

There was a change. It must have been the pressure that changed first, although we did not know it. The eyelids are sensitive to touch. They must have been weary of being shut. When the pressure upon them weakened a little, they opened. But there was no way for us to know that. It was too cold for us to feel anything. There was nothing to be seen. There was black.

But then—"then," for the event created time, created before and after, near and far, now and then—"then" there was the light. One light. One small, strange light that passed slowly, at what distance we could not tell. A small, greenish white, slightly blurred point of radiance, passing.

Our eyes were certainly open, "then," for we saw it. We saw the moment. The moment is a point of light. Whether in darkness or in the field of all light, the moment is small, and moves, but not quickly. And "then" it is gone.

It did not occur to us that there might be another moment. There was no reason to assume that there might be more than one. One was marvel enough: that in all the field of the dark, in the cold, heavy, dense, moveless, timeless, placeless, boundless black, there should have occurred, once, a small slightly blurred, moving light! Time need be created only once, we thought.

But we were mistaken. The difference between one and more than one is all the difference in the world. Indeed, that difference is the world.

The light returned.

The same light, or another one? There was no telling.

But, "this time," we wondered about the light: Was it small and near to us, or large and far away? Again there was no telling; but there was something about the way it moved, a trace of hesitation, a tentative quality, that did not seem proper to anything large and remote. The stars, for instance. We began to remember the stars.

The stars had never hesitated.

Perhaps the noble certainty of their gait had been a mere effect of distance. Perhaps in fact they had hurtled wildly, enormous furnace-fragments of a primal bomb thrown through the cosmic dark; but time and distance soften all agony. If the universe, as seems likely, began with an act of destruction, the stars we had used to see told no tales of it. They had been implacably serene.

The planets, however.... We began to remember the planets. They had suffered certain changes both of appearance and of course. At certain times of the year Mars would reverse its direction and go backward through the stars. Venus had been brighter and less bright as she went through her phases of crescent, full, and wane. Mercury had shuddered like a skidding drop of rain on the sky flushed with daybreak. The light we now watched had that erratic, trembling quality. We saw it, unmistakably, change direction and go backward. It then grew smaller and fainter; blinked—an eclipse?—and slowly disappeared.

Slowly, but not slowly enough for a planet.

Then—the third "then"!—arrived the indubitable and positive Wonder of the World, the Magic Trick, watch now, watch, you will not believe your eyes, mama, mama, look what I can do—

Seven lights in a row, proceeding fairly rapidly, with a darting movement, from left to right. Proceeding less rapidly from right to left, two dimmer, greenish lights. Two lights halt, blink, reverse course, proceed hastily and in a wavering manner from left to right. Seven lights increase speed, and catch up. Two lights flash desperately, flicker, and are gone.

Seven lights hang still for some while, then merge gradually into one streak, veering away, and little by little vanish into the immensity of the dark.

But in the dark now are growing other lights, many of them: lamps, dots, rows, scintillations—some near at hand, some far. Like the stars, yes, but not stars. It is not the great Existences we are seeing, but only the little lives.

In the morning Simon told me something about the Camp, but not until after he had had me check the apartment for bugs. I thought at first he had been given behavior mod and gone paranoid. We never had been infested. And I'd been living alone for a year and a half; surely they didn't want to hear me talking to myself? But he said, "They may have been expecting me to come here."

"But they let you go free!"

He just lay there and laughed at me. So I checked everywhere we could think of. I didn't find any bugs, but it did look as if somebody had gone through the bureau drawers while I was away in the Wilderness. Simon's papers were all at Max's, so that didn't matter. I made tea on the Primus, and washed and shaved Simon with the extra hot water in the kettle—he had a thick beard and wanted to get rid of it because of the lice he had brought from Camp—and while we were doing that he told me about the Camp. In fact he told me very little, but not much was necessary.

He had lost about 20 pounds. As he only weighed 140 to start with, this left little to go on with. His knees and wrist bones stuck out like

the Camp boots; he hadn't dared take the boots off, the last three days of walking, because he was afraid he wouldn't be able to get them back on. When he had to move or sit up so I could wash him, he shut his eyes.

"Am I really here?" he asked. "Am I here?"

"Yes," I said. "You are here. What I don't understand is how you got here."

"Oh, it wasn't bad so long as I kept moving. All you need is to know where you're going—to have someplace to go. You know, some of the people in Camp, if they'd let them go, they wouldn't have had that. They couldn't have gone anywhere. Keeping moving was the main thing. See, my back's all seized up, now."

When he had to get up to go to the bathroom he moved like a ninety-year-old. He couldn't stand straight, but was all bent out of shape, and shuffled. I helped him put on clean clothes. When he lay down on the bed again, a sound of pain came out of him, like tearing thick paper. I went around the room putting things away. He asked me to come sit by him and said I was going to drown him if I went on crying. "You'll submerge the entire North American continent," he said. I can't remember what he said, but he made me laugh finally. It is hard to remember things Simon says, and hard not to laugh when he says them. This is not merely the partiality of affection: He makes everybody laugh. I doubt that he intends to. It is just that a mathematician's mind works differently from other people's. Then when they laugh, that pleases him.

It was strange, and it is strange, to be thinking about "him," the man I have known for ten years, the same man, while "he" lay there changed out of recognition, a different man. It is enough to make you understand why most languages have a word like "soul." There are various degrees of death, and time spares us none of them. Yet something endures, for which a word is needed.

I said what I had not been able to say for a year and a half: "I was afraid they'd brainwash you."

He said, "Behavior mod is expensive. Even just the drugs. They save it mostly for the VIPs. But I'm afraid they got a notion I might be important after all. I got questioned a lot the last couple of months. About my 'foreign ~ He snorted. "The stuff that got published abroad, I suppose. So I want to be careful and make sure it's just a Camp again next time, and not a Federal Hospital."

"Simon, were they… are they cruel, or just righteous?"

He did not answer for a while. He did not want to answer. He knew what I was asking. He knew by what thread hangs hope, the sword, above our heads.

"Some of them… "he said at last, mumbling.

Some of them had been cruel. Some of them had enjoyed their work. You cannot blame everything on society.

"Prisoners, as well as guards," he said.

You cannot blame everything on the enemy.

"Some of them, Belle," he said with energy, touching my hand—"some of them, there were men like gold there—"

The thread is tough; you cannot cut it with one stroke.

"What have you been playing?" he asked.

"Forrest, Schubert."

"With the quartet?"

"Trio, now. Janet went to Oakland with a new lover."

"Ah, poor Max."

"It's just as well, really. She isn't a good pianist."

I make Simon laugh, too, though I don't intend to. We talked until it was past time for me to go to work. My shift since the Full Employment Act last year is ten to two. I am an inspector in a recycled paper bag factory. I have never rejected a bag yet; the electronic inspector catches all the defective ones first. It is a rather depressing job. But it's only four hours a day, and it takes more time than that to go through all the lines and physical and mental examinations, and fill out all the forms, and talk to all the welfare counselors and inspectors every week in order to qualify as Unemployed, and then line up every day for the ration stamps and the dole. Simon thought I ought to go to work as usual. I tried to, but I couldn't. He had felt very hot to the touch when I kissed him good-bye. I went instead and got a black-market doctor. A girl at the factory had recommended her, for an abortion, if I ever wanted one without going through the regulation two years of sex-depressant drugs the fed-meds make you take when they give you an abortion. She was a jeweler's assistant in a shop on Alder Street, and the girl said she was convenient because if you didn't have enough cash you could leave something in pawn at the jeweler's as payment. Nobody ever does have enough cash, and of course credit cards aren't worth much on the black market.

The doctor was willing to come at once, so we rode home on the bus together. She gathered very soon that Simon and I were married, and it was funny to see her look at us and smile like a cat. Some people love illegality for its own sake. Men, more often than women. It's men who make laws, and enforce them, and break them, and think the whole performance is wonderful. Most women would rather just ignore them. You could see that this woman, like a man, actually enjoyed breaking them. That may have been what put her into an illegal business in the first place, a preference for the shady side. But there was more to it than that. No doubt she'd wanted to be a doctor, too; and the Federal Medical Association doesn't admit women into the medical schools. She probably got her training as some other doctor's private pupil, under the counter. Very much as Simon learned mathematics, since the universities don't teach much but Business Administration and Advertising and Media Skills any more. However she learned it, she seemed to know her stuff. She fixed up a kind of homemade traction device for Simon very handily and informed him that if he did much more walking for two months he'd be crippled the rest of his life, but if he behaved himself he'd just be more or less lame. It isn't the kind of thing you'd expect to be grateful for being told, but we both were. Leaving, she gave me a bottle of about two hundred plain white pills, unlabeled. "Aspirin," she said. "He'll be in a good deal of pain off and on for weeks."

I looked at the bottle. I had never seen aspirin before, only the Super-Buffered Pane-Gon and the Triple-Power N-L-G-Zic and the Extra-Strength Apansprin with the miracle ingredient more doctors recommend, which the fed-meds always give you prescriptions for, to be filled at your FMA-approved private enterprise friendly drugstore at the low, low prices established by the Pure Food and Drug Administration in order to inspire competitive research.

"Aspirin," the doctor repeated. "The miracle ingredient more doctors recommend." She cat-grinned again. I think she liked us because we were living in sin. That bottle of black-market aspirin was probably worth more than the old Navajo bracelet I pawned for her fee.

I went out again to register Simon as temporarily domiciled at my address and to apply for Temporary Unemployment Compensation ration stamps for him. They only give them to you for two weeks and you have to come every day; but to register him as Temporarily Disabled meant getting the signatures of two fed-meds, and I thought I'd rather put that off for a while. It took three hours to go through the lines and get the forms he would have to fill out, and to answer the 'crats' questions about why he wasn't there in person. They smelled something fishy. Of course it's hard for them to prove that two people are married and aren't just adultering if you move now and then and your friends help out by sometimes registering one of you as living at their address; but they had all the back files on both of us and it was obvious that we had been around each other for a suspiciously long time. The State really does make things awfully hard for itself. It must have been simpler to enforce the laws back when marriage was legal and adultery was what got you into trouble. They only had to catch you once. But I'll bet people broke the law just as often then as they do now.

> The lantern-creatures came close enough at last that we could see not only their light, but their bodies in the illumination of their light. They were not pretty. They were dark colored, most often a dark red, and they were all mouth. They ate one another whole. Light swallowed light all swallowed together in the vaster mouth of the darkness. They moved slowly, for nothing, however small and hungry, could move fast under that weight, in that cold. Their eyes, round with fear, were never closed. Their bodies were tiny and bony behind the gaping jaws. They wore queer, ugly decorations on their lips and skulls: fringes, serrated wattles, featherlike fronds, gauds, bangles, lures. Poor little sheep of the deep pastures! Poor ragged, hunch-jawed dwarfs squeezed to the bone by the weight of the darkness, chilled to the bone by the cold of the darkness, tiny monsters burning with bright hunger, who brought us back to life!

> Occasionally, in the wan, sparse illumination of one of the lantern-creatures, we caught a momentary glimpse of other, large, unmoving shapes: the barest suggestion, off in the distance, not of a wall, nothing so solid and certain as a wall, but of a surface, an angle... Was it there?
>
> Or something would glitter, faint, far off, far down. There was no use trying to make out what it might be. Probably it was only a fleck of sediment, mud or mica, disturbed by a struggle between the lantern-creatures, flickering like a bit of diamond dust as it rose and settled slowly. In any case, we could not move to go see what it was. We had not even the cold, narrow freedom of the lantern-creatures. We were immobilized, borne down, still shadows among the half-guessed shadow walls. Were we there?
>
> The lantern-creatures showed no awareness of us. They passed before us, among us, perhaps even through us—it was impossible to be sure. They were not afraid, or curious.
>
> Once something a little larger than a hand came crawling near, and for a moment we saw quite distinctly the clean angle where the foot of a wall rose from the pavement, in the glow cast by the crawling creature, which was covered with a foliage of plumes, each plume dotted with many tiny, bluish points of light. We saw the pavement beneath the creature and the wall beside it, heartbreaking in its exact, clear linearity, its opposition to all that was fluid, random, vast, and void. We saw the creature's claws, slowly reaching out and retracting like small stiff fingers, touch the wall. Its plumage of light quivering, it dragged itself along and vanished behind the corner of the wall.
>
> So we knew that the wall was there; and that it was an outer wall, a housefront, perhaps, or the side of one of the towers of the city.
>
> We remembered the towers. We remembered the city. We had forgotten it. We had forgotten who we were; but we remembered the city, now.

WHEN I GOT HOME, THE FBI had already been there. The computer at the police precinct where I registered Simon's address must have flashed it right over to the computer at the FBI building. They had questioned Simon for about an hour, mostly about what he had been doing during the twelve days it took him to get from the Camp to Portland. I suppose they thought he had flown to Peking or something. Having a police record in Walla Walla for hitchhiking helped him establish his story. He told me that one of them had gone to the bathroom. Sure enough I found a bug stuck on the top of the bathroom door frame. I left it, as we figured it's really better to leave it when you know you have one, than to take it off and then never be sure they haven't planted another one you don't know about. As Simon said, if we felt we had to say something unpatriotic we could always flush the toilet at the same time.

I have a battery radio—there are so many work stoppages because of power failures, and days the water has to be boiled, and so on, that you really have to have a radio to save wasting time and dying of typhoid—and he turned it on while I was making supper on the Primus. The six o'clock All-American Broadcasting Company news announcer announced that peace was at hand in Uruguay, the president's confidential aide having been seen to smile at a passing blonde as he left the 613th day of the secret negotiations in a villa outside Katmandu. The war in Liberia was going well; the enemy said they had shot down seventeen American planes but the Pentagon said we had shot down twenty-two enemy planes, and the capital city—I forget its name, but it hasn't been inhabitable for seven years anyway—was on the verge of being recaptured by the forces of freedom. The police action in Arizona was also successful. The Neo-Birch insurgents in Phoenix could not hold out much longer against the massed might of the American army and air force, since their underground supply of small tactical nukes from the Weathermen in Los Angeles had been cut off. Then there was an advertisement for Fed-Cred cards, and a commercial for the Supreme Court: "Take your legal troubles to the Nine Wise Men!" Then there was something about why tariffs had gone up, and a report from the stock market, which had just closed at over two thousand, and a commercial for U.S. Government canned water, with a catchy little tune: "Don't be sorry when you drink / It's not as healthy as you think / Don't you think you really ought to / Drink coo-ool, puu-uure U.S.G. water?"—with three sopranos in close harmony on the last line. Then, just as the battery began to give out and his voice was dying away into a faraway tiny whisper, the announcer seemed to be saying something about a new continent emerging.

"What was that?"

"I didn't hear," Simon said, lying with his eyes shut and his face pale and sweaty. I gave him two aspirins before we ate. He ate little, and fell asleep while I was washing the dishes in the bathroom. I had been going to practice, but a viola is fairly wakeful in a one-room apartment. I read for a while instead. It was a best seller Janet had given me when she left. She thought it was very good, but then she likes Franz Liszt too. I don't read much since the libraries were closed down, it's too hard to get books; all you can buy is best sellers. I don't remember the title of this one, the cover just said "Ninety Million Copies in Print!!!" It was about small-town sex life in the last century, the dear old 1970s when there weren't any problems and life was so simple and nostalgic. The author squeezed all the naughty thrills he could out of the fact that all the main characters were married. I looked at the end and saw that all the married couples shot each other after all their children became schizophrenic hookers, except for one brave pair that divorced and then leapt into bed together with a. clear-eyed pair of government-employed lovers for eight pages of healthy group sex as a brighter future dawned. I went to bed then, too. Simon was hot, but sleeping quietly. His breathing was like the sound of soft waves far away, and I went out to the dark sea on the sound of them.

I used to go out to the dark sea, often, as a child, falling asleep. I had almost forgotten it with my waking mind. As a child all I had to do was stretch out and think, "the dark sea... the dark sea... and soon enough I'd be there, in the great depths, rocking. But after I grew up it only happened rarely, as a great gift. To know the abyss of the darkness and not to fear it, to entrust oneself to it and whatever may arise from it—what greater gift?

> We watched the tiny lights come and go around us, and doing so, we gained a sense of space and of direction—near and far, at least, and higher and lower. It was that sense of space that allowed us to become aware of the currents. Space was no longer entirely still around us, suppressed by the enormous pressure of its own weight. Very dimly we were aware that the cold darkness moved, slowly, softly, pressing against us a little for a long time, then ceasing, in a vast oscillation. The empty darkness flowed slowly along our unmoving unseen bodies; along them, past them; perhaps through them; we could not tell.
>
> Where did they come from, those dim, slow, vast tides? What pressure or attraction stirred the deeps to these slow drifting movements? We could not understand that; we could only feel their touch against us, but in straining our sense to guess their origin or end, we became aware of something else: something out there in the darkness of the great currents: sounds. We listened. We heard.
>
> So our sense of space sharpened and localized to a sense of place. For sound is local, as sight is not. Sound is delimited by silence; and it does not rise out of the silence unless it is fairly close, both in space and in time. Though we stand where once the singer stood we cannot hear the voice singing; the years have carried it off on their tides, submerged it. Sound is a fragile thing, a tremor, as delicate as life itself. We may see the

stars, but we cannot hear them. Even were the hollowness of outer space an atmosphere, an ether that transmitted the waves of sound, we could not hear the stars; they are too far away. At most if we listened we might hear our own sun, all the mighty, roiling, exploding storm of its burning, as a whisper at the edge of hearing.

A sea wave laps one's feet: It is the shock wave of a volcanic eruption on the far side of the world. But one hears nothing.

A red light flickers on the horizon: It is the reflection in smoke of a city on the distant mainland, burning. But one hears nothing.

Only on the slopes of the volcano, in the suburbs of the city, does one begin to hear the deep thunder, and the high voices crying.

Thus, when we became aware that we were hearing, we were sure that the sounds we heard were fairly close to us. And yet we may have been quite wrong. For we were in a strange place, a deep place. Sound travels fast and far in the deep places, and the silence there is perfect, letting the least noise be heard for hundreds of miles.

And these were not small noises. The lights were tiny, but the sounds were vast: not loud, but very large. Often they were below the range of hearing, long slow vibrations rather than sounds. The first we heard seemed to us to rise up through the currents from beneath us: immense groans, sighs felt along the bone, a rumbling, a deep uneasy whispering.

Later, certain sounds came down to us from above, or borne along the endless levels of the darkness, and these were stranger yet, for they were music. A huge, calling, yearning music from far away in the darkness, calling not to us. *Where are you? I am here.*

Not to us.

They were the voices of the great souls, the great lives, the lonely ones, the voyagers. Calling. Not often answered. *Where are you? Where have you gone?*

But the bones, the keels and girders of white bones on icy isles of the South, the shores of bones did not reply.

Nor could we reply. But we listened, and the tears rose in our eyes, salt, not so salt as the oceans, the world-girdling deep bereaved currents, the abandoned roadways of the great lives; not so salt, but warmer.

I am here. Where have you gone?

No answer.

Only the whispering thunder from below.

But we knew now, though we could not answer, we knew because we heard, because we felt, because we wept, we knew that we were; and we remembered other voices.

MAX CAME THE NEXT NIGHT. I sat on the toilet lid to practice, with the bathroom door shut. The FBI men on the other end of the bug got a solid half hour of scales and doublestops, and then a quite good performance of the Hindemith unaccompanied viola sonata. The bathroom being very small and all hard surfaces, the noise I made was really tremendous. Not a good sound, far too much echo, but the sheer volume was contagious, and I played louder as I went on. The man up above knocked on his floor once; but if I have to listen to the weekly All-American Olympic Games at full blast every Sunday morning from his TV set, then he has to accept Paul Hindemith coming up out of his toilet now and then.

When I got tired I put a wad of cotton over the bug, and came out of the bathroom half-deaf. Simon and Max were on fire. Burning, unconsumed. Simon was scribbling formulae in traction, and Max was pumping his elbows up and down the way he does, like a boxer, and saying "The e-lec-tron emis-sion..." through his nose, with his eyes narrowed, and his mind evidently going light-years per second faster than his tongue, because he kept beginning over and saying "The e-lec-tron emis-sion..." and pumping his elbows.

Intellectuals at work are very strange to look at. As strange as artists. I never could understand how an audience can sit there and *look* at a fiddler rolling his eyes and biting his tongue, or a horn player collecting spit, or a pianist like a black cat strapped to an electrified bench, as if what they *saw* had anything to do with the music.

I damped the fires with a quart of black-market beer—the legal kind is better, but I never have enough ration stamps for beer; I'm not thirsty enough to go without eating—and gradually Max and Simon cooled down. Max would have stayed talking all night, but I drove him out because Simon was looking tired.

I put a new battery in the radio and left it playing in the bathroom, and blew out the candle and lay and talked with Simon; he was too excited to sleep. He said that Max had solved the problems that were bothering them before Simon was sent to Camp, and had fitted Simon's equations to (as Simon put it) the bare facts, which means they have achieved "direct energy conversion." Ten or twelve people have worked on it at different times since Simon published the theoretical part of it when he was twenty-two. The physicist Ann Jones had pointed out right away that the simplest practical application of the theory would be to build a "sun tap," a device for collecting and storing solar energy, only much cheaper and better than the U.S.G. Sola-Heetas that some rich people have on their houses. And it would have been simple only they kept hitting the same snag. Now Max has got around the snag.

I said that Simon published the theory, but that is inaccurate. Of course he's never been able to publish any of his papers, in print; he's not a federal employee and doesn't have a government clearance. But it did get circulated in what the scientists and poets call Sammy's-dot, that is, just handwritten or hectographed. It's an old joke that the FBI arrests everybody with purple fingers, because they have either been hectographing Sammy's-dots, or they have impetigo.

Anyhow, Simon was on top of the mountain that night. His true joy is in the pure math; but he had been working with Clara and Max and the others in this effort to materialize the theory for ten years, and a taste of material victory is a good thing, once in a lifetime.

I asked him to explain what the sun tap would mean to the masses, with me as a representative mass. He explained that it means we can tap solar energy for power, using a device that's easier to build than a jar battery. The efficiency and storage capacity are such that about ten minutes of sunlight will power an apartment complex like ours, heat and lights and elevators and all, for twenty-four hours; and no pollution, particulate, thermal, or radioactive. "There isn't any danger of using up the sun?" I asked. He took it soberly—it was a stupid question, but after all not so long ago people thought there wasn't any danger of using up the earth—and said no, because we wouldn't be pulling out energy, as we did when we mined and lumbered and split atoms, but just using the energy that comes to us anyhow: as the plants, the trees and grass and rosebushes, always have done. "You could call it Flower Power," he said. He was high, high up on the mountain, ski-jumping in the sunlight.

"The State owns us," he said, "because the corporative State has a monopoly on power sources, and there's not enough power to go around. But now, anybody could build a generator on their roof that would furnish enough power to light a city."

I looked out the window at the dark city.

"We could completely decentralize industry and agriculture. Technology could serve life instead of serving capital. We could each run our own life. Power is power! ... The State is a machine. We could unplug the machine, now. Power corrupts; absolute power corrupts absolutely. But that's true only when there's a price on power. When groups can keep the power to themselves; when they can use physical power-to in order to exert spiritual power-over; when might makes right. But if power is free? If everybody is equally mighty? Then everybody's got to find a better way of showing that he's right...

"That's what Mr. Nobel thought when he invented dynamite," I said. "Peace on earth."

He slid down the sunlit slope a couple of thousand feet and stopped beside me in a spray of snow, smiling. "Skull at the banquet," he said, "finger writing on the wall. Be still! Look, don't you see the sun shining on the Pentagon, all the roofs are off, the sun shines at last into the corridors of power... And they shrivel up, they wither away. The green grass grows through the carpets of the Oval Room, the Hot Line is disconnected for nonpayment of the bill. The first thing we'll do is build an electrified fence outside the electrified fence around the White House. The inner one prevents unauthorized persons from getting in. The outer one will prevent authorized persons from getting out...."

Of course he was bitter. Not many people come out of prison sweet.

But it was cruel, to be shown this great hope, and to know that there was no hope for it. He did know that. He knew it right along. He knew that there was no mountain, that he was skiing on the wind.

The tiny lights of the lantern-creatures died out one by one, sank away. The distant lonely voices were silent. The cold, slow currents flowed, vacant, only shaken from time to time by a shifting in the abyss.

It was dark again, and no voice spoke. All dark, dumb, cold.

Then the sun rose.

It was not like the dawns we had begun to remember: the change, manifold and subtle, in the smell and touch of the air; the hush that, instead of sleeping, wakes, holds still, and waits; the appearance of objects, looking gray, vague, and new, as if just created distant mountains against the eastern sky, one's own hands, the hoary grass full of dew and shadow, the fold in the edge of a curtain hanging by the window—and then, before one is quite sure that one is indeed seeing again, that the light has returned, that day is breaking, the first, abrupt, sweet stammer of a waking bird. And after that the chorus, voice by voice: This is my nest, this is my tree, this is my egg, this is my day, this is my life, here I am, here I am, hurray for me! I'm here!—No, it wasn't like that at all, this dawn. It was completely silent, and it was blue.

In the dawns that we had begun to remember, one did not become aware of the light itself, but of the separate objects touched by the light, the things, the world. They were there, visible again, as if visibility were their own property, not a gift from the rising sun.

In this dawn, there was nothing but the light itself. Indeed there was not even light, we would have said, but only color: blue.

There was no compass bearing to it. It was not brighter in the east. There was no east or west. There was only up and down, below and above. Below was dark. The blue light came from above. Brightness fell. Beneath, where the shaking thunder had stilled, the brightness died away through violet into blindness.

We, arising, watched light fall.

In a way it was more like an ethereal snowfall than like a sunrise. The light seemed to be in discrete particles, infinitesimal flecks, slowly descending, faint, fainter than flecks of fine snow on a dark night, and tinier; but blue. A soft, penetrating blue tending to the violet, the color of the shadows in an iceberg, the color of a streak of sky between gray clouds on a winter afternoon before snow: faint in intensity but vivid in hue: the color of the remote, the color of the cold, the color farthest from the sun.

On Saturday night they held a scientific congress in our room. Clara and Max came, of course, and the engineer Phil Drum and three others who had worked on the sun tap. Phil Drum was very pleased with himself because he had actually built one of the things, a solar cell, and brought it along. I don't think it had occurred to either Max or Simon to build one. Once they knew it could be done they were satisfied and wanted to get on with something else. But Phil unwrapped his baby with a lot of flourish, and people made remarks like, "Mr. Watson, will you come here a minute," and "Hey, Wilbur, you're off the ground!" and "I say, nasty mould you've got there, Alec, why don't you throw it out?" and "Ugh, ugh, burns, burns, wow, ow," the latter from Max, who does look a little pre-Mousterian. Phil explained that he had exposed the cell for one minute at four in the afternoon up in Washington Park during a light rain. The lights were back on on the West Side since Thursday, so we could test it without being conspicuous.

We turned off the lights, after Phil had wired the table-lamp cord to the cell. He turned on the lamp switch. The bulb came on, about twice as bright as before, at its full forty watts—city power of course was never full strength. We all looked at it. It was a dime-store table lamp with a metallized gold base and a white plasticloth shade.

"Brighter than a thousand suns," Simon murmured from the bed.

"Could it be," said Clara Edmonds, "that we physicists have known sin—and have come out the other side?"

"It really wouldn't be any good at all for making bombs with," Max said dreamily.

"Bombs," Phil Drum said with scorn. "Bombs are obsolete. Don't you realize that we could move a mountain with this kind of power? I mean pick up Mount Hood, move it, and set it down. We could thaw Antarctica, we could freeze the Congo. We could sink a continent. Give me a fulcrum and I'll move the world. Well, Archimedes, you've got your fulcrum. The sun."

"Christ," Simon said, "the radio, Belle!"

The bathroom door was shut and I had put cotton over the bug, but he was right; if they were going to go ahead at this rate there had better be some added static. And though I liked watching their faces in the clear light of the lamp—they all had good, interesting faces, well worn, like the handles of wooden tools or the rocks in a running stream—I did not much want to listen to them talk tonight. Not because I wasn't a scientist, that made no difference. And not because I disagreed or disapproved or disbelieved anything they said. Only because it grieved me terribly, their talking. Because they couldn't rejoice aloud over a job done and a discovery made, but had to hide there and whisper about it. Because they couldn't go out into the sun.

I went into the bathroom with my viola and sat on the toilet lid and did a long set of sautillé exercises. Then I tried to work at the Forrest trio, but it was too assertive. I played the solo part from *Harold in Italy,* which is beautiful, but it wasn't quite the right mood either. They were still going strong in the other room. I began to improvise.

After a few minutes in E-minor the light over the shaving mirror began to flicker and dim; then it died. Another outage. The table lamp in the other room did not go out, being connected with the sun, not with the twenty-three atomic fission plants that power the Greater Portland Area. Within two seconds somebody had switched it off, too, so that we shouldn't be the only window in the West Hills left alight; and I could hear them rooting for candles and rattling matches. I went on improvising in the dark. Without light, when you couldn't see all the hard shiny surfaces of things, the sound seemed softer and less muddled. I went on, and it began to shape up. All the laws of harmonics sang together when the bow came down. The strings of the viola were the cords of my own voice, tightened by sorrow, tuned to the pitch of joy. The melody created itself out of air and energy, it raised up the valleys, and the mountains and hills were made low, and the crooked straight, and the rough places plain. And the music went out to the dark sea and sang in the darkness, over the abyss.

When I came out they were all sitting there and none of them was talking. Max had been crying. I could see little candle flames in the tears around his eyes. Simon lay flat on the bed in the shadows, his eyes closed. Phil Drum sat hunched over, holding the solar cell in his hands.

I loosened the pegs, put the bow and the viola in the case, and cleared my throat. It was embarrassing. I finally said, "I'm sorry.

One of the women spoke: Rose Abramski, a private student of Simon's, a big shy woman who could hardly speak at all unless it was in mathematical symbols. "I saw it," she said. "I saw it. I saw the white towers, and the water streaming down their sides, and running back down to the sea. And the sunlight shining in the streets, after ten thousand years of darkness."

"I heard them," Simon said, very low, from the shadow. "I heard their voices."

"Oh, Christ! Stop it!" Max cried out, and got up and went blundering out into the unlit hall, without his coat. We heard him running down the stairs.

"Phil," said Simon, lying there, "could we raise up the white towers, with our lever and our fulcrum?"

After a long silence Phil Drum answered, "We have the power to do it."

"What else do we need?" Simon said. "What else do we need, besides power?"

Nobody answered him.

> The blue changed. It became brighter, lighter, and at the same time thicker: impure. The ethereal luminosity of blue-violet turned to turquoise, intense and opaque. Still we could not have said that everything was now turquoise-colored, for there were still no things. There was nothing, except the color of turquoise.
>
> The change continued. The opacity became veined and thinned. The dense, solid color began to appear translucent, transparent. Then it seemed as if we were in the heart of a sacred jade, or the brilliant crystal of a sapphire or an emerald.
>
> As at the inner structure of a crystal, there was no motion. But there was something, now, to see. It was as if we saw the motionless, elegant inward structure of the molecules of a precious stone. Planes and angles appeared about us, shadowless and clear in that even, glowing, blue-green light.

These were the walls and towers of the city, the streets, the windows, the gates.

We knew them, but we did not recognize them. We did not dare to recognize them. It had been so long. And it was so strange. We had used to dream, when we lived in this city. We had lain down, nights, in the rooms behind the windows, and slept, and dreamed. We had all dreamed of the ocean, of the deep sea. Were we not dreaming now?

Sometimes the thunder and tremor deep below us rolled again, but it was faint now, far away; as far away as our memory of the thunder and the tremor and the fire and the towers falling, long ago. Neither the sound nor the memory frightened us. We knew them.

The sapphire light brightened overhead to green, almost green-gold. We looked up. The tops of the highest towers were hard to see, glowing in the radiance of light. The streets and doorways were darker, more clearly defined.

In one of those long, jewel-dark streets something was moving—something not composed of planes and angles, but of curves and arcs. We all turned to look at it, slowly, wondering as we did so at the slow ease of our own motion, our freedom. Sinuous, with a beautiful flowing, gathering, rolling movement, now rapid and now tentative, the thing drifted across the street from a blank garden wall to the recess of a door. There, in the dark blue shadow, it was hard to see for a while. We watched. A pale blue curve appeared at the top of the doorway. A second followed, and a third. The moving thing clung or hovered there, above the door, like a swaying knot of silvery cords or a boneless hand, one arched finger pointing carelessly to something above the lintel of the door, something like itself, but motionless—a carving. A carving in jade light. A carving in stone.

Delicately and easily the long curving tentacle followed the curves of the carved figure, the eight petal-limbs, the round eyes. Did it recognize its image?

The living one swung suddenly, gathered its curves in a loose knot, and darted away down the street, swift and sinuous. Behind it a faint cloud of darker blue hung for a minute and dispersed, revealing again the carved figure above the door: the sea-flower, the cuttlefish, quick, great-eyed, graceful, evasive, the cherished sign, carved on a thousand walls, worked into the design of cornices, pavements, handles, lids of jewel boxes, canopies, tapestries, tabletops, gateways.

Down another street, about the level of the first-floor windows, came a flickering drift of hundreds of motes of silver. With a single motion all turned toward the cross street, and glittered off into the dark blue shadows.

There were shadows, now.

We looked up, up from the flight of silverfish, up from the streets where the jade-green currents flowed and the blue shadows fell. We moved and looked up, yearning, to the high towers of our city. They stood, the fallen towers. They glowed in the ever-brightening radiance, not blue or blue-green, up there, but gold. Far above them lay a vast, circular, trembling brightness: the sun's light on the surface of the sea.

We are here. When we break through the bright circle into life, the water will break and stream white down the white sides of the towers, and run down the steep streets back into the sea. The water will glitter in dark hair, on the eyelids of dark eyes, and dry to a thin white film of salt.

We are here.

Whose voice? Who called to us?

He was with me for twelve days. On January 28th the 'crats came from the Bureau of Health, Education and Welfare and said that since he was receiving Unemployment Compensation while suffering from an untreated illness, the government must look after him and restore him to health, because health is the inalienable right of the citizens of a democracy. He refused to sign the consent forms, so the chief health officer signed them. He refused to get up, so two of the policemen pulled him up off the bed. He started to try to fight them. The chief health officer pulled his gun and said that if he continued to struggle he would shoot him for resisting welfare, and arrest me for conspiracy to defraud the government. The man who was holding my arms behind my back said they could always arrest me for unreported pregnancy with intent to form a nuclear family. At that Simon stopped trying to get free. It was really all he was trying to do, not to fight them, just to get his arms free. He looked at me, and they took him out.

He is in the federal hospital in Salem. I have not been able to find out whether he is in the regular hospital or the mental wards.

It was on the radio again yesterday, about the rising land masses in the South Atlantic and the Western Pacific. At Max's the other night I saw a TV special explaining about geophysical stresses and subsidence and faults. The U.S. Geodetic Service is doing a lot of advertising around town, the most common one is a big billboard that says IT'S NOT OUR FAULT! with a picture of a beaver pointing to a schematic map that shows how even if Oregon has a major earthquake and subsidence as California did last month, it will not affect Portland, or only the western suburbs perhaps. The news also said that they plan to halt the tidal waves in Florida by dropping nuclear bombs where Miami was. Then they will reattach Florida to the mainland with landfill. They are already advertising real estate for housing developments on the landfill. The president is staying at the Mile High White House in Aspen, Colorado. I don't think it will do him much good. Houseboats down on the Willamette are selling for $500,000. There are no trains or buses running south from Portland, because all the highways were badly damaged by the tremors and landslides last week, so I will have to see if I can get to Salem on foot. I still have the rucksack I bought for the Mount Hood Wilderness Week. I got some dry lima beans and raisins with my Federal Fair Share Super Value Green Stamp minimal ration book for February-it took the whole book-and Phil Drum made me a tiny camp stove powered with the solar cell. I didn't want to take the Primus, it's too bulky, and I did want to be able to carry the viola. Max gave me a half pint of brandy. When the brandy is gone I expect I will stuff this notebook into the bottle and put the cap on tight and leave it on a hillside somewhere between here and Salem. I like to think of it being lifted up little by little by the water, and rocking, and going out to the dark sea.

Where are you?
We are here. Where have you gone?

Copyright Acknowledgments

Every effort has been made to find the legal copyright holders of the material reproduced herein. If for some reason we have overlooked a copyright holder who should be acknowledged, we have done so inadvertently or because our best efforts to locate that copyright holder failed. Thus, these works are reprinted in good faith. If anyone can bring to our attention copyrighted material the holders of which we have not acknowledged, we shall be happy to do so in a subsequent edition.

Anderson, Kent. From *Night Dogs* by Kent Anderson. Copyright © 1996 by Kent Anderson. Used by permission of Bantam Books, a division of Bantam Doubleday Publishing Group, Inc.

Anise (Anna Louise Strong). "Centralia Pictures." From the IWW Labadie Collection.

Alexie, Sherman. From *Indian Killer* by Sherman Alexie. Copyright © by Sherman Alexie. Used by permission of Grove/Atlantic, Inc.

Axelrod, David. "Skill of the Heart" by David Axelrod. Used by permission of the author.

Barnes, Kim. From *In the Wilderness: Coming of Age in an Unknown Country* by Kim Barnes. Copyright © 1996 by Kim Barnes. All rights reserved. Used by permission of the author.

Bodeen, Jim. "Replenishing the Neighborhood." Used by permission of the author.

Braid, Kate, "*Girl* on the Crew." Reprinted from *Covering Rough Ground* (1991). Published by Polestar Book Publishers, Victoria, BC. Used by permission.

Callenbach, Ernest. From *Ecotopia* by Ernest Callenbach. Copyright © 1975 by Ernest Callenbach. Used by permission of Bantam Books, a division of Bantam Doubleday Dell Publishing Group, Inc.

Churchill, Sam. "Whistle While You Work" from *Big Sam* by Sam Churchill. Used by permission of Dorothy Churchill.

Carlile, Henry. "Graveyard Shift" is from *Rain*, Carnegie Mellon Univ. Press, 1994. Used by permission of the author.

Cooper, Fannie Adams. "West by Train." Excerpt from "My Life as a Homesteader: Fannie Adams Cooper." Edited by Leonard A. Whitlow and Catherine Cooper Whitlow. From *Oregon Historical Quarterly* 82:1 (Spring 1981): 65-84. Used by permission of *Oregon Historical Quarterly.*

Coupland, Douglas. Copyright © 1991 by Douglas Coupland. From *Generation X.* by Douglas Coupland. Reprinted by permission of St. Martin's Press, Inc.

Daniels, Willie. "Willie Daniels, Concrete Worker" from S.L. Sanger's *Working on the Bomb: An Oral History of WW II Hanford.* Used by permission of Continuing Education Press, School of Extended Studies, Portland State University, Portland, Oregon.

Davis, H. L. "Steel Gang." From *Proud Riders and Other Poems* by H. L. Davis.

Esval, Orland E. "Member of the Crew." Used by permission of *Montana: The Magazine of Western History.*

Gallagher, Tess. "Black Money" copyright © 1987 by Tess Gallagher. Reprinted from *Amplitude: New and Selected Poems ,* with the permission of Graywolf Press, Saint Paul, Minnesota.

Gunn, Eileen. "Stable Strategies for Middle Management." Used by permission of the author.

Guthrie, Woody. "The Grand Coulee Dam." Words and music by Woody Guthrie. TRO © Copyright 1958 (Renewed) 1963 (Renewed) 1976 Ludlow Music, Inc., New York, NY. Used by permission.

Hall, Hazel. "Instruction." Used by permission of Ahsahta Press, Boise State University, Boise, Idaho.

Halm, Joseph B. "Recollection of the Fires of 1910." From *American Forests and Forest Life,* July 1930.

Hill, Joe. "The Preacher and the Slave." From IWW songbook, third edition.

Kesey, Ken. From *Sometimes a Great Notion* by Ken Kesey. Copyright © 1964 renewed 1992 by Ken Kesey. Used by permission of Viking Penguin, a division of Penguin Putnam Inc.

Koehler, Pat. "Reminiscence on the Women Shipbuilders of World War II." From *Oregon Historical Quarterly* 91:3 (Fall 1990): 285-291. Used by permission of *Oregon Historical Quarterly.*

Le Guin, Ursula K. "The New Atlantis" copyright © 1975 by Ursula K. Le Guin; first appeared in *The New Atlantis*, Hawthorn Books, Inc., 1975; reprinted by permission of the author and the author's agent, Virginia Kid.

Lesley, Craig. Excerpt from *River Song* by Craig Lesley. Copyright © 1989 by Craig Lesley. Reprinted by permission of Houghton Mifflin Company. All rights reserved.

MacKay, Hamish Scott. From *My Experiences in the United States*, edited by Michael Munk. Used by permission of Michael Munk..

Maldonado, Jesús María "El Flaco." "Memorias de César Chávez." From *The Americas Review* 23;3-4 (Fall-Winter 1995):141.

Millar, Joseph. "Tax Man." Used by permission of the author.

Morgan, Howard. "Recollections of Tom Burns of Burnside."

Murphy, Dennis "Dinny". "I Found My Likings in the Mines" used by permission of Teresa Jordan.

Olsen, Charles Oluf. "Zero Hour in the Factory."

Oregon Labor Press. "If America Should Go Red?" November 17, 1933.

Rember, John. "Post Cowboy Dreams" is reprinted from *Cheerleaders from Gomorrah,* Copyright 1994 by John Rember. Reprinted by permission of Confluence Press at Lewis-Clark State College, Lewiston, Idaho 83501.

Rice, Clyde. Excerpt from *Nordi's Gift* by Clyde Rice. Used by permission of Gary Miranda, Executor of the Literary Estate of Clyde Rice.

Seufert, Francis. "Chinese." From *Wheels of Fortune*, edited by Thomas Vaughn. Used with permission from the Oregon Historical Society Press.

Snyder, Gary. "The Late Snow and Lumber Strike of the Summer of Fifty-Four" from *Riprap and Cold Mountain Poems* by Gary Snyder. Copyright © 1990 by Gary Snyder. Reprinted by permission of North Point Press, a division of Farrar, Straus & Giroux, Inc.

Starck, Clemens. "Putting in Footings" from *Journeyman's Wages* by Clemens Starck. Used by permission of Story Line Press.

Stevens, James. "The Old Warhorse." From *Homer in the Sagebrush* by James Stevens.

"To the Oregon Emigrants of 1846." From *Oregon Spectator*.

Vindex, Charles. "Survival on the High Plains, 1929-1934." Used by permission of *Montana: The Magazine of Western History.*

Winstead, Ralph. "Johnson the Gypo." From *Industrial Pioneer*, September 1921.

Wrigley, Robert. "The Sinking of Clay City." Used by permission of the author.